The Virgin's
Tale

About the author

Sherri Smith lives in Winnipeg, Canada. *The Virgin's Tale* is her first novel.

The Virgin's Tale

SHERRI SMITH

POCKET
BOOKS

LONDON • SYDNEY • NEW YORK • TORONTO

First published in Great Britain by Simon & Schuster UK Ltd, 2008
A CBS COMPANY

1 3 5 7 9 10 8 6 4 2

Simon & Schuster UK Ltd
Africa House
64–78 Kingsway
London WC2B 6AH

www.simonsays.co.uk

Simon & Schuster Australia
Sydney

A CIP catalogue record for this book
is available from the British Library

ISBN: 978-1-84737-186-7

Typeset in Plantin by M Rules
Printed in the UK by CPI Mackays, Chatham ME5 8TD

For Tara

Acknowledgements

I want to thank Pauline Ripat (PhD) for reading early drafts and lending her Classical expertise; this book could not have been written otherwise. I am forever indebted to Miriam Toews, for taking me aside and encouraging me to write, regardless.

Thank you to my agent, Sarah Heller, for her many suggestions, countless hours of discussion and much needed support.

Immense gratitude is extended to Kate Lyall Grant at Simon & Schuster UK for her keen insight and guidance.

Many thanks also to Alain and Carole Smith, Grace Graham, Sherry Graham, Lisa Rasmussen, Joan Rasmussen, Marcie Snyder, and Scott and Terry Nicholson, who have all, in some way, helped in this endeavour.

December 63 BCE/691 AUC
or Ab Urbe Condita

THE TOMB

Voices mingle and merge into a single united murmur as each layer of soil is thrown on top of the chamber; I can no longer call it a door. The bright white sun of the afternoon will soon wane on Colline Gate and the scorning, tsking people will eventually turn back towards Rome. This is salt in the wound, to be put to death on such a sunny day. I would prefer it was raining to show that the gods were dissatisfied, but the cloudless sky is like an apathetic grin or a teasing sneer. Now that my audience has seen my disgrace, the conclusion of the scandal, they will be eager to get back behind the city's walls to eat dinner, drink wine, theorize about my guilt, forget and make love to slaves, wives or one another; I know of such things now. Surely, this entertainment has put many in high spirits. Another's death always makes one feel more alive, more willing to indulge in bodily excess; this too I know. Tomorrow I will be forgotten and the spot where the earth swallowed me whole will go unmarked and unnoticed. I did not anticipate this ending to my life. Not that this possibility wasn't always present, a constant warning that became buried under the deafening sound of treading water, of keeping afloat.

I sit on the couch and try to soothe my spinning heart, rapid breathing and the pulse searing into my chest and neck. Sweat coats my skin and stings my eyes. The air is thick and wet. I thought it would be cold here, but it is as if I am immersed in warm bath water rather than below the surface of the earth, underneath layers and layers of heavy muddy soil. I feel in the darkness for the promised lamp and find it resting on a small wooden table. I feel for flint and am relieved there is some beside the table. I take the flint and stone and scrape, chipping small cuts into my palm, wrist, clumsy not only because of the dark, but also from lack of experience. One would think someone like me would be quick and artful, with fingers so nimble sparks would snap upwards with an easy flick of a forefinger and thumb, but this is not so; I have always tended, never created. I scrape and scrape until sparks finally kindle the lamp and light is born. Perhaps I should try to spread the lamp's flame, spill it on the floor, or hold it near stray twigs and dried leaves. What would they say then? They would see it as a sign. Perhaps they would believe I am innocent, blameless, even virtuous. They see everything as a sign, not realizing it is the reader, not the sign, who bestows significance. Setting my chamber on fire, blending with soil and sand, could exonerate my name. The faultless Vestal Virgin, rescued and protected by Vesta's fire in her burial plot, whose purity surpassed all others. Or perhaps it would be seen as the fiery Underworld impatiently plucking me from my tomb to face relentless punishment for my believed offences. I would burn just as I should.

I am now able to see where I will die. My tomb seemed bigger in the darkness, but it is merely a tiny pocket in the earth. I cannot tell how far underground I've been buried, but my cell is small, only a few feet wide. The sealed ceiling is high above my head so I cannot reach it and be heard pounding against the earth, my pleas unsettling even if muffled. This too would be significant – a sign – threaten their decision. There is a basket of food beside the lamp; its presence soothes their guilt. The bread is dusty, the fruit is bruised and wrinkled, the water is coated with mud. This food is not meant to nourish me; to kill me outright could shake the permanence of Rome, cause civil unrest or an invasion of barbarians, hinder expansion. It is bad luck to handle me, even to bring death upon me, and there is also the slight possibility that they could offend Vesta, that they mistook Her will. This food feeds their belief that they are not my executioners and I am not being executed. I close my eyes.

Nervous laughter has faded above; all sound has receded aside from the distant shrill cries of a crow, my only mourner. Silence is familiar. I decide that my death will not be slow. I will not ration the air. Instead, I will keep the lamp lit, permit the light to breathe the air and allow the flame, as always, to be greedy. This way I should die in a day or two. I do not wish to wait for dehydration to take me, but simply wish to fall asleep with my mouth gaping, hung on my last breath, forced open by clay, frozen by mud. I picture a vine or a tree springing from my mouth, envisage seeds hidden between my teeth. I begin to undress, pulling at the headband first, picking each nearly embedded pin from my scalp, from its cocoon-like scar. The headdress falls to the floor and I shamelessly scratch my itchy cheeks and nose and rub my eyes. I am not supervised here. My coiled hair is dry as ash and smells of smoke. The braids pinch as I try to unravel them; my hair has collapsed, fallen permanently into a web. Strands of white hair once intertwined with black-brown have broken and strayed outward from the coils; this testament to enduring time makes me smile, as if time were an illness that I outlasted and am now on the other side of, my white hair proof of my survival, like pockmarks.

I stand and begin to undo the golden rope below my breasts, string it between my fingers and feel its braided thickness, then drop it. My hands are shaking, straying from my control. I sit and hold them in front of my eyes willing them to be still, but they quiver like the lips of a spurned child. I place them underneath my thighs in hopes of regaining control; force myself once more to look round the chamber, my grave. Roots poke through the ceiling and crawl down the walls, twirling round wooden columns, like tendons or thin, curling fingernails grasping for my throat. It is as though I am held captive in the palm of a giant's hand.

There is a distinct smell, which I can taste faintly in the back of my throat. It is a mixture of moisture mingled with decay, like slaughtered animals dead too long to be emptied and their entrails accurately read. Can I already be sinking towards death? Can my insides be curdling, congealing, hardening into a thick red pulpy mass of bone and blood? Can I smell the process of my own death? It is definitely death I smell. I pull up my long purple stola and examine the flesh on my legs. I am looking for the onset of death, decay, stiffness, broken blue skin, holes, swollen veins.

Suddenly the lamp's light sways, falters and bends towards the floor. I am spinning, dizzy. By my left foot I see a long brown bone sticking out from underneath the couch. My scream is soundless. I reach down and throw it across the chamber. I pull my legs up onto the couch, anxious the bone might awaken and come nipping at my ankles. The odour of death is now putrid. I am gagging, my empty stomach heaving sour air. I press my palms into my cheeks, close my eyes until my breathing slows and my stomach is no longer stretching. I suppose they have buried me alive in a used grave to cut costs.

4

Why am I shocked? Why dig out a new tomb when they can simply toss me in one previously hollowed out? It is not as though I will have a chance to complain.

I turn over onto my stomach and peer underneath the couch. There is a set of bones. Strange how in death we lose our singularity; bones become fragmented into small groups: leg bones, arm bones, hand bones, neck bones. A body is reduced to a collection, a sack of bones, a container, a compilation, much as pages of a book if not bound together are meaningless, disjointed.

I place the lamp on the floor to illuminate my partner in captivity and death. A frayed golden rope lies close to her skull and part of her purple robe is still worn by her naked bones. She too was a Vestal Virgin. Her body is angled in such a way that she appears to have died face down. Her last breath tasted of dirt and dust. Beetles crawl in and out of her spongy skull and spotted bones as though unloading ships from battle. I think of what must have fed off her, lived off her, been born and become embedded into her sockets, in orifices of any sort. There is irony in this, in the life that has sprouted from her bones, her stripped torso, in the life that is now housed there. There is irony in what will emerge from my flesh as it peels and breaks, what will live in my bones when all the air has disappeared. I was half-way through, only fifteen more years to go. I am twenty-one, would have been thirty-six when it was over, but now . . . now I will stay twenty-one. I feel sick. I lie back on the couch and try to calm my crumpling stomach. Tears drip from the corners of my eyes, tickling as they meander through the curves of my ears. I was half done; I am done.

Breathe.

I cannot believe I will soon end, be no longer. He once told me it is only human conceit to believe in eternity, in an Underworld, that death is death and death concludes. Perhaps he is wrong, perhaps afterlife exists in the bellies of insects, or in the leaves of trees, or in one granule of sand, and despite crumbling, breaking down into the finest of fragments and reassembling into something other, something new, I will still be familiar with myself as a whole. The same, but different.

He said afterlife is subject to the memory of the living. Will he remember me? Will my afterlife materialize as a taut muscle between his shoulder blades or a nagging pressure in his temples? Will his memory, my presence, ride on his back? I will remember him, over and over, until he vanishes with my last breath. The dead cannot recall the living.

I turn onto my side and stare into the wall. I am waiting. The light from the lamp brushes against the wall, softening bleak mud into soft brown curves as though this wall once belonged to water-etched shores. My eyes grow heavy, the wall blurs. The surface of my clay-like confines turns into puffy white clouds on a summer's afternoon, shifting and shaping into whatever the imagination, or perhaps delirium, condones. Outlines of faces surface and recede into the wall: a hooked nose, swollen eyes, enlarged lips, a dog, a horse; I see a swinging serpent, a yellow stem, the long blond neck of a giraffe, a noose. My ears ring loud like the harsh shrieks of a hundred voices. I did not see it until now: draped from a protruding black root a broken and frayed golden rope gently sways back and forth. She must have grown impatient and succumbed to her golden rope; wrapped it around her neck and let go. A chaste death, free from puncture, free from piercing; even a knife should not enter us. I slide my hand across the couch and feel for the rope once wrapped round my ribs. The rope was always provided. I did not notice until now that I always had this option.

6

PART I

Men in general are quick to believe that which they wish to be true.

Caesar

CHAPTER I

I was chosen on a windy day. I remember this because even though my hair was tightly braided, the wind kept blowing out stray hairs that tickled my nose and revealed patches of my scalp. My mother brushed my hand away before I could rub it as we walked down the cobblestone path to the waiting litter. I remember this best, not the sensation of her touch, but of being prevented, for the first time, from scratching that which itched.

She'd tried to dye my hair the night before from a dark brown to a reddish-blonde, rubbing a concoction of henna leaves into my scalp until my neck ached, only to have much of my hair fall out, tangled between her fingers like clumps of seaweed. The thinned hair that remained was streaked a sallow yellow, as if I had stripes. Though she was disappointed, she still braided my hair the next morning, instead of a slave. She had never done this before. I did not suspect anything amiss, but thought she might have started taking more interest in me now I was older, six years old, and past the weakness of babies. She also added some of her own pretty beaded combs made from shiny shells and smoothed some white chalk over my cheeks, gently blowing away the excess powder, her breath sweet with apricot.

If she spoke that morning as she readied my hair and face, I did not hear; if a tear was shed, I did not see; if she bent to kiss me, I did not feel her embrace.

Though she had never dressed me before that day, I like to remember she had once or twice perched me up on her bed and allowed me to watch her dress; her combs sliding into perfectly braided hair, dyed a golden-red with saffron. Her deft hands fastening pearl earrings and a matching necklace, or carefully applying crushed chalk to her own cheeks and charcoal to her eyelids, pausing to decide on a fan made of peacock feathers, or should it be a parasol? 'Lavish,' she would say, 'simply lavish.' But I thought lavish meant lather, and would think of buckets of olive oil spilt across the floors in the dining room, people drenched in it, lathered, gooey, slipping, sliding on their bellies from chair to couch to courtyard. She would reach over, eyes remaining fixed on her mirror, and touch the hair of the pretty young slave who helped her get ready and say, 'Such beautiful hair . . . soon,' and I knew she would have the slave's hair cut and made into a hairpiece she could wear, thickening her already long tresses.

To have a daughter as a Vestal Virgin brings respect, notability. We cannot remember our parents, but they can point us out – 'My daughter . . . once, long ago' – and be admired. I like to think of her pointing me out at the theatre or games, even during rituals, vying for a better spot to watch me from. I often pretend she is watching me, filled with pride, and I straighten my back, hold my chin higher. Sometimes I would like her to be seething with regret, remorse, loss, wanting her daughter back, and again I straighten my back and hold my chin higher: you could have had a wonderful daughter. In all likelihood she is dead now, but I choose to disregard this. A Virgin needs inspiration from wherever she can find it, real or not.

Before that morning she had only watched as a slave washed or dressed or fed me. As she looked down at me, a hovering shadow puppet in the distance as I was dipped in a basin or as fine silk was lowered over my head or as I ate a spoonful of squashed apples, her face darkened in the same way it does when one comes indoors from a bright sunny day and one's eyes have yet to adjust to the sudden dimness.

But that morning I can clearly remember her face as she paused to massage the joints of her fingers as she braided my hair; though perhaps she was wringing her hands. Her hair fell loose to her waist, crumpled from the rolls she'd had in the day before. She looked tired, dark circles under eyes, a lined triangle between her eyebrows; she looked nothing as she did with her make-up on.

I was excited and could not wait for my mother to be finished with my hair. I squirmed around impatiently; this I regret, if only I had revelled in her last touches.

My brother's dog had just had a litter of pups and Father had said today would be the day I could finally hold one. My brother was much older than me, and every so often, he lifted me up on his shoulders and walked me round the villa and through the garden as I held onto his neck and chin, his bristles prickling my hands. How small everything suddenly seemed, especially me. He would amble through the courtyard, past the marble pond filled with lampreys with their underdeveloped eyes like two holes, their pointed teeth, and the short silver fish they fed off. A delicacy we would eat some day soon. He would tickle the little slave boy, his brown skin smooth and unblemished, his eyes much like the lampreys' eyes trying to feel up my brother's shoulder to the strange shadow he was carting around his neck.

11

My brother would step on the daffodils that sprung up between the colonnades in the courtyard which I would sometimes pick, guilt-ridden, knowing I was killing them.

That morning after eating some porridge, nuts and bread dipped in honey, a bigger morning meal than usual, my father and brother brought out one of the brown-spotted pups and placed it gently in the crook of my arm, though I still sat at the dining table. My brother would get a cuff if his dog came anywhere near our table. I looked down at the pup, its eyes barely open, its warm, fleshy, spotty skin nestling in my arms like the heat of an oven. Its chest panted rapidly up and down, as if it were worried what it would see once its eyelids sprung open. I rocked it back and forth, asking my father if I could keep this one. 'Oh, please, just let me have this one, please?'

My father shrugged, laughing lightly. 'Certainly, my little one, you may have her. We will keep her here and look after her for you.'

My brother whispered playfully, 'Mothering seems to come so naturally to her.'

'You need to put it back now, so its mother can feed it.' My father sighed, reaching to take it.

I leaned down and kissed the pup on her wrinkled nose, squeezing it gently, so happy I had my own dog like my brother that it did not come to my mind to ask why they would look after her *for* me.

'You shouldn't tease her like that,' my mother said, emerging from her bedroom wearing a new white stola with white dove feathers sewn into the neckline and round the hem and cuffs. Now she looked herself. She rubbed my back between my shoulders, a flaccid sort of patting. My father wrapped one of my

12

mother's shawls round my tunic, a bright patchwork of green and gold, while my mother gently leaned over, her feather cuffs sweeping against my ears, as she placed the bulla necklace around my neck to avert the evil eye. 'Where are we going?' I asked.

She took both my hands and knelt in front of me. 'We are going to the Forum, dear daughter.' She tilted her head and suddenly looked at me very hard, as if maybe I were ill, as if maybe I were dying. I thought of the daffodils I had picked so many times, so limp in my hands, and a sense of dread rung in my ears, tears welled. My mother quickly turned my hands over, kissing both my palms, pretending to eat my fingers, snorting like a hungry pig. I was not used to this, this kind of indulgence from her; I began to giggle uncontrollably, dread forgotten.

Both my mother and father took one of my hands as we stepped from our house. 'Say goodbye to everything,' my mother said.

'Goodbye to everything.' I thought she was still playing, thought it was a game. 'Goodbye, brother; goodbye, puppy; goodbye, house; goodbye, daffodils; goodbye, lampreys; goodbye, nursemaid; goodbye, little boy without any eyes. Goodbye.'

In the litter I watched our house recede, become tucked in behind other houses just like it, fading and become nothing more than a colourful smear I would never find again as we were carried off down the Palatine Hill.

As we rode into the Forum, there were large throngs of people gathered near the Assembly Ground.

'What god is being honoured today?'

I loved not the religious ceremonies but the festivals afterwards, the street performers, the smell of cooked meats and baked breads that filled the air, the way my father jested with other men, the parties at our mansion afterwards. Listening to raucous laughter, muffled discussions as I fell asleep.

'You worship the gods deeply, don't you, dear daughter?' My father asked, as he stared over my head at my mother.

'Oh yes!' I answered, oh yes.

'You will have your wish then!' he said, and before I could ask what it was I wished for, the litter stopped and my father tucked me under his arm and carried me up to the speaker's platform. The ships' prows, embedded in the outer edges of the platform, were decorated with streamers, tied round the necks of wooden busts or long protruding sternposts, snapping and rippling as they flailed in the wind. The busts' splintered faces and empty eyeholes seemed like leashed animals, lost by their owners.

I was so high up, higher than my brother's shoulders; I could see the three-tree square, the shrine of Janus, even the shrine of Venus.

My father's other arm waved to the watching crowd urging them to cheer for me, or really for him. It was his name after all on the ballot, not mine. He placed me in the line of freeborn girls, daughters of wealthy Roman citizens vying for the honour of giving them to Rome. He put his large hands on my shoulders and shook me, a sort of excited hug, turned and strode back down the steps still waving. He seemed so young, so free to draw attention to himself, unabashed at his loud voice; he seemed younger than my mother, though he was much older. He teased her about this, saying how old he was when he was too lazy to reach for a pillow or a cup of wine on the table near his lounging couch. 'Get me that cup of wine, dear wife, I am too old to reach, but you are still so youthful, surely your able

14

body could get it for me.' He'd laugh as my mother, her glazed prettiness as set as a painting on a vase, brought his pillow, and he'd tuck it under his head of black and silver curls and cross one hairy leg over the other.

My mother was lost from my sight by then, in a sandy, rocky bed of bobbing heads. Some of the other girls stood quietly, small downcast faces framed by hair carefully braided into the style of a bride, braided just like my hair. Some enjoyed the attention, cheeks pink, twisting their hands and arms round from the back to the front of their bodies, as if holding them back from flailing wildly, giggling softly. Others cried, eyes closed, arms reaching out, sure their mothers would soon pick them back up and carry them back down.

The platform was covered with long-stemmed daisies, but rows of matrons tossed even more, their faces blurred behind the arches of white daisies cascading down through the blue sky like tumbling clouds. Some daisies fell just short of the stage or hit an attendant, or worse, the wrong little girl, not their own little girl, at whom they were aiming for luck. A daisy hit me in the leg, a light smack before it flopped to my feet like a dead fish, but surely this was some other mother's bad aim. My mother wished me home.

The Pontifex Maximus walked up and down the platform, sometimes lifting a little girl's face up to study it, turning her from side to side, ensuring she was free of blemish or disfigurement, asking her a question or two to ensure her mind, speech and hearing were also free of any kind of physical defect. When he reached me, he smiled a thin dry smile, his mulberry birthmark glinting in the sun, his strands of black hair rustling in the wind. He did not ask me anything, his grey eyes passed over me with a sigh.

· 15

Each stone ballot is inscribed with the father's name and put in a small wooden box. My father was a senator; I know this because only daughters of senators can be Virgins. I've since envisioned many ways my father slipped my name into the ballot box. Sometimes I picture him having done it absentmindedly, otherwise engrossed in an animated conversation with other senators, perhaps while he told one of his jokes. Other times I imagine him rushing past the box, late getting to a meeting or a party or the baths, nearly forgetting to enter my name at all. 'Oh wait, yes, my daughter. What had I planned to do with her again?' and he would pat down his toga, rummage through his purse for the ballot as if it were a missing list of foodstuff to buy in the Forum. But never do I imagine him to have hesitated, winced as he heard the stone ballot hit the bottom of the box. How easily daughters are traded, even for that which cannot be held, slippery as it is and easily sullied: honour. It would be better if I were traded for gold; at least then my worth could have been weighed.

Six heifers were tied together at their necks to be sacrificed once the new Virgin was chosen, their round bodies painted purple, wreaths of daisies pinned to their heads, from which blood slowly dripped. The Pontifex Maximus's toga stretched around him like a swaddled fleshy boulder, pushed tight against his plump chest by the wind as he recited the prayers, asking for guidance to pick the right Virgin, for the right Virgin to be pure and dutiful, for Rome to always be favoured. He prayed, not to Vesta, her appeasement would come later, but to Jupiter 'the best and the greatest'.

This is when I noticed there were only four Virgins standing round a low temporary hearth. Their stolas and veils blew about in the wind, but each stood as stiff as the next – brittle sticks wrapped in silk. I wondered where the other Virgin was; there were always five of those strange purple women, the sixth stayed in the temple tending the fire. The summer sun suddenly blazed into my tunic as if it were a mouth exhaling into the fabric. One Virgin was missing.

As the Pontifex Maximus reached into the box wrapped in purple silk, held by a slave, his lips still moved in prayer. The crowd quieted except for the awkward sounds of babies crying, the girls whimpering and the heifers whining. He drew out the ballot and stepped to the very front of the platform and read the name so loudly that the veins in the side of his neck bulged and his shoulders heaved as if he'd just spent his one and only breath. I heard my father cheer, saw him run back up the platform, taking two steps at a time. He picked me up, swung me around with his nose squished against mine. I tried my best not to smile, not to laugh, not to let him carry me towards the Pontifex Maximus so willingly, but I had never seen him so pleased with me.

'Don't let yourself get so carried away,' my father would warn me, if my brother had made me cry by yanking my hair or if I was laughing too loudly, excitedly, but I let him carry me away like the tide.

What I should have done as my father handed me over as symbolic wife to the Pontifex Maximus, what I should have said as he whispered, 'Beloved,' was cried, kicked, screamed, stuck out my tongue, contorted my face into something blemished and grotesque, drooled like a fool. I should have wriggled free as he held me up, fallen (deemed to be bad luck), given him no choice but to declare me unsuitable. Such cleverness always comes after.

17

The ballot box was still open in the slave's hands and, as the Pontifex Maximus lifted me high in the air, I could clearly see into it. It is believed that choosing the new Virgin rests only on the whim of chance, of luck, on Jupiter's wisdom, each girl having equal opportunity, though some fathers try their best to tip the scales in their favour with offerings to Jupiter. The box was empty. The name had been chosen before all this; this was not a lottery. For a moment I thought the slave had taken the other names out, and once the Pontifex Maximus set me down I would pick up the box, walk to the front of the platform and turn it upside down. My father would be so proud of me; good girls always tell. Though sometimes he gets angry and says I am tattling. Is this telling or tattling? I wasn't sure. My father walked down the steps; he was leaving without knowing what had happened. The Pontifex Maximus thanked Jupiter for enabling his hand to pick the right Virgin, as if he had picked the sweetest apple from the tree. As he set me down gently I ran down the steps after my father, who turned smiling, not at me but at the watching crowds. With an exaggerated shrug, which the crowds laughed at, he picked me up and placed me by the Pontifex Maximus, wagging his forefinger in front of my nose. 'This is Jupiter's will, Aemilia. You will honour me and be honoured. Behave now.' I watched him leave, shaking his head like a father who had just disciplined his child, to a few more stray laughs.

With a wave of relief I realized it was Jupiter who had removed the other names, just as my father said. He had come soundlessly, imperceptibly – from where exactly I wasn't sure – and taken the other stones in his hands, crushed them to powder and blown them away. Or maybe he hadn't come here at all, but had only willed it from afar – the gods need not accompany their own will – like a blown kiss. Jupiter chose me. I believed those sorts of things then, before Tullia told me otherwise. It was easier then. It was easier than to acknowledge that my father had bribed my way here, that this was how much they preferred honour over me.

The four Vestals took me into a huddle, a sort of embrace, each of their bodies hard and rigid underneath their stolas, completing my 'giving away'.

I was finally lifted into a purple litter, completely unlike the one I had arrived in. It was sheathed in purple silk, like a wooden box wrapped up as a gift, but hollow. Around the litter waited a cluster of strange-looking men, each one holding a bundle of rods tightly against his left shoulder, as if worried they would slide from his hands. I later learned this was another of a Vestal's privileges – to have lictors; though we cannot use them to arrest or execute as magistrates can, they still act as attendants to announce our approach and clear our path, although our paths tend to clear on their own. If a pedestrian passes under our litter, accidentally or not, the lictors must execute him on the spot for committing sacrilege. People steer clear of Vestal Virgins.

The wreath of daisies kept falling to the side of my head, my heart beat so quickly it burned my throat. The applause of the people, the hordes of hands waving in the air, reaching out to try to touch me for luck, frightened me. I could almost feel their hands pulling me, choking me.

As we rode back to the Vestals' house in the litter, there were no words of comfort, of reassurance. The carpet of silk and the plush purple pillows on the benches were what I imagined the inside of a heart to look like. But the litter seemed hard. I could

19

feel the jiggling steps of the slaves carrying us. Tears rolled down my cheeks as they soundlessly studied my face as if I were the odd one.

'I have a dog, you know. I have to get back soon to feed her . . . My dog is waiting for me . . .'

The litter was closing in on me. I could feel their breath sucking away my own, their silence ringing in my ears.

One of them reached out towards me, her eyes seemed not any one colour, but a kind of muffled grey that captured shades of many colours in their dewiness. 'I am Tullia,' she said gently. Her hand was flat, turned sideways like a tipped plate being scraped of food. She ran her fingers close to my cheek, but did not touch me, as if the air round me suddenly thickened into a kind of impermeable boundary.

Another one, older, swatted just above Tullia's hand. 'How will that help?' she scolded. Her head reminded me of the stones my brother skipped across the pond, laughing as the lampreys scattered – long and oval with rutted surfaces. Her eyes were embedded in a net of sagging creases, as if her eyelids were melting. 'I am Sempronia, the Vestalis Virgo Maxima. This is Fabia, she is second.' She pointed to the pallid Virgin with narrow shoulders and a small compact body who sat beside her. Fabia's black eyebrows were jagged and sharp against her fleshy pallor that would always be damp to the touch. 'This is Tullia, third, but you know this, because she spoke out of turn.' It was the lack of severity in her voice that frightened me; she said this rebuke just as she said the introductions. Tullia turned as if to look out of the heavily curtained opening. 'Porcia, fourth. The other one, the fifth, is in the temple with Vesta.' Sempronia closed her eyes a moment, then flinched as if suddenly remembering something, which I

20

expected would be the fifth one's name, but she leaned slightly into Fabia. 'Is she able to tend properly?' and they each began to whisper to one another, Sempronia's top teeth tapping into the bottom row like fingers snapping to a song.

I wasn't sure then why they numbered themselves, why each took a number as if in some kind of line, but later discovered that the ranks of Virginity are based on seniority, on time spent. First Sempronia, the oldest woman I could remember seeing; though a child's memory is shallow and often random in what it chooses to keep. She was an odd, grotesque novelty. There was something so grisly about her. Her close proximity to death made her a faded spectre of a full person who did not feel or think or sound as a full person would, and thus was a suspect and repulsive anomaly of a human being. In that moment, sitting across from her, I feared she would lunge and attempt to eat me, swallow the years of my life that had yet to pass. And she would, they each would, just not in the way I imagined then. Sempronia looked up at me; the pink lining on her lower eyelids seemed almost painted on, but her brown eyes were crisp and I could suddenly tell that regardless of her appearance, she was not going to die soon. Good Virgins live longest.

I turned towards Tullia and watched as she fluttered her eyes upwards, the way I suddenly pictured my mother doing when she turned away from my father, but then maybe I looked for familiarity only when there was none, the way one looks for hope in the hopeless. There's no way to tell now.

Tullia unhooked her veil and though she only looked forward, a small subtle smile flickered over her lips; she later said this was meant to soothe me. She said it was all she could do at the time.

Sempronia and Fabia stopped whispering and the lictors'

scuffling pace became the only sound, growing louder and louder, into a defined measurement of distance, an alarm that I was getting farther and farther away from everything I had known and closer to the unknown.

I thought Porcia, being younger than the others, would understand my appeals.

'I have a dog. I have to get back to feed her.'

Her thin face made her eyes seem wider, like two brown bulbs set into a doughy cake, with her nose where the dough was pinched and pulled until the tip drooped down. She had white-headed bumps down her chin and between her fair, faint eyebrows that were barely discernable from her skin. Her breasts were just beginning to bud under her stola. Yes, she was young enough to listen, but she only snorted, her veil bubbling with air in front of her mouth.

CHAPTER II

It was strange to enter the house. My family and I passed it when we went to the Forum. 'That is where the sacred priestesses who care for Vesta live. Isn't it a pretty house? It must be so nice to live there.' My mother would lean back in her seat holding up a small polished mirror in front of her face, hiding from me. Once I watched her offer Vesta a bouquet of flowers from the top step of the temple. As we rode back up the hill I told my mother it seemed to be nothing but a small dark cave with two statues inside. She pinched the back of my arm. 'Your disrespect tempts ill-will towards me.'

The house seemed bigger from the outside, narrower from within. The tall pillars at the front suggested opulence, but it was much more stark and bare than our mansion. Inside the entrance was a vast central atrium with a long rectangular pool, the water so clear I could see the bottom, surrounded by statues of past Vestal Virgins eternalized in stone. A slave was carefully cleaning one with a small brush. The mosaics on the walls and floor were of Vesta or Minerva or simply dull geometrical shapes in black and white. Large vases, also with Vesta and Minerva painted on them, and potted plants set upon long ornate purple carpets were the only other decoration. There were none of the usual frescos, stuccoed designs or clutter of sculptures I was used to. There was little variation in colour at all; in our house there were muslin curtains of rich vibrant red, green, gold – a different colour over each window. The only embellishment of colour here was the shafts of yellow sunlight streaming through the open roof, caught on the water like floating stars. This house seemed drab and uniform, so unlike my home, unlike the Forum, which was a patchwork of vivid hues. It seemed un-Roman, foreign even.

It was very neat, not a speck of dust or a granule of sand on the floor; it smelled strongly of olive oil, as if everything had been rubbed down and cleaned with a strigil – the floors, walls, statues. On both the right and left were sets of stairs leading up to the second level, where the Virgins slept. Virgins are kept up on the second floor, farthest from the doors.

The others led me through the kitchen into the garden to a long rectangular table. It was still very warm, the heat from the braziers the slaves were cooking on in the kitchen was carried to us on the wind. The sky turned a slow sinking pink and the garden was so quiet I thought I could hear the green ivy creeping up over the brick walls, out of the garden, away from my own choking sobs. I was served a plate of rabbit, its sinewy toughness like bits of stringy sponge. I could not swallow it, and spat it out into a napkin beside my plate. A dish of sliced pears came next. I ate these slowly, carefully, exhaustion replacing sadness.

It began then, on the very first day, the teachings.

'You're an important girl now, superior and privileged, so you really mustn't cry. Did you see all those other little girls standing in that line? They wouldn't be crying now; they would be rejoicing to have fulfilled their father's dream, rejoicing to have brought honour to their families and become a safekeeper of Rome.' Sempronia's eyes seemed to rest upon two pink half-moons; they seemed to bore into every honest answer, honest question, until one felt so truthless. Sempronia the bore.

The Virgins appeared so frightening with their matching purple stolas and headdresses, like chirping birds of the same flock, heads dipping into spoons of food between murmuring, clucking. Multiples of one breed, creatures of another kind – purple-crested Virgins.

Soon after we finished eating, a slave pulled out my chair from the table and set it a few steps away. She guided me there by stroking my hair. As I sat down, she began to pull out the pretty combs my mother had put in my hair that morning, brushing out my braids. I could feel her hands, as if she were rummaging through my hair looking for something. Then I felt cold metal shears pressing against my scalp, my fine brown and yellow wisps of hair seemed to hover mid-air, nearly floating away with the wind until the slave snatched at them as if catching flies.

'No,' I cried. 'Those are my mother's combs. I must take them back to her. She is waiting. They are not yours!' Cries turned to screams. My hair, my hair, the hair mother used her very own hands to dye and braid, to beautify. She slid her very own combs just above my ears, brushing against my cheek as she fixed them firmly into place. How will my mother recognize me when she comes? I tried to get up, but another slave came out and held me down in the chair. 'My mother braided my hair . . . She will be so angry at all of you . . .' My legs kicked out

25

wildly. I had never acted this way before, so severely and violently, my body heaving, choking on sobs, sounding distant as if I were another little girl somewhere outside the garden in the midst of a tantrum.

The others stayed at the table, watching. Sempronia smirked at Fabia, as if my tears were nothing short of ludicrous, the empty dramatic antics of a child. They found it funny, amusing.

'We have all endured this. It is for the good of Vesta, so the goddess can accept you. It will grow back.' Fabia pointed to Porcia, who nodded haughtily as if she were much older and more experienced than her fourteen years, never the child I was, never less than the perfect Virgin.

'She didn't cry. No, she was happy to make her offering to Vesta,' Fabia continued as Porcia nodded her head as if made animate by Fabia's voice. '*I* certainly didn't cry.' She said this like a long sigh, as if it were obvious, but also as if she were showing scars and quietly boasting of her own nerve, her own endurance; a good Virgin knows only modesty.

Still, I cried on, trying to grab my mother's combs as the slave placed them on the table. Finally, they sent me into the house, bald and tired as if I had trod water for hours without ever reaching the shallows. Even my skin seemed sodden.

As I lay in bed, hoping for sleep to come so I could wake up again back in my own room, I thought not of my mother or my father, knowing this would require an admission that they had given me up to Vesta, just as my mother once did the bouquet of flowers. No, I thought of my little dog, her eyes still closed to the life before her, cuddled in folds of fuzzy skin, wanting me to pick her up and hold her, wanting me to kiss her nose. Wanting me. Wanting me as a child wants her mother because, though a child is never guaranteed her mother's love, a child's love for her mother is certain. At least at first.

When I awoke, a slave was waiting with a purple stola hanging over her arm.

CHAPTER III

'You've been blessed with the greatest honour and privilege. You will always be fed, clothed, housed, and will learn to read and write fluently. You will have a place of honour reserved for you at all public games and may dispose of your property as you wish. You are symbolically gifted with *imperium*. Wills are stored in this house under Virgin guardianship; we are the safe-keepers of property, position and great fortune; a man's immortality is his estate; his measure of success is how much he has to give away at death. Wills uphold the lineage of Senatorial families, keeping order in the Republic, and this pleases Jupiter. Wills must be deposited with utmost care. But, above all, you are a care-giver to Vesta; your greatest honour and greatest privilege is to offer yourself to maintain Rome's permanence. All in exchange for one restriction, one constraint you will be pleased with anyway. You are the envy of all matrons, but good Virgins do not envy matrons. You are esteemed by all men . . .'

Fabia began each of her lessons like this, right after my morning meal, making me repeat it word for word: 'I've been blessed with the greatest honour and privilege . . .' She was the most diligent of teachers. It was as if she scraped away at the skin on the back of my hands until blood was drawn and a perfect round

28

hole made where she inserted her teachings so they circulated through my blue veins and settled in my brain. She scolded me constantly for not listening, accused me of insolence when I could not repeat whatever it was she had just said, when my eyes wandered from her face, my ears from her words. She delivered long-winded diatribes on our role in Rome, lengthy lists of duties. 'With each piece of charcoal offered to Vesta you must pray: "I beseech thee with this offering of charcoal to continue your safekeeping of Rome." With each piece of wood offered to Vesta you must pray: "I beseech thee with this offering of wood to protect all fires in hearth and altar." With each handful of kindling you must pray: "I beseech thee with this offering of kindling to warm the bellies of Romulus's offspring and keep citizens strong and mighty." If you do not tell Vesta exactly this, in this way, in this exact order, the offering will not be accepted and someone in Rome will starve, be cold, or worse, Rome could be threatened. The health of the citizens and the wealth and stability of Rome fall upon you.'

'The health of the citizens and the wealth and stability of Rome fall upon me . . .' With each recitation, I could almost feel hooks swell out from underneath my skin, like a bumpy rash, could feel tiny filaments loop around them, as if I were a sail guiding the path of Rome. With each recitation I felt heavier and heavier, as if my six-year-old legs and arms were beginning to bloat and extend to a thick mast attached to my stola.

If I stammered or could not remember these phrases verbatim, I would go to bed hungry, my blankets stripped from my bed; good Virgins understand the repercussions of their errors.

Fabia's voice, so constant and steady, whistled past me as I sat cross-legged on the floor, wax tablets in my lap. Although there were chairs, she preferred I sit on the floor. 'Discomfort is more conducive to learning. It is something you should get used to and the quicker the better, and anyhow, you will never know the discomfort of matrons . . . you have it easy, really.' The classroom was behind a hanging tapestry, empty except for the table and two chairs, one Fabia used, the other chair was meant to further ingrain self-restraint by accepting discomfort with comfort so close by. To accept what is, with what if so close by.

I wished I could learn outside in the garden, but this might encourage matrons to engage in intellectual studies, or at least this is how the rule began long before there was a wall round the garden and a passing matron could see in. Once a rule, always a rule. Even learning behind the tapestry seemed as if we were hiding, that we were doing something that needed to be shrouded in secretiveness.

'You must also purify the temple floor several times, so that Vesta is able to see her reflection and be pleased with her high and full flames. You must cleanse Minerva several times, and as you do so you must pray: 'I beseech thee with this sponge and soap to protect Rome from loss of commerce and craft, and to bestow your good graces upon our armies to fight with your warrior cunning.' You will bake the mola salsa cakes and offer them according to ceremonial ritual without imperfection. You, not a slave, must bake the cakes to crumble over the heads of sacrifices, or the gods will find them tasteless, belch them up, unsatisfied and unappeased. You must abide by each ritual accordingly, this is of the utmost importance, this is absolutely imperative . . .'

'Where do the gods live?' I interrupted, because I realized suddenly I did not know where these gods were. How did they hear me? How did they see me? Were they always watching, listening?

Fabia's skin took on a kind of translucent light, as if what I had just asked paled her into invisibility. 'The gods are everywhere . . .' she said seething, her hands flicking upwards in a gesture of obviousness. 'We are among spirits – numina – our world is filled with them. They are in the earth, in each rolling hill, each tree of a forest, each droplet of water in the oceans. They live in the sky and air. They control light, rain, hail, sleet, wind, night, day. These spirits are the gods and goddesses of state worship; they have names and functions specific to their areas of influence. We purchase their help with prayer and sacrifice. We gain their favour by not offending them, by paying them due reverence. Those people careless of the gods, those who are negligent, will flounder under disease and misfortune, leprosy and exile; there have been men and women who have led long, harsh and unbearable lives all because they were too busy or too forgetful to give the gods the appreciation they deserve. In the absence of the gods' goodwill, one is not protected.

'There are other kinds of numina, the kinds without names or shape that lurk about, feeling shunned and shirked, waiting to be called upon, invoked by people who are deformed, by foreigners and crippled magi to fulfill their depravities. There are also spirits that rise up from the dead if they are not appeased properly, especially those who died untimely deaths; these spirits walk among us to do the biddings of their callers. We are surrounded by signs, indications of where these spirits were, are or intend to be, spirits that could leap from one body to another if one comes close enough to the infected. Spirits that will bloat your joints with gout, swell your back with humps and give you cysts and lesions upon your face and body.'

I fell still at the mention of these spiritual predators skulking about; I pictured them to be black swirls that would surface and attack me for errors I had unknowingly committed and would greatly fear sudden gusts of wind, rustling leaves, fog, for a long time after. My anxiety pleased Fabia. 'But good Virgins are protected against these kinds of numina by Vesta, by our bullas, by our purity. Only Virgins not seamlessly devout are susceptible and defenceless, and how better can one achieve seamless devotion than by being an apt and attentive student?'

She frequently nodded her head up and down, as if she were in constant agreement with herself, with the way it is. She would often say, like an answer wrapped in ribbons, the perfect gift for all occasions, 'That's just the way it is.' Sometimes she'd slip elsewhere, into a fit of glee or a trance – she moved so little – and seemed to look beyond me, beyond the house, her moving lips separated from her face. Her lips guided by the gods.

'The general rules of prayer are: first, the right god must be chosen. It would not do one any good to pray to Mercury, the god of commerce and trade, to repel dangerous fire from touching Rome. No, Vulcan must be addressed then. Names are very important, not just naming the correct god, but naming the god correctly. First a god or goddess must be called upon with his or her name so one can be assured he is listening. This is best achieved by naming the gods' parentage, and by listing those traits which are specific to the god and, also, by saying the title the god uses in accordance with what the prayer is requesting. When praying to Jupiter to protect Rome from harmful weather, for example, one calls him Jupiter Optimus Maximus, the protector of cities, god of sun and moon, wind, thunder, rain, light-ning and snow. When praying to him for courage in battle, one would pray to Jupiter Stator; when praying to him for victory in battle, one would pray to Jupiter Victor, promoter of victory. Specificity is key.'

'Specificity is key,' I repeated.

'If a god or goddess is called by the wrong name this will greatly upset them and he or she not only will not bother, but may be swayed to do the exact opposite the prayer requests. If a god or goddess is accidentally referred to as a she when he is a he, the god will be so insulted it could be injurious to everyone in Rome until the proper ceremony is carried out to apologize and gain the god's forgiveness . . .' She would always conclude by reminding me, 'Though you will never publicly pray to other gods and goddesses, it is good for a Virgin to know this so she can tell the Pontifex Maximus, if he is not in attendance, when a priest does it incorrectly. Good Virgins are the eyes and ears, watching and listening, for the betterment of the Republic of Rome.'

She'd instruct me to copy out letters, over and over, until my hand was numb, so that I'd appreciate I was not an ordinary girl, but a privileged girl.

Tullia was entirely different; she taught me in the afternoons and would ask only easy questions and arch her eyebrows as I recited my answer, as if I was telling some sort of anecdote. Her laughter was encouraging, honeyed and inviting.

'Let us unwind,' she would say, her eyelids suddenly heavy, and I would imagine us both untwining, unknotting, our bones supple as we lay back on soft green grass under a hot sun.

Though she only said things like this when Sempronia did not linger about, which Sempronia did sometimes, as if she had wandered into the wrong room and thought it would be nice to stay, pulling out a chair close to Tullia. She would often correct Tullia, looking up, scowling. 'No, not Cerilia, you meant Parilia, festival of Pales. It is Parilia; are you not of the right mind? How could you make such an error?' Sempronia would stomp one of her feet, as if it were a gavel.

And Tullia would close her eyes for a moment, breathe in deeply through her mouth, grip the back of a chair, 'I apologize for the slip of my tongue . . .' and begin again, correctly, 'Parilia is the festival of Pales, deity of shepherds and sheep. Sheep pens must be cleaned and decorated with foliage, and the sheep themselves must be purified in smoke from a bonfire on which sulphur is burned. Milk and mola salsa cake must be offered to Pales, and shepherds must wash themselves in dew, drink milk and leap through the bonfire.'

But when no one was around she would turn her hands into puppets, ask a silly question, 'What is a young pirate, like you, up to today?' and though she never touched me, it often seemed as if she wanted to pick me up and swing me about, even kiss my forehead.

Tullia's face was slowly becoming superimposed on the distancing face of my mother.

She arranged her stola in such a way that it seemed more fitted than that of the others, showing off curving hips. I believed she also took great care to keep her skin pale, plucked the fine hairs from her lips, chin and between her eyebrows and kept her hands manicured, ignoring the fact that we were all pale and all our hands were soft and pretty because we handled nothing but spoons for food, ignoring the fact that tools of beauty had no place here and were not permitted. Even so, if they were sisters, one, two, three, four, she would be the pretty one.

When Tullia taught, she paced, or else sat in a chair staring out of the window, ignoring the pile of papyrus in front of her. Sometimes I'd stare out of the window with her and she would not send me back to sit down. We'd breathe in the fresh air together; there was no such luxury in our rooms. Windows might be confused as opportunities in our rooms. The faint blonde down on her cheeks would catch in the sun, and the outline of her skin seemed blurred, like a portrait painted under the softest of light.

'Sempronia is old, she was born old . . .' I said this one particular afternoon, as I stood at the window with her after Sempronia had picked at each of her sentences, dismembering each one piece by piece, like a bird picking at entrails.

Tullia turned to look at me and for a moment I expected her to order me to copy letters, or recite until my voice ached, but instead she laughed, deep dusty laughs. This was very encouraging. I hadn't heard much laughter since I'd arrived.

'Her nose is so big; what are those red things all over it? Webs? Her lips are like two earthworms rubbing together and that mole on her cheek is really a porcupine in his nest.'

Tullia laughed harder and harder, tears streaming down her face. She wiped her cheeks with the backs of her hands.

'And she's hunched like a skulking dog. No wonder she did not leave here! No man would ever marry such an old beast.' Tullia could barely get it out, choking on her own laughter, but when she finally stopped, tears still fell.

Though she never joined in again, not then anyway, she still let me from time to time mock the others' voices, imitate their mannerisms, ridicule the way they walked, ate, moved. It was their fault I was here, I felt, forgetting it was my father or my mother who had added my name to the lottery, and that it was finally Jupiter who had chosen me. The others were much easier to hate. Tullia would still laugh as I hunched over in the chair, tapping my foot, shaking my head 'no' like Sempronia. But this only happened sometimes; at other times she would sigh, turn away as if she never saw me at all, and I would be hurt, embarrassed and try to gain her attention another way. For a short while, I tried to do this by playing up, refusing to recite or scribbling instead of writing, wanting some kind of reaction from her. But she only appeared bored, fading off mid-sentence in her chastisement as if about to fall asleep, always returning with an apology and a flush of red in her cheeks. At other times she ignored me completely, until I no longer tried this method of attention seeking and instead concentrated all my efforts on pleasing her with my imitations or even quietness. 'Oh, what a wonderfully quiet girl you are!' she sometimes said, her warm smile a kiss upon my cheeks.

When Sempronia wasn't there, Tullia never made sure I was listening with an onslaught of questions and quizzes, and I would never try to wake her from wherever it was she often went. It was if we both disrobed behind this tapestry, shirked off our stolas and any sense of duty and knew the other wouldn't tell. I decided that if she could, she too would rather be playing in the garden; this is how I remember then, now.

When Tullia did teach, her teachings were mostly redundant, fragmentary, shards of glass in need of piecing together. 'June ninth to the fifteenth is the state festival of Vesta. Matrons must honour her by walking barefoot to our shrine, bringing food for the goddess. You must offer Vesta their food with your right hand, wine with your left. You mustn't look at any of them.' Her eyes would flutter up with resentment or maybe derision, but this is something I attached to her mannerisms afterwards and now can only remember her as always that way. She continued on, moving from topic to topic like a poet searching for his next line: 'These are our gods, the gods. Juno is the goddess of light, presiding over childbirth and bringing infants from darkness into light . . . Juno Rumina looks after the mother's milk supply . . . Juno Ossipago strengthens an infant's bones . . . Juno also watches over marriage arrangements (this is when she should be referred to as Juno Domiduca), watches as the bride crosses the threshold to her new home (this is when she should be called Juno Interduca), as the bride's girdle is untied (this is when she should be referred to as Juno Cinxia) . . .' She'd sigh deeply, her face would seem to go flaccid for a moment. 'Oh, never mind the many names of Juno . . . We never need to know them . . .' But Tullia knew them; she knew them well, just in case.

Often she would veer from her lectures, to repeat herself. She seemed to speak aloud, not her thoughts, but something less conscious, a kind of mantra.

'After thirty years you may go . . . after thirty years you may go.' This time she stopped herself and began again. 'Yes, after thirty years of service you may go. But rarely does a Virgin leave. She will stay here at this house, a priestess of Vesta, until death; her thirty years turns to a lifetime.'

'But why would a Virgin stay?' I once asked her, I could ask Tullia such things.

37

Her mouth opened, then closed as if she had been about to say something completely different. 'You are freer here than anywhere else.' She nodded her head and pursed her lips, suppressing whatever emotion played at the edges of her mouth.

There were also times she didn't speak at all, but studied her hands in her lap as if she couldn't see me whispering to one of my made-up friends, pretending to have an excellent discussion with Piso or Livia.

These friends came to me during my classes with Fabia. They were not as apt as I was and certainly less obedient of Fabia's required rigidity, but friendly nonetheless. Livia ripped the papyrus when she was reading aloud, just a little at the edges where no one would notice. Piso, a boy, stabbed the wax tablets instead of writing his notes and rolled his eyes whenever he was told to do something. Once he even kicked over a chair when no one was looking and I was punished. Octavia was younger than me and had to be cared for all the time; I had to dress her, brush her hair, hush her, though this I did only when alone in my room. I think I liked Piso best. If there were others, I don't recall. They left me when Julia arrived.

CHAPTER IV

At the first ceremony I attended I cried aloud, a single cry that sounded more like a broken hiccup. It was the beginning of the festival of Neptunalia, before citizens left to make their way to the outskirts of Rome to build huts made of bay branches and leaves and hold a private feast in Neptune's honour, returning in the afternoons to watch the games, then going back to their huts to feast at night. Wealthy men take their own bulls to sacrifice and try their best to convince Neptune to keep the rivers high so they can water their crops. Appeasing Neptune ensures rainfall and averts drought, pushing it somewhere else, to a place where the people cannot appease their gods as well. We stood on the steps of Neptune's temple, a small altar was brought out and all we were required to do was stand in single file and offer a cake of mola salsa and one single fish once the bigger sacrifice had been carried out and Neptune would be more open to smaller gifts. Though sometimes this was reversed and we'd offer the small gifts first, catching the attention of the god for the larger gifts to come; this was dependent on the god's preference. We would also attend the games later, but not feast in the forest. Virgins belong *to* the public *in* public.

The priest of Neptune whispered the prayers and a bull was sacrificed; I watched it fold into itself as if it had deflated, its white wreath turning crimson, its head slouching forward against its horns. Fabia had gone over and over my role in the ceremony the previous week. 'Offer the fish first, then crumble the cake like this . . .' I repeated it again and again, demonstrated it again and again. What I wasn't prepared for was the odd, expectant, pleading faces of the farmers and peasants. Their dark skin tanned to leather and bleak bloodshot eyes made them seem needy, so needy; it filled me with both apprehension and revulsion. Even the wealthy landowners appeared creased and furrowed. I could not bear them looking at me, as if the world had toppled over and spilled out on its side, everything mixed up and they were the children and I was somehow responsible for each of them.

The prayers seemed to go on and on. Fabia had failed to mention this. 'You will feel a sense of great fulfilment and contentment as you make your offering to secure the favour of the gods. It will wash over you like a warm ray of sunlight.' The sun did warm me, but not the way she said it would: I felt hot and sickly. My headdress pinched and itched. The fish had already begun to smell, its oily skin exuding salt and seaweed; it does not take long in such heat, it was nearly decaying in my hands. Black flies buzzed around my wrists. I began to move with small twitches like the skin on a bull's back trying to wave off flies. But still they swarmed round my hands, crawling up my fingers, up my sleeve, their silver wings and shiny bodies disappearing under the cuff of my stola. Suddenly, I yelped and dropped the fish, tears streamed down my face. I had been bitten by something; I could feel a sting in the inside of my arm. No one came to my aid, not even Tullia; they each kept their heads bowed as if they did not know me. The people went quiet, so very quiet. The priest stopped his prayers, stopped pouring the blood of the bull into the altar's fire. It was as if Rome paused, held its breath all at once. There was a silence that seemed to last for many moments, then the priest went back into the temple. Two of the temple's attendants rushed over, picked up my fish and handed me a new one.

I could hear the crowd muttering, even groaning, some of the wives quietly crying. This is why men don't often bring their wives to public ceremonies, women are prohibited from attending many of the ceremonies – the gods hate crying. I had polluted the ceremony, forecast drought, famine, loss of wealth, fires. I had ruined the lives of all these people; they would die because of me. I could feel a sob, many sobs, edge up my throat, but silenced them by breathing quickly through my nose. A good Virgin should always be composed.

'Composed of what?' I had asked Tullia.

'Two parts stillness, two parts silence,' she had answered. This proved to be much more efficient advice than Fabia's tangled religiosity.

The priest finally re-emerged in a clean toga, a new bull was brought forth and the ceremony began again. I stayed still now, letting the flies crawl over my hands, up my sleeves. When it was finally nearing its close and I had offered up our fish and cake and the soothsayer was reading the extracted liver, holding it next to a bronze model divided into sixteen sections that corresponded to the sixteen regions of the sky, a light misty shower began to fall. It was faint, less than a drizzle. The soothsayer stopped examining the liver, claimed it as pleasing to Neptune,

41

and the priest motioned to the temple's attendants to begin burning the animal fat on the altar.

The gathering of farmers lifted their hands in the air, smiling at one another, suddenly unburdened by unpredictability. Some of the farmer's wives were almost dancing, arms flailing, praising Neptune; some had their eyes rolling back into their heads. Overjoyed, elated, jubilant, delighted, I use these words liberally when I can, like adding more honey to your wine when no one is looking, taking full advantage of opportunity. They could have been carried away if it had not been for their husbands pulling down on their arms like levers. The wives settled down as if their husbands had opened a trapdoor and their happiness, merriment, glee had gushed out. Or at least quieted until later, when the gods were not so close by and could not be annoyed by their high-pitched voices.

Landowners grouped together as if discussing their next move to further better the odds of abundant crops, or maybe finding out what the others planned to sacrifice later in the woods and making a note to outdo them. To sway Neptune to be on one's side, edging out the competition and becoming wealthier than the rest, though they may just have been discussing the games that were to be held later on. I often do this, think the worst of others.

I was now a portent of good fortune. No, not just me, it is one for all. All the Virgins were one single portent of good fortune because of me. If Porcia had been here and not tending in the temple, I'd have stuck my tongue out at her. They would be very pleased; maybe I would even receive an extra piece of pastry later, after dinner.

As we travelled back to the house in the litter I could hear the farmers and their wives saying I had cried 'Victory', others

'Rain', some even said when my mouth opened it sounded like the echo of a seashell and that I must have been infused with Neptune. Yes, it must have been Neptune who stung me.

I looked up to Sempronia and Fabia, trying to find some trace of happiness in their faces, even gratitude, but their veils were pulled as tight as the curtains round the litter and the parts that did show appeared expressionless, unmoved, blank as hard-boiled eggs. Even Tullia.

I was made to practise staying still for days afterward. Fabia wiped my wrists and ankles, even neck, with honey and sent me to stand still in the garden until told otherwise. 'Practise makes perfect.'

Fabia never explained why my cry was punished instead of celebrated, but later I would come to understand that if it had not rained, there were things we could have been held accountable for, not just me; it is one for all.

Sometimes I'd have to stand there as the others ate, ants crawling over my feet and up my legs, bees and black flies buzzing and landing in the folds of my stola, sometimes landing on my cheek. Some slowly crawling up my arm, over my shoulder to the honey on my neck.

The first time I kept my eyes on Tullia, wishing she'd look back, wishing I could hear her thoughts, could carry on whole conversations with her without ever uttering a word, but she would not return my look. Later she said she could not encourage my dependence; it would be better for me in the end to learn to stand without her.

This is when I discovered that counting worked best, counting the leaves on trees, the stones in the cobblestone paths, various kinds of flowers. Then, later, at ceremonies, counting the spots on a heifer or the toes of those in attendance for the sacrifice, the ridges in a pillar or the leaves of the ivy growing up it, in order to keep still, pass the time. It is better to count than to count on.

CHAPTER V

Julia came less than a year after me. I do not remember any details of the Virgin she replaced, other than that she was fifth, and that she was kept behind closed doors. But I do recall her cough was violent and echoed through the central atrium, until one day it stopped. The others rarely mentioned her, but I knew she wasn't old, because she was fifth and so had to be younger than Porcia. Fabia said her death could be blamed on the weakness of her cycles, which had placed Rome under stress and may have caused the dissension between the two consuls that year, and thus, Vesta allowed illness to befall her. There was guilt and a need to atone when a young Virgin died.

Afterward, there was a flurry of busyness. The others seemed to move in a sudden whirlwind of silent knowing, of synchronicity that left me behind, outside comprehension until Tullia told me I was about to attend a funeral, that now I was fifth. She relayed this as if it were something I should be pleased about, and at first I thought she meant I should be happy this girl was dead, but, later, I understood that without birth, without marriage, only death was left, even a young death, to give signature to the passage of time. Time, Tullia said, is a comatose animal and any occasional heave it gives to show it is still alive is cause enough to be pleased.

I watched Julia very carefully at first, trying to spot some kind of resemblance between us, some commonality that made us both Jupiter's choice. I went over her round and chubby face with its clusters of freckles that spread over her cheeks and forehead, her blue eyes like two baubles of silver sticking out of a sandy shore, searching for what it was that had attracted Jupiter to us. I thought it would be much more apparent since we were both still children, and that perhaps whatever it was faded as one aged, because I could not see why Jupiter would have ever chosen Fabia or Sempronia or Porcia.

I watched as Julia's hair was being sheared, as she sat stiff as a wooden doll, quiet as a mouse, still as stone, not even sure if she were really alive or not. We did not look very much alike – I had no freckles, my hair and eyes were very dark chestnut. But then, as she stood up and the slave brushed the rest of her cedar-coloured hair from her tunic, her face started to shrink into a red, runny mess. Her cries were loud and sharp, as if she were suffocating on them.

Fabia pointed at me. 'She did not cry and she is barely older than you, just seven. She was proud to give Vesta something of herself and be accepted by her . . .' She told Julia my hair was long again under my headdress and that it was only shorn off a year ago. Fabia was lying: my hair was not long at all, not even to my ears, and I had cried worse than Julia. I wondered what else she lied about.

Sempronia and Fabia finally gave up and sent Julia inside, then after a few minutes sent me in to play with her, to distract her from her sadness, make her sound less unsettling, before she turned into a bad omen.

When I entered her room she was limp like a rabbit on the

floor, skinned and ready to eat. I was suddenly tempted to treat her as a lesser; to act as if I knew better than her childishness, that I was as swift and proficient as the others; to click my tongue and sigh so she could admire me and I could feel better. Surely, they sent me here to set an example. But when she didn't look up at me, her back shuddering as if she were trying to grind herself down into flour and escape through the fine cracks in the floor, I said, 'I am fine and you will be too . . . We were chosen by Jupiter. There is a lot to do. You will learn how to read. In a way you get to become a boy, grow into a sort of man, a person who is owned neither by a father nor by a husband . . .' I trailed off, realized that what I was saying sounded more like a series of questions, repeating what I had been told over and over by Sempronia and Fabia.

Then I said nothing at all, but pulled off my headdress and showed her my short hair, just two thumbs' length off my scalp. 'See, we're the same.' My heart thumped in my chest; I wanted her to be my friend. From the moment I knew another was to be chosen, I had confided in Piso and Livia how hopeful I was of having a companion. Not one like Tullia, but one I could do more playful things with, more often.

When she finally did sit up all she said was, 'My mother . . .' then fell back over, her tears renewed.

I simply sat there for a little while, wanting to tell her something soothing, something about my mother and father, perhaps lie and say that they visited from time to time and that her mother would probably come soon. She would like me more for this, and once she found it wasn't true, she'd appreciate the fact that I'd tried to ease her grief. But my parents were already lapsing into silhouettes, drowning in the black sea of the forgotten.

47

'We are one family. Think of us now as your sisters, your aunts, your loved ones,' Fabia had said, always omitting 'mother.'

I decided to tell her about my dog. 'She's a sweet little thing, she visits every so often—'

'You're lying.' She sat straight up. 'My mother said once I was chosen my ancestry with her and my father would disappear and be replaced with a new one, as a Virgin.' She wiped her nose on her fingers.

'I only wanted to make you feel better, ease your grief . . .'

She leaned back on her elbows, grew very quiet, her reddened eyes narrowed. A sudden look of puzzlement parted her lips, then she shook her head at me. 'I am not grieving; these are tears of joy! I am rejoicing, just as my mother said I would.'

CHAPTER VI

The following day Fabia taught Julia the stories of past great Vestal Virgins; it was a lesson for Julia, as I had heard them all before. She took us round the central atrium over and over again, nearly stroking the legs of the statues, if stroking were allowed, as she spoke: 'This is Fulvia; she lived nearly a hundred years ago. Her greatness came when barbarians entered Rome. They approached at night and did not want to be seen coming, so they travelled in complete darkness. Once they arrived they entered the temple and tried to light their torches to set Rome on fire. But Fulvia, always dutiful in keeping Vesta strong and the temple clean with purified water, stopped their attempts at stealing Vesta's fire with her great reverence for Vesta and Rome. Regardless of how long the barbarians held their torches in Vesta, regardless of how much oil they poured over them, they would not light. The smoke from Vesta turned a bright purple, signalling to the rest of Rome the presence of barbarian intruders.' When she told these stories, her half smile curled up like a snarl, her skin turned a faint rose and her dark brown eyes looked beyond us, as if under the spell of something.

'This is Servilia, the Virgin tending Vesta when Hannibal finally fell. She was very young, her coming of age arrived when she was barely ten. Vesta beckoned her early. Though almost a child, she was a Virgin of immense modesty and devotion, she never engaged in childish antics, not even showing interest in toys. When she was struck with a fever, she never once complained. She died while tending Vesta, yet held on with her last breath until Rome captured Macedonia.' Fabia would pause then, waiting for the goodness of Servilia to settle over us, into us, as if we were raw meat marinating in olive oil and pepper; Servilia with the small chip in her cheek, her blank, downcast eyes, her painted skin a shade too brown, almost red as if flushing with utter demureness. Fabia let out a sigh. 'If only all young Virgins aspired to such greatness . . .' She trailed off, giving up on us for the time being, unsure if we were naturals like Servilia.

'And this statue . . .' she waved her arms up and down the largest statue at the head of the pool, or perhaps it was the foot, if the pool were a table and a table were a body. The pliability of words can also divert the mind from the sleepiness of boredom. Men sit at the head of the table, so women are their feet, though men always claim women to be underfoot. Is it better to be the head or the feet? The feet can run away, but then so can the head.

'This . . .' Fabia picked something off the statue's base and brushed the stone hem of the stola clean, 'this . . . is Rhea Silva . . . the first . . .' Fabia's voice broke each time we came to this one, her body shaking beneath her stola, causing little quakes to rise through the fabric, her sagging chin wagging back and forth. 'She is the mother of Rome.' Rhea had just been freshly painted, the female slaves would do it when the cool, wet winters and hot, dry summers had eventually taken their toll and the statues appeared like faded apparitions, or the weathered women who stood round the arena after the games. She seemed almost life-like, her eyes following us; the lines round her mouth and down her chin gave the impression she was suppressing a laugh or a cry. Each of her arms was bent at the elbow in a gesture of eternal receiving, of unrequited wanting.

Fabia concluded her tour, as always, with the same words: 'A Virgin's name is never spoken in public, unless she is dead and revered or of ill-repute; the former becomes part of history and lasts for ever, but the latter is short-lived and forgotten. Only good Virgins are remembered.' Sometimes Fabia would send us off ahead of her and stay behind slumped at the ankles of one of the statues.

Tullia later told me that every Virgin left a will giving her would-be dowry to pay for a statue to be erected in her honour – that is, if she were judged worthy – otherwise the dowry went to the house. A Virgin's worthiness was decided ultimately by the Pontifex Maximus, and in order to gain his attention, a Virgin must be considered extraordinary in her talents of devotion. The most devoted, she said, were thought to embody numina-like powers. These Virgins could cure illness, send tremors to far-off lands and incite defeat, defend our borders with their ethereal wombs.

'But space is limited, only so many can be squeezed into the central atrium. This is every Virgin's aim, to be immortalized as a trophy to her own devotion. The only time a Virgin is ever coveted is when she is stone, and even then only by other Virgins. It's been eighty years or more since a new statue has been erected – did you not notice the dates beside their names?

Why bother? The people have forgotten to attribute any of Rome's glory to us. Why share the glory with a Virgin who is just as readily available to blame when the status quo is shaken?' She also said it was pure irony that the only women in Rome permitted to produce a will had no one to leave anything to.

We were each expected to pay the statues adulation throughout the day, dropping daisies at their feet. Some had toes too thick and hulky and others too skinny and claw-like. I wondered what sort of liberties the stone carvers took, or if this was what they had really looked like. There was a kind of similarity among them, similar head-shapes, noses, all about the same height, even Servilia. They would have had to be carved from memory, but whose memory? Not the stone carver's; he would have been hired only after the Virgin died. It would have had to be the memory of other Virgins, and none would be willing to claim knowledge of intimate details of another. 'No, her chin was softer, more round; it would wrinkle up when she chewed or was deep in thought.' This would not occur. Or perhaps this was meant to be snide, not to offer anything that would make the statue seem different from the others. To have the final say: 'She is who I say she is.' Each had a striking resemblance to Rhea, the first. There were variations, possibly improvements; some had their arms at their sides, smaller eyes, more lowered. The suppressed expression exchanged for one more satisfied and peaceful.

There was an allure to thinking my image could be made into a statue one day, whether or not it really looked like me, my name at least would be there at the base, under my feet. My only heir, the only indelible mark on the world I could make, like graffiti 'I was here . . . really I was.'

Julia and I would stand and stare at the life-sized figures in admiration, bringing daisies, the symbol of Virginity because of their simplicity, lack of colour and innocent shape, to Rhea Silva sometimes three times a day. We would lay the flowers over each of her hands, half expecting them to close and her arms to rest. The more time we spent admiring the statues, the longer we could stay out in the garden collecting daisies. And at dinner, we would be given an extra pastry for our acts of devotion. Sempronia would do this silently, nod at a slave to place another on our plate; a much-coveted token of reassurance and approval, though a mute one that caused a short uplifting swell in my chest. This extra pastry tasted sweeter than any other. It seemed food was the one indulgence a Virgin could enjoy, sometimes to excess. Sempronia ate as much cake as she pleased; she was the one who controlled it after all, and her growing waistline showed she was very pleased with herself.

CHAPTER VII

We were allowed to wander after class, all through the house, up and down stairs, in and out of rooms. We were not yet permitted in the room where the wills were kept, but we did not care. The rest of the house, its airiness, like a yawning mouth, was enough.

Even now, when I recall the brief freedom we experienced in those first few years, it seems it could not have really happened here, not in this house. But then I suppose that sense of freedom was fictional, fabricated in order for us to settle into the house and see it as our home. Our wanderings were only another exercise intended for us to lose our sense of time and the time 'before'.

But while these seemingly unrestricted strolls lasted, the kitchen was my favourite place to be because the others were rarely there. I would hide under a table or sometimes sit in the open eating apples with Julia, listening to the slaves, pretending they were a gaggle of aunts. The casual way they spoke to one another while slicing fruit or chopping cabbage, sorrel or leeks filled us with puffs of white cloud, the wake without the storm. Easing into their complaints about the aches and pains in their hands and elbows and feet or the lateness of the day, so much to do, too little time; the sweet smell of baking bread wafting in the air as they joked to one another, playful taunts, retorting by bumping into each other with their hips. They spoke of those who had died and from what. Though sometimes it was how. Of people they once knew. There was a difference between what one died from and how one died. When it was of what, they shared stories, comparing treatments and cures used in their homelands. When it was of how, they spoke in whispers, lips drooping into their chins like inverted bowls, shaking their heads from side to side in quick sharp quivers.

They were different from one another, some white, some dark, some very black, others pockmarked and scarred pink. Not the same as us; I could easily tell them apart. Sometimes I'd listen to them mourn their pasts. It would happen suddenly. One would be kneading dough to make bread, arms nearly up to the elbow in a large red earthenware bowl. She would stop abruptly, her shoulder sinking until she was almost bowing over the bowl. Another slave would rush over, say something softly into her ear, put an arm round her waist and guide her to the stool in the corner where she'd sit for a while, staring at the tiled mosaic of a hearth and Virgin in the floor, crying without moving, without tears, without opening her mouth. It was this gentleness between them that also brought me here, just to watch it.

Or there would be conspiratorial whispers, just out of our reach, only an occasional profanity caressing the tips of our ears. 'Bitch . . . impossible . . . daughter of a donkey . . . witch does nothing.' Insulting Sempronia, the others, each other, even the dull knives. They would suddenly remember me, look over and switch to another language, each word floating like an empty crate at sea. Their roughness reminding me they were from a separate place.

At first I invited Julia to play games of hide and seek, leap and jump, imaginary explorations of enchanted forests, but she would partake only in religious games. So we would take flowers from the pots placed throughout the house, fasten them into wiry crowns and pretend we were getting ready to be offered up, like a trickle of wine or a gift of gold, as new daughters to some god in the sky. I would pretend to slit Julia's throat and she thrashed about until she suddenly grew very still. Then a smile would erupt over her cheeks and she would reach up in the air, at her beautiful new mother, sometimes nameless, sometimes Vesta or Venus or even Minerva, who would embrace her, having turned her into a little goddess. She'd walk around quite piously, pleading that I go along and make offerings at her feet, until I grew tired of it and told her she was being sacrilegious and could very well be punished by Vesta.

She also liked to pretend I was sick, near death, and soon she'd be sick as well and the only way we could both survive was if we found some secret plant, like a lotus, to offer to the goddess Fortuna. This game I enjoyed; I liked the way she would feel my forehead for a fever, tuck my hair behind my ears and soothe me, saying, 'I'll be back soon, I promise.' She'd return with a leaf plucked from the garden or a pot of flowers and we'd be cured and ready to move on to something else.

Other times we pretended to be Remus and Romulus, snuggling up to our mother wolf or battling one another. I would like to pretend to duel with shiny sharp swords, but Julia preferred we narrated the battle together; neither of us ever wanted to be

Remus. Often I would cajole Julia into being Remus with the promise that I would act him next time, but then would later deny I ever made such a promise. Julia would crumble into a sobbing tantrum each time and I'd feel a strange and panicked satisfaction, before eventually allowing her to be Romulus.

Often we swam away the evenings, flipping and rolling in the pool meant for bathing, counting who could hold her breath longer, our chests nearly bursting, our wool under-dresses rising with water, smelling faintly of wet dog.

I asked if she would pretend to be a Siren with me, luring men from their ships. We were not meant to know what a Siren was, but somehow I had heard of them, likely from my brother.

'They sing love songs and the men sailing by get trapped by them, ensnared like flies in a spider's web, forgetting about riches, battles. They just float towards the song, helplessly. But the Sirens are really pirates in disguise and as soon as the men arrive on their island, crying for their love, the Sirens behead them . . . no, enslave them until they are rickety old men, then they behead them.'

I would open my eyes very wide, lower my voice into a booming note, and she would emit a squeak of fear. I liked to scare her. I would sometimes pretend to be sucked down to the bottom of the pool, towards a Siren's song only I could hear, nearing the Underworld, sinking to my chin, then up I'd come again singing:

> There was an old king named Priam
> He exiled his daughter to Brundisium
> Apollo's seeress was she
> Out she swam to the Aegean Sea

As Troy tumbled down
She nearly drowned
Until Agamemnon's daughter
Bobbed up right beside her
Thus, she held tight upon her decapitated head
And old Cassandra gave her best tread
Until Agamemnon's ship sailed by
And pulled her up and out by her thigh.

Grabbing at her legs, pulling her under as a game, but of course she only kicked and screamed. Fabia would come and tell me to get out. 'The bath is not a pool to splash about in. It's a place to wash . . . A clean Virgin is a good Virgin.'

Julia would swim up to the side then and stare up at the statues with awe and Fabia would let her stay in the pool as a slave dried me off.

It was the slaves who bathed us, brushed us, cared for us when were sick; at least this wasn't any different from our first home. The others couldn't spend themselves that way; having children in the house was dangerous for them as well, it could awaken something.

In the garden we'd eat our lunch sitting on short stools, quickly swallowing dried figs and nuts, gulping down cheese and bread and olives, so we could have time to play. We'd sometimes go over to the small statue of Priapus, round and fat, sitting naked on top of one of the walls enclosing the garden, an inscription in his bronze back claiming: 'I, god of gardens, will rape any man, woman, boy or girl who enters this garden uninvited and with intent to steal, killing any intruder by penetration.' We discovered him one day, hidden under some vines. A funny little fat man with a vulgar grin, one hand holding a scythe, the other holding himself under the fold of his belly like a weapon. In other state gardens he is much larger, life size in height, his stone body sculpted like a soldier's, though I do not know how lifelike the other part is. In our garden, he is subdued and supposed to go unnoticed; a necessary measure of security that is to be ignored by us, as if made invisible in the path of our purity.

Though the presence of this god, any god, could not occur inside the house, outside is beyond their control. After all, such lewd depictions are everywhere, painted on chariots to ward off envy, hanging from shops in the Forum representing Roman strength, outside the temple of Ceres encouraging fertility in women. Weapons like Priapus's swing on shop fronts, made into wind chimes, begging to be looked at. Control what you can, Tullia used to say, and I suppose this is true for all of us; a Virgin can always close her eyes, though Tullia likely meant open eyes.

The front of Priapus faced outwards, so Julia and I would lift one another to see it, the long wide stick jutting from him. At first we thought it was only a stick to beat the intruders with, before we were taught the word 'rape.' Fabia taught us this as well, though it was a question better meant for Tullia. Julia, obviously preoccupied with the word while we were copying out letters, simply asked its meaning with the same ease as if asking about Minerva's shield or Jupiter's lightning.

Fabia didn't snort or press her mouth thin as a pin, become silent as she usually did when a stray question was asked. 'An irrelevant question incites an irrelevant answer. Ask only that which will better you,' she would finally say and continue with her teaching, and slowly we understood that relevant questions were those which were asked in order for her to expand her teachings in greater detail.

Instead she came in close towards us and motioned for us to stand. She bent over just slightly because she was barely taller than us, even then we nearly reached her shoulders. 'Rape is something that can happen to you if you do not follow the ways of a Virgin, just as not eating all your dinner would result in fever.' She spoke in that cautioning way she sometimes did when she wanted to emphasize the gravity of her warnings or the severity of a god's wrath; soft and low and so out of the ordinary we could only believe we were being given sound advice that would keep us safe.

'Virgins have three eyes, and the third is hidden there.' Fabia pointed to the V-shaped crevice between our legs that had yet to be given a name. 'It is the eye within.' Unlike our arms, legs, neck, elbows and ankles, this spot could not be precisely identified, and with its namelessness and its use for passing water, I believed it was considered as revolting as foul odours and excrement, as these too were not something a Virgin commented on.

An eye, a third eye.

'But why can I not see out of it?' I asked, feeling myself clench, attempting to blink, see. How unfamiliar I felt to myself then, as if my skin was a stola with secret purses sewn into it and I was just discovering their contents.

'It looks inward at your purity. It is the eye that watches for Vesta and sees your dedication, purity and worship. You must watch out for this eye, as the eye watches out for Vesta. It is tender and delicate and, like your other eyes, this one could turn red, swollen, even fall out if scratched. If you poke the eye below

60

it blinds Vesta to your purity and so you must use the sponges and sticks in the chamber room very carefully, just one poke, one jab and it would break and Vesta would know. Careful preservation of the eye is what makes one a Virgin.' Fabia turned, about to continue with her lessons, but Julia called after her, 'But what of rape?'

Fabia stilled for a moment, as if Julia had thrown something at her and she was stunned by the impact. Even I was amazed at Julia's forwardness; she should have known better by then. I expected her to be punished, maybe have her tongue lassoed up with a long piece of string, the other end tied to her thumb as I had once been punished for speaking out of turn in my first year.

'Control your tongue,' I waited for Fabia to say, for her white skin to flare red and her chin to tuck into her chest so that the sagging skin underneath bulged up like a frog's inflated throat. Any moment she would beckon to the slave standing at the arch-way to inflict the string punishment upon Julia.

But Fabia only returned to hover just above our heads; a twitch travelled down her nostrils to the corner of her lip.

'Rape is getting this eye purposely poked out by another.'

She said this as if it were plainly obvious but she peered down at us with such disgust that I wasn't sure if it was over the act of rape itself or because Julia had demanded an answer and Fabia had been required to give her one. When I think back to that moment, I realize Fabia may have shuddered with disgust that she herself was born at all with this third eye, the eye within, and though it was imperative to teach us its existence it complicated her own complete denial of its presence in her own body and thus the vulnerability of her own Virginity. As she wrung her

61

small, childish hands, we waited to hear more about the one who rapes, what sort person was he, how could he be recognized, how exactly would it occur, was Priapus the main perpetrator? But the spell of secret-sharing was now broken, the invitation to ask anything more was over and the constant shrillness in her voice returned as the rest of her words spilled from her crooked mouth. Her breath smelled as sour as stale wine or over-ripe fruit.

'Now, matrons have eyes also, but their husbands prick them so they can deposit their seeds and make them mothers. This is why the matrons swell as they do. Their eyes have turned inside out into pockets so they can hold the infants until they are ready to be born. When the infant finally comes it inflicts writhing pain upon the matrons, which is most often fatal. Luckily, matrons have very different sets of eyes than both of you. Be thankful Vesta sees through your eyes. Remember, good Virgins keep all their eyes to the ground. In the end, rules are for your own good.' Before she turned back to her chair I noticed the whites of her dark brown eyes were slightly yellowed, with a small bump knotted up in one like a miniscule pile of salt that could be pinched off.

CHAPTER VIII

Later, when Julia and I walked around the garden, we took careful steps, our legs pressed unusually tightly together, using only
our feet and legs beneath our knees to carry ourselves forward.
This lasted for only a few days – that is, until we later came of
age and this style of walking became innate.

It was Julia who first suggested we take a stroll closer to where
Priapus squatted on the garden wall, though of course she didn't
mention Priapus, only that she wished to get a closer look at the
daisies in that part of the garden. 'We should look for some tall
ones to grace Rhea's hands.' She glanced at me sideways, wanting to see if I would comply with her dare, and so I did by
pretending I was unaware Priapus was so close by. We stood at
the edge of the path over the patch of daisies, teetering slightly
as if we stood on a cliff over the sea.

'They are best like this, on a sunny day. So vibrant.'

'Yes, their yellow centres are like a cat's eyes.'

The mere mention of 'eyes' made us both burst into a shy
giggle. Julia waded farther into the daisy patch, turning to see if
I'd follow her. 'There's a rabbit over there. We should get it and
toss it outside the garden before it eats everything up.'

'Where?' I did not see a rabbit. 'We could never catch a

rabbit,' I said, trying to sound guided only by logic and not by fear.

'But maybe we could find the hole it sleeps in and tell the slaves,' Julia retorted, smiling. I could not think of a good enough reason to dissuade her unless I mentioned Priapus, and if I did so, I would have to admit I was afraid and Julia would have won the dare.

She waded in first, her legs disappearing in the daisies of desertion, all the way up to her knees. I followed her, staying slightly behind her. Julia suddenly crouched down. 'I will look here for the rabbit hole. You look over there.' She pointed to her right, towards the rows of cypress trees in front of the wall where the daisies' green willowy stems unabashedly arched forward to get out of the shadows cast by the trees. Again a goading smile crept over her face: do it, just to see what will happen.

As I walked slowly towards the wall, stopping frequently and making a show of closely examining the ground for openings, Julia hissed at me, 'That bush there, it's rustling. Quick! Priapus!' I started to run, but tripped beneath the daisies' white heads into a dark earthy forest I was suddenly lost in. The sharp taste of dread peppered my throat, over my tongue. Priapus would grab one of my legs any moment and pull them apart.

'Quick!' Julia hissed again. She knew better than to yell, to draw attention, even if I was suffocating down here or my eye was being scooped out. I stood up and ran to Julia, who was nervously bouncing up and down on her toes. We both ran back towards the path, a gleeful panic bursting in our chests. Julia held my hand tightly as we ran towards the house, letting go just before we reached it as Porcia, sitting quietly on a bench, came into view. I noticed then the dirt down the front of my stola.

64

'Walk!' Porcia commanded and ordered a slave to let Sempronia know we had been running. Julia and I glanced at one another; we hated Porcia then. We resented taking orders from her; she was directly in the middle. If we must be further refined and our faults sifted away, it was somehow worse for it to be brought on by Porcia. When the slave returned with a rope to tie round our ankles so we could not take such long strides, Porcia watched, almost mirthful. She would get an extra pastry at dinner.

Even so, Julia and I made it a game to circle round Priapus, always under the pretence of admiring the daisies. It excited a mixture of horror and exhilaration that made the constant dullness of each day more bearable. We'd squeal at the other's claims that it was turning around to point towards us. 'Priapus is coming for you . . . watch your eye,' I'd call out to Julia and we'd stumble on, the rope chafing our ankles. She would always reach for me as we loped away, linking her arm tightly through mine or gripping my hand; she always liked to be touching in some way, she said it warded him off to see two Virgins so close together.

Eventually Priapus no longer evoked such fear, and Julia decided it was silly to fear him.

'This is our garden, we are not intruders. Why should he be interested in us? It is us he is protecting! We are Vesta's servants.' She said this one day after I claimed to have felt the earth move and was sure it was Priapus coming for us in the shape of a slug. She laughed at me drily with her nose wrinkled up. 'You should know better than to be frightened. I know better and you are older than me.'

'Well, I can list all of Jupiter's epithets.' I felt betrayed by her sudden departure from our game; it was made worse by her waiting for such a moment so she could belittle my ignorance that we'd outgrown fearing Priapus. She had done something similar a short while ago, when I suggested we act out a sacrifice to Mars, something Julia was always eager to do. This time she said she thought it sacrilegious and pretended to have always believed such games to be impious. I am not sure what happened next – we likely squabbled, as we tended to do, over who knew more than the other.

Julia still liked to go sometimes and look at Priapus's blinding stick, but now she would justify our visits as acceptable, considering he was a god and the attention we paid to him was, in a way, a form of worship. Julia needed this now, a link to religious devotion, no matter how weak or flimsy. I suppressed my fears and went along. She was becoming more virtuous by the day; I had to keep up with her.

Though I no longer appeared to fear Priapus in front of Julia, at night I often thought I heard him punishing an intruder outside, and I'd sit up in my bed, clutching at the blankets. Or I'd think he'd mistaken me for an intruder earlier in the afternoon and was waiting to pounce on me at night, while I slept. This is when my nightmares began.

CHAPTER IX

My favourite slave was a short, round woman with dark bushy hair and a toothless smile. She laughed easily, her tongue falling out of her mouth, and when the others were not around she'd tickle our ribs, pull our noses. Once when Julia fell climbing up out of the pool and hurt her arm, the slave scooped her up, carried her into the kitchen and tied bacon round the fractured bone, without ever hushing her. When my ear was sore and burning and dizziness seemed to tip me up and down, she laid me on my bed and gently cleaned my ear with warm water and inserted a mixture of the gall of swine and oil of roses, warmed with leek juice and honey. It slowly trickled down my ear, soothing the burning. Then she rubbed it with a blend of vinegar and the old sloughed skin of a serpent, wrapped up in a ball of wool. I called her Altrica after that, nurse. Sometimes she sang as she bathed me, nonsense songs without much of a story, more just humming with words which I couldn't fully understand or repeat, but I could feel the vibrations of her voice travel down her arm as she rubbed me with olive oil.

But she was my favourite for only a short while, until I found Cupid, a stray kitten. It was mewing by the kitchen door, the one that opens up to the grain storehouse. I gave it tiny slices of bird meat I was able to swipe when the aunts were busy rushing in and out, tending to laundry or weaving.

I called it Cupid because I immediately loved him, struck by his sharp arrow. I knew 'it' was a he, like the boy-god of love, because it seemed, according to the plays put on at the theatre, boys best inspired love.

I did not even bother to ask any of the others if I could keep him; it was useless, I knew. We are not to mother, not now, not then. Though I did tell Julia and soon we were both caring for him.

'We must protect him at all costs.' I needed her to promise.

'Yes.' She agreed, and then added more quietly, 'Let's pretend we are his parents; I am the husband and you are the matron.'

'Happily!' I answered, pleased with her sudden transgression and relieved we were, even if just for a little while, able to resume any sort playfulness.

'Though I suppose it would be better if he is adopted.' Her freckles sunk in a brief rush of red.

We led Cupid close to the cypress trees, where we could visit him unseen. Or at least we thought no one would see us. Children are so obvious. I see them at the games; they think they can get away with anything just a short distance away from their parents. But then we must have got away with it for a little while at least; it would never have been allowed to go on otherwise.

It lasted for more than a week, our secret meetings with Cupid. We stripped twigs of leaves and twirled them around Cupid in the garden behind the row of rose bushes, giggling as his big furry paws swatted and missed. He would roll on his back, back and forth, catching sand and leaves in his long fluffy

68

orange fur as we stroked his belly. I kissed him a thousand times, his whiskers tickling my nostrils, his rough tongue scraping against my cheeks. Julia didn't kiss him once but she liked to watch the way Cupid would reach up to my lips. We dug him burrows, tiny caves as his home, and when he did not go in, I tied together some sticks into a sort of tent and was relieved when he happily rolled on his back, shaded from the hot sun in his new home.

Julia would come up behind me and place her hands on my shoulders; twice she wrapped her arms around my waist. Her hands would blaze into my skin, and I would worry sweaty fingerprints would give us away. Once she pulled me back into her, hugging me tightly, I could feel her stomach swell and shrink against the small of my back, her rope nudging into me as she breathed. She was always very soundless when she did this. I assumed it was because neither of us was quite sure what a husband would say to a matron.

It was Altrica who noticed the missing meat and discovered Cupid begging by the back door. She swatted at him over and over with a broom, as I stood there silently watching. Julia was there, sitting on a stool, nibbling on olives. Her mouth fell wide open and I couldn't tell if she was laughing or crying, and I could see green bits of olive speckled over her pink tongue like a disease. There was nothing I could do. I couldn't stand it, the sounds he was making. I ran to the door and tried scooping him up. If Altrica hadn't known before it was me who was caring for Cupid, she knew now. She laughed, her tongue again dangling out, but this time it was not sweet or playful, almost as if she were laughing at me for thinking there could be any other outcome. She pulled me back. 'You know better than that,' she said.

Later, when she bathed me, I tried my best to seem indifferent, as if I did not know or care for the beggar of an orange cat, but I could not help cringing at her touch.

Altrica must have told Sempronia because I was not allowed to eat for two days. Julia said nothing of her own role in keeping Cupid, but told me she was very sorry over what had happened. I said there was little point in both of us suffering and she agreed, though during dinner, as I sat and watched the others dine, Julia seemed to take a new pleasure in eating, as if each bite was a rare delicacy.

Over dinner Sempronia usually tested us, between mouthfuls of stuffed dates or pastry. 'March, tell me about March,' she would demand as crumbs spilled down her chin.

'The month of March belongs to Mars. He is the god of war and promotes victory and glory for Roman armies. He also oversees Rome's agriculture. On the first day of March we attend Mars's sanctuary in the Regia, the symbolic home of our Pontifex Maximus, who really lives in the State House, where twelve young aristocrats perform rituals to encourage the growth of crops . . .'

Julia and I would alternate answers, and Sempronia would offer the extra piece of pastry to the one who answered best. To be right. To be better than Julia.

If either of us smiled, the pastry would be taken away; gloating is foreign to a good Virgin, Sempronia would tell us. This was untrue; even the way Sempronia waved at one of the slaves to take away the pastry seemed too pronounced, a gesture that revelled in its own weight.

This evening, only Julia was quizzed and she was more talkative than usual, answering all Sempronia's questions with a kind of vigour that seemed put on; she did not look at me at all, none of them looked at me. I seemed a spirit, though powerless, more like fog in the early morning. I thought of how on the first day I arrived the others seemed to be only multiples of one and how now, when I stand with them at sacrifices, I must also seem indistinguishable. I watched Julia very carefully across the table, transfixed, and realized we were like two shades of the same colour that could be told apart by the others from here forward only when compared, and that she already knew this. She licked her lips more often than normal as she spooned up her pastry.

I think perhaps I am wrong when I think that children are so obvious; it seems that battles can be waged and go unnoticed.

Cupid disappeared; at least this is what I told myself, because disappearing is open-ended.

I stopped going to the kitchen after that. The aunts dissolved like snails in salt, and slaves could not be trusted.

A few days later, after I had eaten my lunch in the garden, I wandered out to the place where we found Priapus. I had planned it the night before, a slow, careful, methodical wandering, nothing obvious; I even pretended I was chasing something, a frog, or perhaps picking berries. Once I reached the edge of the garden, I grabbed some of the vines growing along the wall like matted hair and tried to pull myself up. I expected someone to get me by my waist and pull me down, a bell to toll, even for Priapus to lean over and blind me, but no one came. I heaved one leg over the wall and sat there, with a leg on each side. Still no one came. I could leave now, slide straight down this wall, maybe even find Cupid in the Forum. The Forum itself rippled with movement, the way sun glints against shuddering water, streaming from one place to the next. I could see outlines of carcasses hanging in butchers' stalls, the swinging of various coloured cloths through the air being beaten by fullers like falling leaves in autumn. I watched litters being squeezed through crowded streets, down alleyways and between temples, a man juggling, another on stilts, both vying for coin. Slaves carrying boxes of goods on their heads, or silks round their necks to bring back to their owners. A cacophony of shouts, laughter, flutes and lyres. I could get lost there; they'd never find me. But I already knew that beyond this wall was only another and another and another that would lead me right back here, behind the very one I was sliding down.

Any feelings of guilt that I once experienced picking daffodils were gone, replaced with a sensation of great release and empowerment. Anything with white will die today, I had decided, and pulled out clumps of flowers, though never daisies. I could feel them wilt between my fingers; I pulled off their heads, snapped the stems in bits and pieces, rolled the petals between my fingers until they tore apart.

CHAPTER X

Since Julia's arrival, Sempronia oversaw most of Tullia's classes. I never wondered until later why the others seemed to spite Tullia, what it was she'd done; their spite seemed very acceptable at the time, as if it were the natural order between them.

But today Sempronia wasn't there, and Tullia told us to draw whatever we wanted on our wax tablets, then pulled her chair closer to the window and, instead of gazing out, stared at the floor.

We each wanted Tullia; she was the only one who would verbalize fondness. Any morsel of attention she offered was accepted with a smile that could last for days. 'My, you look healthy today!' she would say to us alternately with an affectionate blink, or 'What a lovely shine to your skin', or 'How tall you are getting!'

These encounters with Tullia occurred almost always outside the classroom in the central atrium as she breezed by and we were being readied for our baths, or as she passed us on the stairs, or outside as she walked by in the garden; she was always much livelier, more endearing, when she was moving.

They weren't specific or consistent compliments. What Tullia complimented me on one day she could say to Julia the following week. But somehow that didn't lessen the effect of her words and, in fact, may have only added to the desperation with which we clung to her praise, as we knew it was so fleeting. In the short while after one of us was complimented, our mannerisms would change accordingly. If it was a comment on our skin we would stroke our cheeks when we knew the other was watching. If it was a comment on height, we'd lean into our toes for that extra bit of stature.

It was a secret, these compliments from Tullia. We knew she shouldn't be saying these things to us; it incited vanity, and vanity hindered devotion.

Or at least that is what Fabia would say when every so often we answered something correctly and unknowingly imparted an expectation in the lull that followed. 'If you expect praise, you vain girl, stand corrected. Praise is for Vesta and only Vesta. Devoted servants do not crave a slice of their goddess's praise. Devotion is beyond matter, substance, material and thus, its carrier must also be beyond matter, substance, material; vanity clogs the arteries devotion must pass through.'

Often Fabia would answer this lull with, 'Be modest; the greatest compliment for a Virgin, second to a statue in the central atrium for her heightened devotion, is to go unnoticed during her lifetime.' I would become confused with the contradiction, what was the difference between non-existence and unnoticed?

Tullia enjoyed revealing the presence of contradictions. But a contradiction is like a crack in the wall: once it's been noticed, one cannot help but always notice it. Tullia hadn't meant it this way, but she only enforced how irreparable being noticed is.

Devotion is indeed a careful negotiation, something each

Virgin can never have enough of, but it is not something one can show proof of, like a scab or a wound, or even a mole. There aren't any marks of devotion that can be flashed around like a gash, half healed, half oozing that which hasn't turned or ripened to devotion. Though I suppose, if one eats enough of the cake Sempronia offers for correct answers, one can show the fat around one's middle, evidence of gorging on devotion. But I can't seem to get fat.

Our time with Vesta is carefully allotted by our bodies, from when we start to bleed to when we stop; time itself is not a sign of devotion, though the longer one's body bleeds, the more devout the Virgin is believed to be. But it is modesty, in the interim, that is one's best attempt at proving devotion on a daily basis, and modesty is best demonstrated with one's face in a constant state of repose, an apathetic merriment around the eyes, a slightly sagging mouth. Most importantly, the eyes must lack any unnecessary sheen of alertness, as this can easily be confused with secrecy or smugness. The devout must, at all times, seem at once austere and tranquil.

Julia and I were not yet devout or modest, but modest in the making. We theatrically sparred over Tullia's attention like two actors waging war over an invisible crown. I wish I could say that when it was my turn to act haughty, I took into consideration how I felt when Julia had done it to me and refrained from perpetuating the same cruelty onto her, but we were both ruthless in our imagined exclusivity with Tullia; by then Julia and I were both friends and enemies at once – from circumstance. We became friends because of our close-ness in age – in another place we may not have liked one

75

another at all – but we also enacted the petty rivalries we saw around us.

We would each think of ways to get Tullia to look our way on the off-chance she would offer us some kind word we could gloat over. Sometimes one of us would speak more loudly or lag behind the other if Tullia was approaching, in the hope she would single us out. Afterwards, we'd accuse each other of cheating. I would exaggerate stories to Julia about how well Tullia and I got along before she arrived and how we'd spent the afternoons together alone. 'We would drink wine and unwind. She told me how advanced I was in reading and letters and how she felt I had a special purity.' I would tell Julia about the Neptune Festival, how I'd been celebrated, considered a portal. Of course, I left out the punishment I underwent and the reason I cried out. Sometimes I'd even put on a concentrated expression and tell Julia I was having a vision, but she soon imitated me and eventually we were both afflicted with mystic visions. This led to many futile arguments between us, arguments we could not prove or disprove as we'd not tell the other our vision but only claim after the fact to have known something would pass.

'I envisioned we'd be served marrows for dinner.'

'No, you did not.'

'Yes, I did.'

'No.'

'Yes.'

In the end Julia finally won; she was clever enough to become extra tight-lipped about her visions and would only mysteriously nod at her plate of food, or as a bird landed nearby. This I found especially irritating and as a result played up my own turn with a compliment from Tullia.

76

Tullia's compliments made each of us all the more determined to make the other feel that one was 'in' with Tullia and the other 'out'. Sometimes we would try to undo the other's compliment by a quick pinch on the arm, or a scuffing kick to the ankle or a push so the wax tablet was dropped, anything so that the other would get angry or cry ouch and Tullia would sigh with annoyance and the compliment would shatter.

On this particular day, I am not sure who it was who last received a compliment from Tullia, though I suspect it was me, considering what happened next. We had Tullia all to ourselves, cornered in the classroom, and the air was filled with a kind of fretfulness to seize this chance to impress her. I thought I would draw an elaborate garden with grand detail paid to various flowers and shrubs and trees with a large spouting fountain in the shape of a swan. I knew she loved the garden, the way she stared out at it. I could give her a new garden to look at, but each time I pressed my stylus into the wax nothing resembled what it should. I wanted to create something beautiful Tullia could take back to her room and hang upon her wall, glance at and think of me before falling asleep. I wanted to bring forth my drawing and have Tullia compliment my artistry in front of Julia. I couldn't think up another garden other than the one outside. I thought of the sun, the way it shimmied into the garden and made everything shine as if of silver. I will draw a silver garden for Tullia, yes, one filled with broad unyielding trees with branches made of shiny filaments that could be broken off and twined around the neck like jewellery. But each time my stylus dug into the wax I could not design anything other than the oak trees outside and the brick path between them. The blank tablet stared up at me, perforated like a bee-hive resting between my knees.

I looked over at Julia, who was drawing a picture of Vesta's hearth, with a long stick-like Minerva warming her hands over the fire. Minerva's fingers were almost claw-like, long as legs, and descended deep into the hearth.

'Her fingers are too long and would catch fire that way,' I whispered to Julia. 'You should shorten them.' I meant this as friendly help. Though this is how I remember it now, maybe I meant to be malicious right from the start. Maybe I wished I had thought to draw Vesta piously first.

'No . . . Vesta would never burn Minerva . . .' She shook her head without looking at me and continued drawing. This annoyed me, being dismissed as if I were younger than her; she was acting like Porcia.

'Yes, in your picture Vesta is roasting Minerva's fingers like piglets on skewers.'

'No . . . no.' Julia grew somewhat agitated, looking more closely at her sketch.

'It's an ugly picture and you've likely greatly offended Minerva and Vesta by making them so hideous . . .'

Julia jumped from her place on the floor and came towards me with the wax tablet held high over her head. I wasn't sure at first what she was about to do, then realized she intended to bash it into my skull. I blocked it with my arms, but it still clapped against my ear.

I screamed, my ear ringing. Julia held it up and was about to try to hit me again, but Tullia quickly tore it from her hands. She then leaned down and took mine, stepped back, her eyes wavering back and forth as if she could not recognize us, trying

78

to understand what it was we had just done. She held the tablets in front of her as if they were shields. She stood that way for a while, as if she had suddenly turned into Minerva. She finally placed the tablets on the table, pressed her palms to her cheeks or maybe over her ears and sat down again. Her upper body bent forward so that her head sunk towards her knees. The afternoon passed this way, with us watching Tullia slumped in her chair. 'Look what you've done,' I wanted to whisper to Julia, but when I looked over at her, she had pulled her headdress round her head as if hiding under the sheaths of silk until everything smoothed over, or maybe incubating her head so her modesty could hatch, and she could re-emerge an ideal Virgin. A coming-out. Fabia said modesty came from the head, not the heart.

That evening Sempronia did not quiz us at all, nor were there the usual pious conversations about upcoming festivals, preparations for state rituals. I noticed we dined quite silently as I picked mushrooms off the roasted turtle dove covered in honey and poppy seeds, trying to drop them inconspicuously under the table, hoping the sauce would not make a splattering sound. I hated mushrooms, their limpness and faint dung flavour. I looked up at Tullia sitting beside me, to see if she had noticed what I was doing, but she was busy stirring her spoon round in her plate; she barely ate anything. Maybe she knew what would happen next.

Sempronia clanged her knife against her cup. 'I listened to you teaching today, Tullia. I hid on the other side of the tapestry; you didn't even know I was there. I must say I am very disappointed that you cannot even properly convey the basic

79

rudiments to your students, although I am not surprised. I expected this, expected you were just putting on a show for me and did not really teach as you are required. From now on I will teach in the afternoons and when I am too tired Porcia will take over.'

Porcia straightened her back, perked up like a dog's ears. Julia waved at her, spoon in hand, making a soft gleeful sound. Maybe she knew then that Tullia was a sinking ship that should be abandoned.

I waited for Tullia to protest. Surely she would want to protect the time she shared with me, our bond, but she stayed silent, and grave disappointment crawled down my neck. I even willed her to reveal how Julia and I vied for her compliments, that our immodesties were the reason behind what had happened. To lose the afternoons with Tullia would be the worst punishment.

Instead Tullia sighed, a hard long sigh I could feel against my hand as it hovered over my plate picking at mushrooms. I would later interchangeably read this sigh as release from having to deal with Julia and me again, and fury at having her time with me stripped away. It was very dependent on how I felt about Tullia at the moment when this memory felt compelled to be conjured up and milled about my mind.

Memory is moody in this way.

As we continued through dinner, I felt my face slacken, open up as the lip of a cup that Vesta may drink from at her leisure. Modesty is consistency, and in that moment I solidified, my face hardened to the consistency of stone instead of skin, any expression was replaced with a fixed impression of modesty, as if I'd been branded and all that remained of my cheeks, lips, lids was the gristle of scar tissue. The ringing in my ear quieted to a distant tolling and a faint murmur I can sometimes still hear now; a constant reminder of the perils of the immodest.

CHAPTER XI

Our classroom began moving from room to room, no longer a door to enter or exit, teaching and learning never ceased. We could be called forth at any moment, expected to describe a prayer, the request, to which god, what was sacrificed, why, how, when; every minute detail bore itself into my core and became moored to my memory.

> Convector is the deity of binding and sheaths and must be
>   offered a pig wrapped in tree bark.
> Felicitas is goddess of good luck and is celebrated two days
>   after the nones of October.
> Spiniensis presides over the digging out of thorn bushes and
>   must be offered three droplets of blood from a pricked
>   thumb and five droplets from an ox.
> Sterculinus is the god of manure spreading and must be
>   offered one horse and two bulls.
> Robigus is the god of mildew or grain rust and must be
>   offered a rust-coloured dog ten days after the ides of April.

Late afternoons were now for exercise, and Julia and I would be sent out to the garden; our legs had long lost the urge to run.

We were now referred to as young women. My hair had grown long enough to be braided and rolled snugly into my headdress. More than two years had passed since Julia's arrival. I was nearing ten and would soon begin tending Vesta under Fabia's supervision, until I came of age and could tend alone. There were greater expectations of us now.

Julia and I had settled into a formal rapport; we discussed little outside our studies or the order of rituals, but sometimes we shared a laugh as we quizzed one another. We were never friendlier than we needed to be, and at times our quizzing could take on an antagonistic tone; at times Julia would laugh softly when I answered something incorrectly, a menacing sort of laughter meant to belittle. At least that is how it would strike me every so often, but then perception can be temperamental. I would feel a slight pull to do the same back to her when she jumbled the proper order of a festival, but I would quickly suppress it; the devout cannot be antagonized, I thought optimistically, though this optimism would prove to be fleeting.

We never mentioned what had happened that day in the classroom or how it served us both as pivotal points towards modesty. We never spoke in any depth about Tullia, and really, spoke of her only in the context of baking or dining, as in 'Tullia mixed the dough quite thick' or, 'Tullia commented that the beans were too ripe and she was right, they were horrible, that stupid cook cannot get anything right of late'. Slaves were something we could freely belittle. Though, even at Tullia's mention, I could not help but detect a slight mockery in Julia's voice, something she seemed to have picked up from the others. Sound was all I had to go on for the most part now, my headdress was like blinkers, like cupped hands round my eyes; it was better not to look directly in the others' faces, better because one could not risk pausing a moment too long, allowing a glance to turn to a gape and all the effort one put into one's modest demeanour to be undermined. But there was also another risk in that pause: it didn't matter with whom it was shared, even Tullia. That was disconcerting, as if we waited for the other to say something, as if there was a sudden strain similar to trying to see in the dark, for anything to emerge from the other's shadowy throat and take shape.

Julia and I spent our late afternoons like this, circling the garden, preparing ourselves for Vesta. There was an excited anticipation about turning ten, to begin tending even as an apprentice. I repeated the festivals again and again in my mind, each little intricacy, until the landscape of the garden turned to a map of symbols to jog my memory. I listened more keenly in the classroom, and found my errors were becoming fewer, that I was achieving a greater level of comprehension and memory each day. At rituals I stood perfectly still when required, perfectly poured what was needed, my expression was a perfect arrangement of modesty. That is how I felt, arranged, this was all arranged. I am part of the gods' arrangement, like a centre-piece in the middle of the table they feast from.

I felt that even if nothing else was, I could be filled with promise.

Things would be different now if things had gone according to plan, if Fabia had been my teacher and not Tullia. I would be different now. I would be what was promised.

CHAPTER XII

One night I dreamt again I was alone in a garden. Its paths were paved with brick and lined with roses, lilacs and statues of Jupiter, Juno and Ceres. Minerva was missing. The sun blazed and burnt my skin; the scent of grapes was strong and ripe. Bees and butterflies buzzed and hovered, working steadfastly in their tiny worlds, oblivious. Wind rustled through olive trees, whispering like a polite child. I meandered down the path, occasionally picking up sticks and tossing them into long, swaying grass. Time seemed endless, plentiful, an abundant crop. When I reached a river I stopped; it was clear and mirrored the blueness of the sky and the yellow sun. I climbed down the banks and peered in at myself. My hair was loose and framed my reddened cheeks. My lips were moist and my nose freckled. My dark brown eyes were shaded, appearing shapely and exotic. I was surprised that I was beautiful. I splashed the water and waited until its ripples faded, but my face was still there, exactly as before, beautiful. I moved closer, my nose grazing the surface of the river. I realized my face was coloured with paint, heavily decorated like that of a matron trying to sustain the attentions of her husband. I cupped my hands and drew water up against my face and tried to rub it clean. Suddenly a branch snapped.

Someone was behind me, watching from the bushes atop the river bank. Frightened of being caught this way, without my headdress, looking ornamented and enticing, I plunged my whole head into the river. Shaking to and fro, splashing, scrubbing, ridding myself of this unsightly vanity. I finally stopped, breathless, and waited for the water to calm. I looked again. I was still the same, coloured and tempting. Dried leaves cracked. Whoever was behind me was approaching. Again I bobbed my head in and out of the river, faster, barely able to gasp for air, nearly drowning. Still I was the same. I picked up a rock beside my knee; it was rough enough. I began to grate it against my eyes and cheeks. It was better to lose my face than be caught with this one. My skin stung, burned, and just as I was about to dunk myself again into the water it abruptly struck me that it was the protector of gardens, the god Priapus, who was coming for me; he would not know the way. I could run down the river bank and swim into its middle and be unreachable. But then I realized I'd had this dream before. I would be caught. Now I was only curious what he would look like this time. Sometimes he is fat and lurid with a good sense of humour; other times he is dark and toothless, and other times cruel like a pack of dogs. Once he was a boy with long golden hair, reluctant but dutiful. Laying me down softly on the grass, sickle still in hand, entering me, not much like rape but more a warning. He was moving swiftly now, leaping over hills, gliding down the embankment, naked and shameless. His stride was strong and graceful. His chest youthful, legs etched with muscle. I blinked and he was beside me. I did not want to see it, its enormity pointing, beady black eye winking. I lay back, positioned, eyes closed, submitting. But, instead of entering me, punishing me for whatever he

86

mistakenly believed I had stolen from this garden, he laughed. He laughed like a growling animal. I don't know why, but I reached for him.

'Aemilia? Aemilia?'

I opened my eyes, I could feel a strange shadow bent over me . . . Priapus is here in my room! I nearly shrieked, but a hand went over my mouth and muffled it.

'Shhhh . . . it's me, Julia. Shh!'

'What are you doing here?' I went still, my breath caught in my throat. 'What has happened?' Julia sat down on the edge of my bed for a moment, then she turned round and sat facing me, cross-legged. I knew she was facing me because I could feel her odd breathiness, although I was not even able to see a trace of her face. Maybe that was why it was easy.

'I had an odd dream,' she said quietly. I waited for her to say more, to hurry and finish and go back to her room. This was explicitly forbidden, to go to another's rooms. Aside from the first day Julia arrived, I had not been inside her room again. I knew it looked exactly the same as mine: windowless, a bureau, a bed, a potted plant, hooks to hang the stola and headdress from, two oil lamps fastened to the same wall, in the same spot. Over her bureau, where a mirror should be, hangs the same tapestry of Minerva standing very erect, with a wide-eyed owl perched on her head, a scroll in one hand, an orb in the other. In our bedrooms she is not depicted with her spear as she is elsewhere. A modest room, fit for a Virgin.

'What of?' I finally asked, I suspected she needed me to ask as it would confirm I was consenting to her visit.

'Of Cupid . . . Do you remember Cupid? It was such an odd dream. I think it was a dream. It was horrible. Cupid was in my room, but I could not see him. More so feel him, hear him. He would brush against my legs, I could feel his soft fur against my neck as if he kept stepping over me as I slept. I could feel the pads of his paws walking up and down my back, leaving behind damp, sweaty prints. I could hear him scratching and scratching, under the bed, at the bureau, at my stola, at the door frame.' She shuddered.

I thought of Cupid lurking in the house all this time, hidden away in the shadows, but there is nowhere to hide here. 'How did you get to my room without being noticed?' A slave stands in the hallway each night in order to ring the chimes to wake the next tending Virgin and summon the dressing slaves. I felt the now familiar prickle of panic. Any moment we would be discovered and who knew what punishment would be doled out to us.

'I waited until the chimes rang for Tullia and as all the slaves went into her room, I came out to yours.' Julia's stealth surprised me, as if she were revealing a new side to herself. Why I did not call out to the slaves then, did not scream and have Julia removed from my room, I can only surmise was due to my own dream and that I too did not want to be alone. It was also the way she spoke to me, so openly and filled with a sincerity that seemed to materialize in the dark as an exhumed relic from a distant time. It seemed both a heightened feeling of reality, a kind of waking from a lengthy delusion, and a descent into another dream-like realm that by its very improbability – to sit here in the dark in my room with Julia, another Julia, a better version of the one I've always known – brought a feeling of safety.

'I just couldn't stay in my room any longer,' Julia continued. 'I finally woke up because I could feel Cupid on my chest, but he was much bigger in my dream, and so very heavy, I couldn't

88

breathe. He was like an expanding boulder and when I did awake, for a moment, I could see his yellow eyes like two burning keyholes in the night. I couldn't stay there, Aemilia, do you understand? I was so frightened, even after I woke up I could still feel him rubbing against my skin. Will you let me stay here with you for a little while? I have to anyway, until the slaves go to wake Sempronia, near sunrise.'

I let myself believe there was little else I could do but let her stay.

'Do you think it means anything? This dream?'

If Cupid had wanted to come to one of us in our dreams, I wondered, why would he choose her and not me? I had cared for Cupid much more deeply. I was the one who discovered him. I felt a pang of jealousy that threatened to burst the calm, crack this sheath of safety.

'I think maybe he came to you to give me a message,' I said very solemnly, expecting Julia to disagree and us to spend the rest of the night at odds with one another.

'Yes, I think so as well. I think Cupid misses you and wants me to let you know he thinks of you often, especially the times we played matron and husband for him. Actually, part of my dream was Cupid whispering to me to go to your room and tell you his message.'

I revelled in this for a moment: of Cupid returning to recount his affection towards me, of Julia's generosity to follow through and deliver the message.

We slowly began to speak of other things.

Julia told me how horrible she found Fabia's breath, offering a perfect impression. 'Now this is what I do . . . watch what I do . . . no . . . like this, like me . . .' in an especially breathy way so I could feel the wet heat of her breath against my face. She imitated Sempronia's gurgling and Porcia's bleating, Tullia's dreaminess. Though I was bothered by her teasing of Tullia, I decided to take it as indication that she had given Tullia over to me. I felt that she had conceded defeat and, in some way, that I had won. This warmed me even more towards her; it was as if we really were suddenly close friends, in our own secluded, secret corner, like two matrons in rushed conversation in the Forum just outside a shop.

We talked about what we saw at the games, the Circus Maximus, the making of mola salsa cakes, the tiny white worms found in livers and entrails.

We giggled as quietly as we could together.

Soon we were lying down, face to face, mirrored shadows, our words growing sparse as our drowsiness slowly began to take over. I wanted so badly to stay awake all night, talking, telling. I wanted to know what her kinship with Vesta felt like. I wanted to know if she felt the gods. I wanted to ask if she felt hard lumps growing in her chest, if she also was scared of her eye and if it was a different colour to mine. There was so much more I wished to say, tell, but I couldn't conjure the words; like disinterested spirits they just wouldn't come, or maybe they were wise spirits who knew better than to reveal too much.

I could hear sleep nearing her, see her chest rising, falling. I could feel the shroud of sleep gently lowering itself over my own face and the gentle lifting of my body.

It's as if she kissed me to replace these absent words, these words too many and long and heavy to be negotiated by the tongue in the usual way. As if to fulfill what would not come to my own lips, to transfer words in another way.

90

She missed my mouth at first because it was so dark, kissing my chin. But I tilted my head down and our lips met; her hands against my cheeks, my hands on the back of her slender neck, each of us pulling the other further and further in, until she softly pulled away. A long silence ensued, and I knew Julia only pretended to sleep, I knew this because her breathing was quicker than the soft, slow breathing of one asleep. A brilliant kind of exhilaration swirled around my collarbones mixed with excited horror and descending into an otherwise silent, unmoving cistern of absence, causing a surge of wrinkles to skip across the surface. I made a point not to lick my lips as if I would somehow wash it away, so that I could continue to smell her as sleep finally came upon me, the smell of a lush leafy outdoors, the taste of absence turning to longing.

I am not sure when Julia finally left. I didn't hear her leave, but I knew she returned to her room without being discovered because when I saw her in the garden the following day she seemed intact and the others moved about as they always did. The day was very warm, the kind of heat that sunk into one until one's limbs felt like steamed rags. I went and sat next to her on the bench. 'So you got back safely?' I looked around to ensure none of the others were near. Already I had thought of ways each could sneak to the other's room for nights to come.

'Yes,' she answered, her voice tired, faint.

We sat for a few more moments; I waited for her to say more, but she did not. So I made some sort of attempt at humour. I think I may have imitated Fabia in the same breathy way Julia had the night before, but I am not sure. Either way, Julia did not laugh, but looked at me with a slight smile that only later I came to understand bordered on a grimace, an expression I mistook for affection, later to realize it was equally filled with revulsion.

'I am going to be bathed now,' she said flatly. She stood up and walked under the portico, into the kitchen entrance. I decided to wait a little while and then follow her to the baths. We could still bathe together then so long as it was unplanned, an infrequent coincidence, before our routine with Vesta became set and there was no longer such a thing as coincidence.

After the slaves scrubbed us both and we were rinsing off in the pool, Julia finally seemed rejuvenated. She waded back and forth, taking light buoyant strides. The sun streamed down through the atrium infusing the beads of water on our arms with light like glistening pearls, refracted through the water so that it seemed we waded amid shoals of luminous fish.

I once wished I could dive into the water, dunk my head, undo my hair and let it spread out around me like a swirling cloud of dye. I used to be tempted to act as if I'd slipped in the pool, just for a moment of underwater quiet, to feel the water rise over me, though I knew that with the weight of the headdress I'd surely drown.

The sun stirred the surrounding statues, illuminating the bland paint, the faded purple stolas and yellow ropes, their jaundiced or reddish brown faces with a fresh gleaming coat. The whole central atrium seemed criss-crossed with silky webs strewn with white glinting dewdrops.

Julia and I said little to one another, the slaves were all round us, but we circled one another in the pool like coiled eels. A safe distance but closer than necessary.

'Aemilia, your headdress is coming undone.' Julia suddenly

glided up behind me and I felt her hands brush up my neck and re-tighten my rolled headdress, clumsily tugging the loose silk back up into a swirled hat. I still liked to picture it looking like a basket on my head, regardless of the fact that on the others the headdresses looked like a half-melted candle; there were still times I could conceive of my appearance as different from the others'.

Julia struggled slightly. This was a slave's task; we could later, over dinner, let Sempronia know that the slave who had tied my headdress had failed to secure it properly. It should not get wet; we must remain covered under the open sky, the unfurled eye of the gods.

I looked down at the black-and-white tiled floor of the pool, a mirage of smooth stones. I wanted to lean back, fall into the water with Julia and make a gurgled promise that I would look after her as she did me, that if her headdress were to come untied in the open I would re-tie it. Let's make an alliance in this way, just as the others seemed to have made one against Tullia. Let's make one of our own; a guarantee that out of the other five, one will always be on our side, you and I. It need not be spoken, acted upon, but only known. To only know this connection existed would be enough to get us through the daily maintenance of our own Virginity, of living. An alliance so impenetrable it would last our lifetime so we can last here, outlast this. Share knowing glances over the dinner table, inside smiles, breathy laughter detectable only by the other; respite from constant modesty that would only be enhanced by these brief breaks, as a soldier needs sleep to regain his strength, a traveller needs nourishment to continue on. It would assure our endurance. A melodramatic, desperate promise that the slaves would hear nothing of but the vacant airy bubbles rising to the surface.

Julia's hands stopped abruptly and I thought maybe one of the others was close by. I looked up just as she pushed me, not hard, but enough that I stumbled slightly forward. I glanced round, past the hunched impassive slaves waiting with linens to dry us off, the fence of statues, but could not see if one of the others was there, though maybe whoever it was had gone by already. Maybe Julia had been quick enough and she had seen nothing at all.

This was before I came to understand Julia pushed me because things were different in the light.

CHAPTER XIII

I went to sleep hoping Julia would come again to my room. I thought of her sneaking down the dark hallway in her under-dress, the soundless padding of her feet against the smooth stone, silently avoiding the cracked-opened doors, crouching by the slave standing dully with chimes in her hand. I thought how white her arms would look under the moonlight, if there had been windows for the moonlight to shine through, stripped of the light dusting of freckles on her shoulders. I liked this scenario better than the frenetic dash she must have made when the slave rang the chimes for one of the others to waken; it was over too quickly. It made waiting for her easier, to think she was delayed due to skulking in the hallway, to think she accidentally slept through the chimes that rang for Tullia to tend and was now forced to come to my room in such a dangerous way.

I waited, fending off sleep as long as I could, brimming with words. The questions from the night before came forward, writhing on the tip of my tongue, impatiently begging to be asked. Each question, like a slender silver chain shimmering on my lap, I wove and embedded into the others, then ripped away again to be posed alone. I laid them straight, made them

95

poignant. I bent them in the middle to assume an answer, then straightened them. I arranged them in order from long to simple, from direct to wordy and complex, until each question curled round the others into a medley of overlapping circles that, as the night deepened, became less discernible.

I was slowly losing the words I wanted so badly to be there, ready, so our lips need not meet again, not out of fear or modesty, but because there was too much silence out there to waste this seclusion with more.

When Julia did appear in my room, it was not as I had hoped. She stood alongside Fabia and Sempronia by my bed. At first I thought I was still dreaming, laughing softly at Julia's mockery of them: Oh, now she is even dressed like them. But Sempronia pulled me up by my braided bun.

'You depraved, incestuous girl. Your vows of chastity extend to one another, both men and women.' Her grim ashy face was nearly green. 'Can you not control yourself, you perverse girl? Preying on the purity of others. Your fertility cannot be split up, cannot be spent on another. Such a waste. Going into her room tonight, making such a suggestion. At least she had the sense, the morality, the goodness to send you back to your room and not to fall victim to your immodesties, otherwise you'd be in a much worse position. We are the untouchables, to one another, to ourselves. Repeat! Repeat!' Sempronia was shaking my head back and forth. 'Repeat!'

'Www . . . ee . . .' I could not keep her words, could not say them back. All was a blur, like the intense buzz of a fly in the ear, as if the chute from their mouths to mine was suddenly blocked by some kind of stray debris, as if the roof of my mouth had been abraded and my tongue was too stunned to lift itself into the now infinite darkness.

'Repeat!' She pulled my head back. She was touching me now. You are touching me now.

'We are the untouchaaaables, to one aaaanother, to ourselveeees.' The words stretched out to match my neck, now stretched to the length of a goose's.

'Again.'

'We are the untouchaaaables, to one aaaaanother, to ourselveeees . . .'

This went on for some time. My head folded into the middle of my shoulder blades; the words, like tiny bubbles, slowly wound their way up to my mouth.

Out of the corner of my eye I saw Fabia nodding, a mixture of both controlled and uncontrolled shaking, agreement and disgust. Her arms were folded in front of her under-dress, her breasts slightly spilling over each of her wrists as if they were small leather sacks filled with water.

Julia had not told them we had kissed, only that I had entered her room asking for a kiss. The kiss of doubt, the kiss of death, the kiss-off. If I told the truth, then we would have committed an act much worse than the one I was accused of, and the likelihood of my being believed over Julia was nil.

When Sempronia finally let me go, I fell back into the bed and tried to pull the covers over me, to hide myself, but Sempronia ripped them from my hands and forced me to lie there exposed in only my under-dress. She turned to Fabia. 'What should we do with this . . .' It was a mock conversation, the kind your punishers have to let you know all the ways they can punish you, like browsing through a tray of various weapons, discussing which one will inflict the greatest pain. I thought they meant 'about this', until I realized I was the 'this'. I'd been reduced to a 'this', stripped of being, an inanimate bowl of jellied flesh. I was no longer shaped as they were, no longer fit the mould, but lay here formless. They had the power to do this, to hollow out my stola and discard what was inside, to pick me clean of it. I am only the hook the stola hangs from, no, only my womb provides a clasp to drape the stola from. The clothes make the Virgin. I vanished then, disappeared into the fringes of sound, where sound and silence met, a rift that closed round me like a fist.

When I returned I realized that to go unnoticed does not negate one's existence. I stopped chasing singularity then, as I once had chased Tullia's compliments, and ended any hope of an independent friendship with Julia. My existence is significant for Rome, as a pillar's is in holding up the roof of a house, but a pillar is silent and should be taken for granted. Its existence is measured by the fact the roof has not yet fallen in, and from the outside one cannot tell which pillar bears more weight than the other. But inside, the pillars know, and if the roof should threaten to cave in, they know which pillar is to blame. One's best defence is not to draw attention to one's own fragility and, in the end, what Fabia said is true: if one is known outside this house, if not for her eminent devotion, it is only because she buckled.

How simple Virginity seemed, in that moment, as black and white as the mosaics scattered throughout the house, but this simplicity would not last, just as the tiles, when stared at for too long, would not stay still, but shifted and distorted.

I looked up at Julia, thinking she would not meet my eyes,

would be ashamed by her betrayal of me. But something had happened after she left my room; she had convinced herself of another truth and her absolved mouth turned down and began sinking off her face.

Fabia decided it was best and most effective to lock me up in the latrine by the kitchen for three days. Some Virgins are born good, others are made. Modesty must be more than a mask, it must be a light emanating from a Virgin's centre. A sullied, sullen Virgin should remedy her base behaviour in the basest of rooms. 'There she will come to understand that there are two choices for a Virgin, that of wastefulness and that of usefulness. There she will see it is better to be used than wasted. Waste not, want not.'

In the small dark latrine on the earth floor in the heat of summer, with the chirping and whirring and clicking of insects, I waited for it to be over. Curled up, knees tucked against my chest, farthest from the hole that is meant to flush our waste into the sewers below the street but often becomes clogged because the kitchen slaves toss in vegetable skins, rotting cabbage and leeks, chicken bones, sour milk. Their arms gusted in and out like a sudden wind, dumping the contents of terracotta jars, bowls, chamber pots. The smell of waste was so horrific I vomited any food and water that was given me. I'd listen to the slaves drinking leftover wine or finishing off half-eaten plates of food, their hushed laughter as they prepared meals. I heard Fabia come in and complain she found a hair – or was it a nail clipping? – in her food. Again waves of hushed laughter.

The others came into the kitchen to prepare mola salsa cakes, though there wasn't a sacrifice for another week. This is when Julia's voice took on its light, airy calmness.

'Oh Fabia, how does this look?' A pious voice, untroubled.

'Near perfect, very good.'

They carried on a good-natured banter I'd never heard before, light puffs of laughter floating into the latrine. Proof of how easily they could go on without me.

Tullia would often try to visit me during the day when the others weren't looking and talk to me through the door. But rather than soothe me, her visits at first infuriated me. She was not outraged, did not speak of how unjust it all was; she did not ask about the crime, ask if I was innocent or guilty. She did not even offer sympathy. Instead she rattled on about the weather, flowers in the garden, what she'd had for dinner.

'Do you think that concerns me right now?'

Tullia went quiet. Then, as if I had said nothing at all, carried on.

On the third day I welcomed her chatter. At least it was something to listen to other than the insects and the choking drain. When it was finally over and I could barely stand due to thirst, hunger and the cramping of my legs, Fabia put a bowl of peppercorns on the floor in front of me and handed me a spoon. 'Your lips will remember this way.'

The kiss is why I began tending to Vesta under Tullia's supervision. I can still see Fabia discussing this with Sempronia in the garden, her black eyes shifting back and forth so very quickly as if in spasm, searching for the contagious invisible powers looming in the grass that had possessed me that night. Sempronia would agree because, if nothing else, it is always better to be safe than sorry when it comes to the malice of ill-tempered numina. If nothing else, it is better to test the malignancy on someone else, in case of repercussion. Yes, this is likely why I was paired with Tullia and not passed on to Porcia: two lost causes belong together.

Fabia and Porcia would share Julia the following year; she did not exhibit such ominous traits. I tried to be a better Virgin after that. I tried to prove I was a dutiful and chaste Virgin, not at all perverse or incestuous, but well versed, well read. Modest inside and out. I tried so hard to believe wholeheartedly, to believe in my own usefulness for Vesta and Rome, to follow carefully Fabia's edicts, but Tullia was always there, shedding her doubt upon me like a blanket I could not shake off.

CHAPTER XIV

At the time I thought it was good luck to be with Tullia, though now I am undecided. Luck, good or bad, is as deceitful as a two-headed coin. I was also curious to take my place beside the fire named Vesta, the goddess I had been chosen to serve and would dedicate the rest of my life to. I had been inside the temple before, of course, but never as Vesta's servant. I hoped for a sense of serenity, for sense to be made of my life and gratefulness to emerge. For the feeling of warm sunlight to burst in my chest with such utter reverence for Vesta, just as Fabia said should occur at each sacrifice, each ritual. I wanted to feel the presence of the gods as heavily as I felt my head-dress, but as clearly as if seen without a veil. I wanted the mysteries of gods and their mysterious ways to be suddenly smoothed out and become rational.

In that first year, Tullia was like a chained hummingbird inside the temple, chattering endlessly about what she had seen the day previously through the temple's entrance, which really meant overheard. We can only see what the half-oval entrance frames, and it's not as though a Virgin can stand out on the steps like a nosy neighbour. We must stay inside the temple, like the roots under a tree, unseen, to imply we are relentlessly engaged in our task of fastening, so Rome can stay fixed; one only sees the roots of the uprooted.

But still Tullia would always claim to have 'seen' something. 'I saw two peasants wrestling just over there. I could see them screaming and smacking one another, grunting all the while like animals.' She really meant she had heard them. She would do this, exchange a word for one more subversive, a word that would give an impression of autonomy; heard was saw, heard was felt, thought was said.

Tullia tended overnight, so there was only the odd matron who entered in the early morning to make her pleas to Vesta. Only women sporadically visit and offer small sacrifices of flowers, clothing, sometimes silver or gold. Each household is graced with a smaller version of the goddess of the hearth. It is the hearth that a home is centred upon. It feeds and heats and thus must be honoured every day. Vesta is the hearth of Rome. Patrician matrons come here not to request food or warmth – this can be done at home – but to beg for the end of civil strife, a favourable verdict for a son on trial, the election of a husband. Their embroidered stolas swirl round their ankles, lips and eyes coloured, as they make an impatient offering while their children pull at one another quietly by the entrance. Sometimes they attempt to appeal for a larger home, an address on Palatine Hill, or a lover. They assume we can't hear.

Tullia gorged on the matrons as they knelt next to Vesta, drinking in their clothes, their hair, eavesdropping on their prayers. I was always surprised they never felt her stare, but in the temple we blended into the walls and bricks; they don't suppose we have eyes.

Once they had left Tullia liked to pick over each of them, as if they were figurines she could turn and examine in her palms. 'Her stola was stunning. The yellow as bright as day and it went so well with the blue ribbon of her shawl. Though her hair was coming down at the back, did you see that? She should not have offered so many pins, I am sure her hair will be down to her waist by the end of the day! Oh, and did you hear what she said about her son?'

Plebeian women were different, their offerings were a stub of bread, a cut of meat with little fat, always food of some sort, that which they needed most. The gods preferred offerings that were most difficult to part with; they better bent their ears. These women requested health for their children, or to have no more children, for their husbands or fathers to be fair this month with the state ration of corn. They entered self-consciously, heads already bowed, already making their quick, anxious prayers as they fell to their knees, lingering behind to watch their offering burn as if to make sure it was accepted.

Tullia didn't speak of them after they were gone; the matrons were the jewels to be dazzled by.

The mornings were short. Just as the squeaking carts could be heard approaching in the distance, filled with goods to sell to the merchants in the Forum, Fabia appeared to relieve us. It was the night we waded through; the morning we waited for. With Tullia there was always the feeling of moving towards something, the light of morning, the bath once we returned to the house, the next meal, the next day, the end of our shift with Vesta. It was as if the temple was a stagnant pond we had to loosen ourselves from rather than an oasis for practising our devotion; a place one departs reluctantly, sadly, and all the other parts of a day are that which we must endure as the hurdles towards returning to this retreat. As if, with Tullia, things were backwards.

Tullia would ask me what I liked best to eat, to drink, which instrument I preferred to listen to and would play if I could, what colours I adored, how I would wear my hair if I could. It became a game of sorts. 'If I could, I would . . .'

'If I could, I would wear my hair long, almost down to my ankles, and it would be as soft as the finest wool so that whenever I grew tired, I could wrap myself up in my hair and go to bed anywhere, at any moment, or even suddenly hide from anyone, almost like a snail!'

Tullia would always follow my answer with a long detailed answer of her own, as though she only wanted to pose the question to herself in the first place, as though she had thought long and hard about her answers before I arrived.

'If I could, I would weave my hair with dove feathers, or dye it a golden red and roll it into a mass of plaits piled high upon my head, so the curls would seem to graze against the sky. I'd also wear wigs, sometimes Eastern black, but only for special occasions or something sombre like a funeral. Mostly I'd wear Germanic blonde and I'd braid the wig with pearls so under the sun my hair would appear to have flecks of dew that would catch in the light and I'd look as beautiful as Flora's flowers, as young and new as Flora's springtime . . .' Tullia would close her eyes, eyelids flickering, her smile wide, her teeth even showing. Good Virgins keep their mouths pressed shut. Only when eating or drinking should a Virgin's lips part, opening just slightly, as if sipping food through a straw, never wide enough for teeth to show.

She still complimented me for a time, every now and then, verbal strokes under the chin or across the cheek I would have to brace myself against. 'How straight your nose is', she would say or, 'Such a lovely chin', and I would have to abstain from her praise, before its intoxicating effects took hold. I would nod demurely, silently counting, letting her praise bump off my nose or chin like floating ash. *My face need not matter, my face is matterless.* There were times she'd even pull me into her hip; the first time I went stiff, unsure what she was doing. I leaned awkwardly into her only to have her hip bone jab into my stomach. But after a few times, I fell into her embrace and could have slept my life away there. 'If I could, I would have one just like you,' she'd whisper, and I would say nothing, because I knew it was wrong for her to say so, but also because I wanted to revel in this brief closeness, so grateful to have felt I pleased someone.

'Boredom does not settle well with people; it erodes our minds,' she often said, followed by a defiant peek outside the door, then she'd turn back, arms outstretched, pulling me into a quick makeshift dance, spinning round Vesta, backs arched, laughing wildly until our headdresses felt they were hanging from a pin and we were nearly sick.

She taught me how to arrange Vesta's logs carefully. 'Lean them up against the side of the hearth . . . be careful not to catch your sleeve on the fire or the others will think something more of it.' She told me what to do if I heard someone approaching and a thick, high flame was quickly needed. 'Grab handful after handful of leaves, the drier and more browned the better, even these little twigs here work well, then lean down and blow. Keep your headdress firmly tucked behind your ears so as not to let it accidentally drag over the flames, otherwise you will become a disfigured Virgin and, as you know, Virgins must not be blemished in any way, never mind half melted!' She said this lightly, as if it were funny.

'What would happen then?' I peered into the hearth, Vesta's flames seemed less beautiful, less glorious. I pictured them travelling downwards, through the bottom of the hearth, through the floor of the temple, spreading out under Rome like a cupped hand. The danger of Vesta never occurred to me, nor did I consider taking the ordinary precautions one would with simple fire. Surely, Vesta possessed a sense of discrimination; it was Vulcan who burned uncontrollably, not Vesta. When Tullia turned the other way I placed my hand on a brick in Vesta's hearth and immediately felt scorching pain and flinched away.

'Oh, you really wouldn't care what would happen to you then! Remember, there is nothing in the temple to re-light Vesta with. She must never go out.' She went over the prayers for Vesta and Minerva that must accompany their offerings, how to wash Minerva and the temple floor, keep Vesta high and strong. But this was all. If I asked about the gods and goddesses themselves, she'd change the subject, or say, 'Later, there is so much time for that', but later never seemed to come, though once, as I was kneeling at the box of kindling, Tullia said, 'You'll find out for yourself.' I had not asked about the gods that night, but I took it to mean that the gods would come to me when they were ready, that Vesta would shine inside me once I'd convinced her of my devotion, that I was worthy of her light.

But, as I methodically washed down Minerva, murmuring her prayers, she only looked on, stone-faced and removed. I'd read the etched band below her feet a million times already,

'Protector of Cities'. It was said Aeneas brought her and was the reason our temple was built in the first place, to guard her as she guards Rome. It was only after her removal that Troy fell. It was also believed that Aeneas stored many other sacred objects, too sacred to be named, from Troy in our temple, but they must have long ago been carried off to the homes of rich senators or generals, if they ever existed at all. A cupboard just to the right of Minerva was said to house these sacred goods, but it was empty. She shouldn't have, but Tullia opened it to show me. 'An empty cupboard can still hold pretence.'

Tullia fought off silence well. Her mouth like the swirling clouds in a storm, delivering a rhapsody of words. Her hands like trees in the wind, never still, flapping and waving, smoothing out the front of her stola or pulling at her headdress, picking the bark off a twig. She'd skip round the temple, telling me to follow, and we'd hop on one foot round Vesta. 'If we are caught we only need to say we hurt our other foot . . .' Her eyes widened in mock fear, mouth open, laughing as if she had outsmarted the others.

'If only Vesta's image materialized not in fire but in a statue,' she'd say. 'If there were just one other statue to look at, other than Minerva, maybe we could compose a dialogue between the two . . . I know, I'll pretend to be Diana, you be Minerva.'

'What are you doing here, Diana?'

'Same as you, Minerva . . . basking!'

She rarely paused, her mouth restless, tireless. 'The lyre is my favourite instrument, of course; it is like a gentle rain that one can feel just ever so slightly, almost a mist that spreads over one's cheeks like kisses and drives one to beg for rain.'

My ears stung from the word 'kiss', until I convinced myself

I had misheard, and then convinced myself for some time that I did not even know its definition.

'The lyre was made for dancing by an old man with crippled legs. He invented it so he could remind others to move as he could not, to twirl and bend and twist, just like this.' She bowed forward, then back, into an elegant arch, one hand over her head.

'How do you know all this?' I asked.

She said she listened, watched and filled in the rest. 'I just make them up really. Stories I distract myself with. Living in one's head isn't such a bad thing, until, of course, it is no longer enough.'

This was the sort of wisdom Tullia imparted to me in that first year, practical advice on how to maintain devotion, or maybe sustain it. She taught the necessary motions of devotion, the physical aspects, with a sense of detachment that I, at the time, often believed was the even surface of unremitting calm. At other times I was sure she was missing something, leaving something out, some ingredient of devotion that prevented the airy well-being to fully rise in my chest like warm cake and overrun my being with serenity. The quiet, for one. In the quiet one could hear Vesta, be assured of her purpose. One could hear the earth rumble with each offering, each prayer and the subsequent tightening of the earth's grip on Rome and the lengthening reach of the gods' hands on new lands. I knew the others stood very quietly beside Vesta. As the year passed, I would turn back when it was Fabia's turn to tend and catch a quick glimpse of her and eventually Julia, as the slave escorted Tullia and I back to the house. They stood not side by side, as Tullia and I often

109

did, but across from each other with Vesta between them, hovering over her flames with matching subdued smiles, their mouths firmly closed.

The quiet can snuff out impatience, edginess, boredom, if one is given the chance to get used to it; the head can match the quiet, can live in it, with it, stop.

CHAPTER XV

There was an abundance of time. Wide gaps throughout the day; time when I was not tending to Vesta, not bathing, not sleeping, not eating, not learning to deposit a will, not standing at an altar at a state ceremony. So I spent my time, as I still do, in this chair, in my room. But because a slave was always a stone's throw away in any direction, it was never a good time to appear idle. So I'd sit, as I still do, with a history book in my lap, one of the three we were allowed to read, appearing studious. I had already read and re-read all the books so many times I could recite each one verbatim. The legends of Rome's early heroes demonstrated the Roman way of determination, constant devotion and duty to state. Farmers who, through discipline, austerity, duty and diligence, transformed the small agricultural community nestled between seven hills into the world's greatest capital city. Another book told the story of Remus and Romulus, born of a Vestal Virgin and Mars.

Usually, I spent this time wondering. Did the Vestal Virgin allow Mars to impregnate her? Did he rape her or did she simply wake up one day pregnant? Will it happen to me? Will I feel it? Did she feel it? Would Mars be anything like Priapus? Did she lie? Did she really have a lover but blamed it on Mars? How could there have been a Vestal Virgin before the inception of Rome? What hearth did she watch over? The legend said it was her uncle who turned her into a Vestal so she could not have children who would one day threaten his throne. She is Rhea Silva, the first Vestal Virgin and the first to break her chastity and be punished for it. Fabia omits this part from her admiration of Rhea Silva, omits it from her teachings, perhaps because Rhea can be forgiven as she gave birth to Romulus, or perhaps because she had little choice in the matter if Mars really was the father, though I remember what Fabia taught us about rape – a Virgin is not absolved even if a god was the perpetrator. The book is without details, only that Mars chose the purest of Virgins. Possibly this is why it is forgivable now: if she was good enough for Mars she is good enough to be revered by Virgins today. These are the folds not meant to be unfolded; Virgins shouldn't wonder, or is it wander? Both mean the same. Revere blindly, unconditionally.

Sometimes I secretly hated Rhea Silva, blamed her for setting this precedent, thought it somehow her fault: for being in the wrong place at the wrong time, or for something she did or did not wear. But I know this is absurd; the gods always get their way, have their way. At other times I felt sorry for her and invented a new ending for her, without a Mars, without children, without an uncle, without Virginity.

Our third history book told how Jupiter founded Rome, or better, led Aeneas to Rome. We were to ignore the inconsistencies and incoherencies of the three texts. A people as great as the Romans are born many ways. History need not be true, only interchangeable.

CHAPTER XVI

I can pinpoint the exact moment I knew Tullia had moved elsewhere, as if she had finally come unhinged from whatever it was that kept her standing upright. Of course there were earlier indications: the disparities between idle chatter and nervous giddiness were becoming greater, longer, like abrupt cliffs. Once she squealed when it started to snow lightly and jumped up and down, wringing her hands. 'Look, it's like tiny albino spiders gently lowering themselves to the ground with their silky thread!' As if under a spell, she began to step out of the temple until I pulled her back by her elbow. If I looked closely enough I could see she was wearing the faintest line of charcoal round her eyes, which I think was really ash she wiped on her fingers from the temple floor. I'd spot stray light brown ringlets falling loose from her headdress, close to her ears, and again suspect that she did this on purpose, pulling them out quickly when no one was looking. I suspected she did a lot on purpose.

She began to count the years she had left to go, even the months and sometimes the days. She said it made her feel better to see not how much was left, but how much time had passed. 'I have survived twenty-four years. What is another six?' She'd grow very still then, although her lips would still be moving, calculating, reasoning, emitting only breathy whispers. Sometimes she'd do this for days at a time, barely speaking, just tallying her time. I couldn't draw her out with questions – 'If you could' – she had to return all by herself.

Over dinner she alternated between slumping over her plate barely eating and eating too much too quickly, her movements as sharp as a finch picking at a seed. She would clunk her cup down, clang her spoon against her bowl too loudly. At times she was argumentative; if Sempronia raised her cup in praise of an earlier ritual, Tullia would say she thought so-and-so was a bit too slow, the sacrifice not quick enough, the banquet meat undercooked. She would wave away the raised glasses with her knife, olive oil dribbling off the bread down her other hand. 'No, it was much better when so-and-so did it. He was much louder and it wasn't raining so hard either.' She would say this still chewing, food flipping over on the back of her tongue like fallen freight on the seashore sinking under skipping waves. Sometimes she snapped at the slaves, 'How dare you take my plate! I wasn't finished with my bread!' smacking the table close to the slave's hand.

Once I asked her when my coming of age ceremony would be. I'd soon be turning fourteen and Fabia had said the better the Virgin, the sooner her coming of age, though Julia had yet to, and I wanted to be first. Tullia grabbed me by my forearms and shook me. 'Be thankful it is coming late; there's no turning back once it arrives. You'll have to stand here alone, all alone, for years. I've been trying my best to keep it away from you . . . Why? Have you grown tired of me? Are you becoming like the others?'

She started to cry, nearly falling into me, holding onto my

arms until fingerprint bruises indented into the back of each of my arms above my elbows. I watched the back of her headdress shudder, waves in a purple sea, and felt her tears drip onto my feet and was almost relieved she was holding my arms so tightly at my sides, because I wouldn't have known what to do with them otherwise; good Virgins do not cry.

She tried to make me laugh after that, asking me silly questions, telling fantasies of a life away from here, where she could see me right now, if I had not been chosen. 'You'd have long rich brown hair, some even say almost black, and you'd be sitting in a garden sewing patches of silk, nearly sewing your own hair into the patches because it felt just as smooth as the silk . . .'

But underneath, her voice was flat, tired.

CHAPTER XVII

The exact moment of Tullia's exodus came one May afternoon during the festival of Lemuria. Each year for five days, Rome feeds the unhappy, restless dead to prevent them from feeding on the living. This is how Romulus appeased his brother's spirit.

It isn't a popular ritual because there are no free games or theatrical performances offered during or even after, and no one is allowed to marry for the whole month of May. Happiness should be hidden, suppressed so as not to tempt the malevolent spirits to rise up with envy.

A corner of the Forum is cleared and banqueting tables are set up beside a small, crude altar. Cows, bulls, sows, chickens and a horse are sacrificed by the feast organizers, the Epulones, a college of ten priests. The sacrifices are then carved up and placed on the tables, which are also set with bread, wine and milk. Two by two we were required to attend, after or before our time with Vesta, sitting silently at the table as though dining with the dead. After the five days are up, the food is buried in a deep hole dug underneath the table. There, the spirits of the Underworld can rise, feast and be placated. All we had to do was sit and endure time. Day after day, people tiptoed by us, as we kept our eyes firmly on our empty plates and the meats turned from a pulpy pink mass to dark brown to black and rancid. Black flies picked and took away as much as they could carry. Ants stormed through, crawling up over the lips of cups, stealing honey.

On the last day, when the scent of rotting flesh was so strong all we could do was breathe through the corners of our mouths, Tullia began to whisper, 'Mmmmm, this looks delicious. Yes, two please . . .'. I was taken aback; she'd broken the silence and offended the dead.

'Such a lovely spread . . . Surely I am not deserving.' She brushed my shoulder with hers, placed her hand to her chest in mock surprise; she was mocking the priests, the ceremony, the dead, all of it. As if some defiant spirit had slithered up out of the Underworld and slipped into her body.

As much as I fought it, nervous laughter intertwined with the gasps of shock bubbling out of me.

'Is this a special recipe? I've never tasted anything so delicious in my life!' She was no longer whispering, feeding off my amusement. She looked up and down at the ten priests, took her fork and reached over and plucked a chunk from the side of a decomposing chicken – or was it a pig? – by then they all looked the same, aside from the horse's leg lying in the middle of the table like an ornate centrepiece. 'Oh come up, you dead, come for your libations.' She poured a cup of wine to the ground. 'Still hungry? Eat this.' Tullia then flung the meat to the ground. 'This is absurd . . . The dead are not hungry any more.' Her voice changed, quivering, hiding tears as she began to rage at the Epulones; she was no longer joking. Dread flushed up my cheeks, into the roots of my hair. One of the Epulones waved over a slave and had him drag Tullia away for Sempronia to deal with.

Tullia went missing for a week, punished in some unknown corridor of the house. I didn't look for her. At first I thought maybe she was in the latrine and so I said little in the kitchen and never laughed, but when a slave opened the door to the latrine to toss some peels, I saw that Tullia was not there. I didn't search for her. I didn't sneak down hallways whispering her name, or explore walls and floors for some hidden door she could be starving behind and I could whisper comfort through. I didn't because I felt she was deserving of her punishment, I felt a kind of satisfaction that she was somewhere in the house and justice was being carried out. Though as the week went on, I realized it was not her mockery of the festival of Lemuria I wanted her punished for but her cracking. I felt vulnerable to losing her to whatever was thinning her Virginal veneer and, more selfishly, worried such cracks would provide windows for the others to suspect that I wasn't learning a passion for Vesta.

In the week she was gone I was paired in the temple with Porcia and Julia. It happened to be Julia's week with Porcia and not Fabia. I stood before them, feeling trivial, an annoying bother as trifling as rinsing one's mouth in the morning. But at the same time, I felt large and awkward, an unwelcome stranger who did not know where to stand or how to look, or what to do with her hands. The temple itself seemed slanted, like trying to manoeuvre in the dark; I kept brushing against Minerva, bumping the box of kindling. They sighed even more with annoyance: what a dismal thing I was.

Porcia's nearly bare brow seemed lower in Vesta's shadow.

Her pale eyebrows, I decided, must have been singed off by Vesta long ago and had never come back. Julia had grown and was taller than me. This bothered me. Her extra bit of stature made it seem as if she were the plant that had been doted upon and was now quickly flowering while I was wilting around the edges. I hadn't noticed this before, but I suppose I rarely stood so close to her anymore.

Julia's freckles had faded as well, and her eyes seemed more blue in contrast to her lightened skin. But this was all I really saw of either of them. It was a week of avoiding looking at them, for if my eyes were to even lightly set upon either of their faces, they would whisper bitterly, 'Stop looking at me! I will tell Sempronia about your gawking if you don't stop right now.' But each time my eyes accidentally fell on Julia – and fall is what they did, in the silence I was not used to, dropping down heavy as stone – she was always already looking at me. Serenity felt much like sleep.

Porcia did things differently and Julia imitated her precisely. I still like to think that Julia only copied, mimicked and was not really learning or advancing. Her lack of originality somehow made me feel better; at least Tullia allowed imagination and I could change the pace of my offerings, the volume of my prayers. Tullia allowed such creativity, or even if she didn't, she never noticed. Tullia's temple was filled with stories, and furtive dances, and spoken games, 'If I could, I would'; maybe Vesta enjoyed this, found it comforting, like the sound of familiar voices when one is about to fall asleep, like the whispered chatter of the slaves as they readied one of the others down the hall. I still had moments when I could deny devotion was a rote activity. Though I realized I expected Vesta to be higher and stronger under their care than mine and Tullia's; but Vesta burned on just the same.

Porcia's prayers were slow, silent songs that seemed to last as long as the length of time she tended; Julia was her constant chorus. There were more matrons entering during the day, though not as many as I expected. When one did enter, Porcia retreated into the brick of the temple, arms folded in front of her, deaf, dumb and blind. Julia fell in beside her, but she kept opening one eye, peeking at me to see if I was watching her or the praying matrons. Her eye would shut again, and she would flinch when she saw I had not closed my eyes; afterwards, she wanted to reprimand me for this, but then she would have had to admit she had opened hers, so instead she took it out on me in other ways. She'd point out to Porcia something I was doing wrong – that the kindling I chose was too wet, for example. She did this by asking innocently, 'Is that dry enough, Porcia?' A gentle poke into the otherwise perpetual quiet.

The hearth then became a set of reins they would not hand over to me for long. 'That twig is not dry enough to offer Vesta,' Porcia would sneer as I picked through the kindling for offerings. Under the serene surface was a bed of delicate inflections that released a range of other emotions. A word said harder than need be meant anger, softer meant disappointment, though sometimes these would be reversed. The nuances of pronunciation became their own language, a more detailed language made up of a wider vocabulary.

Once, just to hear something other than Vesta's continuous crackling, I asked, 'Should I use more water when washing Minerva?' Tullia had already told me that too much water would wear the paint and so to just dampen the sponge.

120

'Incompetence begets incompetence,' Julia answered, looking directly at me. She flickered back and forth from familiar to unfamiliar as light sometimes does when the sun shines behind a banner fluttering in the wind. The surface of her voice held the same singsong cadence as any other set of words, but underneath was another vein, filled with nervous spite, older than both of us.

CHAPTER XVIII

When Tullia did return she moved more slowly, carefully, like a dog favouring his hind leg. She stopped watching herself, nothing censored. Disdain mingled with her every word, until she finally cracked open like an egg, dripping out a tirade on the futility or even idiocy of some of Rome's most sacred rituals. 'The gods are always hungry, always more, more . . . And why do all gods enjoy a good gladiator show? A good horse race or banquet? Are these the interests of gods . . . or men?'

She scorned Vesta, once even kicking the base of Vesta's hearth, spitting into her fire. 'Look, Vesta does not rise up and burn me down, Jupiter does not strike at me with lightning, Minerva's spear is still only stone and not plunged through my heart. Oh no. Consequences come not from the gods but from each other . . . from them.' She laughed at this. Not the easy lilting laughter of before, but a shrill nervous cackle that came out suddenly, almost uncontrollably, like a squawk that was beginning to punctuate each sentence.

I backed away from her, wishing for a corner in the round temple to hide in. I could feel myself shaking, feel the consequences she spoke about bear down on me, knowing that while it may not happen here, now, there *would* be consequences.

Fabia said there were consequences for those who did not honour Vesta: that those who degrade her slowly decay from the outside in.

'How many offerings will it take to undo what you have done? How many recitations to Vesta will I need to offer? What amount of purified water will I need to cleanse the temple of your repelling words? How can I convince Vesta not to neglect us? Not to abandon us to the spirits of the dead that seem to have materialized in you right before my very eyes? Spirits that will leap into me if I do not get away and crinkle up my spine or scatter my skin with leaky sores . . .' I was shaking, my hands in front of my face, as if she were about to toss a bucket of boiling water at me. I stepped backwards, ready to trip down the steps, dash to the house, tell Fabia what was happening – surely this would ensure my own protection, display my own devotion to Vesta. Vesta comes first.

Tullia stopped suddenly, grew quiet. Only her head shook, no, no, no, and the demon jerking about inside her seeped out. She was Tullia once again. 'I am sorry, so sorry . . .' Her voice thinned with pleading. 'Please don't tell, please. Here, let me purify the floor . . . I want to purify the floor.' Her face softened. 'I beseech thee, Vesta, with this offering of cleanliness to continue to embody this temple's hearth, the hearth of Romulus . . .' She prayed in threes, scrubbing in quick successions of three round circles. I was surprised she still knew how to honour Vesta properly, something she had left to me to carry out for some time. She even offered prayers to Minerva, but I knew she only did it for me, not because she thought it necessary, not because she felt compelled to repent and recant her rage.

A little while later, she tried to be her playful self again, list-lessly weaving stories of the matrons at the theatre or games. 'Arria, wife of Paetus, once sat four rows directly behind me at the games. She took her own life for her husband. Paetus committed patricide; it is said he did it before his father could change his will and leave his estate to the son born of his second wife. Rather than face the usual punishment of being beaten with blood-red rods, sewn into a sack together with a dog, a cock, a viper and an ape, and thrown into the Tiber, his wife encouraged him to take his own life. She unsheathed his sword, looked directly at him and plunged it into her own chest, then handed the bloodied sword to her husband and said, "Paetus, it does not hurt." She concealed her tears as she died so her husband would have the courage to do what was necessary. Now she is praised as a heroic wife and is said to have gained immortality for her remarkable compassion. She's famous. I heard one man joke at the tracks that if only every man's wife showed such dedication, the divorce rate would not be so high. His friend berated him for abusing the name of Arria. She's divine now, for pursuing the welfare of her husband.'

Tullia sighed and slipped back to her own life after here. Her after life, her after now. 'I will one day host the most extravagant party and invite the wealthiest matrons, and you as well, of course! I'll serve a spread of rare delicacies: teats from a sow's udder, pigeon dripping with grits, blue oysters, sheep's womb filled with delicious sausage meat . . . or, no, maybe rabbit . . . No, that won't do either. I'll only serve cake, long tables of delectable pastries . . .'

But she kept getting confounded in her details, confounded by her own intricacy as if she were attempting to stitch a design too elaborate for her hands, and thus she'd stand silently until inspired to try again. Two half moons swelled under her squinting, searching eyes, as if she were looking for something very small she had dropped on the floor.

I felt sorry for her, she looked so weak, like a child who had grown arthritic overnight, waking confused at her body's sudden waywardness. I decided to cling to my devotion of Vesta, caring for her for the both of us, to ward off whatever misfortune Tullia roused through her rage. Surely Tullia, the one who hugged me into her hip, played games with me, the one who said I would be right next time when I answered wrong, never chastising my improper questions, was deserving of this.

For the first while, I waited for sores to erupt, for a hump to bulge, for spirits to tremor inside me, but nothing so heinous ever occurred. We were saved because I served Vesta so well.

Tullia's tirades eventually tapered off into a soft trickle of mutterings; as she stared into Vesta, she began to say such strange things through a smile that seemed to be stolen from someone else and sewn over her own lips. She was always smiling by then. 'Oh yes, I adore the gods, of course I do. But there are other ways to gain their support, other gods to gain support from. There are gods other than those they've told us about, better ways to worship and be heard. No, not just be heard, but be listened to.' She would talk of other ways to gain control . . . of what or who, I wasn't always sure. Of burying curse tablets, love potions, spells; of twining hair round and round a rock then throwing it into the Tiber. 'I have spirits on my side now, protecting me, working for me. *I* caused the rain to fall yesterday, not Neptune . . .'

She said she'd put the curse tablets in the cupboard beside

125

Minerva, but whenever I opened the cupboard to check, it was always empty. 'Spirits have them now,' she'd say with a shrug, smiling into Vesta, or else she'd change her mind, saying she had buried the tablets in the garden. I didn't ask whom she wished to curse or where she learned to curse, hoping that if I did not exhibit curiosity her tiresome tangents of curses and potions would be shorter lived, but I let her go on, just as a pillar goes on holding up a roof.

'There's a restlessness in certain Virgins; it's in me and I can see it in you. A restlessness that kicks inside you like an infant; not all Virgins are empty. You will not stay here for all your days. No, maybe you will move next to me, down the road in a little house surrounded with flowers . . . If you could, what sort of flowers would you plant most of?' She would return once again, for a little while, languidly detailing what could surely come.

This only happened when we were alone; she revised herself in public, in the presence of the others. I could only recognize how she was in the temple in her carefully set smile. Though I didn't want to abandon her to her conjured spirits, I started to look forward to tending Vesta alone.

Along with her blasphemous ravings of the supernatural came something else: a decision, a mind made up, her eyes fixed on a place far from here. 'I'm still young, you know,' she would say. Just one of her many bursts of self-acknowledgements; they were rhetorical, I need not agree or disagree. Or sometimes, 'I am still attractive' or 'I am not drying up here, drying out like the others' or 'Someone will have me' as if she were a pastry no one wished to eat or to throw away, in case of hunger. 'Someone will have it,' they say to console or absolve themselves. This last was the most baffling. Who would have her? How would she be had?

Thirty years is only a prelude to a lifetime. Where is there to go? Who is there to go to?

Maybe he asked her then. The man she spoke to in hushed murmurs by the temple's entrance as I stared down at my feet or counted the bricks in Vesta's hearth. She would turn back to me every so often, a slight smirk on her face, her lips wider, her eyes brighter, begging for my curiosity, a question. I could not bring myself to ask her; I did not want to know.

CHAPTER XIX

My coming-of-age ceremony came in the middle of the year I turned fourteen. Tullia couldn't stop its arrival for ever, regardless of the tricks she used, the numina she tried to incite. At least Julia had also yet to become of age. This was one small triumph: Fabia could not declare my own lateness as another proof of my inadequacy if Julia was also late. Maybe Tullia arranged this somehow, but maybe I am attributing too much to her.

I woke up to something itching, a slow trickle between my legs. I did not dare to scratch, not there, not ever there. I placed my hands underneath me, my own weight pressing down so I would not be tempted to scratch.

When I woke up next, there was a hot stickiness over my hands and the familiar rusty smell of blood. It was Mars after me, pricking my eye, impregnating me as I slept. I kicked in the air hoping to get him off me. I thrashed around and squeezed my legs shut. 'Off,' I hissed, 'off me . . .' I cupped myself, trying my best to do so without touching, while providing another barrier, a thicker eyelid, but still the blood flowed and a throbbing pain beat through my belly. It was over. I was over. I would just have to wait until the others found out, until Fabia noticed a bump in my belly and sent me away. I'd be alone, carrying the son of a god. Would they let me have the baby at all? Surely, they would let me keep the son of a god. Perhaps it was not the child of Mars, perhaps Jupiter took me. Or maybe it wasn't Jupiter but Priapus. Yes, it was likely that sinister Priapus, sticking it into my eye as I slept. I knew he'd get me, but would I not be dead? Maybe I am bleeding to death now, or is it just my eye turning into a pocket? Even Priapus would want a son.

I needed to wash the blood away and wait for my son to arrive. I would not send him upstream, even if he was the offspring of Priapus; I would care for him as I once did Cupid, and in return he would help me one day build a house up the road from Tullia.

What will Tullia say? She will say she always knew I was meant for greater things.

I stood up and called for the slave to lead me to the chamber room. When she held the lamp high she saw the blood on my hands, droplets on my feet, went to the hall and rang the chimes.

As Fabia entered, I waited for her to seethe, but instead she stepped towards my bed and pulled the covers back to reveal the small circles of blood on the mattress. She turned and took one quick glance at my feet and said, 'Well, it's about time. You've finally come of age.' She lifted her chin; I was already a head taller than her, more without her headdress. Fine red veins webbed round small bubbles in the corners of her eyes where sooty sleep had gathered. 'I didn't think you would, considering, but yes, you have finally become a full priestess of Vesta.' She walked in front of me down to the chamber room.

I had known I was to become fertile, but there had been no

mention of blood, she had never said there would be blood. For a moment I was sad I was not with child, with a god's son to build me a house.

Fabia took me into the chamber room and gave me a loin-cloth with a strip of wool inside to tie round my hips. I waited, checking, for the blood to finally drench the wool, pacing back and forth, as she instructed, to urge the blood out.

The chamber room is my favourite room. It is small but has two high, open windows near the ceiling, allowing the air to circulate. In spring and summer there are bunches of fresh, sweet-smelling lavender in the vases in each corner. There is also a door that can be closed, not locked but firmly shut. This would be the best room in the house, if not for a slave who waits outside the door under the pretence of making herself available if a sudden need should arise, when she is really there listening.

I knew this because I'd seen them leaning against the door when others were using the room. Listening for what exactly I could only guess and my guesses changed as time went on. At first I thought it was because they wanted to make sure I went and would not wet the bed, then I believed it was because they wanted to check I was not in any way trying to beautify myself by plucking or applying faint shades of charcoal. (It did not occur to me then that having these things would be next to impossible.) Now I think they listen only for the sake of listen-ing, not for anything in particular, and maybe they no longer hear what they listen to. But this act of listening rules out pos-sibilities, even if they have yet to be thought of. Even with their ears pressed against the doors, we are not allowed to spend great lengths of time in here unless we are ill (in which case, a slave would be with us).

There are six chamber pots, not because more than one of us ever uses this room at once (as this would mean we'd see each other), but because it enforces chasteness in that our bodies never touch, even inadvertently. Six pots of separation. Yet none of us knows who uses which pot and so we must certainly 'touch' all the time, but the very presence of six pots somehow annuls this certainty. In the middle of the room are three baskets, one filled with strips of wool and triangular loincloths for when it is a Virgin's time of renewal, the other with sponges, and the third with sticks and a large basin of water. Afterwards I take a sponge and clean myself. I poke it with the stick and rinse it out in the basin of water much longer than necessary because I enjoy those brief moments of being behind a closed door, the façade of privacy. Each time I drop the sponge back in the basket with the five others, I wonder again why the sharing of these sponges is not considered 'touching'.

As soon as one steps from the chamber room, a slave scurries in after the chamber pot to empty it in the latrine by the kitchen. Sometimes I wondered what would happen if they found the pot empty. What sort of conclusions would they draw then? What else was possible in this room?

When the wool was finally sodden, I was to place it in a box in one of the corners and replace the wool with a fresh strip. 'The bleeding only lasts five to seven days, seven if one is more akin to Vesta such as myself . . .' Fabia said. 'Each time your strip of wool needs to be changed, place the bloodied wool in the box with the yellow dot on the side; this is now your box. The first blood of a Virgin's cycle needs to be offered to Vesta in a ceremony so she can accept you. Each cycle afterward, you must take your box to the temple as an offering to Vesta.'

131

The slave went to wake the others. It was just after dusk, and soon all six of us were in the temple. Porcia looked surprised, as if we'd interrupted her. Fabia sprinkled purified water round the temple as Sempronia poured wine into Vesta, along with a bowl of fat from the roasted chicken we'd had at dinner and a cake of mola salsa, before she began prayers. 'Oh, Vesta, safe keeper of Rome, honoured in every home, who presides over preparation of food and warmth and is the centre of each household, you who were born with Rome's inception, you the preserver of the race of Romulus, you who instils comfort to the body and family, you who . . .' Once it was assured the attention of Vesta had been gained she continued, 'We chaste Virgins beseech you to accept your new attendant.' Sempronia offered the strip of wool to Vesta, 'Please accept the first blood of this Virgin, who vows chasteness in your name, who vows to honour you, who vows to keep your flames high and strong, though you are already mighty. Who vows to . . .' As Sempronia continued a long list of vows on my behalf, I was waiting for something to happen, for Vesta to spit out my strip of wool, but also for something good, for Vesta to shoot up, growl out more flames, for anything to happen. Tullia stood beside me, and in the light of Vesta I could see her eyes were damp, but she could get away with this here, pass them off as tears of happiness, of gratitude towards Vesta, of seeing the Virgin she mentored advance. Tullia would not look at me, as much as I willed her to. But Julia stared at me during the ceremony, her eyes wide and unmoving, as if looking for changes in me, on me, for me, or maybe what was to come for herself.

Part of the celebration was to take the night off, be rewarded, stay in bed and allow my fertility to course through my body. I

132

was even served a piece of pastry, wine and some pears in my room and presented with a new stola, freshly dyed a bright purple. I heard the chimes ring for Tullia and the slaves enter her room to dress her; on any other night I'd be woken too, dressed, brought to the temple – how nice it was to stay in bed. How nice everyone was so pleased with me. I felt a lurch of excitement in my stomach now I was a full Virgin, a full priestess. I turned onto my belly and let sleep slowly trickle in.

CHAPTER XX

The first time I tended alone with Vesta I expected to hear the temple hum, Vesta to speak to me in some way. To hear a hushed soothing song, faint to the human ear, emanate from Minerva. Hear some divine message in the absence of Tullia, something that I may have missed due to her chatter, or that was not said in her presence. But the temple was a den of dead air; without Tullia it seemed a bell without its hammer, a deserted cave. Maybe because the quiet had never had a chance to take hold of me, I never slipped into its undertow, became awash with it, turning into part of the seascape as fodder for fish, a grotto for algae. I was too old now to merge with it; like heated clay, I'd been set. Tullia had wasted my malleable years, ears, and maybe it was only after this merger one heard the gods.

I arranged, then re-arranged the kindling, washed the ash from Minerva. I watched the dried leaves and parched wood sink into Vesta's flames, char, then detach into sparking and glowing birds.

I stared at the sacred statue of Minerva perched atop the low pillar embedded in the wall, until I thought I saw her spear move and her eyes blink; in here she is allowed a spear. Then I walked round the temple counting my steps, the cracks in the walls. I re-arranged the kindling again, counted the logs and twigs, surveyed the dried leaves. I gazed at Vesta ceaselessly twitching, her iridescent light calming, lulling. Watched until she nearly reeled me in too far, mesmerized, before blurring the line between sleep and wakefulness so much that my head would knock against the wall.

As the hours wore on I began to ache, so thoroughly ache, as if the weight of a thousand slabs of stone were strapped onto my back. My knees and ankles grew stiff and brittle, as if I had suddenly aged several years. As the days wore on, I fended off lethargy by standing close to the temple door, at first for the fresh air, then to eavesdrop on passers-by.

I wrenched my ears as if stretching them out like fishing nets to trail over the heads of those who lived outside this temple, this house, scooping up words not meant for me. Words devoid of Vesta, purified water, mola salsa cake, purple stolas, the reading of entrails, of Mars, Jupiter, Mercury, Minerva . . . the litany of upcoming ceremonies.

Like a forgotten old woman holed up in a back room, holding a cup to the wall to better hear her sons and daughters-in-law, I pried.

I listened in to old men's ailments and young men's remedies, the stern discussions on economy, the secret conversations between men, speaking offhandedly, casually, as they scurried down the road between the Regia and the temple, when they were rushing towards the Forum and its bordering shops looking to buy delicacies, barter for fine silks and linens and scrutinize speeches early in the morning. Or their excited debates over new policies, the political disparities between rising businessmen and those born into wealth and nobility, the utility

135

of slaves versus the poverty caused by unemployment, the unfairness of political representation for the masses of plebeians and the political domination of the many by the few. Heated arguments over the short supply of land owned mainly by the rich and worked by slaves, sending peasant farmers into the streets of Rome to live from grain dole to grain dole, which policies of land reform would be best for all. They spoke of the dangers of private armies, which were loyal only to their commanders rather than to the state, of those who had too much power and needed to be prevented from snatching up more. From their conversations, I discovered that the many despised the power of the few, though the few do not fear the power of the many, but rather the culmination of power in one. This seemed backward to me, but then these are the affairs of men.

I listened carefully to their whispers of who they believed was lying about being the recipient of omens and divine messages to gain approval for a bill by the general assembly. Which trials had been won or lost and the cost of bribes to ensure either outcome, which wars would soon be won and which wars would soon be waged, of the incompetence of the Republic to lead over an ever-expanding Rome and a multitude of alternatives. I weighed the ideas of supporters versus radicals, of conservatives and reformers, as if I had the intellect to judge or be swayed from side to side, as if I knew more than brief bits that must be re-arranged, extended, filled in and combined with others so that I could follow enough to feel distracted from the stiffness in my body, Vesta's silence.

When mouths became looser with wine, and men headed towards the Circus Maximus, stretched between the Palatine and Aventine hills, to watch chariot races, I strained to hear complaints about losing at the track, about their wives, their sons, their slaves. This is when I pretended to think like a man; my thoughts mimicked what I overheard and were coarse, even vile.

'My slave is a whore, not only does she sneak about giving it away to my neighbour, but she gives it to his slaves as well . . . greedy whore . . . dirty bitch . . . That fucking limp-legged horse . . . I bet Green, but Quintus took my money and placed it on Blue. His throat should be cut, such stupidity should be punishable . . . At the baths . . . he was so young, so soft, so new, so beautiful . . . My apartments will soon bring me profits, perhaps I will close down Plubius . . . The plebs are never satisfied . . . The senate is run by pigs . . .' My tongue flickers behind closed lips, shaping and enunciating the words which wander like leaves carried by the wind. This is my secret, prying open this other Rome, the lives of men. These are the things one must do to pass time, to stay awake.

As the months wore on, Tullia found ways to come into the temple. She would offer to get the purified water from the sacred well, or pretend she had lost a hairpin. If Sempronia or one of the others found her there, she would act as though she were answering some pressing question, as if I had called her in to help me with something as I stood there silent, looking incompetent. For a while, because I was still new to tending alone, she could get away with this, and later, when it was her last year, she had nothing to lose. So there she was, in and out, like a bee in a hive, an ant in a hill, a bird in a nest. Carrying pieces of knowledge to and fro, regurgitating, feeding me mouth to mouth. She would try to bait me with her questions, urging out curiosity.

137

Once she asked me to keep any spiders I saw in the temple.
'Why?'

'Oh, well, so I don't get pregnant too soon. Not until I've left. I need spiders for this. It is most effective as they carry a worm inside them that can stop a seed from settling . . .'

I pictured Tullia's eye with a worm wriggling around in the middle; my stomach turned.

'I am going to a place, somewhere far from here,' she would say, 'where I will do what comes naturally to women. This place isn't natural. Vesta is only a fire. Rome is not the centre of the world, you know.' Or she would take my hand, pet the back, remnants of her once maternal ways creasing the corners of her lips. 'I've met someone and look, Rome didn't crumble.' Tullia slipped away a week earlier than her designated last day, after thirty years, fed up and in love.

There were times I would think I heard her passing by the temple, her children following like little yellow chicks. She would pause – wondering if she should go in like the matrons she had once envied and watched so closely or, for old times' sake, to make Vesta just one more offering – but decide to continue on to the market, children in tow, letting bygones be bygones, letting go of a life once lived long ago.

This is what I think. Tullia will hear of my disposal, believe it unjust and come here and dig me up. She lives in a villa in the countryside, far from Rome, where no one thinks of her as anything more or less than a wife. Her husband is a small landowner with a tiny plot of land; he grows olives, apples and grapes. There is an orchard at the back where Tullia strings up her family's laundry and saunters easily through its paths, sometimes stopping to stroke the unwanted soft willows that sprout up along the way. Petals from the thriving crab apple trees float downwards like rotating, abandoned boats. She takes a basket and picks up some olives that have fallen from the tree, ripe and fresh and smelling of sun. Her children call after her, two boys, one girl, and just as she leans down to pick up the young girl, her face much like her own, pale, full, heart-shaped lips, darting eyes, hair a reddish brown, she will think of me.

She will remind herself to write another letter later enquiring about me to a nameless source. Tullia always has her ways, a do-gooder will write back, include all the sordid details, but when she goes into her house to collect another basket, she sees a letter already waiting for her. And what will Tullia do? She will tell her husband, who is down working in the vegetable gardens. Tilling the same soil I am now under. He is thinking of planting more carrots, beans, maybe adding more oak trees, as he calculates the current price of acorns. He often worries about how much time they have left here before the wealthy elite in Rome come and buy up his land for their large sheep and cattle ranches, run by their slaves, and he will become a slave of another kind. What will he do? How will he care for his

139

family? Or maybe it will be some rich politician or general – what's the difference any more? – wanting to guarantee loyalty from his long-standing soldiers and thus granting them farms they can settle on until they are needed to fight again. So rich and powerful, the politician only need blow on you, bully for low prices, pulling the land out from under you like a rug. It happens all the time in an agricultural crisis, families forced off the countryside into the urban centre, into the only city that matters – Rome, with its cramped shoddily built apartments, overcrowding, incessant fires, hazardous housing, traffic jams, aggressive stall-holders. He will look up to see Tullia, her stola – not purple, she will never wear purple again – hiked up, leather sandals kicked off, running down that slight dip and over the hill they still sometimes sneak out to, when the children are asleep and their handful of slaves are having their supper, to make love. When he looks down at her, just before he pulls her up and they return back home to the sensibility of their beds, he feels lucky. He does not believe in the gods. This is the hill she is sprinting over now. Is it one of the children? His heart jumps: a caring father. When Tullia finally reaches him, breathless, red, he asks about the children first. 'They're fine . . . Not . . . them . . . it's . . . Aemilia . . .' She will wait to catch her breath to tell him the rest. Yes, I just have to wait.

I wish I could sleep away the waiting time, but I can't get comfortable; the couch is too hard and smells faintly of urine. Funny thing, we were not allowed, any one woman, to laze about on a couch like men. Too licentious. I'd envy men at banquets, spread out, at ease on a couch's cushions, shameless, like sunbathing cats on their backs, panting ever so lightly.

I think of the places I never saw, the different quarters of Rome: the artists' district, the foreigners' district, the outcasts' district, the widows' district. The inside of a public bathhouse, an apartment building, a whorehouse, a eunuch's temple, a ship, a shop deep inside the market, the black market. I am much too superstitious to walk about; too many things to be wary of, bad luck, a premonition, like an evil eye cast upon a newborn baby. Seeing a Vestal Virgin anywhere but where she is expected to be is something worth mentioning, baffling, nerve-racking. Why in the world would she ever be there? I will never see Sicily, the countryside, Pompeii, Egypt, Carthage, Athens, Asia Minor or the Black Sea. At least I know there are places other than here, and their names. He told me all about them. Maybe it was better before.

I do not feel as though I am dying yet. But I don't know what it feels like; we only die once. I lean over the couch, looking at the nameless scattered bones resting below me to see if I can tell how it is to die, but I cannot. Death must be like an inexplicable scent or taste or sunset one person cannot describe to another.

'Who are you?' My own voice sounds stiff and contrived, like a bad actor's. 'How long have you been down here? How long did it take?'

Maybe I could snap a bone in two, see rings like a tree and count how old it is. It? She. How old she is. She is likely from long ago. Guilty as a thief. Breaking her vows of chastity as easily as a hen's neck. Had by so many men, men who were not afraid of being fortune's enemy, who scoffed at bad luck and basked in the novelty of it all. She is nothing like me. I had good intentions; there was a greater purpose. I will not be reduced to this – an it. Stripped of flesh we are all the same sex. I want to climb up the sides of this tomb, quietly open the door and eject these bones, coughed up by the earth – no, belched up, rejected.

Wait . . . I only need to wait. Come, Tullia, please come.

PART II

January 63 BCE/691 AUC

Memory is the treasury and guardian of all things.

Cicero

CHAPTER XXI

Today is a day of beginnings dedicated to Janus, the two-faced. One nose to the past, one to the future. Like a door he opens on the new year with its newly elected consuls, shutting on the consuls who have finished serving their year-long term. The new consuls, Cicero and Antonius, will be here soon, after they sacrifice twelve white bulls at the temple of Janus, and the Etruscan soothsayer gives his nod of approval with a liver in his palm. There is always a good liver, indicating the gods are pleased, if one digs around long enough. Through the half oval of the door, I watch the morning rain pelt down through the temple's columns from a smudged sky, a fingerprint in silver. Yes, the new consuls will try to hurry here and finish their inductions because the rain is falling steadily and sightings of Jupiter's lightning will want to be avoided; from the east favourable, from the west unfavourable.

The ceremony of beginnings ends here, in our temple, where each pillar is a copy of the next, set to encircle Vesta's round brick temple; a complete circle, infinite, without beginning or end. Symbolizing that while those serving may change, the system will not: the Republic will go on and on and on.

Janus, the rotating door.

In spite of this, I spend this day rehashing a broken narrative, much like piecing together a scene on a broken jug, but it turns out slightly different each time. Something is always left askew, but it still works the same as a pinch, a way to know I am indeed still awake. Alive.

This day I despise more than any other, and I wake up cringing. It is the one day a year we are all together in the same room. Each tries to outdo the other, showing off talents in the temple with Vesta that otherwise go unseen.

'Sprinkle the purified water all the way to the edges, that is how I do it. Pour enough for it to seep down through the brick floor.' Fabia's short arms will sweep out in front of her, her hands barely poking out of her stola, flickering as if each held a string attached to our backs.

'No, too much could be slippery . . .' Sempronia's long drooping face will shake from side to side, a face that doesn't seem to move even when speaking. We know it is her speaking, though, because her voice is low, raspy; some say this happens to Virgins, we become mannish from lack of use of our feminine attributes. This is true for Sempronia, though sometimes I wonder if she ever had any feminine attributes.

Fabia will wave her arms again, giving up, though she thinks she knows better, for who can argue with Sempronia – she is the oldest. Fabia turns to another instead. 'Oh, not like that, bundle the leaves tightly; they burn more slowly and more brightly then . . .'

Though I've cleaned Minerva carefully with the purified water and sponge, until there is not a trace of Vesta's soot, I know Fabia will still run a finger up and down her thigh, bring it close to Vesta's light and tell me to do it again.

The temple will become a warren filled of shoulders not to brush, gazes not to meet; my tongue will thin and fall dislocated inside my mouth, curl like a snail in the fleshy pocket behind my bottom teeth. I will feel intruded upon.

Yes, this day is usually tedious. The others swarm around, quickly wiping, sprinkling, pointing, demanding, sweeping up soot, adding more kindling, like bees in a hive. Beginnings imply there will be some kind of change, but nothing changes here, not for us. Though today *is* different. Today, we have a new Pontifex Maximus, Julius Caesar, elected for life, his life. I do not know much about him other than that he has been in charge of public games and the upkeep of buildings and temples. Two years ago he built in the Forum an arena for gladiators where they emerged from hidden corridors dug out underneath the ground. He also had many beautiful colonnades built and funded grand exhibitions all over Capitol Hill.

But nothing really changes here, and Caesar will just continue where the last one left off, the same but with a different face. Virgins are an edifice that must always be kept up but never renovated.

The last Pontifex Maximus died a month ago, the same short, slothful little man who held me once as child. His chest grew puffy until it bulged all the way down to his hips like a robin's. His breath left him easily, until one day it left and never returned. Even when he came up the few steps of our temple, sweat would bead and drip down his ears, his mottled face reddening, matching the mulberry birthmark on his cheek that had intensified to the deep colour of wine. He would lean against the wall with one hand until his breath returned and I would try my best not to look at him, at the strange colours his birthmark would turn as it slowly lightened against his whitening skin, but regardless of my efforts my eyes would stray there as if it were an embedded Siren and I could not control myself. And he would catch me, sputter out a look of disdain and repulsion at my lack of modesty. I only hope the complexion of this new one is free of such curiosities.

I turn and try to warm my back with Vesta's eternal fire and peel the damp chill from my skin; I feel as though I may never be warm again and wish to be back in the house, in a heated bath or under a heap of blankets. The cold rain on the wind blows straight inside the temple, snarling at my legs and arms; a door to close would be nice. The closeness of the house is no comfort; it is just a few steps away, twelve if taking long strides, twenty-six if walking delicately, so close I can almost feel the warmth of the braziers aflame on each side of the entrance, feel my toe dip in the pool in the central atrium, feel the heat of the hot room just off to the side of the pool and the cold slip away, but the closeness of the house does not mean I will be relieved of this biting cold any sooner.

I can see the purple litter approaching; on this day Virgins must leave early, just when sacrificial rites have ended. It is preferred that we are arranged neatly in the temple, and neatness takes time. I stand demurely next to Minerva and wait. Chin lowered, eyes on feet, trying to appear natural.

I hear Sempronia first, her voice a grating gurgle. 'I will take Claudia and collect the cakes from the house . . . Julia, get another bucket of water . . .' I can hear her slow shuffling in the trail of gravel to the house.

Sempronia will lean heavily against Claudia, taking advantage of her close proximity to youth, drinking in her fluid and solid

148

steps, strength and straightness of her back, her damp bones, and try to recall a time when she suffered not from the dry rigidity of her own bones that are chipping to a fine powder and are slowly passing through her sieve-like skin, through the large pores of her face and vent-like folds on her neck. Claudia's cheeks are rosy and high; they're cheeks that have yet to be dried from Vesta's heat, that boast she has been here for only two years. Claudia is Tullia's replacement, the refill to Vesta's never empty cup.

Fabia enters first, Porcia just behind her, and peers into the hearth, half mumbling to Porcia as though I am not here. 'Vesta should be much higher . . . mmm . . . yes – much more kindling . . . should have more logs . . .' Porcia moves in rhythm to her words like the soft powdery pulses of a moth's wings around a flame, her eyes fixed, with the slight smirk the competent wear when in close proximity to the incompetent. Or so it seems.

Fabia glances at me when she trails her finger down Minerva, then brings it up close to her face, examining, her eyes slightly crossed.

A clenching tingle travels through me, as if I am biting down on something hard, holding something in, but I am used to this. Silently, I list the profanities I know as I meet her gaze; this makes it easier to obey.

'One can barely see Minerva under all this ash.' She points over to the bucket and sponge, Fabia always prefers to see a Virgin busy.

I can hear a shift in the crowd, voices hollering, even jeering, growing louder and more distinct. They are following behind the consuls' litters; behind Caesar comes the lictors; behind them tax collectors, judges, tribunes of the plebeians and so on;

149

a sea of senators, aristocrats, farmers and slaves spreading forth like a frothy wave, bypassing the Sacred Way and parading diagonally across the Forum, past closed shops and the Regia to the steps of the Temple of Vesta.

Julia and Claudia are each holding one of Sempronia's arms, helping her hobble quickly up the steps; one has a bucket of water and the other a bowl of cakes. The water sloshes a little, one cake drops to the ground, and Claudia quickly bends to pick it up. Fabia clucks her tongue, which at first could be mistaken as sympathy, but by the way she shifts from one short leg to the other, her hands dropping from her hips, it is obviously impatience. Sometimes I suspect she is impatient not only with her aged rickety bones that no longer bend quickly or with ease, but also with her place as head Vestal Virgin.

We each take our positions. Sempronia and Fabia by the door, backs against the wall, or at least Sempronia tries to, but her back is too hunched over as if she is slowly tipping towards the Underworld. Porcia stands closest to Vesta holding out the bowl of mola salsa cakes. Her smirk now gone, replaced with requisite demureness, her mouth a string pinned over her chin, though her eyebrows remain arched high in her forehead as if she had turned to stone before she could answer your question with the wittiest and most knowledgeable of responses. It is a look she has practised for many years. Claudia stands beside her, her hands clasped together around her stola, her little round face flushed like a fresh rose. She looks up at Porcia and arches her eyebrows just the same, a little clay doll in the making being rolled between the palms of the others before being placed in the oven and solidified.

Julia and I kneel across from one another around the fire; we are to appear as Vesta's couriers, guiding the upcoming sacrifices and prayers. If Claudia were older she too would act as a courier, but she has not yet come of age. The others' fertility is not considered as potent as ours because they are past twenty-five and only the most fertile Virgins are to be Vesta's couriers. Other gods and goddesses may not care, but Vesta is particular in this way.

There was a time, shortly after Tullia left, when I could actually feel words gliding through me, beginning at my toes or fingertips or sometimes my mouth, beating through my limbs, mixing along the way, translating into a language only Vesta knew. I could feel her sacrifices whirl down my throat and through my stomach, converting tissue and bone and breath into pleadings and gratitude, into pleas and thank-yous, into fodder for her resilience, for her loyalty. For Rome. Gods and goddesses do not bite the hands that feed them. Then I'd feel so tired afterwards; now I am more tired from the clenching, the holding in.

The two newest consuls enter the temple with Caesar, stifling the end of a shared laugh and replacing it with the sighs that come before starting a new task. Immediately the temple seems to shrink in size. It is much too small even for the six of us, but with men and their wide shoulders and long flowing togas we need not even reach out our arms all the way to touch one another. As the men step by me, nearly over me, their togas brush against my cheek, dragging across my face. It would be better to be where Julia is, at the back of the temple. As the two consuls find their places on one side of Vesta, Caesar on the other, Fabia and Sempronia begin to dip their fingers in the new bucket of purified water and flick it out over

151

the temple, while Porcia and Fabia each begin to crumble the mola salsa cakes into Vesta. They must think this is how we always look inside the temple, well-prepared, harmonious, always in the midst of duty, always a resplendent sight of carefully measured movements. Not a bone of cruelty in any one of our pure sanctified bodies.

Cicero pours wine round the hearth, most heavily by my knees so the people outside can see. I can feel it splash through my stola. This is so Vesta will relax, loosen up, be more willing to listen to our pleas of filling the new year with greater expansion, to ensure Rome's permanence.

Caesar then begins reciting prayers: 'Oh, Vesta, Virgin goddess, we praise thee for thy guardianship and continued safekeeping of Rome. It is you, Vesta, who came at the inception of Rome, who ensures the Roman people have food and grow in strength. It is you, Vesta, who guards the scared things, too precious to be named, and the statue of Minerva, brought by our forefather Aeneas. For your good graces we provide thee with the necessary powers of six Virgin priestesses, and their fertility, as carers for thee in thy preservation of Rome. With these offerings we beseech thee to be bountiful and continue to give Rome success and the descendents of Romulus sustenance unto eternity . . .'

His voice falters, quivers here and there; he must be nervous he will err, make a mistake in one of the prayers and be forced to start all over again. Each step, each phase of appeasing the gods, must never be altered in sequence or flawed with stuttering. The gods are vain and enjoy flattery; lack of preparation is insulting. I look at him now, after studying his toes, worried that the bushes of hair on his toes may reflect something equally

152

bushy on his face, but instead his complexion is smooth and free of any eye-luring growths. His hair recedes, making his nose seem stronger, more perfectly aquiline. His eyes are closed as if trying to remember each line, or perhaps he is truly impassioned, it is hard to tell. I cannot look at his face for long; he may feel my gaze, think me immodest.

Antonius then offers a poem, his slight shoulders and narrow neck heaving with each inflection, each morsel of praise. Vesta's light touches his face as he tosses the parchment into the fire, his cheeks shadowed, hollowed.

Now a sudden silence runs over the officials, quieting the damp crowds outside. Caesar adds incense to the flames and the temple fills with sweetened smoke. A flute player begins his song, as a small heifer is dragged forward beside Caesar. She is in heat as required; her agitated snorts sound scornful and offensive. The flute grows louder, trying to drown the cow's ominous whining. Caesar begins another set of prayers, but speaks much louder now, nearly shouting so his voice mutes the heifer. He should whisper his prayers so that anyone wishing Vesta ill-harm cannot hear and cast an evil eye or an abusive thought towards the goddess and force her to turn away before hearing out the request. Paranoia is an affliction of the gods and must be respected.

A sudden squeal and the calf's thin legs are bending, a spray of hot saliva trickles down the side of my face, the smell of urine overpowers the incense. Though Caesar's attendant has entered and bashed her in the back of her head, she is not knocked out, a poor sign. She should go willingly to Vesta, or at least appear to.

Antonius's thick fingers lightly tap against his thigh, shiny half moons at the end of each one. Cicero clears his throat, more than once, as if he is trying to swallow his voice back down. Around his ankles are meshes of purple veins, like drips of spilt wine. Caesar straddles the heifer, his long purple toga a sudden cape on her spotted back. He cuts her first across her spine to transfer ownership from human possession to Vesta, then he wraps his broad hands around her snout, jerks her head upward and slits her throat.

I am surprised he does not begin again, bring in another calf to sacrifice – there are more just outside the temple tethered together by an attendant, there are always more, just in case. The sacrifice must be devoid of resistance; a quick death is essential to Vesta's placation. There is something impatient about Caesar, as if he is worried that if he doesn't finish this quickly, confirm his post, it will be stripped from him.

Sempronia stands before the dying heifer, the bucket shivering in her shaky hands, catching streaming blood. Once it is full, Caesar takes the bucket from her – it is gold with the solemn face of Minerva etched into its side – and makes an offering to Vesta once more, pouring the blood into the fire, cautious not to extinguish her flame. He stands with his legs farther apart now, as if trying to take up as much space as possible and become immovable.

This time he remembers to whisper, but so quietly that I am not even sure he is praying until a lyre's careful strumming penetrates the temple, ending his prayer.

Romans, their slaves and curious foreigners all begin to disperse like wafting smoke, heading off to begin three days of games, dances and theatrical performances. Caesar nods at us as the butcher brushes past him to collect and carve up the remains of the heifer for public feasting. It is not a gesture that speaks either hello or goodbye, but instead an apprehensive acknowledgement that he is now our Pontifex Maximus, our overseer, our symbolic husband, something he's been saddled with.

As each of the men turn and walk out of the temple, the temple grows again and we unclasp ourselves from our positions of incessant devotion.

CHAPTER XXII

When I return to the house there is on the bureau in my room a basin of water and a sponge with which to wash my face. This is meant to wash the last year off, just as if it were a dried dribble of soup on my cheek and chin. Cleansed of the old year to face the new year. This act always reminds me of a trick my brother once showed me: he'd run his hand over his face, quickly turning his expression from smile to frown, sorrow to glee and back again as if his hand were a curtain his face changed behind.

I dip the sponge in the water and feel it gush between my fingers as I squeeze, a feeling of exhilaration comes over me, just as it does each year. I rub the sponge against my cheeks, forehead and nose, softly at first, then harder, nearly scrubbing, as if I were washing Minerva. Balls of dry skin collect under my fingernails. Water seeps into my closed eyes, tears flowing backwards, relieving a dry soreness that wasn't felt so strongly until now. I drag the sponge up and down my neck; I know this is going too far, but the sponge laps up ash and waters down the smell of its residue that seems to have settled in my cheeks and under my nose.

There will be only a few moments of this, of freely touching my own face, cleaning myself, before the slaves enter and take over, replacing my hands with theirs. Up, down and round the sponge climbs and descends, weaving small watery circles, crisp strokes, quenching the small flaking fissures in the skin of my lips. Water catches up my nose, its sharpness twinges and seems to dislodge clumps of cinder, soothing the passageways attached to my throat as if I've inhaled olive oil or breathed in new, tender, soft skin. I could do this until I hear footsteps clicking on the floor, approaching eyes, but the slaves are barefoot and soundless. I drop the sponge back into the basin; a small splash leaps upward and spills onto the bureau. A slave enters, takes the basin and sponge, and I wait out the afternoon until she returns and leads me downstairs to the dining hall for the evening meal.

In the middle of the long wooden table are trays of olives, cheese, dried figs, leek soup, sour pork and a shiny honeycomb for decoration.

The dining hall isn't really a hall at all, but a round room with a never-ending mural of a stiff Minerva floating in a boat to Rome from Troy. I know Aeneas is supposed to be steering the boat, but he is absent because depictions of men do not fit in a house of Virgins. I like this mural, the white-capped waves dipping into a vastness of blue, the green shores of distant places, the strange cloud at the boat's helm where Aeneas should be standing, feathers floating up from the cage of sacred chickens to sacrifice to Neptune. When I was younger Tullia told me it was a Virgin who blotted out Aeneas, adding sadly, 'You think it would have been a Pontifex Maximus . . .'. But I am glad he is gone, because now it is Minerva sailing across the sea alone who invites me into the mural, far enough to fill the cloudy blot, steering the boat the other way.

It's been two years since Tullia went. All I've been left with is an imprint of her, an indentation made in fine sand or maybe dust, because that is what is usually left behind. 'Eat my dust,' a charioteer will yell to his competitors. That is what I must now guard, block the winds from blowing her away by weighing her down with intricate, finely wrought details that reconstruct a whole. Two years without another voice, murmured indignation, a shade of friendship to break up the steady stream of eating, sleeping, bathing, tending, attending. Another to side with, another side of this. Though, of course, it is easier to side with her now that she's gone.

Claudia fits in nicely; she must. We are each a double and have a double somewhere, ready to replace us. But it is really me who has taken Tullia's place, the others are wary of me as they were of her. It is the natural order, to have one to be wary of. Exclusion is still a factor on a scale so minute that outnumbering is dependent on the stance of one other Virgin, this is the problem with even numbers. Small scales still tip. Not that it is always me, sometimes Porcia will do something, spill fish sauce that will accidentally run into Sempronia's sleeve, and then Porcia will be the recipient of weary sighs next time she nods at a slave to ladle on more sauce. Or sometimes it is Julia – her cakes tend to turn out too runny – and the others will shake their heads and she will be relegated to grinding corn. Sempronia never becomes frustrated with Fabia; they are too alike, two peas in a pod, one spool of the same wool. Not that this means friendship, they are constant rather than united. Both fill out their stolas evenly, so much so that if their stolas were cups one could not tell wine from chalice. They've coalesced so completely with their duties that there is never a ripple

158

one can correct the other of and so it is the shifting of others they must finger out. 'Shape up,' they warn.

The slaves weave in and out between our elbows, filling empty plates. Sempronia is bent over her plate at the head of the table. Her elbows seem to grip the table as if she is slipping from her chair. She looks up, her milky-white eyes widen. 'Where is Porcia?'

Julia taps the table to get her attention and bows slightly forward. 'She is with Vesta, as she always is at this time.'

Sempronia's memory is slipping out from under her like a rug. She asks this from time to time, regardless that Porcia is always absent for the evening meal. She tends Vesta from noon to near-dusk. We each keep the same hours with Vesta. In and out we circulate through the temple as though we step to the back of the line the moment we are finished, in the same order; an unalterable arrangement day in, day out, until our fertilities shift. I suppose that is how he always knew when to find Tullia. We all keep the same hours.

Julia tends from near-dusk to midnight, after which I tend, until early morning. She and I watch Vesta the longest and tend overnight when Rome is considered most vulnerable. Fabia only tends for a short time during the early daylight hours when Rome is thought to be least susceptible to surprise attack, and thus, her watered-down fertility is enough. Claudia will take most of Fabia's time with Vesta once she's come of age, and after her new fertility has had a year to settle in, she will take over my time and I will be bumped forward to tending during the day. Sempronia need not ever tend, as she no longer bleeds.

'This cheese is rather dry.' Fabia spits it out on her plate, a glob of white; a slave takes her plate, replaces it and serves another slice of cheese. 'It was a lovely ceremony celebrating the new consuls, who will surely lead the Republic well.' She says this about each new consul, each year, on this day. 'I am also very grateful for our new Pontifex Maximus.'

'As I am,' we each answer together in a kind of chorus, but without any of the harmony. I can feel a slight breeze from Claudia's swinging legs, kicking back and forth underneath the table. Her face is as tight and subdued as the others', as if she is mature on the top, still a child on the bottom. Twelve-year-old women are said to be centaurs because of this.

Silence ensues for a few moments aside from the discord of slurping, clanging, sipping. I cut through my sour pork, so tender I only need pull it apart with my hands; I place bits of it on my spoon. Some of Sempronia's wine swishes over as she shakily brings her cup to her mouth, a slave leans in and wipes it up. Sempronia utters a low quiet sneer, as if it were the slave's fault her body is overwrought with tremors, like a satchel filled with writhing whelps.

'Hopefully there will not be any rain for the games tomorrow,' I say lightly.

'At Neptune's will, Aemilia.' Julia nips at my words piously. I thought that this would stop when Claudia arrived, that Julia would use her as a means to flex her virtue. But it seems this will not happen. Maybe Claudia's newness or youth would make it too feeble a challenge, but this I don't believe. It is something else altogether, an aversion that she seems unable to overcome, not that I think she wants to. If she did she would not always seem to be watching me, ready to pounce and turn my words over on their side, an attempt to expose an underbelly of contrary meaning, cruelly batting them like a cat does a mouse.

160

'Yes, at Neptune's will. Rain would benefit the farmers,' I say, alluding to my shining moment as portent to Neptune's benevolence. I believe this still bothers her.

There is a brief onslaught of enthusiastic comments on the weather, like a puff of smoke that hovers before quickly travelling over our heads and dispersing.

CHAPTER XXIII

After dinner, I sit in the chair beside the bureau and wait to be undressed. Two slaves enter and I am happy, one is the blonde slave. I enjoy this slave best; she was donated to us a short time ago, likely a spoil of some conquered land. I wish I knew the names of distant places. Though her face is long like a horse's, her skin is fair, her hair a soft gold-yellow and her eyes crystal green; a face matrons always try to paint over their own. Sempronia often has her play the lute as we dine, and she plays beautifully; a kind of music that soothes and lulls and drowns out the silence.

If I could, I would make her my own – would have only her hands wash, feed and dress me – but instead I must share her with the others; exclusivity could only bring wrongdoing, or so it's suspected. A state cult is furnished with state slaves, slaves who watch – extra eyes for the others and for the men who cannot enter here. They come and go, easily replaced or inter-changed with other discards or donations. But this one is unlike so many others, who are rough and take pleasure in spilling when serving, or scratching while dressing or yanking back one's hair as if it were the reins to direct the head. They know we cannot punish them in the usual fashion. It is not suitable for a

Vestal Virgin to brandish whips and carry out such punishments. We must assign another slave to punish a slave and surely they are easier on their equals. Spare the rod, spoil the slave.

She stands in front of me and unties the braided rope that sways at my knees and as always I resist the urge to rub the skin under my breasts. The rope is to be pulled tight, secure, to risk not a shred of possibility that it may loosen or, worse, fall silently unlaced. A Virgin should never come undone, no, a Virgin would never come undone. When I was a child and new to the stola of the Virgin, the rope had chafed my skin raw and sore. Each step, each breath, each swallow of food seemed to burn and erode away another layer of skin.

Now, the skin there has thickened into a hardened strip that if I could see it, would look as a healed burn does, or maybe as if a snake had coiled round me so long my skin grew over it. Three knots, one after the other, the slave's hands move quickly, deftly, an elegant blur of purpose, like beating fins. Our stolas resemble the stolas worn by matrons, but without any decoration or variety of colour and with the security of the rope.

She pulls the rope off, winds it from hand to elbow into a perfect loop and hands it to the other slave, who places it on the bureau. There are no drawers in the bureau. She then drags the chair out from against the wall – I step backwards to meet the chair just as it meets me – so she can unpin my headdress. This always comes next. We are without our headdresses only when we sleep. Whether this is for the sake of comfort, a lapse in piety or assurance of smooth silk free of tears and creases does not matter; the hours without such weight sinking into our scalps is a small indulgence.

A greater indulgence would be to have the tight roll in our

hair untwined, laid loose and flat against the pillow. However, our hair is only released from the roll at the nape of the neck when washed or cut by a slave, alone in our respective rooms. Even while we bathe, our hair remains rolled, our headdresses fixed on our heads, like a crown that cannot be detached, a permanent extension of ourselves, as if we were really taller. Each time my hair is cut and I watch it fall to the ground round my feet in dark brown lumps, sticky and wet, I try to will the slave to take off more. More than mid-arm, mid-back, more, more, more; cut until the roll is wispy thin and light and will bend easily into the curve at the base of my head at night and ease the heaviness that is a basket of stones perched on my head during the day. Tullia once said Virgins are born with stronger necks, but somehow this does not ring true, at least not for my neck – I cannot be sure about the others.

The slave moves round me, pulling pins, carefully lifting the layers of silk that cascade down my shoulders, past my elbows to my hips, a headdress that hooks into a veil when required. My head turns, tilts, arches back and forward in rhythm with her hands, as if we are partners in a carefully rehearsed dance.

After she unpins all the silk, she hands it to the other slave, who hangs it on the hook to the right of the bureau. Under the lamp's light, its rippled folds appear like long straight legs huddled together. The blonde slave then lifts off the thick gold headband with the tiny pearl that lies in the middle of my forehead. I seem to fall forward for an instant, unsteady, a decapitated stem limp without its purple petal head. It takes a moment to regain steadiness, adapt to a sudden sense of buoyancy. She hangs the headband with the silk, turns and both slaves then begin to unclasp my stola at my shoulders and slowly lower it over my arms, elbows, hips, knees, until it is flat round my ankles, as if I've collapsed and can step out of myself. My under-dress remains on, fused to my body to just below my knees like an upside-down sack with three holes cut out for my arms and head. Made of white wool in the winter, linen in the spring and summer, it's to be changed only when necessary – when washing both the under-dress and our bodies at the same time during our baths is no longer effective and the under-dress has yellowed or greyed with ash, or if an odour has begun to stick and fans outward while we walk, or if the fabric has frayed or torn. This is done with the slave turned round, facing the other way. As I pass her the dirty under-dress, she passes back a clean one that I slip over my head, a refreshed second skin. It is a quick exchange, as if too much time seeing ourselves could lead to some unspeakable inclination that perhaps our bodies could be used in other ways. Or worse, that our bodies are here, attached to our heads, and not out there hovering over the Republic of Rome.

But in that brief gust of nakedness, I peer down at my body to see what I look like beneath these clothes, to see if I already sag and droop like an old woman or if I retain a body matching my age, or am scaly like a fish or coated with hair. Sometimes I worry that I am covered with thick black hair; my breasts like a camel's dusty hump, my belly and legs sheathed like those of a bear. There are times I explore myself with my fingertips – an act of seedy rebellion, curiosity or maybe just vanity – under-neath blankets at night, to understand the shape of my thighs, hips, belly and breasts, just to ensure they are intact, smooth, that I still have a body shaped like a woman's. Night is a time when one can get away with such things.

When the blonde slave reaches out, I put my hands in hers, not because she offers, out of consideration, to guide my step out over the stola that is a puddle around my feet, but because it's what comes after, always. She picks up the stola, but doesn't place it on the hook to the left of the bureau; instead she will take it and soak it in beet juice to renew the deep shade of whelk dyes. Now that I see it tucked under her arm it does seem to have faded slightly. It will be brought back when I wake, more purple, and the dye will seep into my skin as I tend to Vesta, more so if I sweat.

My under-dress is tinted purple from the running dye and I wonder if I will soon be able to change it and catch a glimpse of myself. I sit on the edge of the bed and pick at the wool under-dress.

The slaves pull the door half closed, not shut and locked and the key tossed or swallowed. All doors here are without locks. Locked doors can be confused with opportunities of another sort.

CHAPTER XXIV

The litter carries us to the games, five of us swaying on ten men's backs. The curtains are drawn tightly over the litter, a mauve silk screen I can see through, just a little. Outlines. Violet men walking, smiling, joking, slapping one another on the back; violet matrons following closely behind, heads held high, almost floating just above ground, elegant, flowered and bejewelled. Light purple throngs traipsing through the Forum, past closed purple shops, purple trees, altars and temples. Deities glazed with violet. Farmers, bewildered in this violet land. I can smell Sempronia's breath, sweet silent decay from the inside out; teeth are always the first to go. If I could see her breath it too would be mauve, not light, but dark and pulpy. I glance over at Julia, seated diagonally across from me, but she, too, is lost in the purple world just outside the window closest to her. Fabia and Claudia are next to her, leaning in like wobbly milk jugs on a serving tray. Sempronia's stiff-jointed legs are stretched out, unlike her, but one inevitable day age overthrows formalities. With each slight dip and quiver she coughs and belches, croaky belches that catch in her throat, her cheeks fluttering. Her stomach rumbles and casts out excess air; we pretend we can't hear or smell her, and she pretends we can't hear or smell her – reciprocal pretence.

Fabia fusses with her stola, tucking and brushing the folds in her lap as though ridding it of crumbs, of evidence of something sweet she didn't share. Her veil drops round her shoulders and her skin below her chin droops, bumpy and red with heat rash. Spikes of hair sprout from her chin like planted onions ready to be yanked. She is always occupied or preoccupied, doing or planning. 'Glory to Janus, may the new year serve Rome well,' Fabia concludes, maybe thinking aloud.

Claudia ages Fabia when she sits so close; maybe she ages us all with her cherry cheeks and dimpled chin. A cherub next to withering widows. Her eyes alert and mouth always on the verge of smiling. Simmering eagerness. Her face has yet to tire. She begins to hum, an absent-minded hum, until Fabia squeezes her forearm to make her stop; music is for entertaining men. This does not interrupt her persistent prelude to a smile.

Draw a line from her to Sempronia, connecting the dots of Fabia, Porcia, Julia and me to form a chronology. We all begin here unblemished, begin here pretty, but this does not necessarily stay true, for whatever reasons blemishes arise and prettiness sinks away. We begin without blemish and end blemished. Start to finish. Linear corrosion. A quilt once beautifully woven, now with tattered edges, slowly coming undone with use, or better, uselessness. Sempronia's head falls back and forth, eyes fluttering open and shut, white to brown; trying to stay awake or maybe trying to sleep. She is frayed. I am fraying. A future after this would be nice.

I am near twenty-one now; fifteen years have passed, fifteen years to go.

Even as we take our seats, a row behind Cicero and Antonius, the crowds are already growling out cries in favour or disfavour

of the gladiators readying themselves for mock battle to enter-
tain Janus on the flat stone slab over which we hover, ever
brutal. The stands are shaky and tremble with each burst of
applause, each shout, each stamp of feet. Parts of it have collapsed altogether in the past, people falling into one another like
water spiralling down a drain. My heart beats much too fast
when I am here.

Though the seating is newly erected I still feel wobbly, as
though perched on the end of a rotting tree branch. The smells
of sausage and roasting dates waft through the air, turning my
stomach. Sempronia and Fabia are closest to the aisle, while
Julia, Claudia and I are marooned farther in. I can feel my
thighs sweating regardless of the cold wind and light rain. I look
round our isolated section, trying to find comfort in the idea
that surely it would not fall. Senators sit to the right of the consuls, Caesar, some augurs and governing officials to the left.
These are the hands of Rome and certainly cannot be severed.
When Cicero and Antonius stand, we stand also, my legs shaking, and point our thumbs up, high in the air, as the rest of our
section also stands, flashing upright thumbs. The arena bursts
into a roar of approval and disapproval, and hecklers turn their
thumbs up, down or to the side. Peasant women and men up in
the back seats across from us, browned by sun, call out to the
consuls for more bread, spit foaming round their mouths, their
faces all too alike. Unlike Tullia, I like to watch the peasant
women, so unrefined, their bodies as broad and strong as their
husbands', so free in their tattered tunics from the physical
tightness of the matrons. They sit in groups, men and women
together, appearing to talk to one another in the same bawdy
language, using the same lively gestures as if they were friends.

169

Minutes pass and Antonius sits, but Cicero stays standing, as if savouring the commotion, a sign of vanity. Finally he sits and the show can begin. The gladiators separate into two teams. On one side are the Gauls, on the other Romans, even though they all look like exports of Carthage. The announcer goes into a lengthy background tale of how the Romans were creeping up to attack a small sleeping village early in the morning when they were suddenly confronted by some of Gaul's strongest warriors: will Rome prevail? And so on and so on. I don't know why they bother with this. They all end up dead or nearly dead anyhow, and if the last gladiator standing was initially designated a Gaul, he suddenly becomes a Roman; Rome never loses. I watch the men, their brawny chests and thick legs, wearing only loincloths, shields and screened helmets, circling one another with swords, lances and nets. Poking, piercing, trapping, cutting, until the amphitheatre shudders with grunts of pain, wails of agony and last breaths. It looks so easy to make someone fall, writhe, spasm, die. There is one who is especially wily; his smooth hairless chest manoeuvres just out of reach of his opponents' weapons, his thin wrist swings his sword with great finesse. He is younger, maybe just sixteen, but he is one of the last of three standing until a shield bashes into his skull. His mouth drops open for a moment in disbelief. He teeters and the crowd cheers him on to continue fighting; his skilfulness made for a compelling fight. He falls, I watch the way his stomach inhales, exhales, his fine ribs bob up and down, until a puddle of urine darkens the sand round him.

I am not repulsed, as the matrons often claim to be, their husbands teasing them as they leave together, secretly impressed and reassured by their faintheartedness. Repulsion would be the wrong word, more so bafflement at the ease with which death comes and how a man's life can end so quickly with a few swipes of a dagger. Bafflement at how another man's death is always, *always* so pleasing to the men round me. Somehow this reduces the mystery of men, makes them seem weaker, simpler, not all that different from us. I find this troubling, preferring to see them as governing giants capable of understanding the complexities of Rome, as ambassadors to the gods, reasonable, sensible, not as vulnerable ragdolls dropping to the ground or rolling back and forth atop one another, so embarrassing to watch – or the bloodthirsty boys they become up here watching, so emotional and frenzied that if they were women they'd be called hysterical. This sudden flip-flop between the matrons, who sit quiet and reserved, looking at their hands in their laps, looking away repulsed, and the men, who lurch back and forth in their seats, biting the backs of their hands, teary-eyed from yelling, squirming with fervour. If the gods are watching these games held in their honour, as they are supposed to be, what will they think of the men's excitability; if they dislike women crying, why are men crying here in their presence?

Abruptly the bench trembles underneath me. I cling to the edge of my seat, apprehension prickling the hairs on my neck, tingling my legs as if pepper was suddenly mixed into my blood. The gods are disgusted at the men, repelled; surely we will collapse on one another, bones gnashing, heads crushing, a fleshy landslide. I dig my fingers more deeply into the bench. I look over and see a group of senators jumping up and down in the stands. Beads of sweat gather under my headdress, drip down my cheeks and forehead. I need to compose myself before the others notice and think I am afflicted in some way or another once again.

171

I study the back of Caesar's head, the way his fair hair is combed forward from the crown in an attempt to disguise his growing forehead. His neck, perfectly groomed, is still tanned by the summer's sun. A neck that leads into strapping shoulders like those of a farmer or slave. Laurel leaves are wrapped just above his ears, ears that don't stick too far out or are too thin so that tiny red veins show throbbing just below the surface. As he turns side to side, following the action of the fight below, I get glimpses of his profile; folds of skin ruffle his forehead, wrinkles of determination. His nose looks as though it has been broken more than once, its bridge sloping. His cheeks are meticulously plucked of all hair, making him look younger than he is.

Caesar suddenly turns all the way around, his lips curling up round his teeth, dimples spreading over his chin. For a moment our eyes meet and thunder pounds deep in my chest, quakes under his fleeting gaze. Eye contact with a Virgin is bad luck for the men; they can wilt for ever if having an indecent thought and meeting our eyes at the same time. We can be glanced at, but not for long, like staring at the sun, though perhaps this indicates the frequency of their indecent thoughts. And to better their odds we keep our eyes down, like heeled dogs.

Stunned, I delay averting my eyes, but he looks past me anyway, waving, and I realize he is smiling at the row of matrons deep in the back row, at his wife. I think her name is Pompeia. She is much younger than me, only fourteen or fifteen; her sweet smile drops away quickly once he turns back round.

The stands are still again, so I focus on the arena. The battle is over; slain bodies are being dragged off to the side, a trail of blood staining grass and stone. The presenter returns. 'The exotic and vicious animals of Africa are upon us . . . Let us hunt!'

Four of the tallest creatures I have ever seen are towed into the middle of the grounds by their muzzled snouts and spindly legs. Their necks are long like climbing vines, disproportionate to their horse-like bodies. Swaying back and forth, up and down, they try to shake free of the ropes, each movement a graceful dance. Their bodies are spotted brown and tan, a painted labyrinth. Spiky manes of hair trace all the way up their elongated necks to the tips of their heads, where pointed ears pop out beside tiny dense antlers. Their sinuous muscles, meandering veins, knobbly knees are beautiful, strong and stunning. I will there to be a different ending. Ten gladiators posing as hunters cut the ropes and surround the animals. They do not gallop away, or produce disembowelling fangs, but stay standing in one spot, showing their checkered teeth in a sort of apologetic polite smile. The hunters go after the smallest one first and spear it in its side over and over, blood spurting as it finally submits, disoriented, its skinny legs collapsing into its hooves, its long neck contorting, slamming against the stone in utter surrender. The hunters leap onto the now dead body, hacking away. The crowds are disappointed: it was too easy. The other three animals scatter as the hunters chase them with whips, antagonizing them, attempting to urge and taunt them into fierce man-eating brutes. Instead they snort fearfully, trying their best to avoid the next lash, trotting backwards, confused, getting trapped against the fence. One actually tries to jump over the fence, into the first row, full stride, and the crowd roars; its agile legs, swift and elegant, are quickly cut down. As they encircle the next animal, its head pointed directly upward as though damning the gods for their tastes in entertainment, neck posed in the most exquisite arch, nostrils flaring, I look away, down at my hands, counting my fingers again and again. This is what I can no longer stand, the lack of anticipation.

CHAPTER XXV

Over dinner, the games are not discussed; they are never discussed, as it would require noting the actions of the men. There is only the occasional 'May the games please the gods.'

'More cakes must be baked for the festival of Lupercalia,' Fabia pronounces, as if stretching out these little bits of easy conversation.

The festival of Lupercalia is more than a month away. There are sixteen other ceremonies in between, and there is always a great surplus of cakes stored; but it gives us something else to do, to bustle over, like one collective busybody. We attend only to crumble the cakes at Lupercalia, and then leave before the men, who sacrifice goats and a dog in a cave near Palatine Hill, arrive. They must smear their foreheads with blood from the sacrificial knife, then wipe themselves with wool dipped in milk, laughing very loudly throughout the whole sacrifice and getting drunk. They then dress in pieces of skin from the goats and run through the Forum striking women with thin strips of goat skin to encourage pregnancy. The origins of Lupercalia are unknown, as if whatever god it once honoured misplaced his invitation.

But we still must carry on with the ritual, just in case.

Still we must go back to the house, in the litter, pretending not to hear the laughter or the whipping.

'Yes, we must do so soon,' I murmur.

Sempronia asks again where Porcia is, and Julia tells her she is at the temple. I hear Claudia swallow her wine, a kind of childish gulping. Her hands stiff with scarring. Sometimes I think I can still smell the bitter, charred scent of her hands.

Some months after she arrived she had taken to flapping her hands. An odd manifestation, it was believed, resulting from blood clots. Good circulation was imperative for Vesta to receive full offerings from Claudia once she came of age; she was still only ten then.

We had to break Claudia of this habit. We watched her as she sat in a chair in the kitchen, assessing as her hands came out of her sleeves and flopped back and forth in quick succession, as if each was on a scheduled visit to the other.

'It is a difficult case, because she will need her hands to make her offerings to Vesta.' Fabia reached for a pear from the basket of fruit on the table, examined it for dents and bruises, then waved at one of the slaves to slice it up for her.

'It is,' I agreed.

'Tie her hands up. Let's see them.' Fabia handed me some rope, some of it sticky with pear juice.

I knelt in front of Claudia, took her small white hands and bound them to the arms of the chair. I wrapped the rope from her wrists to her fingers. Claudia watched as her fingers still flailed out in little twitches. 'I really don't mean it! I look at my hands and beg them to stop, but it's as though they have a life of their own.' Claudia's round face scrunched up in concentration as she again glared down at her hands, willing them to still.

Fabia circled her. 'We could tie some long spikes around her wrists, so if her hands flap they'll be cut on the spike.' She bit into another slice and thought about what she had just said.

Claudia's eyes widened, finally understanding what needed to be done. 'Oh, I am sure it'll go on its own; it's nothing, just a little infection in the joints maybe.' She tugged at her arms, feeling the tightness of the rope. Her fingers twitched faster now, in spite of her best efforts, twitched and shook even more uncontrollably.

'Why not try to bend them forward, so the palm is arched over the wrist? She could still use her hands then, though they'd be shaped more like paws . . .' Julia tapered off, realizing the foolishness of her suggestion.

'Vesta wants her offering made by an animal's paws?' Fabia shook her head at Julia. 'I prescribe that she hold two smouldering pieces of coal to get the blood moving and then the skin will be too crisp to allow flapping, forcing the blood onward.'

She motioned to the slave to go out to the fire heating the cauldron in the garden and collect two pieces of coal. Claudia blinked. 'No . . . no. It's fine, look.' She crammed her fingers stiffly together like a spiralling staircase.

'Be steadfast. It's not as if you need pretty hands. Vesta only cares for efficiency.' Fabia loosened the rope from Claudia's hands.

The slave brought the pieces of coal on a serving tray as if they were cakes and bent towards Claudia.

'I can't . . . I just can't!' Claudia's two legs started wagging. I willed her to keep them still, or else her legs could also be considered a clotted area.

'Take it!' Fabia demanded, and just like that, Claudia reached for the coal, screaming out with pain. Her face turned a deep red. 'That's it, that's it,' Fabia encouraged her. 'I can see it flowing again. Just a moment longer until it passes through your head, down to your heart . . . think of Vesta . . . think of Vesta.'

'Think of Vesta . . .' Julia began to chant with Fabia, and I, too, joined in.

'Think of Vesta . . . think of Vesta . . .' a slow clumsy chant that wore into Claudia like a foot pressing harder and harder into her back.

Finally Claudia's face turned from red to white – so white. 'Let go!' Fabia told her and the two chunks of coal thudded on the floor, rolling slightly despite their awkward shape.

Claudia fell from the chair.

'Tend to her hands.' Fabia waved at the slave and we left the kitchen, leaving Claudia in a heap.

I listen to knives screech across plates as meat is cut, spoons clang, the soft tap of cups being set down – the repetition makes a kind of monotonous patterned beat. Like water slowly dripping.

I add more kindling, wash the floor, sponge Minerva, add more kindling, wash the floor, sponge Minerva . . .

I sit in my room. The potted plant has recently produced what would be a white flower if it was not greyed by soot from the black smoke of the two hanging lamps, one on each side of Minerva. I pull off one of its petals and rub it between my fingers, wipe it white again, then let it drop into the middle of the tile mosaic of Vesta's hearth, a perfect circle that is the core, an orb in the middle of the marble floor, in the centre of my room. This is not really my room; it belongs to the Republic, as do I. These are not my possessions; I did not bring them with me, nor will I carry them out when I go, if I go. All I brought was a meagre dowry that would have been for a husband, if things had been different, but here it serves as a symbolic gesture. We are deemed privileged enough to own 'property'. How can property have property?

I add more kindling, wash the floor, sponge Minerva, add more kindling, wash the floor, sponge Minerva . . .

I enjoy my lunch one day, detest it the next. The lentils in the bread range from too hard to just right; the sesame-seed oil I dip my bread in varies from too sticky to a perfect viscosity. These are variations I cling to, markers that one day does indeed lapse into another.

One morning Claudia comes of age. They enter as I tend, gather round Vesta and offer freshly sprung blood. I watch the browned strips of wool shrivel into smoke. Claudia hooks her veil snugly over her mouth so she does need to try to suppress her smile. She need not worry again about clots.

Time wears on, wears off, like paint in direct sunlight.

I add more kindling, wash the floor, sponge Minerva, add more kindling, wash the floor, sponge Minerva . . .

As if weaving a tapestry or knitting a colourful shawl, though of course I am not permitted to do either as such is the work of wives and widows, nothing so tangible, I craft and devise other scenarios. I do this until my hands feel sore, arthritic, until I am too tired.

I count the creases in the palm of my hand, which seem deeper, older in the light of Vesta; I kick at the small pile of sand and pebbles by the entrance, then spread it out with my foot and count the pebbles. I list the items one finds in a kitchen: cup, bowl, spoon, flour, hearth . . . I list the remedies I know, or at least think I know: earwax for a human bite, the first hair cut from an infant's head to cure gout. To prevent inflammation of the eyes, bind the two middle fingers of the right hand with linen thread; urine can be used to rid specks upon the pupils. Use fresh cheese with honey to rub away bruises; a limp may be cured with goat's dung, applied with honey and raw beef. Time is boundless here.

I add more kindling, wash the floor, sponge Minerva, add more kindling, wash the floor, sponge Minerva . . .

Time is useless here, like a horse with broken legs.

CHAPTER XXVI

Caesar visits the house. Once a year the Pontifex Maximus comes in and walks through the house to make sure it is secure and leaves assured that no one can get in and no one can leave without being caught. The slaves have been instructed to wash the house so it glimmers under the rays of sunlight coming in through the central atrium, the statues especially. Fabia stood by watching the slaves wash each one, tapping her foot, inspecting, having them do it again and again. Over lunch everyone was especially light-hearted; even Sempronia seemed to have a better appetite. To have a visitor! We discussed the cleanliness of the house, and Julia mentioned she was worried about a slight crookedness in the way the door to her room hung from its frame but hoped Caesar would not notice. I said I was glad to have discovered a dead mouse beside a potted plant. 'Slaves would have missed it otherwise.' I did not mention that it had been stepped on or crushed somehow, likely by one of the slaves, and that its belly had been split open and tiny translucent heads of its unborn litter poked out.

We pretended it was more than a symbolic visit. The Pontifex Maximus does little to actually check the security of the house other than look.

Caesar plods through the first level, round the baths, peeks into the will room (peeks, so as not to be accused of meddling in the future), kitchen, dining room. Up on the second level he walks more quickly past our bedrooms, doors half opened; he doesn't peek here. All five of us must follow as Porcia watches Vesta. He looks tired, a bit distracted, like a landowner who knows he knows less than his enslaved farmer. He nods yes too much. He bides his time. Fabia takes *her* time, though, explaining the functions of each of the rooms, our routines, placement of slaves. He furrows his eyebrows, a disinterested uncle who cares just enough to feign caring. He strokes his chin and cheek with his palm. He offers a question here and there: 'Was the house sufficiently warm this past winter?'

Fabia leaps each time, her eyes on his toes. 'Oh yes, very warm! We have ample braziers . . . though perhaps we could do with a few more . . . The heating in the floors can often be uneven. Also, last winter, the hot room in the baths was certainly not hot enough, maybe a leak. I am not sure how such things happen, but the slaves quickly sorted it out—'

He cuts her off with an easy comment, spoken playfully, with humour, so as not to offend. 'I wondered and now I know!'

This is the only time we all turn pink together, emit breathy, nervous laughs together, embarrassed glee, because we are in the direct shadow of a man. He, larger than life in this house, has our undivided attention. When he tells us the house is safe and rather lovely in that conclusive sort of way one does when preparing to leave, there is more breathy laughter through our nostrils, down the front of our stolas to our breasts; the way breath blows when one's head is bent down at an angle. Even I cannot help myself. I smell the air that passes through him as I

182

trail behind, the scent of sour wine and busy sweat. I watch his feet, wide in his sandals, the sprays of hair on his toes a contrast to the sparse hair crawling up his bulky calves, light brown.

His strides are broad, brisk, each step sure. I think of the things I've heard about him – overheard – anti-aristocrat, flashy, supporter of plebs, briber, flatterer, vainer than a woman, one-time lover of the king of Bithynia, opportunist. He rubs his hands together, a muted clapping; it seems he'd be at ease every-where but here. His toga is slowly coming untied, falling loose around his waist, but he does not notice.

As he struts to the doors, about to leave, he turns again towards the central atrium and pauses for what seems to be one last admiring glance at the statues of past Vestal Virgins; one hand is on his hip, the other scratching the back of his neck, then rubbing, stretching, arching. He stops, mid-arch, straight-ens up and begins to walk towards the statues, as if he sees someone he recognizes. He lingers, meandering through the lines of statues with an odd fascination. There is something unseemly in this, the way he is looking at them, pinned down as they are by marble and death, as if this is how he would scruti-nize each of us, if we weren't so eerie. He leans in to read the names and dates. 'These Virgins have each been attributed to having brought Rome some kind of gain?' We are quiet, unsure if he is asking or simply stating. If he is asking, I can feel each of us shrink slightly with outrage and embarrassment that the impact these Virgins had on Rome was so fleeting.

'Yes,' Fabia is first to answer. She rushes over to the statue Caesar is now gazing at, like a vendor ready to exalt the quality of his merchandise.

'What did she do?'

'This is Agrippa, of course! While she was tending, she offered Vesta three cumin seeds, the same day the last king of Rome bought the remaining three Sibylline books. It was this Virgin's devotion to Vesta that eventually led to the expulsion of kings and the birth of the Republic.' Fabia tells him this as if it were common knowledge, her voice verging on indignation. But Caesar does not seem to notice.

'Expulsion of kings.' He releases a light whistle as if discussing the speed of a horse. Again, we are not sure if he is asking or stating. Fabia is about to continue, offer the finer, more elaborate details, but he cuts her off.

'And this . . .' He is standing in front of Rhea Silva now, daisies wilting across her reaching arms. This somehow makes her appear even more mournful, as if she is trying to give the daisies back, begging some unknown entity. Her face should be painted again soon.

'Is Rhea Siliva.' Fabia flings herself in front of Rhea, as if to protect her from the abomination were Caesar to ask who she is. Or maybe in a fit of jealousy, from his gaze, though I am unsure if it is jealousy of or over Rhea.

'Yes, I very well know the mother of Romulus and the people of Rome.' He turns towards us, smiles amicably, and we each sort of chortle, which, for Sempronia, turns into a sharp, uncontrollable cough. 'Well, yes, very nice, very secure.' He moves awkwardly to the doors, unsure how to leave, charming us again with his boyish discomfort. He nods, content, his dark brown eyes two opaque saucers that graze each of us, nearly bows and turns to the three slaves he left just outside the front door, like boots, turning back to wave at us or maybe to wave us away.

CHAPTER XXVII

I sit in the garden and watch dragonflies float, bumping into one another, connecting then disconnecting, strangers again. I gorge on the fresh air. Winter has segued to an early, warm spring, like a well-rehearsed play; one scene to the next. It is late afternoon and the skies are filled with grey tufts of clouds, dirty ice-capped islets.

Porcia is out walking along the garden's path. I watch her unnatural short stride, as if her legs are bound together round her calves. Each small step led by her levelled chin, her movements sharp and jolting; this is considered delicate, elegant for a Virgin. It is preferred Virgins always appear to be in a state of physical distress, at odds with their bodies. Such awkwardness displays the fact that a Virgin's body is nothing more than a source for Vesta to draw upon; it would not to do for a Virgin to saunter, sashay, even stroll. Smooth, graceful, liquid movements are not cohesive to Virginity; this is the walk of matrons. Tullia envied this most, I think, the way matrons could move along with such fluidity as if they were putting on a little dance with every step, and now, as I watch Porcia's jagged marching, knowing I look just as she does when I walk, it sparks envy of my own.

Porcia glances up and sees me, then quickly looks away, as if she hadn't seen me at all, as if acknowledgement is something she must use sparingly.

Off in the distance thunder rolls. Porcia jumps, turns and heads back towards the house. Four male slaves are pruning various bushes, sculpting away excess branches, pulling weeds. They suppress grins and smirks as Porcia bustles by, looking not at her but at one another. I can tell they have yet to notice me, and now that Porcia's back is turned they are raising their eyebrows, lifting one side of their mouths in baffled amusement. One shakes his head, and I can tell they are laughing inwardly, thinking of something funny to say later on when they are alone, out of earshot, lying side by side in their room.

Though I am expected to go indoors, as if Jupiter beckoned, I pretend I do not hear the thunder. Long ago there was a Vestal Virgin struck by lightning out here in the garden. She was still alive when she was found on her back with her legs splayed, stola hiked up over her knees. Some believed Jupiter had punished her for being impure, but whether she had been chaste or not did not matter because being struck made her unchaste, so she was punished shortly afterwards. But this is something I've been doing more and more lately, playing deaf and dumb; Tullia said it is a way to get away with things and I want to stay in the garden longer. I like the rain – no – when it is about to rain. How the clouds reel one another in, spinning, stewing, plotting. It is rain, or even the threat of rain, that keeps them inside and gives me the garden all to myself. And round and round the garden I go.

I walk along the paths, a light mist cascading against my cheeks as a smooth crisp rain falls, as though I am stepping through a grey cloud, stirring up rain. I step into the small puddles gathering on the path, enjoying the way my shoes begin to squish against my toes. Tiny black balls cluster together, another kind of cloud, loitering flies. I pluck a leaf from a tree, bend it in and out, hold it up, its winding veins like tiny streets, pick it apart until it's only a drooping spine, its green skin shed, lost. The smell of wet grass is as sweet as peaches.

Some of the slaves are fixing loose bricks in the wall, others are building another wooden bench, while three or four others are bent over, planting seeds. They move round me as I pass, a breezy wake on their cheeks, a shadow travelling by on a wet breeze. If they do look up, their eyes only reach the hem of my purple stola, then fall down to the pointed white tips of my shoes stepping out one at a time like the hushed rustle of a fluttering moth. They are not to look at me at all, but if they do look, it is for less than a moment, then I am batted away. I snag their eyes with as much hold as fishhooks made of cotton. They need not look; there is nothing here to see. But once the sound of my steps has passed and the airy whisper of my stola is gone, do they again turn back to one another smirking those mysterious smirks the way they did when Porcia bustled by? As I move down the cobbled path, where they are carefully sowing more seeds, maybe radishes, I turn back just to see if I am acknowledged, to see if they roll their eyes. Try to read their faces. I tell myself there isn't any harm in looking.

There are two slaves, one with an odd-looking back as pink as meat and speckled with moles. The other, skinny and dark, is bent over, ribs trailing down his back like gills, dipping his spade in and out of the black soil, stabbing holes, making tiny wombs. He turns and looks at me, but I cannot tell if it is because he would have anyway or because he feels my eyes on him, spying. He has a short beard, up and down his cheeks and chin like dark paint. And down through his beard stream tears, tears I know nothing about. He is new, some upcoming politician's gift to the state, a cast-off, like an outworn toga, a frayed belt, a bent ring missing its insignia. I am sure I've seen him before today but have not noticed him – there but without detail. It's his beard I've noticed. Unlike Roman men, who go to such great lengths to keep their cheeks as hairless as a newly hatched skylark, he has a beard that sticks out. It is not the usual curly mess of a long matted beard belonging to a neg-lected slave. It is groomed, neatly cut against his face. It glazes his sunken cheeks, concealing his thin neck, accentuating his dark eyes like a veil that leaves nothing else to be admired. He is veiled just as I am. There is something so sadly beautiful about him, hunched over, crying, watering radish seeds with his own salted tears, watering his own beard, a hairy vine. He meets my eyes, unashamed and unafraid.

I realize I've stopped walking and am not just slightly tilted the other way, glimpsing, but fully turned around, facing the wrong direction, facing him, ogling. As if waking up from a dream in which I could fly, the owner of two wide wings or feathered legs that can leap up and tread air, I have a feeling of disappointment. I have betrayed myself, shown lack of control. Just before I swing back round I see him rub his eyes with his wrists, leaving behind streaks of soil like old scabs and two black eyes. I pretend to look for something on the ground.

'There it is,' I say loudly, over-enunciating, and pick up a pebble, carrying it the rest of the way as if it were some prized jewel, the pearl from my headband, until I am sure he is no longer looking, then I drop it in the grass.

*

188

The rain stops as quickly as it started. I sit under the portico and watch tiny droplets run off the edge of the roof. I settle into the rhythmic sound of the slaves working. Their movement is much like the stirring one sees when one stares at a patch of grass for any stretch of time; there is constant movement, blades bending and swaying from the busyness that must take place over and under the soil. I hear the occasional grunt, low voices discussing how to move something heavy. I don't know why, but I listen for the one who is crying. 'Heave,' I hear a slave call out, followed by a loud grating noise. I see something large and white being hauled and I think they are dragging a heifer to butcher, but the sound of it is too vexing.

I stand up and peer into the garden from the steps of the portico. They are pulling a slab of Luna marble to the back of the garden, to the darkest corner. 'I want a tent to be erected tomorrow. The stone mason will come the following day. The canvas is thick, so many lamps should be set up inside.' It is Caesar. I can see his furrowed forehead glisten in the now resurfacing sunlight.

He is speaking to a small gathering of male slaves. Our garden is Caesar's garden now that he is Pontifex Maximus, but rarely does he enter. The Pontifex Maximus usually only glimpses the garden, the fountains or benches, or the relief scenes on pillars he has paid to have made in his honour on the same one day he visits the house.

'He must be guided to and from the garden entrance because he will put on a blindfold at the entrance, and when he leaves the tent and is inside the tent he will be out of their sight.' The slaves already know this; this is always how they are done if they are done inside the garden. Most often fountains and pillars are sculpted elsewhere and brought here afterwards, but if the monument is particularly ornate, it will be sculpted here to minimize chipping and cracks when moving it. Caesar must be planning a fountain of enormous proportions; it is usually fountains they have erected in our garden. It is overflowing with fountains: there are the small fountains of long ago, of modest decoration, grey, with dark patches of moss under the basin. They are short and stubby and the water has dwindled to a trickle, spouting from the mouths of Juno and Diana, Minerva and Ceres, and still others too eroded to recognize. The newer fountains have become increasingly elaborate: they depict not only heads but fully sculpted bodies, surrounded by birds, fish and even deer, miniature stone forests with running brooks. Each Pontifex Maximus tries to outdo the one before in size and splendour.

'What is it?' Fabia comes up behind me and sighs, appearing inconvenienced, but this is how she always looks outside the temple and away from an altar. Sempronia comes out a moment later and shuffles towards us, grabbing onto a table and then a stool for support.

'It is Caesar. He is bringing in marble for a new fountain, I suppose.'

'Oh?' Fabia sounds impressed, cheerful even. She enjoys these offerings, takes them personally, as if they were placed here as tokens of appreciation.

'What did you say?' Sempronia cups her right ear, her usual rasping is sometimes pierced by these shrill outbursts. The tunnelling between her mouth and ear is slowly collapsing.

Fabia leans into her and repeats what I just said. Sempronia nods and hobbles back inside the house; wet air swells her joints and a new fountain isn't interesting enough to sustain such pain.

190

Caesar must have heard us, or rather heard Sempronia. He approaches the portico. Fabia and I quickly step down the stairs and bow. The path is still slick with rain; diluted bird droppings have spread into runny gobs. I can't tell if the hem of my stola is dipping into them.

'Honoured Virgins.' His voice is genial, but brisk.

'Honoured Caesar.'

I can tell by his feet that he has shifted his weight and is now looking behind us at the slaves dragging the slab. He mutters something under his breath and is about to step round us as if we are nothing but a small bush or large rock.

'You grace us with another fountain. I am sure it will uphold your name and draw only the favoured birds of the gods,' Fabia calls out. It is strange to hear such flattery from Fabia; it falls from her mouth in one single glop, like spit, like the white bird droppings, thin and semi-transparent.

Caesar turns back, or at least his feet do. 'No. Not another fountain. Surely there are enough fountains here!' He gives a light, forced chuckle. 'Instead, I grace you with a new statue for your central atrium.' He tells us this distractedly, as if it were some unimportant bit of news he hasn't time to share. A trifling matter. Or maybe it is not the matter of the statue that is trifling, but us, here at his knees, having to talk to us.

Fabia makes a little sharp sound, as if something hit her, a mew-like thud. The eighty-year dry spell has ended, and if a Virgin has already broken it, then Fabia cannot. Nor can any of us. This Virgin has taken away the prize, the incentive of becoming a prize on which we all subsist. Each Virgin hopes her life will coincide with an extraordinary event so her devotion will be acknowledged as having had a hand in it. Or womb in it. What

191

is there to subsist on now? What is there to strive for? Glory is the pastry that we've been gorging on. This new Virgin has bettered our chances of becoming for ever obsolete upon our deaths. No two statues are erected of Virgins whose lives have overlapped; it would ruin the incentive to be better. 'And who, might I ask, is the Virgin?'

'Veturia, of course!' I recognized the name but wasn't sure why; the only past Virgins we discuss are the ones already there, dead, in the atrium. 'She died the year I returned to Rome. It was her devotion that aided Caesar back to Rome.' He tells us this as if he wasn't himself, trying on how it will sound when others say so. Veturia, the fifth, the one Julia replaced. The cougher. She was associated with the dissent between the consuls that same year. Vesta rejected her. I suppose he found her name and year of death in the records. Now Caesar is resurrecting her, rearranging her place, her relation to this place, his time. He has reversed time, reached back and made a quick duplicate of Veturia, and is now propping her up beside him. Her significance is his significance, or at least the precursor to his envisioned significance. Omens litter the threshold of great men after they've stepped into their greatness, but not before. How lofty of him, Tullia would say if she were here right now. But Tullia isn't here, so it is I who must think this, though I do not condone deriding the Pontifex Maximus.

We have not only doubles but duplicates, infinite chances to make a come-back, to be a statue in the atrium. My life could be meaningless for centuries after my death, until perhaps one day I will be exhumed and redressed, rewritten and reiterated.

This should cheer me, but it doesn't.

192

'Veturia was a Virgin of exceptional quality,' Fabia states, her voice again a solid calm. 'I will happily provide the details.'

'As I had hoped.' Caesar skirts round us, pulling the drape of his toga further over his shoulder. I can tell this because he momentarily exposes his calves, two oblong hairless precipices that can go where they please.

Fabia and I return to the portico. Fabia slumps onto a stool, not slumps, this she would not do, but perches on it more heavily than normal. I notice one of her legs is bouncing up and down. We sit this way, quietly, apart from the soft rustling of her stola, until the slaves have untied the slab and disappeared back into the brush of the garden. Fabia gets up. 'Such idleness,' she suddenly chirps, scowling at me, and whisks into the house. The kitchen door slams, bringing a gust of boiled boar that quickly recedes into the garden.

I should go up to my room now, read, wait to be beckoned for dinner, but I suddenly have an urge to look at the slab of marble.

I circle around it once or twice, before actually stopping.

The slab looks like a dead fish, a white distended belly with swarms of inflamed blood vessels, a belly that holds a swallowed Virgin; I think of her face being muffled in the stone right now, begging to be let out. To live again and on and on.

I wish it were Tullia in there, just to see her again.

CHAPTER XXVIII

Over dinner Sempronia develops a fever. Her skin takes on a tinge of yellow, which at first seems only to be an odd glow from the candlelight, even leftover excitement from Caesar's visits and the news of the statue, but as the evening wears on, a red rash spreads over her cheeks as well. She looks almost pretty, as if she were wearing make-up, with her cheeks coloured in that way. Cupping her mouth from time to time, as if suppressing a girlish giggle, she appears younger, though of course she is only trying to keep down what she has swallowed.

Fabia relays Caesar's plans of the new statue in a way that hints she always knew of his intention. She is of course aiding the carver so 'Sempronia need not have the worry,' which really means Sempronia can barely recall the morning, never mind fifteen years previously. Once she is finished, she sits again, wearing a serene, secret smile. She must always appear to be the insider with Vesta, the gods, the Pontifex Maximus.

I take another bite of boar; the sauce is a tad too sweet, too much honey and not enough wine, too little salt. I mix in the accompanying basil and pepper to tart the sweetness. There is a mute sombreness as we dine, of hopes dashed, of disappointment. I find I am basking in this unification. If we could, we would stroke one another and tut sympathetically, 'I know, I know.' Perhaps we should celebrate the new statue with a toast – at least one of us is chosen, at least we are acknowledged to have a few tricks up our sleeves. They can't tell us apart out there anyway. Is this not better than to be blamed for some misfortune?

'You were her replacement,' Fabia says snidely, glaring across the table at Julia, a twisted accusation: if it weren't for you she'd still be here, in the flesh, not being moulded from stone, stolen stone meant for me.

It is always more fulfilling to blame the living.

Claudia shakes her head, feeding from Fabia's ire, an occasion to better warm herself to Fabia, who gives out the pastry now.

Julia puts down her spoon, dabs her mouth.

There is no sense of camaraderie here, never. Even now, I cannot help but feel pleased Julia is the recipient of the others' dissatisfaction.

The stone Virgin has taken her place at the table, another cause of chasm. We fissure and fizzle in our own pettiness.

Sempronia gets up and goes to bed before finishing her dinner and stays there.

As I ascend the stairs back up to my room, I notice the white stain of bird waste on my stola, near my ankle. For some reason I am not bothered; it seems appropriate.

The following afternoon, as we bake the cakes for the festival of Mars, Fabia announces that a fever afflicts Sempronia. 'Virgins become more prone to illness the longer they've been dry.' She lowers her head, pulls her veil in an act of sadness, maybe even pre-emptive mourning. Perhaps thinking that her own time with Vesta will soon end. I know this because I heard her in the chamber room once or twice crying – no, not crying, something else; she is too dried out to cry. It was more as if she was trying to cry, but all that came out were little choking emissions of dust and ash. I could hear her before I even approached the door, before the slave blocked the door and told me it was occupied. 'Not yet . . . please . . . please come . . .' a hoarse weep crawled under the door and I knew she was pleading with her own body to continue its cycles of renewal. There have been other signs as well, sudden flashes of heat, having to fan herself between bites of food, an even greater nervousness that shows her womb is shrinking. Tullia said most Virgins should beg for the day they are released from Vesta one way or the other, but the ones who stay, and they nearly all stay, can reap all the benefits of their Virginity and not have to stand in the temple for hours tending Vesta once their wombs have finally shrivelled and hardened, turned as misshaped as ginger root.

Just then, in the quiet after Fabia's announcement, a most impious thought comes to mind. If Sempronia dies, a new Virgin will be chosen. I experience a flutter of hope. Perhaps I could train the new one, as Tullia had trained me. When no one was looking I'd rub her with hemlock, down her arms and legs, and the others would think her ill-marked in some way and send her off with me. Fill this box of silence with words, the temple with words, my throat and mouth with the buzzing shapes of sounds. I'd decongest, the heaviness in my chest would lighten, like spitting up phlegm.

'We must all appeal to Vesta, remind her of Sempronia's years of servitude . . .' Eventually, even the goddess we serve forgets us, once we've been washed up, washed out, like a scrubbed empty bucket.

Fabia places her hands flat against the edge of the small round table as if she needs this support. 'The only cure is to call Vesta's attention to her and I will offer my own blood of fertility to be smeared on the bottom of her feet.' She presses her lips tightly together, steadying herself against the table as if this upcoming act of goodness, supposed selflessness, has already exhausted her. She awaits admiration, clucks and sighs of awe and appreciation.

Instead Porcia raises her hand, as we once did as students. 'But, surely, considering your age, my blood would be much more effective, or Julia's.' She glances over at me. 'Claudia's as well, her fertility being so new and fresh . . .' This happens between Virgins, a shared cycle, bleeding together almost at once as if we share one big womb.

Fabia snaps her head up as if slapped, lets go of the table, eyes wide, picks up a bowl and begins to mix, thrashing the spoon against its side: thud, thud, thud, like beating a drum. 'Quality always comes before quantity.' She starts to say something else, but stops, then tries to march swiftly to collect some eggs from the basket in the corner. Her legs look as if they will twist over one another and she will trip.

Porcia puts her hands in the flour and grain just beside her, begins to knead, the sleeves of her stola rolled back above her wrists. Julia sits at the table and measures out some olive oil. They are all suddenly quiet under the pink light of late afternoon streaming in through the windows and, with the smell of baking mola salsa cakes, it's as if I am with a real family, sisters, mothers and daughters, aunts and nieces. Each stilled and made

197

into statues under molten rock. For a moment I feel utterly disappointed and I don't know why.

I am tempted to stand closer to Porcia, to ask her something, or even whisper my agreement to her. 'You're right, Fabia's potency is nearly depleted.' This is what I do, look for opportunities to wheedle my way in, or maybe this is what I used to do, because as much as I am tempted to do this, I am also tempted to do something rude, like wink or just grin unflinchingly at her. Something Tullia would have done. When Porcia finally realizes how close I am, she jerks up, her hands covered in dough as if they were melting.

I pick up the two jugs and go to the purified well to collect water.

I walk through the garden to the sacred well; it is barricaded with high walls, without a roof so the gods can drink from it when they please. It is very warm out and I can feel my back quickly dampen with sweat. I set the jugs down by my feet and try to draw up the water needed to purify the temple's floor, to bake the cakes. Nothing happens. I pull and pull but the bucket is stuck at the bottom. The pulley is jammed. A cry snarls up in my throat, kicks at the back of my teeth, scratches at my tongue to be let out. I try to swallow it back, bite it, chew it into pieces, hold my breath until it breaks and half sticks under my tongue and all that comes out is a whimper. The other half of the divided cry sneaks up, up, up and my eyes moan tears. Bad luck follows me like a tick embedded in skin. I try to pull again, but the well refuses me. They will think the gods are denying me water and probe for wrongdoing.

I try again to twist the wheel, spitting first into my hands under my veil, wiping the wheel. Nothing, not a budge, not a squeak.

I step out from behind the walls, walk into the garden and wave over the first slave I see. I try my best not to look at him and use as few words as possible, 'The well . . . please fix.' This is the first time I have spoken to a man other than the Pontifex Maximus. For a moment I am not sure if he can see me, or if he speaks the same language, not because he is foreign, but because for a moment I wonder whether I was even taught words a man can understand or maybe my voice will be too high and inaudible.

He follows me and jiggles the wheel, his tanned sinewy arms popping with veins like a map carved into his skin. Nothing. 'Lysander, he is Greek. I'll get him, he knows of these things.'

The slave ambles out like a baited bear. I ignore the limb I now hang from. Here behind these walls, with a man, a slave no less, the things I could be accused of. Lysander enters. It is him, the beautiful weeping slave.

'What is wrong here?' he asks, as though we are standing in the street and I am a young maiden overwhelmed and lost in the Forum. Silence.

He leans over the well, examining, making mechanical utterances, a tug here, a tug there. He goes out and returns with a long piece of metal and a nail. I watch his back bend and twist over the well. The quick flashes of the tattoo on his forearm written like stripes: 'I belong to the Roman state. Capture me if I have run away and return me to the Regia for reward.' Both 'Roman state' and 'Regia' are written under two blotted-out spots, his last owner scribbled over.

Faded scars and old lashings are stacked one upon another, stairs leading up to his shoulders or descending down below, depending on where one starts. Freckles are splattered on his chest, arms, shoulders, back, like little villages. Veins run up and down his arms like canals. He takes hold of the pulley, arches back, arms over head; his hips jut out like two flat stones on a shoreline the wind has slowly unburied, shoulder blades two stubs where wings may have once been; his collarbone sinks down, collapsing into a hidden pool. Metal clanks on metal. If the others hear, see us . . .

He pulls the rope, each muscle pulsing under shallow skin, and up flies the swooshing bucket, spilling water onto his ridged stomach, dampening the trail of hair that stops at the rectangular piece of wool tied around his hips. He rubs the water in, away, touching himself in the way only men can, like small children picking at their belly buttons, full owners of highly explored bodies. As if he owned his body.

He grins, proud of his mechanical genius. 'I am new at this physical sort of labour.' He turns, stops, my purple stola a smack against his lips, a cuff in the jaw, a pincer on his mouth. He steps down, out from behind these walls without a roof, mute.

CHAPTER XXIX

Over the next few days I see Fabia round the house, her palm flat on her belly, sometimes even whispering, as I've seen matrons with child do. Even when she is entering and exiting the stone carver's tent, her hand is there on her belly, negotiating with her bloodless womb. Or maybe she feels a pull, slight contractions as she gives birth to Veturia's face and body, as she was.

Fabia snaps at the slaves when she re-enters the house to get her water or fruit, or when they take her to the baths where she will soak longer than she ever has before, amidst the battalion of deserving statues. I know this because I have to delay my own bath until she is finished, as does Julia. Yesterday, I found Julia at the end of the stairs still waiting.

'She's still in there,' she whispered to me, though she didn't turn around. I always bathe after Julia; the statue has thrown off the precise routine in the house; I would normally find this pleasing, if it weren't delaying the same, or only, parts of the day I enjoy most.

I could smell Julia, rain mingled with smoke and sweat. I must smell the same.

Julia sighed, then asked hopefully, 'Has it been decided if we will make cakes today?'

'I don't know. Nothing was said at dinner last night.' How could Julia look forward to making cake? All we do is make cake.

I felt oddly rooted as I stood behind her, as if rapt by this brief exchange so unfettered by the usual callousness. I felt I was about to say something more and yet could not find anything more to say. There was no comment on the weather I would venture uttering, no remark on Fabia's inconsiderateness or her brooding. Good Virgins do not brood, so this I could not risk saying. I could not remind Julia how we once wandered the house, how we may have stood like this on these stairs so long ago, in the midst of some silly game. No, nostalgia hints at longing and good Virgins do not long. Opening my mouth meant not only my words coming out, but her words going in, a tangled mess of intended and unintended meaning. Cake was all there was, the last slice of neutral fluffiness.

'Well, I'd be better to return to my room and read.' She turned swiftly to go up the stairs, bumping into me. She froze before me as if in utter fear, nose to chin. I could feel her breast against my arm, a padded fist. She pressed further into me, just slightly, but I could feel it, mostly her breast, a hardening nub. Her face swelled red, deeper than the purple of her stola, and for a moment I could again see her freckles, like dead fish, surfacing in the sea of her milky white cheeks.

She suddenly wrapped her hand round my wrist, tight as an asp's jaw, and pulled me down from the step I was standing on. I stumbled, my thigh banging against the corner of the wall. Fabia turned and looked at me from the pool and I knew it looked as if I were spying. I turned, wanting to catch Julia by the ankle even and pull her down with me, but she was gone.

As I passed the pool, I expected Fabia to call out to me,

declare me a deviant yet again, but I realized she never really saw me, or the stumble, or my face, only my shape and colour. Her eyesight is fading; a good Virgin is indeed short-sighted.

Now as I tend Vesta, I pray for Sempronia, though the potential admittance of a new Virgin becomes a kind of subtext in my prayers. 'Vesta, keeper of the hearth, baker of bread, heater of home, safekeeper of Rome, preserver of Romulus's people, I pray and beseech thee to ward off disease from all your six servants. Please permit each Virgin an able body to serve you, permit each Virgin a lengthy life to serve you, permit each Virgin to offer unwavering fertility unto you . . .'

Vesta could take it either way: return Sempronia's health or deliver a new healthy body to tend her. Specificity is key, and thus omission of specificity leaves room for interpretation. Though mentioning fertility may have been a bit obvious.

Sempronia goes untreated for days; her illness wafts down the hall, and the smell of sweat and bile and unwashed skin settles over my face as I try to sleep.

Once Fabia finally bleeds, she makes quite a show of it. She has a slave carry the saucer of blood on a gold tray, as if serving some kind of delicacy, through the house, taking the long way up to Sempronia's room to ensure we all see. A self-satisfied smile hooks up one side of her mouth.

As I pass through the kitchen to the garden to look for the weeping slave, I notice there is a freshly slaughtered chicken, its limp neck hanging over the table, bleeding into a bucket.

Fabia spends the rest of the afternoon until dinner standing

203

outside Sempronia's room, peeking through the open sliver of the door. Over dinner she reports how much better Sempronia is feeling and we each pretend not to hear Sempronia's faint groans drift into the dining room as we eat. I do this by counting the minutes, sometimes seconds, between groans as one does between Jupiter's lightning bolts and claps of thunder to see how soon Neptune's rain will arrive.

After a few moments Fabia sends for the blonde Germanic slave to play the lute. Soon music fills the dining room. The blonde slave's eyes are near closed, her cheeks puffed, a strand of her gold hair is caught in her eyelashes, but she doesn't seem to notice.

She plays a subdued melody, not shrill and loud as the lute players do at sacrifices; she was called to drown out cries of another kind. The music sounds like lapping water. For a moment, I think I can see the water round Minerva's ship begin to ripple and the mast of the ship slightly sway. I feel charmed by the music, like a hypnotized snake rising from a basket. Oh, how talented she is. Sheer enjoyment comes over me, and I notice I am the one swaying.

But as a dish of stoned apricots is placed before us, Fabia begins to tell Claudia a story and the lute becomes broken into irksome fragments. 'There was a Virgin who lived to be eighty years old, her fertility never running dry. A Virgin of such extraordinary purity that those stricken with illness who crossed her path were cured.'

There is a kind of grandiosity in Fabia's story, an exaggeration of a Virgin's powers to nearly divine status that is irreverent. Vesta, not her attendants, is the divine, the goddess. It is as if Fabia is spreading a rumour, lending us divine attributes,

204

making us goddess-like; humility is the backbone of Virginity. Had she not said this over and over? Fabia looks the mirror image of wide-eyed Claudia; both listen intently to the potential powers of a good Virgin, as if Fabia is making it up as she goes along and is excited to hear what comes next.

'There was once a little girl born a mermaid; it was said her mother was cursed after having bought cheap figs and olives from a foreign peasant. The peasant had ignorantly stolen from the fig tree and olive bush near the consecrated waterhole, the pool of Curtius, where the ancient chasm occurred and only fused again with the sacrifice of a Roman soldier. Thus, the infant's legs were fused as one, her feet joined at the heel as fins. The mother of this child knew once her husband discovered this he would take the infant and place her in the Tiber to swim out to sea where she would either sink or swim, depending on whether Neptune deemed her worthy. So the mother of the child hid the tail, wrapping the infant tightly in a blanket and telling her husband she had a bad rash that the air would only make worse. She was able to hide her only child this way for many days, but soon the husband grew suspicious and said that night, after his dinner, he would unwrap his infant daughter. The mother knew it would be the last day she would spend with her daughter, and so took her to the Temple of Vesta. She wished for her daughter to have been in the presence of Vesta at least once before swimming out to the beyond, and also to pay due reverence in the hope that after her deceit was discovered her husband would not banish her from his home and hearth. She came to the temple just as this Virgin of extraordinary purity passed by her.'

Fabia leans in over her plate, basking in her story as if it is a ray of sun on her skin – not that Fabia would bask in the sun; good Virgins are ashen Virgins.

'After dinner, her husband unwrapped the infant and, as the mother braced herself for a beating . . .'

As Fabia continues, it suddenly strikes me that there is something odd about this piece of history she is serving us up like cake, knowing we are obligated to hold our plates out. Why has this story not been told before? Why is there not already a statue of this Virgin healer?

'The husband grew very quiet . . . whispering something under his breath. The wife thought he was cursing her, but then heard he was counting, two legs, two feet, ten toes. The Virgin had healed her, separating the infant's legs with utter purity. Do you know who this Virgin healer was?'

'No,' Claudia answers, sounding more childish than she should.

Fabia takes a long pause, revelling in Claudia's anticipation. She takes a sip of wine, holds it in her mouth, savouring.

For a moment I think she is about to say the Virgin healer is herself. This is why she would not allow a younger Virgin to offer her blood: Fabia wants to use her own, for if it cures Sempronia, she will be deemed a healer. If Sempronia is not cured, Fabia will still be made Vestalis Virgo Maxima. She gains either way. But for now she is already distorting her own history, mythologizing, so she can be remembered for something even grander, more than bleeding into a saucer. A healer who reached beyond the house, to Rome, to an infant mermaid. She is getting to her posterity before anyone else does, trying to elbow her way into the central atrium. What's good for the goose is good the gander; history in the making, history is man-made.

'When the Virgin passed away, she burst into flames shaped as a bird and flew back into the temple, straight into Vesta. This Virgin was Veturia.'

How quickly she has changed camps and allied herself with Veturia! A hanger-on. Soon, she'll be telling stories of how she spotted Veturia's talent for devotion before anyone else; she'll claim she has an eye for devotion.

'When I first arrived, I fractured my arm by the pool. I was in agonizing pain when suddenly a bird flew in and landed directly on my arm.' Julia waves her arm around as proof. 'Veturia, I exclaimed! And the pain was gone.'

No, I want to shout, it was Altrica the slave and a strip of bacon that healed your arm.

They each eye me, waiting, forcing me to lie; there is nothing I can do but go along. Fabricate, because we are all cut from the same long winding fabric. I tell how Veturia healed my ears. I heard a melodious chirping first and so I knew it was her.

The truth is an agreement; together we can convince our-selves of anything.

CHAPTER XXX

If it isn't raining I go for a walk. I am taken by Fabia's and the carver's silhouetted outlines, especially apparent in the grey overcast, bent into stools, the slab between them like a table ready to be set. Elsewhere the carver would have assistants, but this location does not allow for it. It could invite an accident. The statue will take months to finish alone. Fabia isn't in there for long – time enough to describe a nose or an eye, the day after a mouth or chin, the following day the thickness or slenderness of a neck. Perhaps this is the other purpose for the lamps, so their bodies are always illuminated, distinguishable inside the canvas. The blindfolded carver leans sideways; his shadowy legs are spindly and unnaturally long, as are his hands. He nods every so often, obviously thinking Fabia is observing him and his gestures of attentive listening. But she is turned away, her narrow back facing him, she too knows she can be seen and will not miss an opportunity to appear extra chaste. When she leaves, the carver rips off his blindfold and rolls and moulds her details into a small clay model; his long fingers are nimble, moulding Veturia in swift pinches that are, I imagine, sharp as flea bites.

But this isn't why I find myself more often in the garden. No, I find myself in the garden looking for the weeping slave.

Walking up and down the paths more slowly than usual. Stopping at every rustle in the bush. No, not stopping – that would appear too suspicious, as if I am trying to find something, like a buried love note – but pausing, as if catching my breath. Virgins are easily short of breath. Stamina is suspect.

When I see him, I try to do something so he will look up at me directly again. I scuff my feet harder against the cobblestones, snivel, cough, sigh. Today he is on his hands and knees, snipping the grass. His spine bulges out like knots in a rope, climbing up until hidden under his black hair. His loincloth, soiled with streaks of mud, sags round his hips so he has to keep reaching and pulling it up from behind. Sweat trickles down his brown back and is absorbed into his stained loincloth.

I make sure to step on a twig as I pass him, but he does not look up from the scissors in his hands.

Suddenly Fabia comes out of the house and waves me in. A will has arrived and she wants me to deposit it so that she can toddle about the garden with Claudia; it is a lovely day after all. Maybe she also wants to catch glimpses of the carver, moulding the subject of her description, her Virgin healer, relishing her post as commander of both the carver and the carving. What good is contempt? I tuck my hand into the sleeve of my stola and wave goodbye at him, no, rather 'see you soon'.

There are three, not one, new wills to deposit. We must log them in a book – date of arrival, family name, content of will – then deposit the original in a box with a lock. Most wills are just revisions, usually striking off a name here and there, a son who has died or defied, or a new wife and thus, new heirs. Or else a man, who, wife after wife, is still without an heir will declare one, a nephew, a cousin, even an uncle. Then there will be a

disagreement and he will disown this heir and claim another –
an heir by another name is an heir just the same – or leave his
riches to the best soldier who once served him, then later question his loyalty and change his mind once more. Alliances are
made and broken like twigs in a storm; rich men are dubious
men. Virgins are the best keepers of their wills, most objective;
our house most secure from a scorned heir bent on destroying
his dead father's will before it is read. What good is inheritance
if one has invoked the wrath of the gods? Sometimes I peruse
their wills as if they were diagrams and visualize the farms, vine-
yards, even the tables and couches in their homes, the jewels
their wives must wear, read them as if they are diaries and give
insight into the inner workings of men. All I can gather is men
value much. Tullia once whispered that the reason Virgins are
depicted as so unnerving has nothing to do with Vesta, but is to
protect the properties of men from other men.

Before I leave the room, as always, I stroke one of the locks,
feeling its weight in my palm.

I pull myself up out of the bath and a slave runs over, towel
outstretched like a hammock or a merchant selling sashes. I
can see her belly is beginning to swell with child and I wonder
who enters such women. She rubs me dry as I stand there
watching her hair vibrate and fall out of her bun with each pat
of my feet, calves. The back of her neck is spotted with black
moles sheathed in black hair, her nails too long, nearly curling,
yellowed, though she is still prettier from this angle. Maybe
he entered her this way, angled like this. Stupid, she'll soon be
gone.

Julia walks past the bath as the slave unrolls my headdress.

This irks me, this intrusion. 'Surely you've bathed already, Julia?'

'I must pay respects to Rhea.' She waves the twigs of willow in her hands; it is too cold and wet now for daisies. She places the twigs over Rhea's arms, and folds onto her knees in admiration, as we were taught to do.

'Are there not more appropriate times to pay one's respects?' She is doing this more and more since pulling me from the stairs, since Fabia's accusation, closing in on me, a peripheral watchful eye. A dutiful circling dot.

Julia whirls around. 'Do you imply there is an inappropriate time to revere those who have bettered Rome?' She sounds appalled, but I know she is really daring me to say so and show I am less devoted than she. But to what end? What end does she want me to meet? When will this end? I feel a momentary surge of aggravation; I can feel it seeping out of my eyes, burning my nose. I sniff it back up. Good Virgins keep their noses clean.

'Of course not,' I answer, because it is the right answer. She always wins these verbal skirmishes. If only I could find words without antonyms.

She turns back towards Rhea, but not before purposely eyeing me up and down in my wet under-dress, claiming her victory.

CHAPTER XXXI

As I step outside the house, the slave holding the torch comes up behind me. I stop and look back at his face, trying my best to seem as though I am only concerned the doors are firmly shut. Each night I hope it will be the bearded, weeping slave who met my gaze, the one who spoke to me as if I were not a Virgin. Each night I hope he is holding the torch trailing behind me, lighting up the temple's steps. I wait and wait.

When I enter the temple it is choking on its own smoke. The vent in the ceiling must be broken. This happens from time to time – some kind of refuse catches in the wind and settles over the vent.

I can barely breathe, the smoke, is like a strangling thumb pressing into my throat. I take swift gulps of air, sticking my head out of the door just ever so slightly, like a heron dipping for minnows. When Fabia comes, she will send a slave to fix this; he will have to do it from the outside, once it is light. This is annoying. In and out, my lips are shaped like a lamprey's, round and ready for suction. Today is the day. I've been here exactly fifteen years. I am half done, only fifteen more to go.

I am twenty-one now, I'll be thirty-six, just as Tullia was, when it's over, if it's over. Claudia was chosen when she was nearly ten. But I believe it is better to come earlier so one can leave younger; so one can still try to develop some sprightliness in the step, wiggle in the hips, still have some plumpness in the cheeks, escape before a myriad of lines splinter across the forehead, below the eyes, in the chin and mouth. Maybe pass for someone younger. Reinvent a past: perhaps a recent widow married to a merchant who died of hard work before he could give her children; or a dutiful daughter whose healing touch kept her at home, unmarried, whose father weighed her worth more precious as his nurse. Smart man – knew he'd be sick some day. Or . . . what? These are the only two viable lies available. I could be a noble wife from somewhere far away who prefers to live in squalor and poverty in Rome than share her bed with a man who cheats corn from the peasants. It would be a story I would only tell when bent over a heating pot, cooking when the widow from upstairs is visiting. She will tell me I should meet her son.

But we Vestals can't disappear in Rome or reinvent ourselves. We are branded in some way. Maybe it's the way we move: too rigid, prim and proper. The way we smell: of fire, smoke, godliness, reeking of virginity. Maybe it's our eyes, crossed and crooked, too long fixed on fire; our hands gnarled from being still too long at our sides, from never touching another. And when it is discovered we were once Vestal Virgins we are shunned as foreshadowers of imminent disaster, of illness, of loss of wealth. In the open we are thought of as penetrated, though no man would ever lay a hand on us. Who could afford to tempt Vesta's indignation? Any of the gods' for that matter? Fabia didn't leave. Porcia won't. Who would want to give up such honour and privilege? And there is peace in numbers.

Under the thick haze of Vesta's smoke it's almost as if the temple is disappearing, falling into dusty ruins, and I am homeless, walking through a windstorm in the desert. I imagine it must smell like smoke, but then I cannot imagine not smelling smoke.

CHAPTER XXXII

It is the blonde slave who comes this time to wash my hair and I am so relieved and grateful that the thick smoky smell of the temple will be reduced to its normal haze and that her deft hands will wash me. As she bends over, unfastening my head-dress, I can't help but stare at her hair, so beautiful, like a curtain of wheat, natural, not dyed. It is the colour Roman matrons covet and try their best to attain with dried saffron, but most end up with an orange-yellow colour. Sallow, now that I've seen her hair. I would like to touch it. I can almost feel it between my fingertips, like finely ground sand or crushed gold. As though I could grab a handful, cup it in my hand then blow ever so gently and it would scatter like dande-lion seeds drifting from garden to field to meadow. Well travelled and with good intentions. She tilts my head back slowly into the basin, moving with me, not pushing, waiting for my trust. As I am immersed in the warm water she kneads my scalp, loosening and smoothing lumps, massaging away the weight of the headdress, the tightness of the gold headband, the perpetual tapping of the white pearl against the middle of my forehead. I close my eyes, become clay under her finger-tips, the slight flickering of the oil lamps like a kiln ready to make me into a pot or bowl, whatever her hands wish me to be. Surrender.

She is offering her hair to me – a gift. What use does she have for it any more? I weave it quickly, one hand on the spindle, the other full of hair, into a shawl, the most beautiful shawl ever worn. I wrap it round my shoulders, sun-kissed and silky, not caring that I may very well be stuck, unable to move either arms or legs, entangled in a shawl made of golden hair.

She shakes me awake, motioning to the oils she must now apply. I sit back up, embarrassed. As she is brushing through my hair I envision flakes of ash falling to the floor round my chair like snow. I wonder what she thinks of my hair: an abandoned nest, brittle as a blackened fingernail, as plain as splintered tree bark. I am suddenly self-conscious, ugly, as though standing naked in front of men who are examining me the way they do when buying an ox, a cow, a horse. Bartering for a lower price because of my deficiencies: she's too fat, too tall, too wide, too hairy, too weak, too dark, her hair is as arid as a camel's mouth. She begins to part my hair into sections, ready to be folded in and under, back into braids.

I wonder if this is what she had to go through, standing there appraised and sold and resold. I know she could not have been treated gently because she is much too novel with her golden hair, too pretty to have been overlooked; this is what slaves hope for, to be overlooked. Maybe there are few differences between us. We both must abide. We are both novel. My being mistress is as much of a façade as her apparent servitude towards me. She is not really my servant; we are both servants. Slaves without amity, we are not on the same side, we can both turn each other in. I've ruined these few luxurious moments of having my hair hang loose with too many thoughts. I am beginning to think something more is wrong with me.

After she leaves, I stare up at the ceiling from the chair, open history book in lap, and pretend its wavering light is actually stars strewn across the sky, and when my imagination strays, I rub my eyes as hard as I can with my fists and the stars are real. Vesta's smoke is still in my throat, tightening my chest like a vice, squeezing out the last of me.

When I dine later, everything tastes even more strongly of smoke, the barley soup is liquid ash, the snails crispy pieces of burnt wood, even the cucumbers are slices of cinder. I eat in my room. I am too ill to eat with the others. If I am not able to keep this food down, I don't wish to spoil their appetites. A slave stands at my doorway with a pitcher of wine and honey. I drink as much as I can, trying to still my churning stomach. Each time I wave the slave over and she fills my cup there is such pleasure in the sound of the wine splashing against its side, the way the slave waits for me to nod to stop pouring, the simplicity of this exchange, of fulfilled expectations. In a different place, I am the customer and she is the shopkeeper trying to woo me for my money and my business. She entices me with her product: the purest of wines made of the finest grapes, just a touch of honey – surely I will be pleased. I tell her about the dinner I will be hosting, a menu of poached fish with pepper and coriander seed, the wine preferences of each of my guests. A good hostess knows her guests well. She convinces me to buy two or three bottles, ranging from heavy to light, climbing up and down a small ladder, hugging them in her arms. She places each one carefully in a small crate so they can be easily transported back to my house on Palatine Hill, smiling. I count out my coins on

217

the table and she tells me to have a good afternoon and wishes me good luck with the dinner. I smile back, impressed with her doting ways, thinking I will come again, even recommend her at the party. I have never bought anything before, but this is what I imagine it to be like, except we'd both be men. Idyllic, clear, both customer and clerk as easily distinguishable as though it were branded on their foreheads. Uncomplicated and pleasant. I eat slowly, carefully ingesting, waiting to see if the last bite will stay before I take another. Once I am finished eating, I lie back in my bed and try to rest. The ceiling of my room spins.

I try to sleep, but Sempronia's groaning has turned to deep ceaseless coughing that sounds like thunder rolling up her chest and out of her mouth. Just as I am about to drift off, her rough hacking shakes me back awake. Fabia insists that Sempronia is feeling better, that the coughing is just a sign her fever has broken. As she reports this, her hands seem to involuntarily fold over her belly, as if congratulating her inner self.

As I lie here, it seems I can feel Sempronia's illness. But it is not a fever, it is loneliness. Loneliness is a cough I can't seem to shake, right here, embedded in my chest, narrowing my breath, congesting airways, a stuffed nose, eyes, heavy head. It will only worsen. Unlike a regular cough this will not loosen and seep out. Unlike a regular cough it is silent and incurable. Maybe we all die from one kind of cough or another.

Tullia once said loneliness is not an old woman, as most believe, but a woman who is not yet old and no longer young. Old women have made it through and are set in their ways, deaf to the quiet. Young women are filled with hope that the quiet will one day be filled. Women neither old nor young still hear the quiet seething but know it cannot be filled. They fester best in the quiet. Loneliness is a woman who stands right in the middle of her life filled only with fear when looking forward and only with remorse when looking back and has no one to tell about either.

When Sempronia finally seems to quiet, or maybe my ears have grown accustomed to her sharp chokes, sleep slowly trickles in like the light of dawn into the temple.

Again I dream of Priapus. His blond hair flaps in the wind as if it is not really hair at all but a patch of yellow wool. Each time I turn another way to escape, he cuts me off. He is quicker than usual and I realize he is riding on the back of the speckled long-necked creature I saw at the games. He backs me into a stream; my stola fills with water, lifts up. I turn away from him, but in the reflection of the stream I see his legs are wrapped tightly around the creature's long neck. Its head is bent forward, nostrils opening and closing like dilating eyes, a set of perfectly square teeth, large as bricks, white as sandstone, grinning down at me, no, not grinning, but sneering a horse's sneer.

Priapus laughs loudly, gratingly. He is taking his time. Sometimes he likes it better this way, filled with slow anticipation. He pulls out a strip of goat skin and begins to whip my back.

I wade farther into the stream; the water slowly begins to simmer, tiny bubbles ascend from the rocky bottom. Priapus follows, appearing wobbled and rippled in the steaming water.

The creature nudges my back, or seems to, until I realize its reflection in the stream is no longer a reflection, but real. Up comes the snout first, flaring out mist; up come the pointed ears, a rip in one, with two flat stubs beside each; up come the creamy eyes with pretty lashes; up comes the neck, up, up, up, long and slithering, a gold-spotted tan, up, up, up, crisped islands speckled in a sea of yellow, thrashing with a head barely attached.

I stand stricken with a queasy dread, feeling Priapus's lashings cut into me, over and over.

CHAPTER XXXIII

I do not expect it to be the Greek slave. As I glance back the torch seems to eclipse his face for a moment, but then he kind of fumbles it, switching it from one hand to the other, nearly dropping it. 'Oh,' I hear him say, and I know it is him from his voice. So few voices to choose from. He moves the torch upward, like a parasol made of light, and I see it is him. Finally, Lysander walks behind me, though tonight I wish the slaves led, then I could study him from behind, find out little things so that later I could pretend to know him. 'Lysander shouldn't bite his nails so short,' or 'Lysander needs to tend that blister on his heel otherwise it will become infected.'

Just as I am about to walk the path to the temple, just before my pointed white shoes reach out to step on pockets of air and I attempt to make even smaller steps to prolong his presence, I ask him quickly, suddenly, because I genuinely wish to know. I ask with a rush of muted breath mashed with a diffusion of muffled words, 'I wanted to know . . . What are those animals called with those terribly long necks? They are spotted brown and tan. I saw them some time ago at the amphitheatre.' My voice sounds weak, inarticulate, underused and now misused.

I think he doesn't hear me. How could he hear me? I barely spoke. I feel a light brush of air as he leans slightly down, but he could do this because I am not walking, I have not taken a step towards the temple. He thinks I am ill, that I am panting, and he will knock on the house doors to beckon a slave inside. I will have to fake illness, retch violently on my shoes, faint and the others will suspect Vesta caused it because she did not want my care, because I suffer from insufficient devotion.

'Are they really tall?' he whispers back like a breathing stone as if he speaks directly from the knob in his throat so he need not move his lips, an adept whisperer, one who knows the perfect pitch of invisibility, inaudibility.

'Yes,' I answer. I watch the temple, one leg in front of the other, ready to appear mid-stride if Julia peered out, my face already shaped to show indignation that she would so needlessly turn her back towards Vesta. A look that threatens I will tell the others at dinner of her violation of peeking outside the temple.

'Ah, they are called giraffes. They're imported from deep in Carthage. Beautiful creatures, aren't they?'

My ribs suddenly seem to pop out, one by one, undone, disassembled. Beautiful.

'Yes, very beautiful . . . thank you.' I also want to thank him again for helping me with the well, but he seems not to recognize me as the same Virgin. This pleases me, his lack of awareness of my ineptness.

Later, as I stand over Vesta, I hear him whistling a song not yet crushed by wind or night or time and decide he isn't afraid of much.

*

222

Today we are to clear out the storehouse next to our temple, to symbolize the cleaning out of storehouses everywhere in readiness for the next harvest. Today, we represent good daughters and wives by eagerly performing a woman's expected duties, setting a good example. Luckily for us, it is a small storehouse and there is little to clear out as it only houses some old broken statues with chipped noses or ears or necks or completely without heads, or statues of men no longer respected, cut down and hidden back here. They once graced the Forum, but have now been replaced with newer, bigger versions, with finer detail and brighter colours. There are many storehouses such as this, filled with fallen statues that no one wants to dispose of blatantly and thus risk incurring the fury of this god or that goddess or have a spirit resurrected, angry, from the Underworld. Lines of faded stone, of stubby necks and shoulders, of eyes and mouths, expressions as blank as brick and as indifferent as the randomness of death, breathe down one another's necks, a graveyard with standing room only, a line-up to the funeral pyre. All we can really do is sweep, put the dust in small satchels that were once the stomachs of pigs and place it outside the storehouse's door to be thrown into the Tiber. So this is what we do, we sweep and sweep, uprooting cobwebs, dislodging the moss that grows in the creases of the lips, tumbling down chiselled chests or covered bosoms, like green drool, envious of the living. We carefully extricate mice with hardened curled-up bodies, and try to step on those still scurrying about, flinging them out by their tails. We do this while a lyre gently plays outside and the odd passers-by gather here and there for a short time.

It is Julia, Claudia and I, and there is almost an ease, almost as though we really are sisters waiting for our father to get home to impress him with our thoroughness.

'Oh, look at how filthy it is over here in this corner,' Julia will gasp.

And Claudia will shake her head, sighing, affirming, 'It *is* filthy, how dirty things become over the winter,' imbuing a new resolve in Julia to conquer and dispel.

From time to time Julia sweeps over what I just swept and so I go back and again sweep the same spot, which she in turn sweeps again. It could have gone on and on, so I relent and let her follow me with the broom, pretending not to notice, after which she eventually stops.

It feels nice to clean, to do something with my hands and see an immediate result. Wipe and the dust is gone, sweep and the dried leaves are gone, out down the three steps of the storehouse, to settle somewhere new. Each time I am by the storehouse's door, I can see Fabia trying her best not to be seen watching us from inside the temple. It is her turn to be with Vesta, but I can tell she'd rather be here. Who wouldn't be if one could choose between the two? Though she does have the choice, really, tending on empty as she is. She will not admit it, though, and the others will not accuse her of it either; how could they prove it? We can't go sniffing round her like dogs. Even the fact that Sempronia is still ill seems not enough. Only Vesta could prove it somehow, maybe turn to a fiery squall and burn her out. Fabia wants to be known for bleeding right until the end, up to her death.

One year Tullia and I had that one hour in this storehouse completely alone. It was her last year here. The sun was near setting and in through the storehouse door a wide ray of light cast itself on the floor.

'Come here, Aemilia, look.' Tullia tugged at my sleeve, took the broom from my hand and pulled me down with her onto our haunches.

'What?' I snapped, flustered and annoyed. Her excursions into the temple when I was tending Vesta were becoming increasingly frequent; she stayed longer, criticized and grumbled more. She was beginning to seem old. She seemed to think that time was something she could freely borrow from me without asking; she unabashedly ignored my obvious annoyance. Her words tangled, rife with too much useless detail about matrons or else too abstract and confusing to follow, blurred with scepticism and doubt. She was always ruining my persistent attempts to be more like the others via steadfast duty, making it seem I always needed her help in the temple, ruining my attempts at forgetting the last bit of hesitation she had left me with, soiling my belief with shades of her disbelief, time and time again.

In the storehouse hovering over the floor, looking into a ray of sun as though it were a rare sliver of stained glass, she asked me what I saw.

'I see dust, just dust.' Tullia pulled me closer to her, not roughly, but urgently, like a mother not wanting her child to miss a falling star.

'Aemilia, you need to train yourself to see more than what is there. Do you know what I see? I see a thousand moons circling round one another. I see a million bodies, confused, not knowing where to go. I see us suspended in the middle, trapped in time, the before and after, uninterested in our lives. I see infinity.'

I took her hand and we sat that way for a moment, hand in hand, staring into dust, infinity. When we got up, we just walked through the storehouse, looking at the statues, reading their names aloud: 'Jupiter, Neptune, Mercury, Lucius Gallius, Aulus Flavius, Marcus Metellus, Venus, Ceres.'

Tullia started to speak to the statues. 'Why hello, Lucius. How are you today? Uh huh, not feeling so well. Hmmmm. Shall I make you better with a kiss?' She leaned into him, planted a kiss on his cheek. 'Blech.' She wiped her mouth.

We laughed and laughed and soon the statues became animate, people at a dance, an audience, the Senate, we arranged them into couples. We played Cupids.

'Well, Ceres dislikes drinking so therefore Marcus is out, as he enjoys wine so much that if each cup of wine adds another year of life Marcus will never die.' I stood behind one, Tullia another, and we were their voices, a gentleman from the Forum, a gladiator, a charioteer or a matron from Palatine Hill, a scorned mistress, a whining daughter.

Tullia sat on the edge of Jupiter's toes. 'Tell me, great Greek philosopher, what is a good life lived?' Silence. 'No answer for that one, eh?'

I went behind Jupiter, my hand in front stroking his stone beard. 'Well, I don't know what a good life lived is for you, but I do for myself. To me a good life lived is one that follows first duty, then virtue, diligence and discipline.' I changed my voice to sound like Fabia's, but this was just to cover up that I believed what I was saying. After the latrine punishment I was much more prone to believe Fabia.

Tullia answered, 'No, a good life lived is one that leaves something behind. An imprint, better than stone and statues and epitaphs, a life that leaves life behind. Children are the result of a good life lived, for then one is remembered. A woman's life resounds long after she is gone in the voices and actions of her

226

children, and if one cannot leave children, leave change, leave something or someone changed.' She eyed me up and down for a moment, as if assessing me.

'Oh, matrons lead a far better life than Virgins and soon I will be one.' At this she seemed to clench up with excitement. 'Aemilia, so very soon I will be a true matron.' Her eyes gleamed, as if made of glass with the sun glinting in them. For a moment I felt as if she were bragging, and the mood changed. I was tempted to ask her for details, clear concise details, such as what she would do when she was shunned by the other matrons, for surely none would want the eerie company of an ex-Virgin. What would she do when her children were mocked and treated as bad omens for coming from a Virgin who opted not to stay a Virgin? Did she think this future husband of hers would stay when his friends and colleagues avoided his home for fear of becoming ruined by misfortune? Fabia has warned us all about this; Virgins are home bodies, Virgins have only one house.

Instead, I only nodded and then quietly, as though we were out of words, dried up, exhausted, we picked up our brooms and continued to sweep.

The statue is taking shape behind the canvas. The thick contours of a portly torso, of stubby forearms and half legs, a misshapen head, all in pieces, spread across a workbench. The carver now seems a murderous madman, flitting behind a curtain, with blade-like fingers, cutting, reshaping. His emery stone searing across her in agonizing shrieks. He is wheedling out a body. Or body parts. He pegs them together once they're finished. She will then be reborn, hairless and

227

always dressed, with eternally still hands, the third eye absent. Fabia must envy the statues for this solidity, their incapacity for pockets or sticks, prohibiting two bodies to occupy the same space at once, their perfect but unattainable-in-life denseness.

CHAPTER XXXIV

Every night when Lysander walks behind me from the house to the temple, I ask him another question. Each night after he ushers Julia back to the house he secretly returns to the bottom of the temple's steps and I, directly beside the door, my back flat against the stone wall, listen to his answer. At first when he told me to wait, as if I do anything but wait, I was nervous he would not return to answer. When he returns, I am nervous we will be caught, and I keep hearing phantom sounds of the house doors swinging open and Fabia calling my name.

I ask him the name of the drooping sad tree along the path in the garden on the north side, though I already know the answer. I do this just to see if he will answer as easily as the night before, or if last night was some kind of fluke, a lapse in judgement, and during the day he has come to his senses; good Virgins already know all there is to know.

'A willow tree,' he hisses into the temple, his voice coiling round it like leaking water, or a gust of wind. For a moment I wait, just in case, for any changes in Vesta, in Minerva, but there are none.

Then, because it is the only safe way to peer over the wall, I ask him to name all the places in the north, and he does, one by one, and a world outside Rome arises, other places, another map.

'Ameria, Arretium, Pistoria . . . Rubicon . . . Helvetti . . . Treveri . . . Belgae . . . and most northerly, near the edge of the world, Britannia.' He lists them rhythmically, like marching footsteps, until the north rises like a listing ship righting itself.

'Is that all, Vestal?' he asks before he returns to the doors. An undertone of laughter plays just below his voice, not as if he is humouring me as the slave must sometimes humour his owner, but as if I am humorous to him.

'Yes,' I answer, flustered by his blatant delight in 'educating' me. As if he is gloating. Oh, how the tables have turned, the cloistered Virgin with her haughty walk must look to him to be filled in on simple subjects such as geography.

'Well then,' he pauses, as though to ensure I will not change my mind, become confused by what he has told me and ask another question, 'goodnight.' I listen to his footsteps crunch against the gravel, eight quick steps, as if he skipped back showing off unrestrained movement.

The next night, though I tell myself not to, something comes over me and I cannot help it, like a starving peasant eating spoiled meat, I ask about the east. And again other hills, other rivers, other villages, pop up and confound; our horizon is not the end, just a parentheses, a circle within a circle within a circle. A centre with spiralling rings. The next night it's the west and then the south which he answers before I ask, knowing I will ask the following night. All roads lead to Rome, they say, but from where? When I was younger I pictured these roads much like veins in a leaf, travelling inward from its edges, from nowhere, from the abyss. Then they became binding cords, like

230

branches squirrels can scurry up and down, bringing winter fare back into the centre of the tree. He sketches in as much as he can, shading in distances, ports, length of rivers. Other places spring up fully shaped with distinctive attributes: 'Sicily grows more tomatoes; vines and vines of tomatoes.' His words are the topography of where the roads that lead to Rome begin and all along the way.

'You will never know good tomatoes, unless you've been to Sicily.' He seems to revel in his role of guide, growing more and more detailed, his voice taking on a knowing arrogance.

Then, though I am not sure why, perhaps because I am who I am or because he seems so willing or even that I sense he wishes to tell me, I ask about the gods in other places and he scoffs, the first time, 'Well, you should know, they're all in Rome now.'

But from this night he stays longer until the sun is nearing the brim of the horizon, about to kiss the earth's lips. He speaks eloquently, rising, falling, emphasizing, pausing, but never forgetting he is telling me a secret, a series of secrets. 'Roman gods are only Greek gods by another name. Or they are gods that once belonged elsewhere, to the Etruscans perhaps; your gods are only imports, like silk from Hispania, just cargo on a ship. The only difference is, here, they have no personality, no story. If they did, it would be revealed they once belonged elsewhere. Thus, Roman gods are vague and shapeless like a black robe lying on a stone floor. Roman gods have no beginning of their own.'

'And Vesta?' I ask.

He chuckles. 'No, Vesta is not entirely a Roman creation. Vesta is our Hestia, the eldest sister of Zeus, a goddess who

231

nearly left Olympus to stop the other gods from arguing over marrying her. Instead of marrying she remained a Virgin goddess; she is as gentle as a woman could be. She presides over the hearth in the hall of Olympus and ensures alliances between smaller settlements and the capital city. Rome needs a Hestia, a Vesta or whatever, because a capital city needs a hearth in order to be a capital city. It's symbolic, a mere talisman warding off conquerors and aiding in conquering. It makes the people feel settled.' He pauses. 'Just as the dead make better heroes, because no one speaks ill of the dead. Every great nation needs hearth and heroes.'

'I don't know what you mean,' I tell him. And I don't.

He laughs again as if trying to shush himself at the same time and sounds as though he is clearing his throat. 'You rename our gods and what do we get in return? We get treated like children, brilliant children, imported to teach philosophy, teach Roman sons oration.' He thinks this over. 'But I suppose that is better than being treated like stupid children as are the Gauls . . . better to compare one's situation to a worse one, much more consoling than the other way around. Though I cannot help it, sometimes. I watch you Romans basking in your spoils, your gods, as if they had always belonged here. Praising Jupiter as if he were not truly Zeus, Juno as if she were not Hera, Mars as though he were not Ares, Minerva just as if there weren't Athena . . .'

He is talking to himself now, for himself, saying things he wishes he could say to Roman men, Caesar, shout out in the middle of the Senate House. 'Rome has only acquired our gods, diluted them, then made them appear as if they were always Roman, just as they do with each new conquered territory. And yet, the Romans describe *us* as wearers of masks, deceivers, degenerates of our past greatness, underhanded quick-wits. The Romans claimed Athens' greatness; we are good enough for them to take our gods, our literature, our philosophy, our art, our architecture, to teach their children and yet never considered equals. Greeks may be the slaves here, but the Romans are also enslaved to the Greeks. No, not only enslaved, but also indebted and that is worse . . .'

I will have to do, at least I am something, someone. For a moment I want him to go away, defend Rome. 'If your country were so much better, then maybe you wouldn't be here now.' Throw a stick at him. Surely Rome has it right. Surely Rome is correct. Surely we are predestined to dominate. Vesta is different here, has more power here, protects better here. I want to remind him he is just a slave, a conquered little Greek slave. I want to speak against what he is saying, but each time I am about to open my mouth, my tongue ties, thrashes, rolls back. It is against my nature to do so, I tell myself, that is all. But then, it is against my nature to speak to him at all.

'Ah, well, what does it matter? You have your gods now.' He sighs. 'You know them as you do. I don't believe in any gods anyway.'

A sudden throb of insignificance washes over me, up and down, shoulders to toes. Insignificant. An eyelash falling, an aphid crawling up a blade of grass, a chrysalis swallowed by a bird, a spider dragging a crushed leg. Insignificant. 'What does it matter?' The weight of Rome resides on my shoulders, relies on my belly, using it to expand, though I do not swell, do not feel any pulls of labour. This I take their word for. But this weight, this reliance, lifts for a moment. 'What do I matter?'

I do feel not unsettled but soothed, as if his hands are petting me over and over my rolled hair. I feel soothed because he does not ask why I solicit this information and I do not ask why he answers me, and in the absence of such accusation, we excuse the other of any wrongdoing and become accomplices.

'And does your Hestia have six attendants such as us?'

'Oh no, what you are is entirely Roman.'

Later, when he walks me back to the house, I feel as I do without my headdress, more flimsy.

CHAPTER XXXV

We are perched on a platform, elevated, towering over the crowd below. It is the first day of the festival of Diana. Even Sempronia has somehow managed to get out of bed to be here, though still pallid and half choking. She quickly swallows her coughs that seem to come in fits and starts and sound like muzzled snorts. She knows a coughing Virgin is a blank slate that could be written many ways, and does her best to suppress her illness; not that they'd suspect her of anything, not at her age, but still, she is mindful of what could be imagined.

Fabia is enjoying Sempronia's meagre recuperation, helping her up into the litter, though she has never before displayed such concern. Virgins should not nurse as nursing is akin to mothering. It's as if she is now responsible for Sempronia somehow, or maybe she only wants to ensure her blood works.

The first day of the festival of Diana is one of the eight days of the year that slaves are released from service. Diana is revered by slaves. They stand at the back of the crowd, skulking about, trying to appear as if they are enjoying their day off, but their hands look clunky and confused with foreign idleness, awkwardly placed at their own sides and on their own hips for a day.

I wonder if he is here, watching us, trying to work out which is the one he has spoken to the last four nights and deciding it is the one with the dark, pretty, wise eyes, eyes like windows into hearth and home. What will he do today, a day without having to be anywhere at all?

Caesar starts the prayers in his alto whisper, thanking Diana for unifying Rome, praising her chasteness, her hunting skills, grace, sensibility, beauty, imagination.

His wife is sitting primly with the other priests' wives at the bottom of the temple steps. Imagine if we had a table of husbands just to our right. I can only imagine a title, the selection of the letters. 'P' sitting back sipping on wine, flat, misshaped for the chair, constantly slipping off onto the ground, ONTIFEX MAXIMUS, the rest of them, half in their seats, a little drunk, laughing too loudly, obnoxious when they're all together. Then, for a moment, I imagine Lysander, stroking his beard, head tilted to the side, peering up into himself, arranging his words just so. Finding the best way to convey that Diana does not exist.

'Oh, Diana, I pray and beseech you to be kind and well disposed. Oh, daughter of Leto and mighty Jupiter, sister of Luna, twin sister of Apollo, you were born on the island of Delos . . . Diana, queen of forest, treasurer of oak, protector of the race of Romulus . . .' A smaller statue of Diana, said to be a copy of the one in her dedicated temple way up on the Aventine Hill, is at the front of the platform. She wears only a tunic, her legs exposed from the knees down. A stone deer is beside her, her hand is on its antlers, taming; both sets of legs melt together into the base. 'We call on you not to let plague or ruin enter Rome. We call on you for the water from the sources of the river. We call on you for plenty in the forests and grain sprung from the earth.' A basket of arrows is strapped onto her back; one hand reaches behind as if to draw one, as though she were once truly alive, doing just as she did, and was caught off guard and sprayed with stone. Hunted by her worshippers. Underneath she is still alive, cramped and hot, in a shell made of marble; if I knocked her hard enough the stone would crumble and she would run away, arrow finally drawn. 'Oh, Diana, you who were born beside an olive tree, we beseech thee to be kind and well disposed; we offer you the purest of animals, one that has yet to touch the earth.' Caesar has the cow towed up the platform, her skin about to burst, her stomach about to split.

'You who relieves the agony of childbirth, we beseech thee.'

The attendant leans down under the cow and slices her open.

'Oh, Diana, it is thee we worship. I beg you to prevent, ward off, keep away infertility, bring to us riches.' Caesar continues as the cow caves in, slowly, onto her side and his hands enter her, digging. 'And give health and military success to the children of Romulus. May you be strengthened with this offering . . .' He takes a breath and pulls out the unborn calf, purple and wet, slits for eyes, and places it in the small fire, which we encircle: Sempronia, Fabia, Claudia, Julia and I. Porcia is with Vesta. I watch the calf burn, turning from purple to grey. Once it is reduced to ashes, the remains are poured into vials and presented to a handful of landowners standing near the stage; they, no, their farmers will sprinkle it on their farmland for better fertility. The prayer is over and Diana is appeased.

The litter carries us to the Circus Maximus where Diana will continue to be honoured with horse races. The Circus Maximus is the loudest and most offensive place in all of Rome. We are

237

only permitted here during state festivals, just as we are permitted anywhere. Soldiers are stationed round the track ready to break up fights and unruly riots due to discontent that a team lost or overexcitement that a team won; to separate friend beating friend who bet on the opposing team. Civility departs the moment the first horse is whipped and victory is bet upon. The audience here is larger than that at any gladiator games or theatrical performance. The basest sort of language fans through here like the scent of seasoned meats. Crazed fanaticism does not edit. Once it was difficult to stay sitting, to be only the accompaniments of the consuls and the Pontifex Maximus; to be state statues in the stands, not to get caught up, not to pick a colour, a faction, and cheer aloud and provoke those cheering for the other teams. For a while I picked a colour in my mind, usually Red, sometimes Blue, and would root for them, imagining I was sitting on the other side with the plebeians, that I was a plebian also. But I would catch my lips moving and feared they'd be read. I would be read. Now, I watch neither the horses nor the charioteers, nor cheer for Red, White, Blue or Green, but wash myself in the tide of profanities. I lather in the flow of obscenities that do not ebb for a Virgin, a matron or a maiden. I slip into the vulgarity that is emitted from the lips of men of all classes, even the odd swear word of disappointment from the matrons sitting far up behind us. Or the raucous bitching of the peasant women crowded down on the other side with their peasant husbands, who do not reprimand them but extend their swearing with an expletive of their own; a joint cuss. Between races, I study slang used by bragging men. Piece together what is meant, how, which way; my Virgin ears sullied. I store it up, feeling an inexplicable twinge with my

238

growing vocabulary, a cupboard within a cupboard filled with vile words.

I watch thousands of flailing arms waving coloured flags, bullying one another, cursing their opponents by evoking demons to kill the horses and their drivers. After the races, I've seen little bits of papyrus with curses and spells littering the aisles, circling in the wind. A curse must be recited without errors, like a prayer, otherwise it won't work and neither demon nor god will bother listening. These I do not memorize. I watch the kiss of two strangers who just happen to be on the same side and sitting together. I watch oils from sausage drip down the chins of wealthy men who are impeccably dressed in their pressed white togas and who, in any other place, would be furious and embarrassed. But here they just let it drip down onto their togas, like babies drooling. At the track refinement is forsaken upon entry. I watch men pass out. They just fall over, over-heated from excitement, not wanting to miss even a moment for a drink of water. They are not considered hysterical, but fervent. Like a child's game of marbles, everything here is measured and measured again, just to be sure who won. The track is a place where we are not ignored but simply not noticed. We do not sit from behind an invisible border, a glass wall, but here at the track we are completely forgotten in the frenzy. Here we are just veiled faces in a crowd. So I like to think.

As the horses outstrip one another or collide, head over hooves, chariot over charioteer, legs popping, spines snapping, I see Lysander. Something happens, my heart lurches . . . no, clenches, I clench all over. He is leaning against the railing just in front of the section open to slaves for the day. The wind parts his black hair to the side, a vein sticks out in his neck. He is shouting. Maybe he is even pretending to have placed a bet as I used to. Green crosses the finish line and his arms fly up, cheering. He hugs an even smaller man beside him. Then he climbs up the stands and disappears into an ocean of Green. Three more races pass by and I do not find him. I stand up, the others tilt their heads up, like sunflowers at midday.

'I need to visit the facilities,' I explain. Two lictors climb up the steps towards me, to escort me. I want him to find me, see me, a purple Virgin meandering through the crowds, the one he speaks to through the temple walls.

I walk slowly, the lictors trying their best not to bump into me. I enter the private chamber room, used only by us, one at a time, as the lictors guard the door. Private chamber rooms, locked until needed, are everywhere we may be, just in case. On the way back, I want to raise my hand and wave at the slave section. I want to pull his eyes towards me. You will recognize me, because I walk a little bit differently from the rest, a contemplative and reluctant sort of walk, toe to heel, as if underneath this walk is a better, smoother, more matronly walk. When I climb up the steps to sit back down the others watch me, like sunflowers at dusk. Something in me sinks. I feel breathless, tired. Only their monotonous eyes follow me, unwanted as that may be.

That night I ask if he saw me at the track. 'I saw of you, but perhaps not you exactly.'

I wanted to explain how I walked down the steps, trying to get his attention, but know better, thanks to Tullia: forwardness repels, coyness attracts. 'I am as coy as a coin,' she used to say, misquoting the phrase we overhear at the tracks. It is 'I'll be coy for a coin,' something the prostitutes call out to entice men who appear to have the taste only for the timid, leaving and entering the tracks or theatre. Coins are not coy at all. She missed its meaning. She was wrong sometimes.

I decide to ask him about his wager instead. 'Green was strong,' feeling suddenly uneasy, asking such usual questions, inciting such a usual discussion, as if it is a kind of lull and in this lull he will leave and return to his usual position.

'Oh yes, what a wonderful day for Green. If only a slave could wager, have something to wager with, I would be a rich man today. Though I suppose this is why we are not permitted; it would encourage us to steal, they say' – he spits this out – 'but I think it is because a rich slave would be a frightening paradox. They couldn't stand to see a slave earning something for himself. I knew Green would win, I always know who will win. I could be very rich, Vestal, very rich at this very moment.' He seems to want to continue, but then, as if changing his mind, he abruptly begins complaining about how some of the Roman peasants treated him at the tracks. 'Sneering, throwing things at me, calling me such ugly names, saying I take their work away from them. As if I choose this—'

'Are you certain you were not in the Red section?'

At this he laughs, thinking I was trying to be humorous, and something turns inside me. I realize I've soothed him.

'What is your name?' he asks casually, as if asking were an afterthought.

I do not answer right away, if I tell him and anything were to happen, he may not be able to point me out, but he could say, 'It was Aemilia whom I spoke to, Aemilia who asked of other places, other gods.'

241

The male slaves should never know our names; such knowledge can only mean they've interfered with us. Slaves suspected of interference are tortured to death, at least that is what we are told. It never happens though: their interference. Until now. Under such circumstances he couldn't help revealing my name even if he tried. For a moment I think to tell him my name is Porcia, maybe Julia. But I brought him here with my questions, I'm the interferer. Though this is never considered, it is backward: Virgins are put to death for being interfered with, males for interfering.

'Aemilia,' I answer him, realizing I want him to know my name, so he can know me rather than of me.

'Aemilia,' he turns it over on his tongue, 'Aemilia,' getting to know its texture and taste, feeling the weight of it on his tongue to see how easily it could slip out. 'What do you wish to know on this windy night?' he asks playfully and before I can answer he begins once again to let me in on all that is wrong with Rome as though he is offering another way, an *other* way to view my place, my Vesta, my Rome. He guides me inside him, props me behind his eyes, two murals which he explains, vivid depictions of another Rome, an other Rome, not tainted, not untrue, but different. I've finally seen another place, an other place, the same place but different. Now like all decent travellers who have gone and returned, I know more than those who never left at all.

CHAPTER XXXVI

My cycle started as I stood holding one of the sacred war trumpets in Shoemaker's Hall. Caesar walked up and down, waving a stick of incense over each of the trumpets and whispering prayers to Mars Invectus to ready the trumpets for the next season of war campaigns. Behind the stream of smoke, his lips moved quickly, his mumblings sounding like a light whistle. A priest sacrificed a ewe, the scent of blood mixing easily with the smell of leather and incense. Caesar then glazed his fingers in the ewe's blood and stroked each trumpet, leaving a reddish streak around each circular opening. Once these five trumpets were finished being purified five more were handed to each of us and the process began again. I could feel it then, the blood slowly trickling down my legs. I pressed my thighs closer together, thankful for once our stolas are purple. I could see one of the Augurs through the entrance, standing on the steps of the hall looking for woodpeckers, the bird of Mars, his head cocking back and forth at every rustle. His hair was messy, standing up a bit in the back from running his hands through it; he looked much like a bird himself. He'll eventually spot one, they always do, and Mars will be declared in favour of conquering new lands. After the trumpets, there are baskets upon baskets of shoes, purified so Mars can infuse them with both heaviness, so soldiers cannot flee, and lightness, so they can move swiftly in attack. The contradiction of this is ignored. At least the shoes need only be purified by the bundle.

Soon, because I was standing, the blood began to dribble to the floor. I was thankful our stolas are so long.

It was only because Caesar decided to include some of his own shields in the ceremony that he noticed the small droplets of blood on my white shoes. As he handed me the shield to hold, I had to step forward and the specks of blood were revealed. He grinned at me, or at least I think he grinned because the smoke from the incense cast a thick haze over his face and the only light in the hall was from waning votives. He bent down and rubbed his fingers in my blood, feeling it between his thumb and fore-finger as if measuring its fineness, putting his fingers to his nose and smelling as if testing the grade of a wine.

Or maybe out of curiosity, to see if a Virgin smells differently from the women he's known.

He flashed his hand at the priest in a kind of serendipitous gesture, his fist tightening, locking. The priest came over, drip-ping blade from slaying ewes in hand. Caesar and the priest discussed me for a moment in hushed whispers, as if I weren't there standing in front of them. Caesar then streaked my own blood against each of his shields just as if it came from a ewe.

On the way back, in the litter, Julia glared at me as if I had asked for Caesar's attention, as if I could have held back but had instead flaunted myself like a cat in heat. Back end in the air. But there was nothing she could say; we cannot go over Caesar's head, but Vesta can. So she must have given Caesar use of my blood. Her blood. I was but a vein for the bloodletting. I stared

244

back at Julia; she thought I was showing off, but I felt sickly and clammy, blood warming where I sat, and wanted nothing more but for her to turn away. I wanted nothing more but to be unseen until I bathed, until I again felt clean.

So now, before I leave for the temple I must collect my box of bloodied wool strips from the chamber room. As I walk towards the temple, I try to hold the box in front of me, one arm folded over it, hoping the sleeves of my stola will conceal it from Lysander. I can feel him steal glances over my shoulder. I should hold this box proudly, but with Lysander behind me I feel suddenly embarrassed by it.

When Lysander takes Julia, who huffs past me, back to the house, I quickly dump the box's contents into Vesta. 'With this offering I beseech thee to take of me, your eternal attendant, in exchange of Rome's eternalness.' I say it quickly, three times, words stumbling out, barely coherent.

I turn and catch him peeking in. 'What is in those boxes you Virgins carry here?' He is sitting on the steps, arms folded over bent knees. He lays his cheek against his shoulder, eyes squinting to see better in the dimness of the temple. His hair falls straight off to the side, the skin round his eyes is lined from sun and work, not age. Beneath that beard he is not much older than me. The tips of his ears are red. The torch is out, lying beside the steps. His knees poke out from under his yellowed tunic like two buns, his legs two loaves of bread glazed with hair. I can see him so well because he is sitting directly below the torch that is attached beside the temple's door. 'Don't you think you should stand off more in the dark, crouch in the corner of the stairway?'

He shuffles over, but not far enough. 'What was in that box?' He asks again.

'More, move over more.' I am surprised at the severity in my voice.

He slides over again, though only slightly, not at all bothered by my harshness. This softens me, the ease with which he takes my direction, without insult or impudence; he is used to harshness. An odd feeling of protectiveness for him comes over me. I sigh. 'The boxes . . . they're just offerings to Vesta.'

'What sort of offering?' He sounds young in his inquisitiveness, his voice curling upward near the end.

'We give all of ourselves to Vesta; it's a kind of ongoing offering to Vesta to assure her of our devotion.'

He turns back and peers into the temple again. 'I think of this temple,' his voice is soft, a brook, I could sleep in his voice, 'when I peer in, as Plato's cave.'

'Who is Plato?' I ask.

'You do have lots to learn!' I can tell he prefers it this way, as teacher, as the one who knows. This is fine with me; there is a lot I wish to know from him and little I wish to let him know.

He then tells me he is an Epicurean and I think he means he is not Greek. He laughs at this. 'No, to say I am an Epicurean means I follow the philosophies of Epicurus, which really, now that I think of it, is good for both you and me, as he included slaves *and* women. He would think us both capable of understanding his teachings.' He laughs again. 'I will tell you about him. Epicurus believed the universe was created by chance, by tiny little particles that combined together randomly to make up everything we see around us. Even humans are made up of particles so tiny we can never see them with our eyes. Our souls are composed of the finest of these particles.'

246

I think of Tullia's dust, how much she would enjoy what he is saying.

'When we die, these particles dissolve and reconnect. You see, only what the particles make are perishable, not the particles themselves. When we die, our particles will recombine into something new. Maybe one day you and I will make a tree together.' Again, he sounds amused as his own witticism, if that is what it is, catches in his throat. 'If one is an Epicurean, the gods cannot exist – worshipping gods is entirely useless. Epicurus himself said the gods are indifferent to human affairs and take no part in directing events, but I think they just don't exist. Anything that cannot be explained by man is not the gods' doing, but is because these tiny particles have shifted yet again, combined in yet another way. Man has no destiny, nothing is fixed, we live in a world of chance. I am a perfect example.' He pauses, 'Even you, you are an example.'

'How am I an example of this?' There is no such thing as chance here. In this house, in this stola, everything is perfectly measured, contained, drawn out, fixed.

'Well, it is chance you were selected to be as you are. You were chosen by lottery right?'

'Yes, but it was not chance.' I think of my father's bribery.

'Ah well, then it is chance you were born in Rome. Where someone is born is only chance; if you had been born elsewhere, say in Gaul, you would not be as you are.'

I had never considered this before.

'It is chance it was me who came to help you with the well. It could have been another slave and then we'd not be here, discussing Epicureanism. I never could have imagined that I would be here with you, that I would have such an opportunity.'

An allusion to a past, illusion of a past – 'we met at a sacred well' – seems to secure some kind of future, maybe not secure, but implies one nonetheless. A beginning, and a beginning necessitates an ending and both beginning and ending means there will be a middle. I am in the middle of something, here, with him.

He knows it was me at the well, as if he is already familiar enough to see beyond my matching stola; he can pick me out from the others; there is something familial in this, as if he and I are related and can relate to one another enough to pick the other out from a crowd, even if disguised. 'Oh there's my wife – could recognize her anywhere, in anything.' I was just too far away at the tracks for him to see properly. This makes me feel closer to him.

He continues, this time comparing a true Epicurean to the distorted Roman notions of Epicureanism. 'True Epicureans know only moderation, not Roman overindulgence. True Epicureans trust in the human senses, unlike a Roman's excess of pleasuring the human senses . . .'

I pull my stola up my forearms and study my arms for spots, as that is what I imagine particles to look like, the spots that gleam over your eyes when you stand up too quickly, translucent dots tinted with colour, ever moving. I look, but cannot see them. Seeing is believing. Trust the senses. Sensibility over senselessness, this is what he tells me. I can't make sense of anything any more.

'This is our second to last night,' he says, though I wish he hadn't. Remorse swims below the surface of his voice like a shoal of fish. I brace myself for what he will say next; will he tell me it was an odd week, an off week? He wasn't himself, not

248

usually so careless, but has regained his usual rational self and his fear of consequence. Sorry, he will tell me, this must end as though it never happened, too much is at stake. 'The tall Gaul takes over next week after my duty.' It's as if he is making arrangements for me. I find this endearing. 'It will be some time until I have this duty again . . . to be able to talk to you in this temple.' He pauses. 'Have you enjoyed our time together?' His voice is higher, strained.

'Yes,' I answer. Dust seems to swarm up my nose, trickle down the back of my throat, into my ears, unsure whether to settle again or not.

'I too have enjoyed this – teaching you. You are a smart woman.' He is flattering me now. 'I like to think of these nights as pearls strung together to make a beautiful necklace, clasped to make a circle that will go on and on. Our meditations on Epicureanism have re-instilled my desire to ensure it remains in its purest form, to protect it from Roman perversion so it will endure the stand of time.'

Go on and on. We will go on. Pine needles plunge into my side, up and down like quills, regardless that his blatant flattery borders on silliness. 'Very much so,' I say, though he doesn't hear me.

'If you are in agreement, then perhaps you would not mind aiding this cause by . . .' He trails off.

He needs me to urge him on to finish. 'What?' I oblige.

'I wish to preserve Epicureanism by recording it as Epicurus intended, but with an exposition on how it is slowly being warped in the hands of Romans and their misinterpretations of pleasure. A true Epicurean has just enough to prevent want because not to want is true pleasure. The Romans believe pleasure is excess, but excess only causes misery as one is constantly in a state of anticipation for more. It is imperative, really, to be free of the anxieties excess causes. I also wish to reveal the falsehood of religion, that the man who clings to ritual as a means to barter with the gods or out of fear is rife with anxiety and will never know peace of mind. Our souls are material; man should not fear in this life what will occur in his afterlife if proper libations are not offered to the gods because there are none. I wish to do this before Epicureanism is lost under Roman direction . . . do you understand? I am sorry, perhaps this is too much for you. I am asking too much. However, the only way a man, any man, slave or no slave, makes his mark, if not by war, is by leaving his ideas behind. I am an educated man, I need to write. Could you perhaps find a way to bring me some papyrus and a stylus?'

His mention of making a mark, his constant chatter, is so reminiscent of Tullia, a pull of longing swells up inside me. I could not even consider the risk of saying no, the risk of him not returning as he is right now, this way, just like Tullia, teaching me, speaking to me, filling this temple with words. I am hooked on him. This risk seems much greater than the repercussions I could face for stealing papyrus. Vesta suddenly sounds like knuckles continuously cracking. 'Yes, I fully understand. I will bring some tomorrow.'

'Thank you. Here, it isn't much, but what can a slave like me buy?' I hear him stand up, rummage through the grass beside the steps. 'Here,' and into the temple come rolling two radishes.

I hold them in each of my palms, their long white drooping roots carefully cleaned of soil, round red bodies picked of leaves so that each looks like a spinning top. I know I must get rid of these. I should toss them into Vesta, turn them into an offering, but these radishes are the first gift I've ever received. I wish to keep them, not give them to the goddess; I wish to keep something for myself. They are from him; she wouldn't want them anyway. I'll eat them after he leaves, his gift concealed inside me, close as possible.

'Where do you come from?' I roll the radishes between my palms, feeling a kneading tingle.

He is quiet, a long-drawn-out silence. I can hear the faint clinking of the chimes outside the temple door. Once when I had just turned ten, I went to tap the chimes as Tullia and I stepped into the temple, just to hear them jingle. They were old and rusted, a long string dangled from the middle of the heavy cylindrical tubes. Tullia snagged my hand, bending my thumb flat into my palm. 'Never touch those! Those should never ring.'

'Where do you come from?' I ask again, assuming he had not heard me the first time.

I hear him breathe in, ready to tell the long version. 'I come from a small village just outside Athens. We had a house, a fine house with a beautiful garden. My father and uncle owned a large olive grove together – it was once their father's and their father's father's. The olives were famous, unsurpassed for miles, thick, juicy, salty, but not too salty. People came from remote places, some even walking till their feet bled, just to buy their olives. Excellent olives. They made the most luxurious of oils. Oil bought by the wealthiest men of Athens. Famous, I tell you. I was my father's only son and so I was to be the best. My father sent me to the academy in Athens when I turned sixteen.

'I studied the greatest of philosophies with the best philosophers. Greeks are the masters of rhetoric, declamation,

251

literature, poetry, reason – the list goes on. This is why you Romans come in droves, so you can brag that you've been educated by the Greeks. You come to us to complete your education. The most celebrated of Roman scholars simply translate Greek to Latin. But how can one ever understand the contradictions of the Romans? Even your Caesar will tell anyone he does not believe the gods. I heard him debate this with the senator I last served. Yet in Caesar's next breath he says he is the direct descendent of Aeneas, and thus son of the goddess Venus. He is the Pontifex Maximus of Rome, and he doesn't believe in the gods.' He is scoffing again. If I could see him through the temple walls, he would be kicking the dirt.

'I was at the academy when my father died. He was healthy when I left, but fell ill suddenly and died. Just like that. I believe he was poisoned. My uncle was greedy; he did not want to share the land, the profits. He had no sons of his own, so he married my mother and became sole owner of the most famous olive grove in Greece. So what did my uncle do? To his own flesh and blood? He sold me to some Roman. He was so sure my mother would bear him a son of his own, and he did not want his brother's son around seeking revenge.

'This Roman just turned up one day as I sat in the field where Plato once taught, at the knees of my most favoured teacher. He showed him the papers my uncle had signed, seized me by my arm just above my elbow and took me back to Rome. Just like that. He sold me to a wealthy senator; made a profit too. I was his daughter's pedagogue. I taught her a girl's education, just enough to flatter a husband. But, as she grew, she kept asking for more. More history, more philosophy, even more rhetoric. She said that if I didn't, she would tell her father I tried . . .' He stops.

Hestia or Vesta, I am still a Virgin, this is fact; I am still a woman, this is fact. 'Well, so I taught her more, but when the senator found out he tossed me out of his house to this house. No, he didn't just toss me, he beat me out. Now, I am a donation to the state. I do, however, get great satisfaction in knowing that the senator lost whatever he spent on me.'

If I could see him right now, he would be spitting on the ground as punctuation.

'Where are you from exactly, before this?' he asks, as though it were as simple as that; a leisurely question to be answered lazily, without much thought.

'There is no before this,' I answer him. I add another log onto Vesta, carefully place some kindling, recite my prayers in a slight whisper. He rests his chin on his knee, looking into the night, waiting for me to be finished. Then, suddenly, I tell him about the little dog my father let me have. 'She had a dewy pink spotted nose, her eyes were still closed. I cradled her as she slept, her slow breathing had a slight whistle that made me sleepy as well, as if her weariness were contagious.' I knew I wasn't remembering it right, filling in where memory dropped off like canyons, but as I went along, the dog took full shape, almost as if my words were resurrecting her, perhaps differently than she was, but still here in the crook of my arm.

'I have a surprise for you. When you take your walk in the garden, pass the willow tree and look at the trunk of the large oak tree behind it.'

'What is it?' My mind races. Will it be something that will give me away, reveal this nightly dialogue? Does he not know the consequence of this, our talking?

'You'll see!' He pauses. 'Nothing anyone else will notice, do not worry. It's just for you!'

I spend the early morning, after he leaves to stand in front of the doors, reeling with excitement. When he returns to exchange Fabia for me, he mouths the word 'Remember' as I descend the temple's steps and Fabia turns, brushing past me into the temple. I rush to the bath, barely rinsing off. When I find the oak tree, there in its trunk is an etching of a tiny stick dog with a big circle nose. It's almost comical, a child's scrawl. He must have done it hastily, when on respite to relieve himself. I bend down quickly, run my fingers over it, run my fingers over where his fingers have been. Tears brim over my eyes from this act of kindness, absorbing into my dry skin before they can run down my face.

CHAPTER XXXVII

That afternoon I sit at the desk in the will room. Maybe when I die I will leave my dowry to Tullia, though I know it would never find her. I can do this, act as if I am writing out my own will, though not for long as the list is short.

I unhook the binding ring and take three pieces of papyrus out of the log book, fold them and stick one up each sleeve, another between my breasts. I will have to wake up earlier and dress myself, to conceal the papyrus like this and bring it to the temple for him. My stomach turns at this thought; I've never dressed myself before. Someone will know. What can I say? I will say I woke up early, could not sleep and so thought, why wait to be dressed? I will say it offhandedly, as though I did them a favour: the considerate Virgin, the eager Virgin. I get up from the desk, to hear if I rustle when I move. Before I leave, the slave asks if she can help me file my will, I tell her that I need more time to consider such things. Later, I place the papyrus under my pillow before the slaves come to undress me.

I cannot sleep. I am too worried the chime will ring before I am ready. The slaves will enter in a flurry of arms and hands, feeding, cleaning, dressing me and I will not be able to get the papyrus to Lysander. Get the papyrus out from under my pillow, out of this room, away from me. I cannot sleep because I am lying upon a broken rule, one much more tangible than the others I've already broken. This is evidence.

Each evening I've pretended to take him to bed and lie him next to me and repeat over and over what he has said the last six nights. I listen to it all over again, learning more, understanding better, until I can pull his voice over me, and butterfly wings circle down my neck and back, cotton brushes the bottom of my feet, my chin, water trickles through my spine, out of my ears, a lapping pillow, calming, a dandelion twirls around my eyes, soft, a sleepy tickle. This evening, I think of how he was plucked from the academy. I can almost see the disbelief on his face slowly turning to rage. I picture him falling to his knees, digging his toes into the ground, making them drag him away.

'*Excellent olives. Thick, juicy, salty, but not too salty.*'

I hear him say this again and again. Something is not right. I cannot put my finger on it; his voice, something is wrong with his voice.

'*Excellent olives. Thick, juicy, salty, but not too salty.*'

Why hadn't I noticed it before? He does not have an accent. He sounds just as I do, as if he spent most of his life here in Rome; he could not be so recently from Greece. Why did he lie?

'*I never could have imagined that I would be here with you, that I would have such an opportunity.*'

What sort of opportunity am I?

I sit on the edge of the bed, fully dressed, but without my headdress. I had to leave something for them to do. And I don't know how to put it on myself. When the slaves ring and enter, the first one stops, stunned, the other two nearly fall into her and at once all their limbs go limp like jellyfish. I smile. Surprise. I open my mouth, take a breath, but stop, an explanation would indicate one is needed. Give nothing away. After they gather themselves together and put away their distressed faces, one offers me a bowl. As I eat the grapes and bread, I notice it's the pretty blonde slave pinning on my headdress. This time she is not gentle; she scrapes my scalp pin after pin after pin.

CHAPTER XXXVIII

'I could not take a stylus. I had nowhere to hide it. You could use a stick or a twig. That will do, will it not?'

I slip the papyrus out from my stola and am about to slide it over to the temple's door. His hand comes up, dark, speckled with pores, as though a needle has pricked his skin innumerable times. I pull the papyrus back, his fingers wriggle, reaching in farther. 'Where are you really from?'

'I told you already. Did you forget?' He takes his hand out of the temple, a nervous snatch.

'You haven't any accent. You could not have spent most of your life in Greece and sound so Roman.'

'I . . .' I can see a blackened shadow pulling on the hair at his temples, his arms bent into a cage in front of his face, 'Maybe I've been here longer, it's hard to say. I can't remember everything . . .' He sounds so agitated, as if he is about to cry. I hear him scuffle about and I think for a moment he is leaving. In a wave of panic I slide the papyrus out of the door, down the first step. I wait, counting. Has he gone back to the house?

'We needn't know another's past to know one another. There is no before this.' He repeats what I said the night before. 'There is only now and after now.' An after now. He is about to say something else, but I interrupt.

'I think . . .' I expect some half-muted scornful guffaw, women only think they think, but he stays quiet. 'I think sometimes this is pointless . . . sometimes I can't stand this,' and there it is, the start of a confession, a lament, the kind Tullia passed down and became lost in. No, not the start; that is all of it, my whole lament in a nutshell, as they say, a cashew in the palm of a hand. I am quiet. He stays quiet. We share a quiet moment.

'You may not have to for much longer . . .' he mumbles in a grave growl, trailing off.

'What do you mean?' I come closer to the entrance, see him rub his eyes with the heels of his hands.

'Think of it this way; none of this will matter in a thousand years. You will by then, the particles that compose you, have been many things: a table, a chair, a field, a great architect . . . maybe even a waddling cross-eyed duckling!' For a moment I think he is mocking how I walk, the toddling of Virgins, but he sounds light again, as though he is grinning.

'No, not a waddling duckling!' I laugh.

'Oh no? You would not want to float on the sea, up and down rivers to ponds of far-off places? You seemed so interested in geography!'

'Well, then I would not be waddling . . . I'd be floating!'

He laughs, a little too loudly, and I nearly shush him, but his lack of reprimand is my condolence, his lack of shock is my acceptance. It is his own self-importance that consoles me, the way he just keeps on talking, no beat skipped. The way he laughed off the enormity of my secret and, by doing so, alleviated its great heaviness.

259

He is now more than an accomplice; he is a confidant. I can trust he will not sneer, disapprove, run back to the house filled with fear that the wicked Virgin cursed him by revealing herself; it is one thing for him not to believe in the gods, another for a Virgin to utter such to him, from the very temple she serves, in front of the very goddess she serves. There is a hierarchy of blasphemy. I trust he will let me say anything from now on.

I watch him pick up the papyrus and hear him gently roll it up.

There are two kinds of secrets. One kind weighs on you, like sand in your ankles, brick in your hips, stone in your shoulders; you need to tell it to lighten the weight. That kind needs to be told to live on, in someone else's ankles, hips and shoulders. This type of secret makes you ugly, like a gash on your forehead or white-headed boils spreading over your cheeks. Inside coming out. The other kind of secret is made of air, it billows under your toes, lifts you up just below the armpits, it bulges out against the sway of your back. It is the kind you like to keep to yourself because you do not want to be punctured, deflated, aired out. This secret makes you beautiful, seductive, like emerald combs fastened in your hair or sapphires clipped onto your ears. Outside coming in. Invited.

When I see him in the garden I walk by him on purpose as he is mending a fence or planting seeds or gathering wood for Vesta. We take such precautions not to look at one another that I am beginning to wonder if anything happened at all. It is only when I watch him from afar as I sit on a bench with my veil pulled round my face, blocking others from following my eyes, that he seeks me out. Now I have an appreciation for the veil. I watch his hands, his hooked nose nodding at another slave, his straight black hair falling off to the side, and wait for that moment he finally feels my eyes on him, and he turns, looks back at me, then looks side to side, before offering a nod. One single splendid nod that speaks yes, we will continue where we left off.

All other times, I tell myself, he watches me when I am turned the other way.

The statue is taking a more cohesive shape. The carver looks less like a murderer and more a lover as he holds the back of her head, chipping in her finer details, or as he polishes her, intimately caressing her torso or leg with a soft stone. How unseemly it all looks and yet I can't stop looking.

Veturia will have been touched more in death than in life.

CHAPTER XXXIX

I add more kindling, wash the floor, sponge Minerva. I count the cracks in the temple wall, the bricks in the hearth. In the morning I count the matrons who come into the temple and make their offerings for the five-day festival of Vestalis. They pad up the steps barefoot with plates of bread, ears of corn, cabbages, legs of chickens, wings of pigeons, morays and pikes.

I take their offerings, slide the food off the plate into the fire with three drops of wine, not too much to weaken the height of the flames. Though not many make their pilgrimage so early in the morning, once in a while, a small cluster of matrons will gather at the base of the temple steps after they've made their offerings, discussing their villas, silks, jewels, paintings, new births, new deaths, new betrothals. 'It is rumoured he will take Gaius Philo's daughter as his wife, but nothing is certain yet, so keep your lips tight.'

'. . . sick with dysentery . . .'

'. . . a little boy, good colour, his breath strong as wind in a storm . . .'

'. . . he brought it back just for me from Egypt. I will wear it to Cornelia's party . . .'

Or they'll complain about poor dinner guests. 'The other day

Marius showed up before water was even brought and heated, looking for a meal. Not only that, he asked for helping after helping, and when he thought we were not looking, he stored up bits of food in his napkins to sell later!'

The matrons disperse once they've shared their little morsels of news or when a peasant woman approaches the temple. Even now, I can hear their voices scatter like smoke in a cross-breeze.

A peasant woman enters, her hands knotted up like conches; she can barely undo her fists to offer the bread she has brought. She falls in front of the hearth to her knees. 'Can you beseech the goddess that with this bread let there be more?' She holds her pleated hands in front of me.

I take the bread, crusts really. Her two children standing at the door look at me curiously, a little girl clutching a rag doll that is nearly flat and ripped under one eye, the last of its stuffing sticking out, and a boy a year or two older. Then I notice they are looking not at me, but at the bread I am holding over Vesta; the boy licks his lips, holds his belly. For a moment I wish I could give them the bread, unfold their mother's hands and tell her, 'This bread serves you better in your mouths,' but I know that it is not what she wishes to hear. I watch the crusts crisp and char and turn to nothing. The peasant woman sighs as she pushes herself up with the backs of her hands, she smiles into Vesta and I can tell she feels, in this moment, unburdened.

As they step out of the temple I hear the boy huff, 'I am so hungry!' She cuffs him with one of her knobbed hands and it sounds like a wet fish slapping against a chopping block.

Regardless of what Lysander tells me, there is no peace of mind without the gods, not now that there has been peace of mind with them. I waver between seething with bitterness over

263

the non-existence of the gods and a gripping futility because I exist whether the gods do or not. But there is also one strange window, I can feel it more than see out of it, but it is there. A window I cannot yet put words to. A window that beckons to be crawled through, fallen head first from.

Though I am better educated than just to flatter a husband's intellect, I am still only educated enough to flatter the gods. Better to draw the curtains shut for now, because windows are opportunities, but also occasions for mistakes.

I count the dried leaves.

I do this because I no longer need count the nights, because tomorrow night he returns.

As he steps behind me in our short walk to the temple, I can smell him: sweat and cheap olive oil, mixed with aniseed. I listen to him on his return snuff out the torch, take his place on the bottom step of the temple, turn towards the door.

'Have you been well?' I ask him, considering maybe I too should store up bits of food in my napkin to bring him. 'Do you eat well enough?'

'I am not much of an eater,' he answers, then laughs lightly. 'Good for me then, considering! Though of late what suppresses my appetite most is the complexity of Epicurean philosophy and how to fully segregate it from Roman influence; it seems the only way to do this is to write it out completely as it was realized by Epicurus himself. I've been trying to do this on pieces of tree bark after the others have fallen asleep, but it is difficult, the bark is too coarse and unrefined. The papyrus, unfortunately, was not enough.'

I picture him, in a stream of moonlight, sitting cross-legged on the floor, struggling with a twig and tree bark, his back sharply angled, the knob at the nape of his neck nearly splitting through his skin. 'I will take more papyrus.' I say it before I knew I would.

'Oh, that would be wonderful! I am greatly indebted to your kindness. You are a philosopher at heart.' He pauses. 'I think we should go on a journey!'

My heart flips and lurches. 'I cannot go on a journey!' The very suggestion boasts a kind of arrogance, the kind of arrogance that gets one caught.

'We must make do with what we have: a slave's slogan! I've seen many places outside Rome when serving the senator. Close your eyes and I will take you there. We'll go together.'

'I am not sure what you mean . . .'

'Just close your eyes,' he hushes me. 'Now, listen to my voice, let it carry you away. You are stepping from this ashy temple into the fresh air. It is morning, a crisp fresh morning. The summer sun is just lifting the night, like a lid on a pot. I am waiting with a litter, an open litter, not the kind you are used to. We sit back upon soft pillows and watch the passing scenery as we are carried through the Forum, past the loud shouting of vendors, the squealing of pigs, the pleas of lawyers, the conspiring of politicians. Past the smoke and scents of fish sauce, soured milk still being sold as good. Past bustling throngs squeezed in by temples and apartments, being pinched by stone and suffocated by narrow alleyways. We cross the bridge of the Tiber . . .'

'We must make our offering then, toss straw dolls into the Tiber to apologize for the impertinence of the bridge . . .' I murmur, riding his voice in his litter going over the Tiber.

'No, we will not stop. On this journey, the gods are absent.

Why would you want to bring the gods along? Hmmm? No, wait, the gods are here. Do see them?'

'Who?'

'The three men?'

'No, I do not see them.'

'Right there, look. We are passing three men trying to drown a horse in a bucket as a sacrifice to Neptune. One has the horse's nose tied up and is pulling the head down into the bucket, the other is on top of it using all his might to push the neck forward, the third man is kicking the front legs so they buckle. The horse bucks, knocking the man off his neck, then kicks the man kicking at him and bites the man pulling his nose into the bucket of water.' He starts to snigger. 'The horse stamps on all three men. "If you want to ask Neptune something, go to him yourself," he whines.'

'The horse talks?' I laugh.

His voice softens into a lulling cadence. 'Yes, he does, and then the horse comes to us because he knows we will not kill him in such a violent way pretending it is holy. He knows I am not one of those men who just like to see things die. This is when the horse reveals his large wings: they spread out from his side to the length of a ship. Now we continue on the horse, soaring above Rome, looking down with a bird's eye view. Oh, how comical it all seems from up here. How plain the temples appear, how small it all is, how contrived!

'We travel in a starry haze, wet dew against our cheeks, until it is quiet; the air is fresh and we spot the softest, most undisturbed field and decide here we will rest, hidden in its long grass. The Pegasus bends forward to let us off, as if we are a king and queen. I lay out a blanket, pour some wine, serve the finest grapes, cheese and sweet bread. All sounds of Rome are lost, as if we are suspended on a plateau, separated, our province ending at the top layer of our skin; I am not a slave, you are not a Virgin. We pick apples from a nearby tree, ride in a nearby boat, swim in a nearby pond; here everything is nearby.

'When we journey back towards Rome, the horse trots, not flies, concealing his wings at his sides, as we both know he would be taken from us otherwise.

'I bring you through the artists' quarter on Aventine Hill. We stop and I pay, because on this journey I have money, an artist to paint a beautiful portrait of you and he does this with the setting sun behind you, cascading a rose light on your skin. When we return I ask you, "Did you enjoy the trip?" and you answer?'

'Yes, very much so, more than you can imagine.' My eyes stay closed, unwilling to return. 'Again,' I tell him.

He sits on the first step now, leaning into the entrance, his fingers drumming so close to my white shoe I can almost feel the small puffs of air they make.

Each night, for seven nights, he takes me somewhere different.

Each night, for seven nights, I give him pieces of stolen papyrus.

CHAPTER XL

It is the anniversary of the building of Jupiter's temple on Capitoline Hill, the highest of the seven hills. It is the hill with the most spectacular view of the Forum. From here I can almost feel I am riding atop a winged horse. From here, it does all seem rather small, less magnificent, even unplanned, messy, thrown together. Usually I find this view breathtaking, but today I see it Lysander's way.

We stand just outside the doorway, round the collapsible altar that has been brought outside for the sacrifice. This is the feast of politicians, or so I've heard it called. Senators, civic officials and former consuls are required to attend and gather outside the temple. Only patrician men can be in attendance; any slave or foreigner who may even just be passing by the temple on this day would contaminate the whole ceremony, and thus Jupiter will ignore us until a clean ceremony is offered. On this day, it is the acting consuls who will sacrifice the animal, not a priest or an attendant. A fire burns in the altar and Antonius tosses in some incense, the preliminary offering, but it is Cicero, with his long white toga stretched behind him, standing straight and proud, who is reciting the prayer. He prays so quietly, his lips hardly move.

Cicero pours the wine on the white heifer's head, his hand slightly shaking, motioning us forward to crumble mola salsa cakes between the heifer's horns. Oats and corn soak up part of the wine that is trickling down into the heifer's eyes. A melting hat. Cicero strikes the heifer, bends over and slices open her throat, but instead of falling over on her side, a willing offering, she squeals loudly, refusing to go to Jupiter. She tries to go forward, skidding on her blood, then tries to back out, falling down the first two steps of the temple. The attendants pull her up with the rope, cut her a few more times and remove her. The flutists try their best to drown the cries and distract the onlookers but it's too late, the ceremony is ruined. Good slaughtering is a skill; one cannot hit too softly, slice too lightly or hit too hard and shatter the animal's skull, scattering bits of bone over the ground. Gods dislike mangled bludgeoned offerings. Or so it is believed.

Cicero sighs, wipes his face with his palms, sweating and annoyed. Once a consul had to slaughter forty-one white heifers because he kept wavering between hitting too softly and hitting too hard. He quickly fell from popularity. Another white heifer is brought up the steps of the temple and the prayers are repeated, the ceremony is repeated; if someone were to arrive now he would think he hadn't missed a thing. This time the blow to the heifer's head is much harder, but not too hard; spatters of blood spray against the altar and she is good and knocked out before Cicero cuts her throat open. Each of us then comes forward, bowl in hand, trying our best to capture the gushing blood so it can be placed round the altar. It rushes out over our hands, but we grip the bowls firmly, as to drop one would bring us back to the beginning. As the liver is cut out and examined,

I glance over at Fabia and Sempronia, two old women with bloodied hands, cheeks tingling, looking slightly depraved as if they had just committed murder together. They leer at the liver, anticipating what it will read. I am also leering at the liver, hoping it will be deemed satisfactory and we can sit down and eat. Sempronia does appear healthier, though it may just be the reflection of the blood on her cheeks, rather than Fabia's blood offering. Blood of any kind seems to cheer a Virgin.

Over dinner yesterday evening, Fabia asked Sempronia if she would write a letter to the Pontifex Maximus, letting him know how well she had healed under the prowess of her purity. Sempronia cupped her ear, unable to hear across the table, so Fabia said she would write the letter herself and Sempronia need only sign it. Fabia, the other Virgin healer. Though Fabia would never be satisfied to be known as the 'other'. Perhaps while Veturia is still in the process of being taken from stone, Fabia will inhibit the mythology she's sewn for her. Like wearing another's stola until they've grown into it. But will she take it off when the time comes or only let Veturia crawl in with her? A two-headed Virgin. One who lies and the other who becomes the lie once it's uttered.

The leaves shudder on the trees down Capitoline Hill, as though they can smell the burning fat of the carcass. As the intestines are examined, approved, cut up and burnt on the altar, we make our way down to a dining room built onto the side of the temple for the many feasts Jupiter hosts throughout the year. Generals and their armies make an offering and feast here before they set off to battle, asking Jupiter to prevent flight from fight and to ensure victory. A butcher carves up the rest of the heifer and brings pieces to be cooked on the hearth in the corner of the dining room. The consuls file in with Caesar and the priests of Jupiter behind them. At the head table on three couches are statues of Jupiter, Juno and Minerva. They are dressed up in lavish red and yellow silks; Jupiter's silk is pulled up and round into a toga, Juno's and Minerva's more like shawls. Jupiter wears laurel leaves round his head. Juno and Minerva are graced with rose petals on their heads and shoulders. Life-size stone dolls, carefully strapped onto the couches. If one should fall over, chip its mouth or ear, the implications for many of the men in attendance, especially the consuls, would be dire. Unless of course someone could think fast enough and proclaim the statue was only kissing Rome, approving the elected consuls.

As we are served pieces of meat from the heifer, we each cut off a sliver and place it on the ground in front of Jupiter's couch; he looks on blankly, as if both his eyes are lazy. We kneel and chant in hisses, like the sound made by drops of water or wine when poured in Vesta. 'We, Vesta's Virgins, honour and beseech thee with these offerings and in return we ask thee to keep Rome in custody.' Flies have gathered on the meat even before we stand again.

Cicero and Antonius spill their cups of wine in front of Jupiter, as does Caesar. The feast continues. We sit at a small round table beside the statues. I think we must look much like distant cousins. We eat quietly as we always do, not conversing about impending festivals or baking or drawing up water from the sacred wells, not here in front of others. Symbolic; symbols don't often speak. Porcia is tending Vesta. Right now I would trade places with her. Trade this stiffness for bodily stiffness, standing straight over Vesta rather than hunched over meat, trying my best to chew without moving, without noise, though the meat is tough and catches between my teeth. Juice from the meat dribbles down Julia's chin as she struggles to cut off more. Claudia's mouth has shrunk to that of a nipping loach.

Fabia once warned us: 'Virginity is worn on both the outside and the inside; any change in the Virgin's state affects the state, any change in a Virgin's state affects the way her stola hangs, the way she sits, walks, carries herself. Nothing gets past Vesta.'

Apprehension thrums up my neck; I must stand out in some way, surely I look different from the others. My features must be more pronounced, my mouth wider, fuller, from all the talking with Lysander, my eyes brighter from glancing more and more out of the door down the steps at Lysander and away from Vesta. I must appear to have a secret, my hips to have more sway; I walk a bit more smoothly. I am wiser than the others, a world-weary traveller, my life has more texture, more assortment. Surely, this must show. Surely I look less rigid and dour than the others.

I notice the water bowls by our plates are pink from rinsing the blood from our hands, a trail of pink eyes looking up, watching us eat the sticky meat, eat what was once itself, or part of itself, our fingers sticking out from bloody cuffs like writhing tentacles belonging to a single creature.

As we travel back to the house, the lictors leading the way look very solemn, sometimes waving at the men carrying us to stop so they can creep forward and ensure the coast is clear. I can see them when we are making a turn down the tiny path because the curtain has a slight bulge in it; if I lean back a certain way I can see through it without the purple veneer. We take a back street, avoiding the Forum – it is too difficult to clear our path in there – and circle through to Etruscan Alley.

I can hear the shouts of vendors quickly quietening, people splitting apart like feeding chickens as we go through them. They look annoyed at the inconvenience, but resume their affairs a moment after we pass; we are an accepted nuisance, like waiting in line.

As we turn off the alley, I see puffs of sizzling smoke billow into the blue sky and smell roasting meats; it smells so much better down here. Peasant women are gathered round communal ovens, waiting for their turn to bake bread, chattering with one another, laughing. It is a beautiful day to be out, buzzing around with chores and errands, bumping into the occasional friend.

Then I see him, Lysander. He is slumped against a wall talking to a man with a belt of hanging knives. At first I think I am only seeing him as a kind of manifestation of wishful thinking, but I blink and he is still there. He holds a roll of papyrus in his hand and seems to be bored as the man shows a particular knife to him, waving his hand as if to hurry him. Lysander shakes his head no, shows the man the papyrus and the man takes out another knife, flipping it to and fro in his palm, the blade catching the sun as they continue to barter.

What is he doing here? He should not be away from the house. Why is he buying a knife?

Lysander looks up and for a moment I think he sees me, but it's the litter he's looking at. He nods at the man, thrusts the papyrus at him, then pulls his tunic up and tucks the knife in at his back. He breaks into a full sprint. We are only a little way from the house; he'll beat us there, scale the wall and no one will know the difference.

*

When we arrive our evening meal is waiting for us in the dining room, though it will consist of only wine and pastry because we just ate. We must still dine together, regardless of the fact that we are not hungry, because this is what routine orders.

'We should eat in the garden, it is still warm out,' I say this with a warm enthusiastic smile, trying my best to convince them. I want to see him.

'Oh, it is much too chilly!' Fabia rubs just above her elbows, gives a little shiver.

This aggravates me so much that I could almost rub her down myself. 'There, are you warm now? Are you ever warm?' Rub until her arms burn off. I want to go into the garden so badly, want to see Lysander using his new knife as some kind of tool to ease his work. Maybe to loosen the soil for planting seeds. But I know this cannot be. If it were meant as a tool, it would have been brought to the house by one of the Pontifex Maximus's foremen. And a slave would never be handed a knife anyway; nothing useful could come from that. Slaves only kill themselves at their owner's cost, or kill their owners. But Lysander wouldn't kill us; we are not really his owners in the usual way; he belongs to the state. Also there are six of us – it would be too exhausting to slice through us all, and he'd be stopped before he could finish. He could never get close enough to the Pontifex Maximus to attempt assassination, and why would he care to do that?

He must plan to kill himself. My stomach turns at this thought.

The dinner conversation carries on as usual.

'Lovely ceremony. Cicero did a spectacular job!'

'Hear, hear.'

And so on and so on. The blonde slave strums the lyre, a pulsing frantic strum, or at least that is how it sounds just now.

I eat the pastries quickly; they seem dry and doughy at the same time, the wine too thick; everything tastes wrong.

Once dinner is over, instead of climbing the stairs to my room and bed, I go into the garden as if to go for a stroll. This I shouldn't do. I am veering from routine.

I see him as soon as I step from the kitchen. He is feeding chickens just behind the willow tree. The tree's drooping branches provide a curtain that he steps out of and behind as he circles round the pen sprinkling grain.

I walk stiffly along the path, trying my best not to appear to be in a hurry. My legs bend gawkily like those of an upright cricket.

When I reach the willow tree I pause, put my hand flat to my chest so as to seem winded and in need of a rest. 'I know what you are planning!' I say through my veil, through the willow tree.

Lysander steps back, but does not look at me and continues to offer grain to the chickens. 'You do?'

'Yes, and you mustn't carry on with it!'

He suddenly stands very still, the only sounds are the chickens pecking, scraping their claws into the dirt, fluttering their wings at one another to gobble up the other's share greedily. 'How did you find out?' His jaw flexes, like a rising roll of bread.

I hadn't noticed how close it is to dusk, the day has dulled, as though the sun is quickly rolling towards the edge of the earth like a marble off a table. 'Just please don't. Not now, not ever, but if you must, please not yet. You'll be sorry if you do, I am sure of it. I'll be very sorry, I know that.' I hear the squeak of the kitchen door open. 'Promise me, at least not yet.' He still says nothing.

'If you don't, I will tell the others that I saw you threatening a fellow slave and that you should be locked up at Caesar's for a few days as punishment . . .' I say this as though it is a question, as if I am asking how to threaten.

He looks up at me with rage brooding in his narrowed eyes, his lip twitches. I hear the scuffing sounds of someone coming, so before he can offer his promise I need to walk away. When I turn, I see it is only one of the female slaves sweeping the left-over crumbs from our dinner into the garden.

CHAPTER XLI

Tonight, time with Vesta seems much longer, an animal hide stretched over a drum – thump, thump, throb. Smoke and ash are a stinging mist, no, a fog I stand in the middle of each night, breathing in, out, in, out. I go over and over what I said to him in the garden, my cheeks reddening at the audacity with which I spoke, feeling frustration with the way I worded things, with what I could have said but didn't. I do this until I am no longer sure what I said at all.

The quiet has returned, set in, settled like ash on Minerva's head and shield, ash that can't be shaken off because one can't move. My neck is stiff with worry, as if it has thickened and twisted into snaking tree roots, firmly attaching my head to my shoulders like an old tree stump. Dumb as a stump; my father used to say that from time to time – to whom I don't know, why I don't know. Maybe me. I smooth out my headdress, it falls to my elbows. I do not need to attach it to a veil tonight. I don't know why I bother when he is here; if we were caught, my veil would not disguise me, save me or make me appear innocent, virginal, oblivious that something reckless was occurring. A veil – behind a veil, that is – provides a secure place to retreat to, back to unawareness. Here it is again, a long-drawn-out insertion of nothing but time. Only now it is more strenuous, like arching backwards until the spine feels on the verge of snapping.

I roll the golden rope back and forth in my hands, burning my palms. I flick the pearl dangling from the headband in the middle of my forehead, one, two, three, four; a drum on my head. I put more wood on Vesta, blow, offer my breath to her so she can grow. I could not sleep before, but now I struggle to stay awake. Sempronia is coughing again; it began in the litter on the way back from Jupiter's temple and led to a loud raucous spurt that carried on throughout the night, striking me awake like pebbles, so sleep was something I could do only between her coughs. Just slight, light bursts of sleep as short as a blink. But even then those bursts were disrupted by fretting over Lysander's possibly taking his own life.

I turn from Vesta and her drowsy flames. Outside the door the sky is black, starless.

Tullia came into my room the night before she left. She said she'd paid a slave to look the other way. I was already asleep, but she slid into bed behind me and stroked my cheeks, patted my braids. When I woke up she shushed me, finger in front of puckered lips, eyes welling with tears. She wanted to tell me goodbye, she said, spend her last night with me. It was strange being so close to her, having her in my bed, feeling her breath on my neck, her belly on my back, arm over mine, in that way. A mother indulging her child, consoling. I was too old to be held this way, but I wanted it anyhow. I wanted it before I felt the way I curved into her, the way she pulled me in, fastening herself into me, me into her. She told me she loved me like her own daughter, sister, friend, whatever. All of it. Love is love.

'Maybe,' she told me, 'maybe you should forget the things I told you. I think I was – am – wrong. Maybe.' Tears ran down her cheeks, dripping on my own cheek, onto my lips. 'Maybe it is better to live a long life than a full life. Maybe it is best to make do, instead of dreaming of far-off places, living other lives. I don't know, Aemilia, I just don't know. What is best? You find it yourself. Just do your best. That is what the others do, really . . . They just seem to do it better than me. I want better for you. Be better than me. Remember to keep Vesta strong, keep awake, follow closely . . .' Sobs came bubbling out of her chest. 'And if you can, wait them out, the thirty years, just wait them out.'

I rubbed the backs of her hands. 'Will you come back for me, Tullia?' Even as I said it I knew she would not answer.

She squeezed me harder. 'We will find each other again.'

I sank into my bed, under my bed, past the floor, through the surface of the earth to its fiery centre into the Underworld, sank with a mouthful of dirt. I began to cry, sob, as though everything inside me had become detached and had fallen into the wrong place: liver where the heart was, heart where the stomach was. Until everything inside me was trying to claw a way out through my mouth: stomach stepping on lungs, lungs climbing on ribs, wanting out, out, out.

Tullia cupped my mouth, trying to keep my insides inside, to stop me from seeping out, collapsing into her. 'Shhh . . . someone will hear. Listen, you are now my mark, you are my after now.' She said this as if she were my mother.

No. I wanted to say no to her goodbye as though it were my choice, up to me. She turned me towards her, kissed my eyelids. 'I will find you, Aemilia. I promise to find you.' Then she was gone.

I wish I could say this is what happened, but Tullia never came, she never lay in my bed next to me or caressed me like a child. Nothing so dramatic occurred. She left unceremoniously, off to another life beyond these seven hills. Memories should be exchangeable, as interchangeable as history.

There is something I hate in everyone I love: their resistance to loving me back.

I sponge Minerva, gliding the sponge up and down her strong, sturdy legs in the slow, methodical way I wish I could sponge my own. 'I beseech thee with this sponge and soap to protect our Rome from loss of commerce and craft, and to bestow your good graces upon invading soldiers to fight with your warrior cunning.'

'Aemilia?'

I stop, drop the sponge back in the bucket. He is dead; Lysander is walking the earth the way those who die too early, too tragically, do. He is dead.

'Aemilia?'

I turn to the door and he is there, not as a lamenting apparition but in the flesh. His hands grasp at the entrance, as if holding himself up or maybe back; his head is cocked to the side as though waiting to hear his own echo. I step out from beside Minerva and move towards him, my hands reaching up to touch him, just to make sure he is alive and well – but he can't be here.

'Where is the other slave?' I walk backwards, pulling my veil into place, panic setting in. 'Go down a step or two away from Vesta's light; he'll see us . . . You shouldn't be here, it is not your time to escort. Our talks will be found out . . . go down . . . please.'

280

'Shush . . . it is all right, he is fast asleep at the doors. They all sleep there, didn't you know? Some of them even go back to the hut and play dice for a while. It's not as though anyone will attempt to break into your house.' A half guffaw, and he is again serious. 'I *need* to know how you found out.' He stretches out *need* like a trawling net.

Whatever fear I felt for him has suddenly turned to anger, maybe because I am so tired from lack of sleep, maybe so tired of fear itself. 'You only used me for the papyrus. Is this that what you meant by opportunity? I am just your opportunity?'

'No . . . no. Well, yes, just at first. But now it is different—'

'I think it best you go! We should both return to our stations as we are meant!'

'I am not meant to be a slave.' He hangs his head slightly forward, his eyes close for a moment behind a band of his hair. Then he shakes his hair back, flipping his head upright to look directly at me. Now I can see his face completely. 'You don't know what it's like being a slave, not having any kind of autonomy, like a rope binding my arms to my sides. I can't do it any more: watch Romans live off the backs of captured men. Every temple, building, mansion up on Palatine Hill has been built by stolen men for Romans to enjoy and claim as a testament to their own greatness.'

'You are not abused here,' I retort.

'Is that all I have? That I am not abused? If we are not abused we are supposed to kiss their feet, thank our lucky stars we are not being fed to eels for breaking a plate or bowl, or being whipped for feeling ill. Oh, how generous the owner who does not beat his slaves, how generous he is to offer three pounds of stale bread a day while he dines on seven courses of meat and

281

cheese in the other room. What a great favour he does us by giving us a cloak to wear while we work in harsh weather as he lies on the couch by the fire with his wine, congratulating himself, saying, "Other slaves have it so much worse than my own. I am a good man." You don't know what its like to live on a lead.'

It's as if he is reading me his suicide note aloud, and something boils in my stomach, burns through my throat. I feel a gush of words brought on by his ignorance, by desperation that this temple will once again fall silent, this time permanently. '*I don't know*? I don't know what it's like? I know what it's like not to have any freedom. I stand here every day, an ash catcher. When I am out there, a blood catcher. When I am not catching I am storing up to make this goddess her monthly offerings. I am just a vestibule for the gods. Every day I wait for something to happen, some sign, some kind of fulfilment – not my own fulfilment – oh no, I mean the gods' . . . Vesta. That would make me stop waiting, but it never comes. I am always waiting for something to happen to me, something different from the day before and the day coming. Do you know what kind of purgatory that is? Waiting out thirty years? Then you come along and something has happened, and now you wish to take that away!'

'Well then, you are not abused either, not here.' He says this in his pedagogical way, leading me to the obvious.

'No, no. I suppose I am not.' I give him the answer he seeks, annoyed that he is using my own reasoning against me.

'And yet you are still dissatisfied?'

I do not answer that. Why bother?

'Then why do you wish to stop me? Something tells me you are not meant to be a Virgin, if only because no one is meant to.'

'So what do you suggest? That I simply follow you?'

'Yes. I think so! Afterwards there will not be any reason for what you are. You will be free of this temple, ideally of course. You've already helped . . . you're already involved.'

This saddens me, how disposable he thinks I am. What will he do? Leave me as soon as I follow him to the Underworld, the way one ditches a bone picked clean of meat? An exhausted opportunity. If there is no reason for me in the Underworld why should I follow him? Maybe it is some final notoriety he hopes to get out of me: a slave and Virgin dead together in a suicide pact. His name would be known then, at least for a little while.

'Why did you come here? Why not steal marble from the garden, or silver from the house when we were out? Why did you involve me?' My voice quivers; if my eyes had not been so dry for so long, maybe I could cry.

'You spoke to me first . . .' He says this in a childish sort of way that almost makes me laugh.

'Only because I knew you'd speak back to me.'

'I only spoke so much because you listened so well.'

We are both quiet now. I add more kindling, mouth my prayers self-consciously as he stands there watching with a furrowed sympathy, as if I am maimed and limping.

'I did see you as an opportunity at first, for the papyrus, but now I see you differently . . .' His voice is soft again, apologetic.

'How?'

'We are much more alike than I could ever have believed.'

'So I should just kill myself as you plan to do?'

'Kill myself? What do you mean kill myself?'

'The knife. I saw you buy a knife . . . Isn't that what you intend?'

'I . . . no . . . oh . . .' His jaw hangs slightly open, his top teeth bite down on his lower lip. He shakes his head.

'If you do not plan to use it on yourself, then how do you intend to use the knife?' I step back, to the other side of the door, where I could fling my hand out quickly and ring the chimes.

He notices right away what I am doing. 'You're already involved . . . You stole the papyrus for me . . . I still have some in the hut. They will wonder how a slave like me could afford a knife . . . Don't, please don't.'

'They'll think you went into the house and stole. I will claim that to be true!' My hand moves up, but he blocks my way.

'I know your name – *Aemilia*.'

'I can say you overheard it!' But I know if he utters my name aloud, it would not take long to sink under the weight of the others' suspicion.

'Think about it . . . if you ring that bell every day will be the same as before and the day coming . . .'

My arm falls limply to my side. He is breathing rapidly, beads of sweat drip from underneath his hairline, his eyes pleading. I can feel Vesta's heat – bland, steady heat at my back. 'Tell me then, what am I already involved in? What is the knife really for?'

'Spartacus started his revolt with a knife . . .'

'Spartacus?'

'Do you not know who he is?'

'Vaguely. He was some foreign ingrate who tried to pillage the provinces with a gang of runaway slaves, killing men and women, tossing suckling babies on their heads, setting fires, terrorizing peaceful villages. He tried to invade Rome . . . I remember, though I was so young, there were daily sacrifices at Jupiter's temple—'

284

'That is only how you were told to see it! It's all perspective. He was running in the other direction, away from Rome. All Romans think everyone wants to conquer them or become them. How far can one really get from their time and place? Not far, unless someone shows them another side of the coin . . . The Spartacus I know of was a brave man.' His low voice takes on the cadence of a melodious storyteller and I feel that odd twitch, a pull maybe, that I felt only once before, as I kissed Julia. Only this time it's stronger. 'Spartacus was caught in Thrace, forced to serve in his captor's army. When he tried to desert, he was caught and sold to be a gladiator. He eventually escaped, some say on the back of a lion. He seized a knife from the cook's wagon as he soared by. As he made his way north, towards Gaul, slaves fled from their owners and joined him, until he had an army of over a hundred thousand slaves – some too old, some too young, some women, but all willing to fight.

'They defeated Roman legion after Roman legion and would have escaped to the north if not for the greed of some of the men. Seeing this as their only chance for wealth, they convinced Spartacus to go back south to pillage more and were crushed. Thousands of their bodies still lie along the Appian Way. Though all that's left is their bones at the base of the crosses and the rags of their clothes, still nailed there as if their bones just slipped out from them.'

The way he is standing now – a vein slightly bulging in his forehead, the grave serious look on his face, his arms spread open from his chest – he looks very much on a cross himself.

'So you plan to become another Spartacus and end up on a stick on the Appian Way?'

'No, not exactly. There's this man, Sergius Cataline—'

We both hear it then, a rustle, maybe sand crunching or the sizzle a torch makes. He slips past me into the temple, tries to shrink into the wall. His finger is at his lips, shushing me. This is my chance. All I need to do is go to the door, call out to the passer-by and claim a madman I have never seen before has come into the temple. A slave is he? From our very garden? I had not even noticed.

He knows my name. Every day will be the same as the one before and the one coming. Silent night, silent temple. Because you spoke to me. Because you listened.

When the sound has long faded, Lysander breathes out and wipes the sweat from his face. He then looks around at Vesta, the cupboard, Minerva, the sponge and bucket, the tinderbox as if he has stepped into a villa he plans to purchase. I expected him to stumble back out; one may not fear bees but still not wish to sit on their hive. But he stands before me without any unease at all, as if I am nothing to cower away from; he turns towards me, looking directly at me. I am aware of his closeness.

'There's this man, Cataline,' he begins again as if nothing has happened. 'He was defeated twice in the elections to be consul and is now amassing power the other way, with the plebs, castouts and slaves. He wants to overthrow the senate, have the slaves kill the senators as they sleep, have his followers storm the assembly, burn the Forum down. He has rallied a small army by promising a cancellation of debts and land redistribution, so anyone from his class who has squandered his family fortune will fight beside the lowliest peasant who is obligated to a life of labour to pay off a few coins.

'The Republic will fall, I believe this. What I don't believe is Cataline's usual promise to slaves of freedom, a plot of land, full citizenship. He's a spoilt man from an old family. He killed his own son when a woman he fell in love with declared she would not marry him until he was rid of any heirs born by another woman. Is this a steadfast man, a man to be trusted?

'I know he will tell the slaves what they want to hear – promises of land, horses, mistresses – but once it's all over he'll keep them enslaved to rebuild the mess. But my plan is that once Cataline has finished, I will carry the slaves to their own revolt and ensure we get what is promised.'

'But I don't understand. What is it you want from me?'

Serving the greater good leads to greater goods, the old saying goes. Of course there have been frequent times of turmoil, attempts at demagoguery, civil war, but such disputes do not touch us Virgins. We remain unchanged. The senate always reigns. Heads on stakes; withering, crucified men; stains of blood; raging fires – we are unaffected. We keep our curtains closed as we travel in our litter to and from sacrifices, filling the litter with small talk of duty. But now fear and excitement sift through my body. What if Rome changes? What if our litter pitches and tips over and we all fall out? What if we are no longer untouchable?

'With the papyrus, I can slowly stockpile small weapons. I plan to bury them behind the hut until the time comes. No one else knows this but you. Cataline's watchmen are all over, and any of the other slaves could report me. Cataline would pay them very well for such information and I would be killed. They'll follow Cataline until they realize the short end of the stick is in their otherwise empty hands, and that is when I'll rally them into an uprising.'

He is asking me to do the unthinkable: to aid a rebellion

against the Republic, the very thing my womb protects, the very reason for my being. Being here. Choice. I turn this over in my palm like the man who sold the knives. 'And Spartacus, why did you mention him?'

'Spartacus led an unplanned, almost accidental uprising. Think how successful a planned one will be.'

I don't say anything. He drums his fingers on his hip, strokes his beard with the other hand. I don't say anything at all because I cannot bring myself to say yes, agree aloud. Good Virgins stand passively by. He realizes this after a moment or two. 'Oh, thank you . . . thank you.' He pulls me in by my shoulders and attempts to embrace me. My body immediately stiffens, turns brittle, and I instinctively pull myself away, feeling the outline of the knife at his hip. He keeps his hands on my shoulders for a moment, holding me still, staring into me before finally letting me go.

'You're my only ally.' He steps out of the temple into the night, back to his hut.

We excuse the other of any wrongdoing and become accomplices.

CHAPTER XLII

I turn back and stand over Vesta, her orange-red flame tall and thriving. If she had a mouth she'd be smiling, if she had a body she'd be bowing. 'You're welcome . . . A lot of girls would like to be in your place right now.' If she had an eye of her own, she'd give me a wink. I wish she had an eye of her own. I add another log of dry wood – she sparks, or maybe that's her salivating. She grows a little taller, stronger. I stand a little closer but not so close that she will singe me; no, for that she will have to come to me.

I whisper, 'Hestia.' Nothing. Again. 'Hestia, Hestia. Vesta is Hestia.' Nothing. 'Lysander says you do not exist, you are not even Roman. Why not show yourself to me?' I kick her hearth, her heart. 'Give me your wrath! Just prove to me you exist.'

I look for something, anything. A brick about to fall loose. Wait for Vesta to spit out, spread, burn me. For a cackling bird to fly into the temple, straight into Vesta or maybe out of Vesta, cackling all the way through the Forum, telling on me. I wait to see if my stola falls, if Vesta strips me of this honour, if my head-dress pops off my head, leaps across the temple floor and hides behind Minerva's shield. If Minerva shakes free of stone and smacks me on my head. Nothing. Minerva is much too catatonic, went stone crazy and never came back. Why is crazy always a place one must travel towards? Crazy is the body, sanity is the wardrobe. Or is it the other way around? What would Tullia say?

Vesta flickers, oblivious to turmoil, either because she is too superior to be concerned or because she is only fire. Smug fire. Virgins are to serve without question, to serve without doubt. Serve wholly and completely; duty is the Virgin's way, duty keeps devastation at bay.

You'll be sorry if you don't. You'll miss the status quo once it's gone, you'll regret it: plague and starvation are just a hesitation away, the gods are fickle and can go either way. This song of threat and warning was sung much more loudly in my head when I was younger. The 'what if' a far greater threat than 'what is.' Now this chorus has faded with age and become faint croaks and chirps like crickets in the dark, replaced with practical chants; duty is the Virgin's way; duty keeps disbelief at bay.

It could *always* be worse.

But Tullia ruined it; it could *always* be better, she would say. Oh, Tullia, if it weren't for you I would be happy, ignorant and happy. I too could fictionalize what I see. Seeing is believing. But if it were not for Tullia, there would be no Lysander. Lysander said this Vesta of ours is a man-made invention, and not even a truly Roman figment, but an imported figment from another place and people. Vesta was not born with the inception of Rome but arrived later, maybe escorted by some warring general. Better late than never. But how could they carry her hearth, her temple, her fire back to Rome? No, the idea of Vesta – a rumour of a state hearth – spread like wildfire to Rome. 'Calmed the masses elsewhere, should do the trick in Rome. A proven method and the wives love it . . .' Somehow this makes it worse, this lack of mysticism, but what else am I to believe? I have kicked her and taunted her and still she does not show herself. If I am not fit for such consideration, then who is? I live by Vesta, but she lives off me. These are my secrets, such thoughts; the 'what is' is much worse than the 'what if.'

CHAPTER XLIII

Today the chariot races are dedicated to Mars. This time we stand and watch from the centre of the track. Ten laps. The horse of the winning charioteer will be sacrificed to Mars here. His head will be lopped off and fought over by two teams of men, and the winners will be awarded the tail. The god of war enjoys a skirmish. The tail will then be burnt on Mars's altar. We must catch the horse's blood and are required to store it in the house for next year's celebration of the goddess of fountains and springs. As the horses race I pick out the smallest one and hope it wins; there is less blood then. It's white with pinkish brown spots. It doesn't win, instead a large brown horse wins. The charioteer brings the horse to the priest. The salii ritual dancers divide themselves into two groups of twelve and leap and dance round the horse, singing 'Carmen Saliare,' their ancient hymn, and purifying the horse. Their robes are tied round their waists, their chests rubbed down with dust from the track; each carries a leather shield and a spear. Every time I watch their frenzied leaps, I expect one to accidentally impale another, but somehow they never do.

The priest of Mars and his attendants bring the horse into the middle, amid frenzied cheers. Red won. We stand behind the priest. Five figurines. The horse sneezes, shakes its mane back and forth, a wreath of myrtle round his neck. The charioteer comes back over and leads him round in a proud quick gallop, a last gallop, welcoming the adoration. Brown muscles flex with every movement, veins travel down each leg, with every step like bursting streams: a perfect animal. The charioteer kisses him on his white streaked snout, tears in his eyes. The priest begins his series of prayers until he motions to his attendant, who strikes the horse three times on the head. Lyres play, their twanging only emphasizing the horse's high-pitched whinnying.

The horse is disoriented, its head half limp, has fallen nearly between its front legs, but it still makes a feeble effort to trot off, trying to reclaim the pride and glory of a moment ago. I almost laugh then, picturing Lysander's face, the way he would roll his eyes and shake his head at the ridiculousness of this ceremony. I almost laugh at the earnestness of the priest as he slits the horse's throat, his tiny dry mouth perfectly pressed with effort. I can hardly wait to tell Lysander about this; I've been doing this more and more lately, storing up what I see for Lysander to laugh at later. He always does. 'What wasteful idiots,' he'll chortle.

The horse falls slowly, graceful as a gladiator, knees buckling in a final bow, a perfect death as we catch his hot, gushing blood in bowls. I think of the Pegaus Lysander and I imagined, smashing nose-first into the earth, neck snapping, wings folding.

The smell of blood, its warmth, is starting to sicken me.

I see him when we get back as I step down from the litter. He is at the side of the house picking berries. He turns and cups his hand over his eyes to shield them from the glare of the sun, raising each of his reddened fingers in a discreet wave. His mouth turns up in a happy grin that I wish I could curl into, feel his smiling chin atop my head as I lie against his chest. He has bronzed under the sun, his arms thickened with muscle. I return his wave by touching my nose.

Julia bumps into the back of me. 'Oh!'

'My apologies.' I move forward quickly.

Lysander turns, laughing into the berry bush. I nearly laugh with him. How easily the order of things can become disorderly.

CHAPTER XLIV

For the last ten nights, he's come to the temple to collect the papyrus I've stolen from the will room. Sometimes I can only get a small roll, sometimes just a ripped corner, sometimes a full roll.

'It's of the Egyptian standard. It fetches a decent price, so anything is better than nothing,' he tells me.

He stays after I give him the papyrus, and because there isn't any news about Cataline yet, he tells me odd little anecdotes.

He tells me about a slave he once knew. 'There was this man, so short, barely to my hips, but strong as an ox, so no one ever bothered him or tried taking advantage of his size, everyone knew better. However, every time a new slave arrived, he would think this short man must be weak as a lamb and somehow try to get the better of him.

'Once, a new slave, very tall and strong, tried to make him carry his load of wood back up to the senator's house, and in just one instant, the short man threw him to the ground. For a week after, the short one took his food, the strong one cowering in his stubby shadow, and let me tell you he could eat. He ate more than any of us! The senator liked to show him off at his parties, have his guests wager on what he could carry. He'd make everyone laugh. He picked up a whole donkey once and carried it round on his back.'

'Surely a man who measures to your hip could not carry a donkey!' I picture hooves and gangly legs dragging over the slave's shoulders, kicking and knocking him in the head. I find this hilarious and sharp hiccups of laughter come out of my nose.

'Well, maybe I exaggerate just a little, but if he was not to my hips, then only to my elbows.' He sounds playful, as if we are having a mock disagreement, the sort I sometimes hear between matrons and their husbands as they leave the theatre or the games, carrying on a kind of good-natured bantering that seems scripted for an audience – one acting appalled as the other teases. Usually the matron does the teasing. Men tell the stories, they have stories to tell.

He tells me about a kind of sweetbread he once ate. 'So perfectly moist and soft, it could have been used as a pillow.' A prank he and another slave once pulled on the senator he used to serve. 'We slowly thickened his wine throughout the night, adding less and less water to the pitcher. He did not notice while he was entertaining. He became so drunk he challenged one of his guest's sons, a boy half his age, to a wrestling match right there in the dining room. He threw this man's son right up onto the table, wham!' He softly claps his hands in an attempt to emphasize the sound, but also tries to be noiseless, so it comes out more like a light stroke, a damp pat. He laughs. 'He landed right in a tray of fish. They left in quite a hurry after that, smelling horrible!'

These details supplemented his usual conversation about the impending uprising. The details are like bridges connecting one oration to the next; I wish he'd slow down, take his time, build up more slowly, more intricately, before reaching his punch line. They make me feel I am out in the world, living next to the secret lives of men. These are the details I secretly beg for.

Each night my heart and stomach reel and stagger at each breath of wind, wanting it to be Lysander. The silence before he arrives is coarser than ever before, like pepper being funnelled into both my ears. I make quick offerings to Vesta, take my place beside the door, back flat against the temple wall, and anticipate him. I've also taken to washing the temple floor and sponging Minerva in the morning, once he's left; neither Vesta nor Minerva seems to mind this. They haven't presented any sign of disapproval, and thus, it leaves more time with Lysander.

When I hear the soft crunch of his feet and the following padded sound of him climbing the steps, I feel myself tingle, anticipating his liveliness. His living, breathingness. His wordiness. He sits on the first step so Vesta's light clears the shadows from his face. When he arrives, his face is sometimes sombre and serious, at other times good natured, as if he finds everything in life humorous. But it is his face that has summoned a calming certainty that the after now is right around the corner. He is a better sign than any.

What does it matter if I illegally speak to a Greek slave at night right in front of Vesta? All of this will soon be gone. None of this will matter in a thousand years.

Even when the lighter blue bleeds through the black of night, he seems reluctant to leave. 'I should go,' he'll say once or twice before actually leaving. Sometimes I even have to remind him. 'You should go,' and he'll agree, staying just a little while longer, telling me one last quick story, maybe something simple about seeing a three-legged dog that outran a rabbit. Or he'll reveal another small note from his past: 'I was too skinny when I was small and always so cold, though you could never tell now.' He'll turn, smiling, flexing one of his arms. 'A soldier's arms, these!' and I'll roll my eyes with mock annoyance and tell him again, 'You should go, soldier!'

'But I am still cold. Maybe that fire in there could warm me just a little?' and he'll pretend to crawl in.

'Oh no! Go!' He'll only relent once I seem frantic, nearly half his body arched over the threshold before he'll finally say, 'Fine, fine. I'll go.'

'It wasn't fair to distract me that way earlier!' I whisper teasingly as he comes up the steps, and I hear the brashness in my voice. Tullia said flirtation is an art form, a man should only suspect you are flirting but never know for sure: mystery is the means. Not that I mean to sound as if I am flirting, but this has been happening more and more lately, as if my voice has caught and snagged on something and is unwinding its careful repression, has become slippery so that words tumble out without first being filtered. Each burst of this shamelessness is always followed by shame. And for a moment I feel unsteady as the sinking inside me returns, as if I am being pulled to the ground by my sternum.

'Who me? I was only welcoming you back!' he replies and I feel light again; my intervals of shame are shortening.

Tonight I tell him about the skirmish at the track. I exaggerate the blood lust in the players' eyes, the plucky precision of the priest, the way the bucket of blood sat in the heat collecting flies. His light chuckles encourage me to greater embellishments. 'The priest raised both his arms dramatically to the sky once he was finished; spatters of blood dripped onto his face from the blade he was still holding. One would think he had just conquered a massive army of Gauls and not simply slit the throat of a near-unconscious horse. I could hear the players grunting, leaping and tackling each other for the tail that had quickly thinned to a few strands. There were small clumps of hair all over the inner field, like weeds.'

'They might as well have been chasing their own tails!' He laughs full-heartedly as I predicted. How comforting that is, to predict what another will say, not out of obligation, but out of simply knowing. I never knew what Tullia would say. 'There still isn't any news on Cataline. It's difficult, waiting this way. After this Republic falls, Rome will be a state governed not by superstition, the gods, or each man clamouring for more of everything, but by reason, rationality, pleasure. One where each individual is free from fear of the gods, free from envy, failure and desire that a life of competitiveness forces upon each man. Freedom from emotional commitments such as this relieves one of ever having to face loss in the future. Man will be in a constant state of fulfilment, of sated pleasure.' He is in one of his serious moods. His words float in one by one by one, like glowing fire-flies. He has filled to the brim with outrage and needs to pour a little out.

'Waiting is not for the weak!' I encourage him, complimenting myself. We are the only ones waiting; it sets us apart from the rest of the world.

'To fall asleep at night I imagine all the things I will do after-wards. Sometimes I imagine I run a school and can even see rows upon rows of men sitting cross-legged before me, hanging on my every word, so eager to shed the superstition of before. At other times I picture the Forum devoid of anyone at all, and I run through it, eating whatever I wish, putting on the most expensive shoes, draping myself in fine silks. I scream as loudly as I can and all that comes back is my own voice.'

Tonight begins our nightly dreams. With Lysander I play a variation of the game 'If I could, I would,' which I once played with Tullia so long ago. But this time, it is 'I want, I will.' With Lysander the temple becomes a cavern of dreams. No, not dreams – ambitions.

'I want to breathe fresh air for one full day.'

'I will write the most comprehensive poem on Epicureanism – in hexameter, of course.'

'I want to spend a day swimming up and down a brook under a hot sun.'

'I will make my own bread, slay my own animals. I will not have any slaves, and the only slaves in existence will be Romans convicted of crimes. I want to write that a race may only enslave their own race.'

'I want to have a vase of flowers, a mirror, a jewellery box, a brush, a tray of saffron, a line of white, yellow, red stolas, a shelf of books, anything to call my own, anything I could openly reach into, flip through, stroke, smell. Anything to make a room my own, different from the others', would be luxury. To be able to dress myself, brush myself, wash myself, braid my own hair, or even lock a door would be sheer opulence. Pleasure would be to speak loudly, openly, constantly. Pleasure would be to shake free of this stern face, loosen my cheeks, lick my lips.'

'I will drink real wine, not the vinegar they give us.'

300

'Afterwards, I want to wear hair my down, completely uncovered. Feel the wind blow through it. I want to feel aired out.'

'And when you do, I want to run my fingers through your hair . . .' His voice is hoarse and I suddenly feel his hand on my ankle, not moving upwards, not pulling or clasping, but just there. 'Why don't you ever sit?'

'I'm not supposed to. It is disrespectful to her,' I whisper and nod towards Vesta.

He looks up at me, his hair brushed back, his mouth curling up. 'I don't think she'll really mind. Here, let me ask her. "Do you mind if your priestess with the very pretty hair joins me for a moment in the very natural act of sitting?"' He cups his hand to his ear. 'She says it's permitted.' He nods to the side, a kind of beckoning dare. 'Sit. Your legs must be so tired . . . The fire won't tell. I guarantee it!'

I slide down the wall, eyes closed, onto the floor. I sit, legs spread out in a V. I sit in the temple of Vesta, another rule broken. We are sitting nearly back to back. He places his hand over mine, both our hands so dry, his calloused, and smiles. 'I think you have very pretty hair.'

'You haven't even seen my hair . . . *I* haven't even seen my hair!'

'No, but I know that when I do, I will think so.'

His hand is hot and slowly becomes damp and heavy, so it is all I feel – as if the rest of my body has disappeared apart from my hand under his.

After that night he leaves me more etchings in the garden. Sometimes in a tree there is the shape of a wine cup or a hairbrush, he once even arranged small rocks to look like a sun.

Constant reminders that we are on the brink of a transformation. Reminders that result in utter impatience, so much so that my hands twist together and I must pinch the skin between my thumb and forefinger – don't get so carried away.

I want to know if I am beginning to change, appear revolutionary, or if the anticipation of a revolution is detectable on my face. I want to quash any indications of my amity with Lysander, practise wiping them off my face. Fend off suspicion. But also, I want to know if I am pretty or not. I stole a dulled bread knife from the kitchen as we were baking the mola salsa cakes. Slid it up my sleeve – just like that. I polish the silver with my breath. I hide behind my door. It is almost closed. If for some reason the door should fly wide open, they will not see me sitting on my bed or chair vainly gazing at myself; instead they will knock into me and in the confusion and apologies I will stick the knife back up my sleeve.

My eyes are not too close together, but I wish they were blue. My skin is lacklustre, just as I expected. There is a faded freckle just above the dip on my top lip. My eyebrows are dark, too thick, but at least they are not joined in the middle.

I hear footsteps in the hall, not the soft smacking of bare feet, but the whispery sound of a Virgin's shoes. A shadow pauses in front of my door. I go very still, but I know the door will not fling open, not if it is one of the others, not if she is alone and I can hear no other sound. The shadow stays for a moment or two, then moves away. I peek through the slight crack of the door and see Julia about to descend the stairs, moving much too quickly for a Virgin. Did she see me take the knife? If she did she would have already told, there on the spot as I slipped it up my sleeve. So what was she doing here, outside my door? She must be looking for something.

I jump up, my legs so stiff I nearly tip back over. I dig the knife deep down in the potted plant. I tumble into the chair, history book in lap. I am a thief, but now I have a knife just like Lysander.

CHAPTER XLV

I take a stylus for Lysander from the will room when I have to deposit a new will. Surely this will bring him something extra, though it must be the last time I steal from there.

Earlier, as I took my bath, I overheard Fabia saying, 'How many wills have been deposited this month?'

'Only twenty,' Porcia replies.

'It seems odd to need to request more papyrus with only twenty depositions. I don't want Caesar to think we are frivolous or prone to making errors and needing to wastefully re-copy.'

'Maybe Claudia made some errors because of her hands.' Porcia sounds as if she is about to yawn.

Fabia doesn't answer, or at least I cannot hear her.

I must think of other things to take for him.

But now, as I hold the stylus in my hand, I feel the same rush of exhilaration that comes over me each time I take something. The rush seems to grow stronger and stronger with my small acts of rebellion.

I trace just above the letters in one of the history books in my room; I do not want to risk cutting the papyrus. I roll the stylus between my fingers, its slender agility tapering into a pointed tip, sharp and threatening. I feel the movement of the stylus between my fingers as I follow the hooks and dips of the letters, the compactness of words, the strangeness of sentences. I write and re-write history, over and over. I would include the stories that are absent from our texts, the love story between Dido, queen of Carthage, and Aeneas. She was Aeneas's dalliance, he was her infatuation. We watch it at the theatre, over and over. It is always the same: in the end Aeneas obediently follows the call of the gods, and Dido builds her own pyre. If only I could dip this stylus, push hard into the papyrus, maybe Dido would live, taking the life of Aeneas instead. Dido would not contemplate the swiftness of the sword over the cliff she stood upon, as she watched Aeneas sail away, his chest puffed out, sails billowing behind him, steadily sailing onward. Though I can only picture the milky blotch from the mural in the dining room. Or they could both die, by way of poison. Or Aeneas could drown at sea, blending easily into the white frothy waves; no one could save him once he'd fallen overboard, and a whole other kind of man, a man not born of a god, would find Rome. But what would he do? The same things likely. I cannot seem to grasp a Rome so very different from this one, not the way Lysander can.

I look round my room and think of where I can hide the stylus. Because of its cylindrical shape I am scared it will roll out from under my pillow, and evening is still too far off for me to guard it with my head. I wish I could close my door, explore my options, take my time, evaluate where the stylus would be least obvious. Close the door and sew it into my pillow, mattress, thigh. Where can I put it? Under the mattress? If they change my bed it could fall out. Behind the tapestry? If they come to clean it, beat it outside in the garden it will fly out onto the grass; they will stand over it, examining, understanding, call

Sempronia. A Virgin has no memoirs to write, so it must be letters, love letters. Get her. Maybe I could coil it up in my hair, a stiff braid. No. There is little texture in this room, no nooks or crannies or crevices. In the potted plant. I stick the stylus deep into the soil, burying it beside the dulled bread knife. Then decide to conceal one of the candlesticks from the bureau.

Before dinner Sempronia is taken ill again, falling in the chamber room. Three slaves have to carry her back to her room, her head swaying from side to side between her shoulders, headdress flopping, one leg dragging behind her.

Fabia announces that it is a new illness, not the one from before – that one was cured. Though she doesn't say so, she will again muster up a cure for Sempronia. Her hands play around her belly as if it is some kind of drum, rhythmically patting, whispering niceties, encouragements. If she could, she would wring herself out, squeezing out her middle as if it were a cloth, urging out just one spot of blood.

I rise before the chimes ring, rise but not wake, because I did not sleep. Sempronia's door is closed all the way – out of sight, out of mind. But the smell of her still wafts down the hall, an awful sour, acidic scent. Her coughs are airy now, hoarse, as if she's lost her voice, but it's the smell that keeps me up at night. Good Virgins have dulled senses; I am the only one who cannot sleep. I dress myself then slip the candlestick up my sleeve, dig up the stylus from the potted plant and slide it between my breasts and wait. The slaves are used to this now. They consider me eager, dutiful, an avid Virgin. One picks my headdress off its hook by my bed and pins it into my hair, tight, secure, as though it is an extension of my head, another layer of hair. Another of the slaves hands me a bowl of honey and some bread. I reach out, but she pulls it back. She is looking at my hand, my nails. There is mud under my nails, round my thumb, between two fingers. I wipe my hands together, dusting one with the other. I can't think of anything to say, so I just hold out my hands again until she gives me the bowl.

CHAPTER XLVI

Tonight it is Lysander's turn to escort. When I meet him at the door, and it has shut behind us, we begin a kind of dance, soundless other than the soft crunching our feet make on the pebbled pathway. What is really twelve steps, twenty-six for a Virgin, has become closer to thirty-two, perhaps more. Not that I am counting, not any more. He walks very close behind me. I can hear him breathing, or rather trying not to breathe at all, as if by doing so he will ruin this careful synchronicity. He matches each of my steps, his legs bend into the crooks of my legs like shadows as I step forward. The gentle flickering of the torch above us is our own personal sun. In this careful dance we merge, our legs fused as one.

When he returns from escorting Julia back to the house, and I hear the 'tssss' of the torch going out, I turn away from him, pull the stylus from my stola, the candlestick from my sleeve and push each towards him. 'Here.'

He picks up the stylus, then reaches for the candlestick, feeling its weight, rotating it, examining it. His face lights up with a wide smile. 'This alone will arm several men!' He shakes his head with disbelief. His hand reaches out and goes over mine and I expect him to shake it, a firm thank-you, but instead he suddenly pulls me, turning me towards him, his other hand on my cheek. Before I can stop him, before I can want to stop him, before my chastity arrests my inclination to tilt towards him, his lips brush against mine, dry lips but soft. I feel his beard prickle through my veil, as if each of his tiny infiltrating hairs is being held there, snagged. He smells of Vesta's fire.

He looks surprised, as if he hadn't meant to kiss me, but then he blinks and I realize it is incredulity. 'So much of you is so unexpected.' To be so described brings a kind of intrigue, and intrigue brings permissiveness. 'At first, I saw little other than your dress. At first I thought human beings, Romans especially, more easily sink towards depravity than rise to kindness. Though I suppose misunderstanding is the downfall of each of us. We misconstrue the gods, the world, one another . . . This is the bane of man.' His voice is measured, lush. 'We all must do what we must do; this I know you agree with.'

He comes towards me again, but this time chastity has overthrown inclination; chastity is strategic in this way. I turn away, and the kiss, more wet this time, lands on my cheek. 'Don't,' the single word, a chaste weapon that is both regret and spotlessness, tumbles out of my mouth like an arrow.

A piece of wood in Vesta snaps and I jump.

He clears his throat as if the kiss is now lodged there. 'It is just a fire . . .' He overly enunciates 'fire' with a kind of exhausted annoyance as he steps away and sits again on the first step.

I slip more kindling into Vesta, and slide down the wall behind him, touching my lips, cupping my hand over them as if capturing his kiss before it can fly away. Feeling is believing. Trust the senses.

'We are still waiting for the word from Cataline. He's assembled an army up north in Etruria and can call on them any time.'

Tullia once said it is the things left unsaid that can be both the best and the worst at the same time. 'Silence is linear, steady but not necessarily progressing.' But I am happy he wishes to carry on without discussion of my rebuff.

'Cataline wants to assassinate Cicero first, something to do with slander. You see, it is all personal; a man like Cataline can take a thousand lives to exact punishment on those he believes have slighted him. But for us, for slaves, it is the end not the means. Each night, I get the men riled up. We spar and wrestle, doing the exercises of gladiators and soldiers. Cataline better hurry, revolts are all about timing. You cannot heighten men's emotions only to deny them action.' He sounds a little more impatient, even bloodthirsty. For a moment I wonder if he is hinting at me. 'Some want to go straight for Caesar . . . others . . .' He looks at me very carefully.

'What is it?'

'Others want to go into the house and take the Virgins. I think they'd take great delight in that.'

I cannot say I had not considered this, but only the fringes of it. It is too unthinkable, too treacherous. Like Cupid, I imagined the others would simply disappear afterwards.

'When things begin to happen, I want you to go somewhere – hide and wait for me. I don't want anything to happen to you.'

'Where would I go? How could I get anywhere dressed like this? They'd likely rip me apart like rabid dogs. Please try to keep them from the house. It is not our fault we are emblems. Remind them we are just women.'

'Women on whom the greatest act of terrorism against Rome can be made.'

'Stop. I don't wish to know any more.'

'I want to protect you. I want you to meet me, to go somewhere safe and wait for me.'

'But where? And how?'

'Go down into the cellar, wait there. It may be a day or two, but by then I'll have a stola for you and can take you somewhere safe.'

An odd kind of panic sweeps over me. I stand up and gather some logs for Vesta. I watch her hungry flames gust up, ebb, then crawl all over the logs like ants. *The cellar is the end before the end.* My thoughts are jumbled, they slip and bounce and I can't grasp them, just as if I am out of breath. I hear myself panting raggedly. 'No, not there. Somewhere else.' *Not there.*

'The storehouse? It's still close enough. Are you not well? You sound ill.'

I think of how I could hide behind a statue. Yes, the storehouse. 'That's fine.'

'Just so you know, once I am finished my escorting duty, I won't be here for the next two nights; I need to sneak off to buy more knives.'

'I have a knife too,' I tell him. I expect him to laugh, to tease me but still be impressed: 'You, a Virgin warrior?' Lighten the mood. But instead he answers very sombrely, 'Good. Very good. Take it with you to the storehouse.'

We sit for a while in complete silence. Soaking in the things left unsaid.

★

After Lysander returns to the house and the sun rises, the remaining heat of the summer night mingles with the heat of Vesta; it's like eating spoonfuls of sand or dust, anything dry and flaky. The heat shrivels my insides, grills my lungs, red to brown, half cooked, as ash settles and sticks like flour on a raw egg or a raw egg sticks to oats. I am thirsty, but there is no water in here other than the purified water that Vesta drinks as we sprinkle it round her hearth, wash her floor, that only Minerva sips at as we sponge her off. I decide that Minerva looks especially smug today, pitying me, a mere worshipper, mortal, thirsty and pathetic. Up heaves a puff of smoke into my mouth, a sandstorm, a clump of feathers, a bundle of wool. I could drink the bathwater of thirty men right now, suck beads of oil and water right off their backs. Water. Cold water. I can feel it rushing round my arms and legs, swimming in it with an open mouth, cool and wet. Rinsing off my insides, damp and red again. I am dipping down to the bottom of a clear green river, ash floating out from under my headdress, out from my parched pores, and settling on a nearby shore. I look over at the jugs and find clean cold water suddenly cupped in my hands. Tullia told me that time begins to slip by like water through outstretched fingers and haunts you into finding another way to get hold of it. I cup the water tightly.

The purified water tastes the same; I expected something crisper, more fulfilling. I fill up my cupped hands again, drinking faster before it spills. And again. And again. The jug is nearly empty. I wait for something to strike me down, for Vesta to crawl out of her hearth, fiery fang nipping at my neck, or for Minerva to lash out, her leg striking me in the mouth. I wait. But Minerva is again impartial and Vesta still burns.

For the first time I do not pray as I offer kindling, wash the floor, sponge Minerva.

For the first time, I feel like a traitor.

CHAPTER XLVII

It is a silent ceremony for Angerone, the goddess of secrecy and keeper of the name and location of Rome from enemies. She heals the pain and sorrow of secrets; those who come here to make reparation are cured of painful swollen throats that often follow the utterance of that which should be withheld. She is kept in the temple of Volupia, goddess of pleasure, so as not to be easily discovered. Though there seems something more convenient in this.

Angerone is painted in dark hues, shrouded with the vines that grow up and round her, so she would be barely discernible from the dim temple walls if it were not for the bandaged mouth with a white finger to her lip.

There is something calming here, but maybe it is just the quiet.

In her honour, we tie the snouts of three dogs while they are held down by the temple's attendants, sealing them up with rope. They've been trained for the last year by the attendants to stay quiet while their snouts are bound. Their onyx eyes are suffused with the slight sliver of light that sneaks into the temple. I think of the dog that was mine for a day.

Caesar moves and stabs under their chins, where sound comes, twisting so that the dogs die with a muted gurgle. Their

314

eyes turn to soft sponges. A ram will also be sacrificed in her honour, though this will be at the arena, to kick off the games.

Though Lysander would have scoffed, I took a small brown feather from the garden before we left, and as we entered the temple, I dropped it. My offering. Surely the goddess of secrets can appreciate such discretion. *Make my secret light as a feather; keep my secret away from the others.*

As we step down from the temple Fabia has cornered Caesar. 'She's doing better. She claims I have had a profound effect on improving her health . . .'

She is trying to say this with modesty but is failing miserably; there is too much inflection in her voice.

Lysander stands stiffly at the rear of the litter, but I can tell he's been whispering with the other slaves because as soon as they notice us, they quickly look away. All the way here, whenever I peeked through the tear in the curtain, Lysander would wink or stick out his tongue, pretending to pant with exertion from the weight of us, and I'd nearly laugh, my veil lifting up with the soft puff of air from the corner of my mouth.

Lysander and I stare at one another, neither of our faces moving, as we wait for Fabia to finish speaking to Caesar. I wish I could go ahead into the litter, wink back at him through the curtain, but then good Virgins move together, like waves.

On the way back, I keep my eyes on him as he carries me, his arms, his shoulders, the vein in his neck, and feel so completely sure of him.

'What's so interesting out there?' Julia leans over. 'Oh, there's a tear in the curtain.' She says this with excited surprise, her face falling the moment the words crossed the threshold of her lips.

She's given the tear away. She could have enjoyed it on another day. But then she catches sight of Lysander, who was about to stick out his tongue again. He jerks his head away quickly, which looks even more obvious; he should be looking straight ahead, or down at his feet, at least looking where he is going. Julia glances at him, then back at me, him, me, her round lips gather pensively. She must know. Dread hooks itself into me like a tapeworm slithering through my abdomen, tapering my throat. I think I am going to be ill.

'Sit over there. That will be mended.' Fabia wags her hand for us to move over.

For a moment Julia doesn't respond, as if preoccupied, in a state of dreaminess. She slides over. I stay by the litter's opening, counting, counting nothing, just counting, waiting for her to spew out her suspicion that I had eye contact with Lysander. Lustful glances, she will call them, dress it up, maybe hold up my arms in an attempt to reveal circles of sweat or point out the pinkish pigment in my cheeks. I imagine my cheeks are pink. I feel hot, suddenly very hot.

I wait.

'Over.' Fabia waves at me again. I move over, closer to Julia. My thigh accidentally brushes against hers. I expect her to jump with repulsion, but she stays still. Apparently oblivious.

Maybe she didn't notice after all. She would say so now, if she did. She wouldn't hold back. She couldn't. She would tell Fabia immediately, revelling in my disgrace. Also, if she suspects and says nothing, she is an accessory, she must speak up now or not at all. I count the creases in the curtain. I count the inhalations and exhalations of Julia's breathing, waiting for it to hitch and deliver the allegations.

We are nearing the house.

Slowly the tightening of fear eases, my stomach unfolds. Maybe my offering to Angerone was heard.

Now I can see only the eclipsed version of Lysander's face through the curtain, as if he has lain down, face first, an impression in violet sand.

CHAPTER XLVIII

Tullia had a lover, that much is true. Who it was, I never knew. It became a sort of game. Sitting at a banquet, theatre, in the stands at the track, I would try to guess. Could it be him over there, with the receding hair? Perhaps he was a merchant who must pass by the temple to get to his shop, or a landlord on his way to collect overdue rent. Maybe he had a wife and caught sight of Tullia as his wife paid her womanly dues, tossing Vesta his hard-earned silver and gold. Nothing is worse than a woman ignored – Vesta, not his wife. Tullia unabashedly lured him, by staring at him over his kneeling wife. She smiled, exuding, like a squirting squid, whatever it is women exude. I know no such word. He met her stare, ensnared. Men are known for wanting what is rare, unavailable, hard to get. He came back later, stuck his nose in, but she was no longer there. It was Porcia or Fabia, their hands fluttered up to their faces like drunken butterflies, flushed, cocooning their heads with their veils, lime worms once more, safe. Not at all dissuaded, he returned the next night. Men are known to be persistent. This time she was there, the one who tiptoed up his toga, up the inside of his leg. He spoke to her and Tullia, lonely as she was, dissolved into each of his words. He asked simple questions: which plays she had seen, what food she preferred, fish or chicken. Clammy whispers through the temple door. When she spoke he felt her on him, down, kneading, his hands became hers. It was always dark when he visited; he stood on the side of the steps so he was sure no slave belonging to her house could see him. She was sure too. They talked, but steered clear of her position. They pretended she was other than she was. And for a little while she forgot – just an everyday mistress, flattered and flattering. When he ran out of safe questions all that was left was to ask her how it was to be her. So he stopped coming and crouching by the temple's steps.

Then she met the politician; he stood next to her during the festival of Mercury, a little too close, he brushed against her briefly once, twice, nothing to notice. Then he did it again, during the festival of Mars, five or six times, and she noticed. He pulled some strings, as powerful as he was, and arranged some time alone with her. He took her and she let him, in that confused, curious way women are known to be taken. She thought she loved him. But he didn't come back for her. He did what no other man has ever done. He wished he could tell someone, wear it as a badge, but knew that if anything should happen, if Rome were to be threatened, he would be to blame, as would she. He didn't want to be publicly flogged. A traitor. He didn't think of her consequences. Men are known to be more concerned with their own affairs; it is just their way.

Then lastly entered the freedman. He had bought his freedom some time ago, but had nowhere else to go. So he stayed on with his master, working for a salary of appreciation, which he paid to his master. Freedmen are known to feel indebted long after manumission. Gratitude and servitude are the freedman's diet. How they met only they could tell – mischance, likely. It didn't matter how they met, because it was how he bid her 'until later' that Tullia swooned over. He tipped his freedman's felt hat, in the awkward way a hat shaped like half an egg is tipped, showing off his freedom, a slave no more. He was taken by Tullia, not the other way around. He wove her a love that she could wear, a balmy robe, invisible but textured. He was a resilient man, the type who could scrimp and save tips and gifts over many years so he could one day buy his own emancipation. He carved her wooden gifts, a horse, a swan, a tiny house, and left them under a bush by the temple's entrance. She would scoop them up quickly, a cat's claw through a cricket. Enjoyed them until noon neared and she had to leave, tossing them into Vesta. Excited about what she would find tomorrow, maybe a miniature chariot. Once one looks forward to the next day, one never wants it any other way. She found places they could meet. She told me where, inadvertently. 'Did you know there's a cellar out in the garden? Its door is just by those berry bushes at the back,' or 'The storehouse is so strange at night,' or 'I never thought my dowry would ever come in handy . . . A slave's friendliness comes rather cheap.' Clandestine meetings – the kind senators have in one place while their sons conspire in another – where plans were made, promises proclaimed, where an after now bit into Tullia so severely she could never be fixed. An inundated dam, fallen and so submerged that one would never know there was a dam to begin with. Each of Tullia's days, months, years became lily pads leading to the after now.

Tullia had a lover, that much is true. Who it was, I never knew.

CHAPTER XLIX

The night is long and dull with Lysander away. I think of his kiss, and the way his hard chest felt against my hand as I pushed him back, so hard I'd think it hollow if not for the beating of his heart. I can still almost feel its vibrations against my palm, and this makes me momentarily sad – that our hearts beat in spite of us, carrying on in the shadowed recesses of our chests, ignorant of our lives.

I watch a black spider weave a web in Minerva's armpit. Up and round, her thin furry legs move quickly, deftly. I decide the spider is a she because she weaves rather than mending or altering as a tailor does. The light of Vesta glistens against the web. She works through the night, climbing down Minerva's side, climbing up her thread, spreading her net, fastening it like a canopy. A good woman settles in swiftly, making a home any place, anywhere. She is inexhaustible, ignoring the dense smoke, the ash getting caught in her web; she simply plods forward, dutifully, weaving artistically on. Diligent. A Roman spider. The intricate detail of the web is breathtaking, admirable, a sticky tapestry. This is what an enlarged snowflake would look like, one that wouldn't melt. Up and round, twirling, scaling, looping, entwining, but all this work of hers will be fruitless; she will starve.

I pluck the spider off her web, cup her in my hand and watch as she crawls up and over my middle finger. I accidentally drop her to the ground, then pluck her up again and walk to the temple door.

If I am fast enough the slave will not see, will not report I tried to leave the temple on the sly. I reach up and place the spider under the eave over the temple entrance, in the darkest crevice; there she can weave unseen. But as I turn I trip. My ankle twists, gives out. I fall, scraping my knee against the steps. I get up, nearly diving back into the temple. Scrambling to the other side, away from the door. I am nearly winded; I've never moved so fast before. I wait. If the slave saw, he will come over to check on me. Please be asleep as Lysander claims. What would I say? I'll tell him he's imagining things, deny it, put him in his place and send him on his way. I could tell him I was tossing out a snake. But a snake in Vesta's temple while I am tending? I wouldn't risk that. I wait and add kindling to Vesta; if he comes at least I look dutiful. I wait. Blood trickles down my calf. I wait. I pull at the web, taking it down, cleaning Minerva. I wait. I sprinkle some of the purifying water on the floor of the temple. I wait. He doesn't come. I am safe. I got away with it.

I bring the jug up to my lips and sip the purified water. Pull my stola up past my knee – what a strange knee, a dimpled knee, an upside-down bowl covered with skin, a rolling hill, dry, red. A strange knee atop a strange leg, white, fleshy, little muscle with webs of red veins up my inner thigh. I pour the water onto my knee and wipe away the blood with my hands. Then I clean my hands. For the rest of my night with Vesta, I check over and over and over for traces of blood and find none.

322

Good Virgins do not bleed from the wrong places or at the wrong times.

When I return to the house and make my way up the stairs to my room, I overhear Fabia insisting Sempronia get out of bed. I can hear her ordering the slaves to lift her up into a chair as Sempronia moans in gulps and bubbles. I hear a thump. 'Never mind then, just never mind.' Fabia closes the door and walks down the hallway, nearly bumping into me.

As I pass Sempronia's room, I peer in. It's as if she is melting, a white face sinking into the bed. A white face that appears detached from a body; her body seems to have flattened under the heap of blankets. Her hacks have grown even more persistent at night; I do not sleep at all any more. Her white eyelids flicker, squint shut, closed for business. Sempronia is dying.

After my midday meal, I sit in the hot room, close to the pool. Tired. The humidity sticks to my ribs, working up enough sweat so the strigil will simply glide over my skin. Steam teases one to submit to sleep – steamed dreams. I struggle to keep my eyes open. When the slave steps forward, I watch the strigil chip away oil and sweat, up my arms, stopping at the half sleeves of the under-dress, down my legs, a careful rhythmic scraping. A second skin shed. Separating cream from milk. Slice from loaf. Hide from hair. Meat from bone. Around my shoulders, down to my wrists. Around my feet, up under my under-dress to my thighs. Against the scab forming on my knee. She feels it on her hands, blood. I try to wave her way, but instead accidentally pull up my under-dress. Haste hinders prudence. Haste draws attention. A skinned knee can mean a lover.

'Look what you've done!' My voice is cruel, accusing. She

tilts her head down submissively and recedes out of the hot room. I sit for a moment sinking in the steam, thinking I shouldn't have scolded her. What does a skinned knee matter now? The Republic will fall before it's even healed.

CHAPTER L

'Veturia is finished, Veturia is finished,' I hear Claudia squeal through the hall. The carver has left the garden for the last time. I put down the history book I wasn't reading and go into the hall. I think again of ripping some of the papyrus from between the wooden panels of the book to give to Lysander. I could claim it to be a wormhole, act dismayed when I mention it to the others, and in only a day or two, the pages would be replaced, but slightly adjusted, brushed up by whoever the Pontifex Maximus has write them. Maybe in a newer version Aeneas will prophesize Caesar's birth.

I go out onto the portico, excited to see finally what the carver has done. I envision Veturia now to be an object of the carver's affection and imagine that he has put this into her body and face. It will reflect in a fine life-like quality.

Claudia leans forward eagerly on a stool. It is late afternoon; the sky is clear and the air is crisp, but not cold. I look for Lysander and find him standing near the tent, which is still up with Veturia still inside. His hair is damp or dirty, I cannot tell.

'We must wait for Caesar to make a proper induction ceremony.' Fabia tells this to Julia as they both come out from the kitchen. We all sit together on the portico and wait for Caesar.

A peacock lands close by, his tail feathers displayed, and obnoxiously screams his odd call. Though she shouldn't, Claudia giggles, but Fabia does not reprimand her for this. For them it is Juno's bird, a sign of the gods' acceptance of Veturia; already I feel more separate. There is an air of quiet giddiness now, between them and me. I am content to be able to watch Lysander, who is no longer standing by the tent but working on some part of the winch. He should wash his hair, maybe I could sneak out some sage to wash it with, though there is no point to washing before the revolt. I will try to keep some in my room, for after.

A slave eventually beckons us for dinner, but Fabia waves her away as if we are waiting for a dinner guest to arrive.

Julia gets up and readies herself for the temple, and a short while later Porcia joins us. The evening has waned into night. Braziers have been lit and the garden looks a whole other place. The steps of the portico now lead into a boundless dark forest and not the secluded islet of the day. The tent itself seems a blackened molar, pushing out of green mossy gums stretched below the tongue of the trees and bush. I can no longer see Lysander. Caesar finally sends word that he will come at dawn instead. He need not explain himself. Surprisingly, I feel disappointed; I will be at the temple when Veturia is revealed. Maybe I am not as separate from them as I would like to think after all.

We each go up to our rooms without dinner. Though as I pass the dinning hall, I see the table is filled with what was meant to be our dinner – pheasant, beans, eggs, bread, fruit sauce, pastry – all left untouched. I wish I hadn't seen it, it will be all I will think of if I go hungry in the new Rome.

I hope the slaves eat it once we are asleep.

*

326

In the morning the others come in and light a tray full of candles, each offering slices of the whitest bread to Vesta, beseeching her consecration of Veturia. They circle around Vesta one by one, adding the bread, mumbling frantically. The temple smells like toast.

When I return and am about to go upstairs to my room, I see Lysander is helping pull the statue into place by the pool. I stumble, stunned. I never considered how the statue would be placed inside; nothing would get done without pulleys and slaves.

I wish I could show him my room, the room I stay in, or where I eat, what I must read, how I deposit a will, where I take the papyrus from, where Tullia once slept. There is so much I suddenly wish to share with him. The others are absent from the central atrium. I would have expected Fabia to be directing the slaves herself, but no, they are likely out on the portico again. Self-imposed exiles until the male slaves leave. Which means I should also go to the portico, and act equally distressed.

Lysander sees me and nods; a wide smile comes over his lips. The statue lightly knocks him in the shoulder. I can tell he could laugh but doesn't, instead he takes the rope and continues to ease the statue into place.

I look up at Veturia's final image – what little say she has had in it. The sun falls directly against the statue and catches on it as if it is adorned with pearl dewdrops. She looks as if she is flying. Her face is paler than the faces of the other statues, her mouth curved down in a slightly anxious expression just like Rhea. Her chin is pointed in the same crest, her cheeks sag into the same pucker that frames Rhea's chin. She is just like Rhea – that is who Fabia described to the carver. The only difference is that her eyes are very dark and her body is short limbed like a child's. But the torso is of a woman, and something else. There is some-one else in her face. As the statue turns slightly on the ropes, I see it, a glimmer of Fabia; she could be Fabia's sister, daughter even, if Rhea was the father. Though unlike Rhea, her arms are folded tightly at her stomach. Unwanting.

When I enter the portico there is a tense quiet, Fabia is sitting closest to the steps overlooking the garden with her back to Porcia and Julia. Sempronia sleeps against the wall.

Porcia and Julia glare at Fabia's purple back, so much so that Fabia must be ignoring them not to feel it. A statue has been twice taken from them. Not just a statue, not just the chance to have one, but the reliance that those who come after can be entrusted to let praise be paid where praise is due.

Who are the statues in the central atrium now? Are they each the faces of those who turned on their predecessors at the last minute? Why not take a little piece of glory while it's still being served up hot? Can't enjoy it once you're dead. Can't let the flaky softness of pastry melt in your mouth when you have none. We feed on, off one another, at any opportunity.

CHAPTER LI

It seems so odd, knowing that there is a conspiracy fermenting, a revolt brewing just below the surface of routine. During the day, life goes on as usual. The day is now something I must get through, like wading across a rushing river, feeling buoyant yet weighted by its force. Moving slowly, careful not to trip, to slip under as the other side beckons.

Lysander came to the temple last night, on his way back from buying more knives. He bought nine more. He had a thin leather satchel thrown over one shoulder and the shape of each knife protruded, some making small tears along the bottom.

'Be careful, you might lose some,' I warned him, but he was too excited to listen. The vein in the centre of his forehead swelled, as if it were a throbbing border between his two bright eyes, leading into his nose, separating his two bright cheeks and down to his hurried mouth.

'It's just another week or two at the most. It's just about to happen. Cataline was taking his time, until he felt all his military arrangements were secured. But the senate have found out about his plot and have pressured him to leave Rome to live in destitution. It is said that just before Cataline left the meeting, he told the senate, "I see two bodies, one thin and wasted, but with a head, the other headless but big and strong. What is so dreadful if I myself become the head of the body that needs one?" What brilliant defiance. What they don't know is he is really on his way to Etruria to his military camp. He left last night with three hundred more armed men and he's left a man named Lentulus to continue with plans here. Ah, I will not sleep tonight! I am so glad the waiting is over!' He sighed, a happy sigh. 'I had better go and bury these knives while it's still dark.' He went to step down, but then turned back. 'Soon the only fire you'll watch is while you cook for me!' I could hear his mischievous laughter before it dissolved into the night.

I've taken to looking out of the windows in the chamber room by turning one of the pots over and standing on it on the tips of my toes. I watch for Lysander in the garden, watch for any sign the Cataline revolt is getting under way – for some kind of knowing nod between slaves or a secret handshake, some exchange of codes or hand signals – but I see nothing of the sort today. If I do see Lysander he is usually silently labouring along with the others, each appearing to have fully submitted themselves to such drudgery.

One would think things would appear different, that there'd be some kind of ominous music carried on the winds, that black birds would be pecking at the temple, that patricians would seem more downtrodden, weathered and rough, that peasants and slaves would have some spry in their step as they pass by the temple in the morning. But the conversations of passers-by are the same. I listen intently for some hint or suggestion that others are in on it as well, but overhear nothing of the sort. I suppose this is the nature of conspiracy: it creeps about on padded feet like a stalking cat ready to pounce. Though sometimes, I feel a kind of guilty sympathy when I listen to those passing by, that the order they know will soon change into sudden upheaval. I feel a slight urge to at least warn and soothe them with what will come after, though I am not sure what that will be. I am too stricken with a black, blurred image of what Rome will be like, as if it will sink into a black sea or be reduced to a giant blank tablet, and I cannot even imagine what will be written upon it next. I try only to think that Rome will be somehow better off, just as Lysander and I will be.

This is what I must think of now, the possibilities.

I have only a few moments of this, of peering, before a slave will ask if all is well. When I am finished, I take a sponge, rinse it in the pot, then squeeze it out into one of the chamber pots. I am getting clever in this way.

When I leave the chamber room, I walk around the house looking for things to steal. I go into the kitchen, only the blonde slave is there, and I ask her to serve me some figs. When she turns, I take her lyre, which is leaning against the wall under the table, and slip out to the garden. I drop it quickly by the willow tree then kick it under the drooping branches. My ears burn, my underarms are damp, the exhilarating rush pounds against my head into the pulse in my neck. I'll tell Lysander about it tonight. Though he's told me there will be plenty of money afterwards, with all the sacking and looting, maybe we can use it to keep denarii aside for ourselves, just in case looting proves too time-consuming. What does it matter now, if we have a lyre to listen to or not? We will soon be dining elsewhere.

CHAPTER LII

Over dinner I realize I can't keep up with the others any more. They sound muffled and distant, like wind hissing through a shut window. I am a piece of driftwood sticking out in the middle of a rushing river. I pick at the sliced eggs and hot chick-peas, look up and nod when I notice a pause. I also tilt my head and squint my eyes, which makes me appear interested. But I am not interested.

Earlier we attended the feast of Fontonalia in honour of Fons, the god of springs and fountains. We decorated a drinking foun-tain in the Forum with garlands and later placed more garland round the sacred well in the garden. As we prayed, I saw Lysander. He stayed close to the ground on his belly behind a bush, but I could see him smirking as we struggled to fasten the garland. Fabia pulled it from Porcia's hands when Porcia let some slip down the well. Porcia blamed it on me. 'She is not watching what she is doing; she is supposed to attach the excess under here.' Her poached-egg eyes wobbled back and forth from my hand to the garland to the well.

But I wasn't watching the garland or the well – I was watch-ing Lysander slithering for a better look through the entrance and nearly laughing. The pruning scissors in his hand stuck up out of the grass, parted wide open like splayed, straight legs.

'Oh, Aemilia, you have ruined the ceremony. Pull off the garland. Yes, all of it! Coil it all up and come back out through the door. All of it. Do not let it touch the ground, Porcia!' Fabia flustered about, her stubby arms shooing us all away. We backed out from the well, took our positions again, single file, each of us gripping the garland as if it were a squirming snake or a writhing eel.

A surge of embarrassment stiffened my hands and cheeks, and I went very still hoping he couldn't see me.

They discuss the upcoming September games to be held in honour of Jupiter Optimus Maximus, and the games to be held in honour of Juno and Minerva. And then, when that is exhausted, they discuss food and baking and exchange complaints about slaves who do not wash our stolas properly. Julia whines, 'They tell me they dyed my stola, but look at it! One can easily see it is still faded.'

We hum in agreement; the incompetence of slaves is something we can all agree on and is the one thing that connects us in a way that resembles a friendship. There is a long silence.

A pine cone has rolled off the table centrepiece, which was only a tray of pine cones arranged in a sloping molehill. I reach over and replace it. 'A competent slave would have noticed this first!' I must say something.

More hums of agreement.

Fabia sniffs at the air. 'I enjoy the scent of pine cones.'

More hums of agreement.

'The Bona Dea is just around the corner,' Claudia exclaims as if it were a surprise.

When another silent lull takes over, Fabia beckons the blonde slave forward to play the lyre, but the slave shakes her head. Her golden hair ripples over her shoulders.

'What do you mean? You don't wish to play the lyre?' Fabia looks at us, incensed, and on cue we are incensed with her.

'No lyre.' She waves her hands in front of her, palms up, empty-handed. Her Latin is weak and broken. 'It is go away. Gone.'

'What do you mean gone? Does that mean you lost it?'

'Yes, lost. It is lost!' The blonde slave agrees, nodding her head at the word she forgot, not understanding she is really agreeing to her foolish irresponsibility.

'Now I have to add a lyre to the month's inventory? Caesar will think we are feasting and dancing here. This is intolerable! If it were her own property do you think she'd lose it? No. Slaves are so careless!' Fabia shakes her head, and I notice we each shake our heads with her, snapping our tongues. 'Unbelievable! Take her out to the garden.'

Another slave, who is short with dark frizzy hair, takes the blonde one by the arm and leads her away. When we are finished eating, we sit on the bench in the portico. The dark and blonde slaves are whispering in their odd language. The blonde's hands are waving in protest.

'Twelve lashes.' Fabia nods at the dark slave, who goes back into the kitchen and collects the long leather whip. She pulls the blonde's tunic down to her waist, her skin prickles in the cool air. Her back is pink and spotless. Her breasts are small and round with pointed nipples. They stretch out over her gasping ribcage when her hands are strung up to a hanging branch.

'Three on the front.' Fabia smiles at us hungrily. Claudia laughs.

334

I watch the feet of the dark-haired slave, her long, yellowed toenails arching up and down as she leans back then forth. I feel sick as the whip flashes against the blonde's back, cutting into skin that was once smooth as sanded pine, and then flays her two breasts into four.

The grass at the dark-haired slave's feet is red. How much more yellowed her toes look against the red. I count her toes, back and forth.

I see Lysander watching with some of the other male slaves, some of whom look pleased at the sight of the half-naked woman, regardless of the blood and gore – or maybe because of it, I cannot tell. But Lysander's mouth is turned down with outrage. Perhaps I won't tell him about the lyre after all.

I meant to give her the lyre back. When it was all over, I wanted her to have it. I thought she could sell it and get enough money to find her way back to wherever she came from. I wanted to tell her it wasn't my intention she be punished in that way, and to offer her the lyre as a small token of my deepest apologies.

But then good intentions pave the way to the bleakest grottos of the Underworld.

For a moment I wonder about the Underworld, what it looks like if it does exist. Will I be admitted into the sacred areas, into the Elysian Field, where the gentle breeze always blows? I was one of the privileged few here. Why not there? Would there be unending gardens? Maybe even a Forum to shop in? Would I see my parents? Surely they could still recognize me, though I look so different now; they'll know by my eyes that I am their daughter. We will all sit together on plush green softness, the sleepy breeze caressing our faces, and they will ask that I fill them in on all they've missed of my life. They will not accept any abbreviations, but only full, drawn-out details, and we'll find that we have been sitting there for ever.

I try not to think of other parts of the Underworld: the mirthless, dark, dank caves that sweep across the landscape, each its own room of misery. The sound of incessant barking dogs mingled with the pained cries of men, even women. The kind of places a fallen Virgin may find herself in. Just like this tomb, but the everlasting version, with a horrific howling ambiance. At least I'd have something to listen to, know I wasn't alone; misery loves company. No, I think only of my easy existence on the sprawling verdant field and of seeing my parents once again.

The oil in the lamp is draining through its flame. He will come, Tullia will come, but just in case I take my golden rope, wrap one end round a wooden column – side by side the Virgins die – and twist the other end into a noose. I will not have this option once it is dark. Just in case.

PART III

What we wish, we readily believe, and what we
ourselves think, we imagine others think also.

Caesar

CHAPTER LIII

Sempronia died early this first October morning. Claudia came to the temple to tell me, her eyes twinkling with excitement over the commotion, over change.

The house is already surrounded by branches of cypress to contain the pollution of death and announce that death has occurred, warning passers-by to maintain a greater distance. Death is a transmittable blemish. Large baskets of branches are still by the house doors. I see the tall Gaul grab a branch and toss it in front of the steps as I turn the knob. I can also see Lysander, just off to the side, and the other male slaves encircling the house with another layer of cypress. Last night he told me it is just a matter of days now, any day really. It is better Sempronia died today, before the only Rome she's ever known changed.

Sempronia's door is wide open. Fabia and Porcia are directing the slaves to bring more candles, though the room is bright; death, like mould, prefers shadowy places, the light ushers it out. If there were windows in our rooms, one could be opened and death smoked out with oil lamps. Though, it is argued, here windows are not necessary, even for death, as a Virgin's spirit is so used to smoke it would have little effect.

The room is horribly stuffy, and there is a veneer of dust on the bureau. Sempronia's room is exactly the same as mine, though the tapestry of Minerva that hangs over her bureau is woven in blue and brown hues. Her bed is also slightly wider and there is an extra chair, I suppose to give the appearance of achievement.

Three slaves have just finished dressing her and now hold a bier close to her bed, while another three try to lift her onto it. Sempronia's stola comes up slightly, exposing a white calf, like plucked chicken skin, deep blue veins scattered just below the surface, colliding and bubbling upward. Her toenails are thick and yellowed, bird's claws. Her head lolls back and forth, her mouth slightly open, her eyes, only half closed, no longer milky but red smouldering pieces of charcoal peering straight upwards. The slaves begin to tie her to the bier; the flesh in her middle under her stola bulges up in wide ripples. It's the straightest her back has ever been. I half expect to hear it crack or even shatter, to see a cloud of dust to puff out from behind her. One of her hands falls loose, a crippled crab, a slave holds it down and secures it more tightly under the rope.

Fabia and Porcia murmur to one another animatedly, their veils tight across their mouths in the hope of siphoning death from the air they breath. It does smell like death. I can feel it pass up my nostrils, down the back of my throat – a bitter rot. They slip her white shoes on, the outline of her long toenails like a sloping fence.

'Aemilia?' Fabia turns towards me, her nose twitching under her veil in tiny quakes. Though she is not a healer at least she is now Vestalis Virgo Maxima. There is still time to make a new

342

myth up about herself – this I am sure she is calculating, sniffing out. 'Aid Julia in washing the black beans with the purified water in the kitchen. And heat some wax for the mask.'

As I enter the kitchen, Julia is bent over a bowl of beans, scooping up small handfuls to scrub in another bowl of purified water. We will later, after the funeral, walk round the house and spit these beans out in order to purify it of the death that came for Sempronia; they will sate death's appetite.

'I can help.' I move beside her. She looks up.

'Please heat the wax then.' She motions to the bucket of wax by the latrine. I think of the kiss we shared, wonder if she still believes it was my fault. If the truth of it ever comes to her in dreams, and if she finds herself enjoying it there because it happens behind closed eyes where no one will know.

I take a block of wax and heat it into a runny mess; some gets stuck between my fingers, like stringy webs. I take it back up to Sempronia's room in a small bowl and watch as Fabia covers Sempronia's face with it, smoothing the wax over her nose, under her eyes, over her lips. We each offer small hushed prayers, urging her spirit to leave now, accept and go gently without disturbing the living. A melting face upon a melted face. Once it's dried, Fabia peels off the mask. Sempronia's sagging skin sticks and lifts far off her face as if it is the congealed top layer of broth.

Fabia holds the mask to her face, breathes deeply so as to inhale any remnants of Sempronia's last breath, and declares three times, 'Unto me, is thy Virgo Vestalis Virginity.' As she moves the mask away from her face, her eyes are closed, her head sways slightly back and forth as if she has drunk too much wine. She is now officially head Vestal Virgin.

Chimes ring. Caesar has arrived to carry out the funerary procession. We open the door; outside are a group of lute players, purification dancers and a small boy in a mock stola. The bier is carried down the stairs. Sempronia's head accidentally hits the wall on the last step when the slaves try to take the corner too sharply; we pretend not to notice. They adjust her headdress and bring her body to the front step, and give the bier to the undertakers, who position themselves so they can hold it in an upright position – good Virgins are never seen on their backs, even in death.

Fabia hands the wax mask to Caesar and falls to her knees. He takes the mask from her in symbolic acceptance of her promotion to head Vestal. She rises again. Caesar then places the mask on the small boy in the stola; he will act as Sempronia's descendant for the day so her spirit can be fooled into believing it has immortality on earth and not be tempted to continue to walk among the living.

The bier is carried with a cluster of lictors preceding it, three hired mourning women behind it, their cheeks slick with tears, wailing, howling, so aptly, one would think they truly knew and loved Sempronia. The little boy is close behind them, the stola is too loose, falling off one of his slender shoulders.

Caesar leads us, his long toga edged with purple sweeping up dried leaves, a burr or two, like a wake trailing a ship. We follow him in single file and behind us are the lute players and dancers, purifying our steps, like sweeping away mud from one's shoes when walking on a clean floor. We walk slowly to the Forum, to the speaker's platform where each Virgin was selected as a young girl.

The bier is stood up close to the podium. Caesar offers a

short, modest eulogy, fit for a Virgin. 'Here is a Vestal Virgin, praiseworthy in her chasteness, honourable in her duty, adept at tending Vesta. A Vestal Virgin who lived long enough to offer all of herself to Vesta and continued to serve until death. One who is worthy of easy and swift entrance to the Underworld. Carer of Vesta, go gently into the Underworld, with the dutifulness and ease you tended our goddess Vesta in life.'

He rubs his forefingers into his temples and slides his palms down his cheeks, pulling his face into an odd momentary droop. A Virgin dying in his first year as Pontifex Maximus does not look good for him. He must be thinking up ways to explain himself.

The wailers begin again, one very thin, two broader. Their mouths are open and black like gouged eyes, empty sockets.

A small group of onlookers have gathered, but most have slunk away. A Virgin is disquieting while alive, unnerving in death. Funerals for Virgins are rushed affairs; if this were a senator, his funeral would be elaborately planned. His body would lie here in the open while his family sat on ivory chairs, his death mourned by the people for nine days, then he'd be carried out of the city, taking the longest route possible, all along main streets, to be seen and honoured. There would be games held in his honour, put on by his son or nephew or brother. The whole ordeal would last nearly forty days. But Virgins die quietly, quickly, so as not to draw attention that Rome is left without the power of six. There will be thirty days of symbolic mourning until a new Virgin is selected; the wailers will stand at the door on each of these days as the sun falls so as to steer away Sempronia's spirit if she believes she is still alive and tries to return to the house.

345

We continue our procession to the outskirts of Rome, where a pyre is already waiting. The undertakers hitch up the bier and Sempronia is cremated. I watch her stola turn to holes, her golden rope shrink and char. Her headdress catches the most quickly, and flames roll down her blackened face in a gentle cascade. The smell of burning hair fills the air, singeing my nose and going down my throat like sniffing up a strip of wool.

We stand this way, in a small semi-circle, until she is at least partially reduced to ash. It is getting too late in the day to wait for her whole body to burn. The dancers continue to dance, the lute players continue to play, the wailers continue to wail in a cacophony of false sadness. Each of our veils is pulled up high, just below our eyes, as if our faces have contracted, shut as a bell-shaped bulb, though we do not mourn. Good Virgins are plucky in nature, determined by Vesta, for Vesta, not one another.

I am surprised how little I feel; it is as if I am watching a sow roast on a spit.

An undertaker stabs a shovel in the embers. Caesar holds out an urn with a depiction of Minerva beside a hearth painted on it, whispers inaudible prayers while some ash and embers are placed inside and the lid firmly secured.

Before we can leave the pyre, we must be purified of death. The undertakers snap the necks of six doves, cut them across their breasts, red spreading over their white feathers as if their hearts turned to seeping puddles. Fly away death, in the other direction, fly away death, in the other direction, fly away death, in the other direction. The blood is wiped on the inside of each of our wrists.

When we arrive back at the house, we step first into the temple and pour Sempronia's remains into Vesta; full circle.

I am dreaming that Priapus is running after me, but he is wearing the wax mask of Sempronia. He chases me through the house, up and down the stairs, round the central atrium, round the dining table, into the kitchen. He backs me into the latrine and wails and wails, condensation fogging up the mask, wails and wails, his waxy face elongating to a long pointed chin, his mouth opens wider and wider. I wake up.

It's the wailers outside; I can hear them in my room, their dark, bloodcurdling wails erupting from their mouths as cavernous songs.

I will not sleep again, not for thirty days.

CHAPTER LIV

In the temple, I can still smell Sempronia's burning hair. Tullia once said a Virgin's journey has only one destination – death. There she is now, at her destination, in Vesta, parts of flesh, bone, hair, teeth, arms, legs, stomach, nose, eyes. Her body reduced to fodder for Vesta even in death. Her body preserved in life as a pickled herring; her womb reserved by Rome as if it were the best seat at the theatre. Her body and womb gone up in smoke, just as my womb, my body will inevitably do also – revolt or no revolt.

The body is something that cannot be trusted, a captor often so benign one can forget it doles out only one merciless sentence. It is a given that it will one day betray us. It is an unsafe home. We deceive ourselves into believing it is safe so we can continue living in it day to day as if settled, or at least as if not unsettled by the looming prospects of harm until it is too late. If it is solely our bodies that govern then we are subjects to tyranny of the worst kind. Death comes from within. All I have is this body, without the gods, without the existence of the Underworld. All I have is this body, just once, while it lasts.

But will it last? Will I be killed in the turmoil of the uprising? I might not reach the storehouse in time, or I might be discovered before Lysander arrives. Beaten and raped, my neck twisted and separated like a hen's. They would enjoy it too, as Lysander said: a Virgin succumbing at their hands, folding into my stola, at their knees. Maybe they'll even drag me through the Forum, stick me on a cross, naked.

This is the problem with the body, it is a one-time opportunity.

'I am sorry for your loss.' I hear his torch go out.

'Touch me,' I whisper. 'Let me feel my body being felt while I am still in it. What does it matter now whether I am touched or untouched?'

He stands in the temple's entrance, his black hair damp from the light drizzle outside, and he searches my face to see if he has heard correctly. I pull down my veil. He moves swiftly and presses himself against me. I lean into his lips. He runs his hands up and down my arms, then pulls me closer, so close I feel I've stepped into him.

He undresses me. First my headdress: his calloused hands pluck out each pin gently, not scraping, as if each pin turns to air at his touch. He does this while looking deeply into my eyes; his dark, dark eyes with long lashes that have crystal tears threaded between them like tiny webs. As he pulls off my head-dress, he presses his thumb under my chin. At first I think he is trying to keep my head steady, but really it is so he can keep my eyes steady, always on him. He unties my golden rope and I turn like a dancer as he unwinds it from my body, tossing it into the gaping darkness. He raises my arms and pulls off my stola, not rolling it down over my body so I can step out of it, but roughly over my head. It catches on a hairpin; we laugh at this. He reaches to uncoil my hair, but I shake my head. 'We won't be able to braid it the same again.'

349

So he skims over my coils. 'Beautiful hair, I knew it.' He says this softly, as if a lie is more forgivable when whispered.

He then pulls off his own tunic, smoothing down his hair as he drops it. He stands there, arms at his sides, his chest rising, falling, ebbing and flowing like a bottle riding the tide, filled with messages that only cautious fingers could extract. His ribs jut out under his skin like a fan, his chest and stomach are covered in an armour of smooth black hair. He allows me to walk round him, take him in with my eyes, touch the veins running through his forearms like inky seams to his tattoo. I feel the slope of his back all the way down and over his white buttocks to his legs. He allows me to stroke the scars on his back, rib upon ribs, down his knobbly spine, over hips that protrude like ledges. He allows me to run my hands over his narrow thighs, the muscular etchings of legs that can run, over the curled hair soft as down. I can faintly smell the radishes he's planted, taste the salty olives he wishes he grew, feel the heat of saturated sun emanate off his shoulders. He is not like Priapus. There is nothing menacing, he does not hold himself like a weapon, pointing towards me. I touch him there also, examine him like a scene painted on an earthen jug, closely, as if turning it round and round to see each crook, bend, shape in the finely crafted details.

He lays his tunic down like a blanket and lowers me to the temple floor at Minerva's feet. It is crumpled and yellowed, and I feel as if I'm lying upon a precipice that is teetering over the abyss; a sudden panic comes over me. For a moment I do not let him remove my under-dress, but he whispers in my ear, 'You must,' and so I must. He strips it off, and I feel as if I can

350

breathe through each pore in my entire body, as if each pore is an open mouth gasping for more air.

I am naked, here, in front of Vesta. Naked, and so easily seen if there were a late-night passer-by, so easily caught if a matron happened to be in sudden need of Vesta's benevolence, if there were an emergency and one of the others came calling. Fear of being caught seems only to intensify the rush of exhilaration and longing that courses through me; I couldn't stop now, even if I wanted to.

He picks up one of my hands and, hand over hand, drags my fingers over my own skin, over my stomach and hips, over my breasts and shoulders, down my thighs and up my thighs again. He stops atop my eye. He urges my fingers to unbury my eye from its own lashes, peel it open, separate its lids, and stroke inside it. My hand flinches, pulls away, but he brings me back, over and over. It feels surprisingly soft, tender; not the texture of grapefruit peel I had expected.

He then takes my hand and places it against his chest over his heart, as he pushes himself up and hovers over me. I feel safe, as if I am hiding under a table. I reach up and tuck his hair behind his ears, run my hands over his beard, over the dimples in his already hollow cheeks, a bowl within a bowl, and pull his lips down to mine. His mouth opens into mine. All his words spill down my throat and nestle into my neck to be swallowed. All my unspoken words spill out and settle into his ears to be heard.

'There's a spider. It has a web under the eaves. It prevents the seed from settling.'

'*Oh well, so I don't get pregnant too soon. Not until I've left. I need spiders for this. It is most effective as they carry a worm inside*

351

them that can stop a seed from settling.' Tullia's words come back to me.

I realize I've made sure not to lose track of the spider.

'Ah yes, I've heard that also.'

I am glad he says this and I am not going by Tullia's counsel alone. It reassures me of its efficacy. Sometimes she could be wrong.

Try not to think of Tullia now.

He gets up, unabashed by his nakedness, then crouches down and I can see the dangling pillow between his legs. He creeps down the temple steps into the dark. When he comes back his hands are cupped. He kneels down beside me, and before the spider can crawl up his arm, he pinches it and it bursts open, a yellow substance spills out over his fingers. There isn't any worm, but he tucks his hand between my legs and I feel his fingers rubbing into me. He then rubs some on himself. 'There,' he says, looking at me for a moment as if waiting for me to say, 'Stop, I've changed my mind.' I say nothing.

When he enters me, it hurts, burns. 'It will ease,' he breathes into my neck, and stills for a moment, and we lie that way until my eye adjusts, opens, and he is able to continue. He beats inside me, the way I imagine the sail of a ship would look if I were lying directly underneath it as it beats against the wind.

Minerva's knees stay unbent, her nose stays stone and does not flare with ire. Her mouth keeps her distant demure smile.

I notice my breath is now coming out like smoke. For a moment I think he has beaten Vesta out of me, put her out, but then when he raises himself so we are nose to nose, I notice both our breaths are frosted and mingling into one. Over his shoulder I see it is suddenly raining. The rain catches Vesta's light and looks like snow, perfectly round twinkling snowflakes, sparkling like jewels. I think for a moment that somehow snow is falling on my face like the minuscule heads of daisies, wet tingling kisses, but it is his wet hair dripping. Faster and faster the snow cascades down, as if a thousand dandelion seeds were blown from cupped hands, drops from in his hair tingling like shattered ice scattering over my skin. The snow seems to thicken, blow into the temple, until all I see is white.

He lies beside me, hand over hand. We watch the snow as if we were riding a raft, floating away on the remains of an ice storm.

We cannot stay this way for long. I get up and notice there's blood on his tunic. There I am, dispelled and smeared against his tunic, my Virginity. He bends over, picks it up, dabs it in the purified water and tries to scrub the blood out as I try to get dressed. 'There, barely noticeable.' He slips it back on. He helps re-pin my headdress, though I know it will sit crookedly on my head. Once we are both dressed, he takes my hand again and kisses the inside of my wrist. 'Tomorrow night, I want us to go to the storehouse. I want to show you how to place boards across the door to secure it from the inside. I doubt it will be of interest to anyone, but just to be sure.'

'I shouldn't leave the temple!'

'You've done lots you shouldn't do!' He says this as he turns to go, with his back facing me, his neck reddening. He continues, 'I care very deeply for you, if you didn't know already.'

'I hope so,' I whisper back, before he leaves.

I spend the rest of the night, until morning, waiting for thunder, for the sound of pillars crashing down, chasms opening, for Vesta to drip from her hearth like molten lava, burning everything in her path. I wait for her to lash out at me, for if I've ever

353

incurred her wrath it is now. I wait for Minerva to tip over, smash to pieces, but there is nothing, and I stop waiting.

My body feels different, sore, but also heavier, earthier, as if I've finally become untangled from the ethereal threads that kept me writhing in mid-air, as if I've finally become part of the living.

CHAPTER LV

The first thing you need to know if you are to take a lover is that there can be no sign of it on your body. No kiss marks, scratches, scrapes, scabs, grass stains, bruises in the shape of fingertips on the thigh. No flush of the cheeks, smiling off into the distance, heightened excitability, sudden and easy laughter, abrupt enthusiasm. Don't dream of your lover as you risk saying his name while asleep. Don't keep anything your lover may give you, regardless of sentimentality; burn it in Vesta. Whatever it is, it isn't worth it. Virgins bathe each day, so be careful to rid yourself of any dirt or sand on your back or dried leaves in your headdress. Don't depend on your under-dress to conceal anything. Don't ever leave anything behind; there would be nothing you could do then. Don't meet in the same places: there's the cellar, the garden at night, the storehouse. You are less likely to be seen if you don't frequent the same meeting place. Develop a clear list of plausible reasons why you may be found in each place you meet. Make only subtle changes to your routine, and any change must be kept up to ward off suspicion. The first thing you need to know if you are to take a lover, Aemilia, is don't ever, ever get caught.

*

Sempronia's chair has been pulled slightly out from the dinner table, as if she had been sitting there but had to dash down the hall to use the chamber room and would be returning any moment. I suppose a new Virgin will soon fill it, pull it up to the table. Empty spaces are quickly engulfed as if they never were.

The centrepiece is an arrangement of ivy draped over and through small thin branches as if slowly constricting, slowly binding the branches together.

'It was a lovely eulogy.' Fabia again raises her cup of wine and tips it forward. We each follow suit. She pours a little on the ground, beside her chair. 'May death be sated now, and not return to this house. May the dead not bother the living.' We will do this for thirty days in a row. If Sempronia's spirit does happen to get past the wailers and tries to dine with us, we must remind her she is dead.

There is a moment of silence, of slurping soup, wine, dinging spoons. I find a long wavy strand of hair coiled around a piece of leek in my soup, I hold it up closer to try to tell the colour but it is too drenched in white cream. I wave at a slave to take the soup away.

Eventually, conversation turns again to the celebration of Bona Dea and the coming ceremony of Janus, as if we cannot wait until this long-drawn-out, grey narrow alleyway of nothingness subsides, until the next religious ritual. November is a lean month, we are hungry for December. It's as though we wait behind, in front and in between one ritual and another as though stuck between two buildings, two temples, two knees. We do not flail at this – this waiting. We will get out, eventually. Eventually. If only they knew that I am not waiting for them. If only they knew their waiting is in vain.

Suddenly I find great hilarity in their restraint, their eagerness to be in close proximity to bloodshed, their need for duty, as if it were a refreshing spring shower that will wash away that which springs up in the quiet. Unidentifiable inklings that perhaps things need not be as they are, if only all could be in agreement, if only someone spoke the first words. I find hilarity in their sealed-up faces, pursed-up mouths, rigid greasy fingers pulling at meat from chickens' legs. Here we are, women behind closed doors, so tucked away we could get away with anything, more than any other women in Rome, but here we sit, stiff as boards, pious as prunes, following the rules, though no one is looking.

A Virgin is quicker to cast light upon another's imprudence than any other, even if no harm was caused. Virgins will always clamour over each other, grasping for more piety. It is funny that we fear each other most, before Caesar, before the gods. The wrath we incur is from each other.

After dinner, I climb the stairs, am undressed and lie in bed in mock sleep. I listen to the wailers emit sharp croaks, their voices weakening, interchanging rasps and high shrieks like abandoned kettles.

CHAPTER LVI

I sit against the wall, by the door, wanting to draw the flames round me like a blanket, a pillow, a bed I could invite Lysander into, but once he arrives he tells me we should go to the storehouse, that it will only be a day or two more until Cataline attacks Rome.

I add several more logs onto Vesta and take the forbidden step out of the temple.

When we pass the house doors; there isn't a slave there and Lysander shakes his fist back and forth to indicate they are playing dice in the hut, then takes my hand. He leads me through the garden, close to thick hedges, through the shadows, though there are few as the moon is full. I can hear the men in their hut, laughing and arguing raucously, as we pass.

When we get to the storehouse, Lysander opens the door, flinching at each squeak, stopping, then opening it even more slowly. We slip in and he pulls the door closed. The moonlight streams in through grated windows, casting criss-crosses of light and shadow across the statues. The chipped stone faces, pale and ashen under dust, look depraved under the moonlight. Together they are unsettling, just as insects are en masse.

'I put the boards here in the corner. Can you see?'

'Yes.'

'You need to take the shorter one and lean it against the door under the latch like this, then put the longer one on top of it. Now you try.'

I pick up the shorter board, turn awkwardly and nearly knock over a torso. He shakes his head, guides my hands. I slide the board under the latch, put the longer over the top.

'Is this how it is done?'

'Good. Now again, but quicker.'

I do it over and over, until Lysander is finally satisfied I will be able to secure the door on my own. Smiling, he cups my head with both his hands and kisses me. He pulls me along a tight narrow row, and against the storehouse wall, he pulls off his tunic, then pulls up my stola and under-dress and lifts me up onto him. The statues seem to shift and face us, turn into a group of giddy, elderly spectators leering at our show. As if we are an exhibition in the arena. I close my eyes and try to fall into the rhythm of Lysander's ragged breathing, but it seems to echo, as though the statues are breathing with him. I open my eyes; they've moved in closer, watching, watching. His mouth covers my neck and lips. I grab onto his hair. I lock my legs tighter round his hips, tether myself to him, and soon we are the only ones here, soon it doesn't matter if we are not.

He mumbles and moans into my cheek. We slide down the wall, together, my legs still round him. We sit this way, in the quiet.

I tell him about Tullia. 'She was my sculptress, my stone carver.'

359

'What happened to her?'

'She served her thirty years, then she went off with her lover to the countryside in Arpinum, I think, somewhere round there. She had some children. I believe she is happy now.'

'Luckily you need not scorch yourself on that fire for another thirty years.' He smiles and I curl further into his neck. 'I had someone like that, a stone carver, as you say.' I wait for him to continue but he does not. Instead he gets up and pretends to draw a sword. 'Here are the senators.' He waves to the statues and pretends to cut them down. He is so beautiful in this moment.

I cannot picture him in battle and tell him so.

'A woman should never be able to; she would either never let her man go or never love him again once he returned.'

We creep back through the garden, the grass is spongy. I love the feel of his hand in mine, its size, its heaviness.

Suddenly, the hut door opens and out stumbles a large slave; he throws the dice back in and shouts something unintelligible. Lysander grabs me, his big hand over my mouth, and pulls me behind a tree. His hand tastes like salt and mud and I can barely breathe. My legs begin to shake and I think they are about to give way. All my flaunting has brought this on, all my flaunting has tempted a despairing fate.

He brings his lips to my ear. 'I will go ahead and distract him.' I grab his wrist over my mouth and refuse to let go. 'Stick to the shadows.' He pulls his hand away.

The garden is bigger at night, a strange place. I run my hands along the bushes, as if I am blind. If I am caught, I could claim momentary blindness, say I had no idea I had stepped from the temple.

I hear them talking at the doors. Lysander has somehow arranged it so that the other slave's back is towards the temple. 'It would have happened by now, don't you think?' The slave complains.

'Patience wins wars.' Lysander tells him.

I dash back up the steps into the temple, relieved for once to be where I belong.

The horror of nearly being caught soon passes and I spend the night humming.

Each morning that Cataline does not storm Rome, Lysander comes to the temple once Holy Way becomes a desolate street and the only thing visible from the temple entry is the pathway leading back to the house, a peninsula that seems to float on pitch black waters and drops off sharply. Each night we eagerly fall into one another again and again, in rushed, soundless encounters.

He assures me each time we can get away with it. 'The other slaves are even sloppier now they know their freedom is so close. They rarely follow their imposed duties when the Virgins aren't close by. Even if they knew we were here, doing what we are doing, they'd still look the other way. It's your Virgins who've instilled such fear in you. Once someone so thoroughly believes they are being watched, the watchers need not look any more. We are kept apart only by the oppression of time and place . . . and all those meddling Virgins!' He laughs, pulls me in, and I am caught only by his mouth on mine.

It is near the middle of October when he finally hears news again. 'It is planned now for mid-December, set on the third night of Saturnalia. Lentulus sent word. Houses are kept open all night to receive gifts and visitors, slaves are let off their duty and will be free to meet and gather arms. They will not be paid any attention upon return to their master's household. Each senator will be massacred. They don't stand a chance! When you look up Palatine Hill you'll see heads rolling down it! And not so long after that, when so many slaves are being fitted for new collars by Cataline, they will need me and my knives!'

Julia has begun to stay behind longer when Lysander brings me to the temple. She is always in the middle of some task or another when I arrive. 'In a moment, just finishing.' She will act startled, as if I have arrived too early. She will dip the sponge in the bucket a few more times and run it over Minerva or the floor. I know she is acting; there is falseness to this lingering, but I am just not sure why she does it.

When she is bent over I shrug at Lysander, who is standing at the bottom of the stairs.

I told him about the statue and Fabia's betrayal, and though he thought it all very funny, he said it could be the reason behind Julia's reluctance to leave the temple. 'Maybe she wishes to cling to the simplicity of the fire, its honesty.' He thinks better of people than I do.

'I thought you would believe Vesta was dishonest.'

'As Vesta it *is* dishonest, but not as fire. If I actually threw you in, then it would be honest. And faster!' He playfully pretends to pick me up and toss me like a log into the fire.

'Stop!' I could not help laughing, biting his neck softly in mock struggle.

362

This night, Julia hangs about longer than ever before. 'I am just checking the kindling,' she tells me over her shoulder. She sifts through the box slowly, bending various twigs, twirling brown leaves.

'I am sure it will do.' I say, after it seems she will never get up and leave.

'*Will do* is not compensation enough for Vesta's benevolence.' She turns round and glares at me, and then through me, at Vesta. I want her to go. She looks so pathetic hovering over the box of kindling, rifling through its dead leaves and wood, as if squeezing each one for its last drop of moistness, of life blood. Finally she stands up, brushes past me, though not towards the door; instead she picks up the sponge and begins to wash round the box of kindling, as if scooping up leftover crumbs from a table. This is why I did not say anything earlier; I knew she would only stay longer to prove her own devotion in contrast to mine.

'Are you not tired, Julia?' I say it politely, my voice filled only with concern. I expect a tirade of how tireless she is in the company of Vesta. But much to my surprise she puts down the sponge.

'I am actually.' She rubs her hands together. 'All done,' and slips through the door and finally lets Lysander follow her back to the house.

'I didn't think she would ever leave.' Lysander chuckles as he comes back into the temple, shaking his head not just at Julia but at me as well, at our Virginness, our odd interactions. Though this I can only assume because I hear a sharp scuffle against the steps. I push Lysander away and lurch towards the temple door. He crouches behind Minerva. I step towards the entrance but see only the sandy path to the house and beyond that only faded yellow grass.

But then I see something move. Someone.

'Julia?'

'I must say I think . . .'

It is Julia. She comes forward, out of the burrow she made in the night, like a mole. She's back. I wish I could see if she has any mud or clumps of grass on her stola. Was she hiding, watching? I try my best to block her view. I plead with Vesta not to let Julia see Lysander's torch by the steps. I plead with Vesta, because I need to plead. Pleading with the gods is my specialty.

'What is it?' She comes up the first two steps. I lean farther out, ready to take the first forbidden step out of the temple in front of her if need be, ready to pretend to slip and fall on top of her, anything to cause a diversion so Lysander can slip away.

'I was about to say you should have the slave fetch more kindling. I don't think there is enough to last the night. But I suppose you've done that, as he is not here.' I can detect the misgiving in her voice.

'I have.' This is not good enough for her and she takes one more step up. 'If it weren't for you I wouldn't have noticed. So I must thank you for your thorough inspection of the kindling box.'

Julia smiles. As if she got what she came for.

Lysander stays behind Minerva for a long while after Julia is gone. We speak through her thighs. Just to be sure.

'She will soon find out if the revolt does not happen soon, or if we do not end these nightly meetings.'

'It will happen soon. I feel it.'

And I am happy that he did not opt for ending our meetings, that he is willing to risk it until the bitter end.

CHAPTER LVII

Though it is only the end of October we bake cakes for December. Each matron likes a cake to crumble on the pig's head at the celebration of Bona Dea, before it is slaughtered, but not all of the matrons receive a cake. The cakes are treated as jewels in a crown, evidence of status, of whose husband is more powerful. If all the matrons received cake then none of them would want any; they would lose their value, their potency. What good is it to have something if it isn't in demand, if everyone else already has one? We are still required to bake an excess of cakes, so those who do not receive one can look at a table filled with unused cakes and envy the ones with them even more. So close yet so far. We will stand by the table handing them out. The hostess of Bona Dea always decides beforehand who will have a cake. At first they claimed whoever held a cake and sprinkled it on the sow's head would become more fertile, would bear more sons. Then it meant youthful skin, a longer life, greater riches, a powerful son. Then it was simply who had a cake and who did the sprinkling, nothing more.

I roll up the dough, pat it into perfect circles, dusty milky-white eyes. Julia is doing the same, but at the other end of the table with the others. There is enjoyment knowing this will all soon end. Religion and the Republic reduced to rubble. We will soon crumble like a cake, roll away. Crumbs of what was. Fabia will be an old woman still wearing her dusty purple stola, nearly in rags, wandering through the Forum, starting fires here and there and watching them. Porcia by her side, mumbling of better days past. Claudia is still so young, she will easily adapt; she adapted easily enough to here.

I think of Tullia and I, together again. We will be doing something much like we are doing now, but in our own kitchens. We will each visit the other frequently, share the workload of our husbands' households. Tell our own daughters, as we teach them how to make cakes, that we were once Virgins back in our day, the day of the Republic. But our children will not be able to think of us as anything other than their mothers. The Republic will just be an obscure and ancient word we utter from time to time. A word their fathers always spit after, punctuating their disgust, a dark look falling over their faces for a moment, but only a moment. Tullia and I will smile to one another. 'What's done is done,' one of us will say. 'Thankfully,' the other will answer. And in our old age, as old age always brings yearning for one's past, we will watch over each other; if one finds the other in front of the kitchen hearth, praying, making small offerings, she will tap her on the shoulder, bringing her back. 'Get with the times,' we will say. 'Of course, of course. I was only warming my hands, it just happened . . .' Our children will eventually grow up and mock our lives, this part of our lives, mock Roman religion, the gods. 'Oh, how could they have been so dim-witted?' They will laugh at us behind our backs, because we all believed in one god or another, at one time or another, before our enlightenment.

Fabia is sliding the first pan of cakes into the oven. Slapping her hands together afterwards so a small cloud of flour appears. She turns round, rubs the back of her hand against her nose, trying to scratch without using her flour-coated fingers. She blows up a gust of air to cool down her dampening forehead, lets out a bit of a grunt, then goes back to kneading another bowl of dough. If she could, she would be humming, a busy bee is filled with glee, a Virgin at work is a Virgin indeed.

Once the cakes are cooked, Fabia tips her nose towards them and breathes in the fresh baking smells as she always does. So pleased with herself, as if she has guests waiting in the other room and is sure these cakes will be a delight to all, sure she will later be addressed in a toast to the hostess. Once Fabia has finished sniffing, the cakes are put in a basket and taken outside to the storehouse. The cakes will dry out, become stale as smoke, easy to crumble. One pinch and the cake turns to powder, though this pinch is done best with one's whole hand, a crunch really. But pinch is much more pious, or at least this is why I think it is preferred to crush. Virgins do not crush.

One pinch and the cakes turn to powder. That is a good cake, a good sign. But still Fabia acts as if it matters whether the cakes taste delicious or not, as if the heifers, bulls and pigs care for flavour as the cake is crumbled down their heads and the knife splits them open. And if these cakes later reach the gods' plates, surely they will jeer at their gritty coarseness. They must have tasted better than this.

It suddenly occurs to me that this is all I know how to cook. Will he leave if, night after night, I serve him one dried corn cake after the other? I am not even sure if these are edible for

368

mortals; they are made for the gods. There are no gods, I remind myself again; it seems I need to do this, to remind myself that I have changed, now know more, better. The gods are pervasive, persuasive; like the milky blotch of Aeneas in the dining room – they can only be blotted over, not out. Not completely. Though I am trying my best, I still see them, in spite of myself, like recurring cataracts. I have much to learn, much to undo. Maybe he will allow me a slave or two, just in the beginning so I can learn. Yes, he will allow this, he'll let me take one of the cooks, though not the one he already knows – better to start fresh.

'It is a shame Claudia must start tending now; she would benefit from more practice baking mola salsa. I do hope the new Virgin is not as old as she was, six is best, more years to practise before coming of age,' Fabia states, her headdress swaying back and forth as she kneads.

'Oh yes, very true. Practice makes perfect,' Julia answers without looking up; she seems never to look up.

'I wonder what the good consul's wife, Terentia, will serve on the night of the Bona Dea.' Porcia pats more dough into round cakes.

'I hope the dining room is painted yellow; it would go so well with our stolas.'

'Last year the shellfish was a little too shrunken, but the pastries were delectable, they melted in the mouth . . .'

'Salted eel, hopefully. I dislike it unsalted . . . or worse when it's still slithering on the plate . . .'

While they are caught up in their conversation, I try to take the finished cakes out to the storehouse – this is my chance to walk through the garden, to see him – but Fabia stops me.

'You do not need to do that, Aemilia. Let one of the slaves

take it out.' Straight down her nose she stares. A halting look that turns me to stone, reduces me to rubble.

The slave washing the bowls dries her hands on a towel and takes the basket of cakes from my hands. I try my best to seem pleased, relieved, and dip my hands into another bowl of dough, mixing the egg and flour. As Fabia brings over another fresh bowl, I notice she has flour on her nose, a goopy smear of egg and flour in the crevice between her nostril and cheek. I am about to tell her, but do not. Revenge can be as small as this. I smile as I stir. This will tide me over for now.

CHAPTER LVIII

A new Virgin has been chosen. A tiny little girl with wide brown eyes, skin so pale she looks as though she is wrapped in steamed linens. Her cheeks sink, so that the outline of her teeth can be seen through her lips. She rolls her shoulders up into her cheeks, tilting her head to and fro in fits of shyness. Her sheared head bobs over her untouched plate of food.

'A good Virgin appreciates the privilege of being fed!' Fabia leans forward, her chin tucked in and sloping into her neck. She will take her round later, give an account of Veturia with a zeal that would be absent in the rest of us. Veturia will be thought of as special. In a hundred years she will usurp Rhea in importance.

The little girl, face a blank slate, block of white stone, nods. Her mouth is slightly open, one front tooth missing, the other only half grown. She pokes a little at her plate, spoons up some pigeon and leaves it sitting on her tongue.

I cannot stand to hear this all over again.

At night, I can hear her whimper. I am tempted to sneak into her room, tell her there will be revolt and she need not worry, soon she'll be going home to her parents. Hush, I want to tell her, hush, hush.

I thought at least I would get some sleep with the wailers gone, but now the new Virgin chases my sleep away. Sleep is something that arrives in fits and spurts, quick kicks in the head, just above the ear. Not enough to be knocked out by, only dulled.

My cycle has been delayed. If it were only a few days, even a week, maybe two, I might not be concerned. But it's been weeks; I've nearly lost count. This should mean that Vesta is dissatisfied with me in some way, has shirked me, rejecting my blood by preventing its arrival. It would mean this, if it were not for the simple truth that my eye has been broken, flipped inside out.

I stand in the chamber room, rubbing my belly the way Fabia did to coax the blood out, though I know it doesn't work, because I know she really used the blood of animals to conceal her dryness.

I must bleed. I must bleed. Bleed. My box is empty, has been for far too long, and I know the slaves have started to talk. It's the way they pause over the chamber pot before picking it up, inspecting its contents, looking for traces of blood, glancing at my box. They are timing me.

I look in the others' boxes – Virgins often bleed together. There is nothing in Fabia's, which is to be expected. Nothing in Julia's even if she were bleeding she would have emptied her box earlier. There's only one stray wool strip in Porcia's and she'll notice if I take it. I need to bleed. My belly feels harder, as if I am already hardening into a shell, cramping and twisting as it shifts shape, opening for the jumble of bones that I picture looking like stripped chicken bones on an otherwise empty plate.

Bones that are now being swaddled with the blood once meant for Vesta. My desiccated insides are dampening into a shallow pool of life, skimming with algae.

How could this have happened with the precautions we took? Though there wasn't a worm in the spider, its tarry substance should still have caught the seeds just as well as a web. I could tip over and cry. I should find a way to shake these bones out of me. Fall down the steps of the temple. Maybe I could somehow flush the bones from me in the bath, if I thrashed my legs fast enough when no one was looking. Perhaps squat close to Vesta and smoke it out. There are the sticks, right here, in reach. Without the sponge, I could insert one straight up myself and scrape it off like mud off the bottom of a shoe. I should do one of these things, if I were not so secretly pleased.

I need only to get through these last two weeks. There is much more at stake now, too much to be caught. I roll my sleeve up and bite my upper arm, where the under-dress will still conceal the wound as I bathe. I clench my fists, wincing, if my mouth weren't full of flesh, I'd cry out as my teeth sink into my skin. I dab the blood with the wool strip and place it in my box. There.

In the morning two matrons enter the temple: one offers Vesta a lamb chop and the other a silver ring. One carries a baby rolled up in a fur blanket, holding it like a trophy. Chubby, dimpled hands reach out from the blanket, grabbing at his or her mother's nose. She brushes the hands away and tries to balance the baby on her hip as she kneels down in front of Vesta. The baby begins to fuss and the mother shushes it, kissing his or her forehead. I come in closer to see what is shaping inside me. Its translucent skin seems to shine with newness. Its shrunken delicate face sniffs for its mother. For a moment I wonder if it is right now inside me, growing Lysander's black hair that curls in the heat, or my odd knees. What if it is born odd, its legs shaped like a mermaid's? I push this from my mind and try to picture it with Lysander's thick black hair and my dimpled knees, the way its tiny hand will feel wrapped around my finger. I try to imagine the sound of its clear lungs and the heat of its cheek next to mine, the tender thumping of its heart, and how we will one day swing him or her between us as we walk, like an anchor binding us together.

The matron absentmindedly shifts the baby from one arm to the other, and I think of how naturally mothering comes to her. How will I mother, if I've never been mothered? How will I know what to do? It will sniff and sniff for me, wail and clench its pink fists, and I will not know what to offer it, and it will die. I will have to ask someone to tell me what to do, find Tullia, she knows all about matrons.

I watch a bubble of spit dribble from the baby's mouth; the matron pats it away with a corner of the blanket. I must remember to do this.

I hadn't noticed I was smiling until the matron pulls the baby back and covers its face.

CHAPTER LIX

The celebration of Bona Dea begins at dusk and will go on through the night when the moon is full and light against the dark sky until dawn. There isn't a statue to praise because none of us are really sure who or what Bona Dea is; all we know is that she was imported from the East not so long ago. Some say she is Cybele, the great mother; others say it is really Isis. Her image has yet to be decided on, her lineage yet declared. This will change the longer she is in Rome.

Fabia recites the prayers to Bona Dea, the Good Goddess, with a precision any priest would envy; she stands a bit straighter, prouder, man of the house tonight. She pleads for the matrons, for their fertility, youth, continuous love from their husbands, maintenance of their position. Braziers and candles give a warm light over the room. A fountain trickles in the corner of the dining room. There are ten long tables covered with deep red linens and each is decorated with platters of olives, figs, fish, cheese and bread. We will sit at the shorter head table. Trays of wine are stationed in reach of every matron here. Long red curtains, red as the wine, hang from windows, drawn shut for this night.

How can everything seem so conventional when there is

something, someone, growing inside me? It's as if I am completely detached from this room, this moment, but then, where do I fit in? I am pressed between Virgin and matron, neither here nor there; there's nothing to explain me. I am indefinable, annulled.

I am afraid the matrons will know I am with child; they know the signs. It is all very obvious to them. They must know. Maybe my skin is a different shade.

Fabia pinches the first cake over the head of the sow and it snorts. Some of the matrons giggle, clamping their hands over their mouths, and a feeling of terror floods through me. I can feel my cheeks redden. They are watching so closely, whispering comments to one another. Any minute one of them will stand up and reveal to all that I am pregnant. They will say they wanted the real thing – verifiable Virgins. They'll feel cheated. They'll call the guards, have them take me away.

Fabia waves the matrons up from their seats, one by one, according to Terentia's list. The wife of the other consul is first, then Caesar's Pompeia, then the wives of praetors, censores, aediles, lastly the wives of wealthy merchants, each taking a cake and crumbling it on the now squealing sow.

The harpists strum harder, faster, louder. The sow pulls on the rope we all hold, burning our palms. The matrons pinch the cakes more quickly. Strum, crumble, squeal. We pull the sow tighter, her pink nipples are swollen, nearly touching the floor, ready for her litter. Strum, crumble, squeal. Fabia waves the matrons to sit and slits the pig clean and clear across her stomach, and I reel with clenching, cold cramps.

The sow falls to her side. Fabia bends over and opens her up and again I almost lurch with pain. We pull out the entrails, declare the liver as favourable, acceptable. There is no other choice here, there's only ever one sow available to sacrifice. The matrons do not wish to spend an evening free of their husbands on the particularities of religion. This part is just necessary penance for the party after.

They sit up straighter, lighter, leaning now into one another, whispering again. We take the sow's unborn piglets one by one and burn them on the altar Terentia has put together for the occasion. They are just the size of my hand, brown like a curled-up kidney with a tail. Listless, lifeless. So close, yet so far. This we do just outside the garden door, then we wash our hands in the basin beside it. Another day, another sacrifice, each day a sacrifice. Each day brings me closer to the last.

I feel gutted.

CHAPTER LX

Lysander comes to the temple soon after Julia is escorted to the Bona Dea celebration. Tonight she goes on time. He seems to appear from the shadows so easily now, as if they are a part of his wardrobe he wears and sheds at his leisure. I notice his beard is less well groomed, his hair longer. He would be dishevelled if he were not a slave.

'So what is it you do there?' he asks, as he leans into the temple entrance.

'Ah, it's a secret ritual. We dance with spirits and cross over into other worlds and meet with seven-tongued witches who sacrifice young men.'

He is quiet. I laugh. I am near giddiness with relief and exhaustion. Soon I can sleep.

'I am only teasing! The matrons get drunk, gossip, and we sacrifice a pig.'

He sighs, and I can tell he isn't listening or hadn't thought what I said was humorous, and I know he is in his pensive mood. He comes into the temple, his arms already reaching for me. I smile up at him and he returns it.

'I have something very important to tell you!' This will cheer him. 'Even as we speak, I am filling with your flesh and bone.

Perhaps I will have the first-born of the new Rome, a son who will run the school with you.'

He seems not to understand what I am saying and watches my lips as if I am speaking too quickly, or he is suddenly hard of hearing.

'My cycles have ended. I am with child, our child.'

His eyes widen, as if I had slapped him. 'No.' He shakes his head. 'No, no, no . . .' I can feel his tears on my cheeks as he pulls me into him, his lips against mine, not kissing, but gnashing, shushing. 'No, no . . .' His teeth cut into my lower lip, he pushes me down to the floor. My stola is round my hips, his tunic round his. He has pushed me into Minerva, the top of my head knocks against the base that her legs sink into.

I allow him this because there is no reason not to, not now, and because I think this may be how men usually react. Maybe they need to feel it for themselves: feeling is believing. Though I feel none of the pleasure of before. I watch as he moves up and down. He looks different, sounds different as well – a faint whimper. He notices I am watching him and turns his face to the side, away from me, and I notice a loose eyelash is caught in the damp crevices round his eye.

Afterwards, he rests his head on my arm, and the weight of his head makes my wound ache. I withstand it because I only have a few moments of having him like this, so still in my arms. He pulls my hand close, placing both his own hands over mine. At first it seems he means to measure his hands next to mine and then, as if he is making a kind of shell, he seals my hand up in his. I wipe something from my cheek and find his fallen eyelash on my finger. He gets up suddenly, pulls down his tunic and crouches on the temple steps, his bottom lip curling out like a

379

cup, and blows some of his hair up across his forehead. I wait for him to say something about our child, but instead he tells me this.

'Slaves are usually encouraged to breed, like farm animals, to replenish a man's stock or, better, offer him a surplus. Not here, though; here we are to abstain, on the grounds of belonging to the sacred Virgins.

'I remember when I was young, watching my first owner watch his slaves breed. I remember looking at the rolls of fat, three perfect layers, one stacked atop the other on the back of his bald neck, and thinking he could store his coins in those folds of flesh – he had a built-in purse. His beloved money always occupied his mind.' He looks up at me, wants me to laugh, but for some reason, I cannot manage it. Maybe it is the sudden downward tone of his voice; he sounds mired with defeat.

'Why did you lie about where you came from?'

'There is a line from an old story that says a man loses half his selfhood the day of slavery. You looked at me as if you would believe anything and it seemed such a gift. I mean this without offence. It was a gift I could not waste, a gift to make up another beginning to my life, a better one, and be believed.

'As I described the olive groves to you I could smell them, walk down the rows in the orchard, feel the breeze on my face. I could go there, have a nobler birth, even if for a short time, because you let me believe my own lies.'

He is paying me a compliment, as if to say that I am a good listener, but instead that I am a great believer. 'And now you tell the truth?'

'Yes.'

'How will I know?'

'Only the truth sounds this way.'

He breathes in, holds it. I want him to go on.

'I think you are noble,' I whisper down at him, to the part in his hair.

'I was born of slaves, of a Greek mother, and I am not sure who my father was. Most likely my mother's owner, but I was sold at seven years as a full-blooded Greek. The man who bought me already had a Greek slave as a pedagogue for his one son, but he was ailing from something or another. The man, Lucius, wanted the old Greek to educate me before he died, so he could get more of his money's worth from having a young pedagogue who would last for years to come. Also, an educated Greek slave fetches even more money, so I was an investment. Lucius had just married a new young wife and thought he would have many more sons for his Greek pedagogue to teach. Luckily that never came to be, considering the kind of man he was.

'He would travel out to see his crops with his son, Quintus, taking me and the old Greek so we could teach his son along the way. He liked to watch me become smarter just as much as he did his son, like watching a bucket of money grow. Once we arrived at a farm he would pay respects to the household god with a quick sacrifice, then go over the usual things with the slave foreman. Then, later, after dining and drinking too much, he would call his son out to the slave quarters, and the son, smirking at me, would wave at me to come along, saying, 'Household slaves need to know how good they have it compared to farm slaves.' He would say this in a very friendly way, as if granting me a favour.

'The man would select tall, strong men, then lay out a few women and have the men go to them, all in a row. Just as he'd sow seeds of any other crop. Their legs and elbows jabbing into one another. If the men tired he'd whip them onward, even push his foot against their behinds. But the women kept bearing weak children, likely from lack of sustenance while they carried the child. The women skimped on their breast milk so the infant would die rather than live such a miserable existence. This, of course, angered the man, just as a weak yield of any other crop would.

'Then one day, he had the idea that he could do better. Why not mate the women with the farm animals – oxen, horses, even dogs – so the offspring would have the strength and swiftness of an animal with the dexterity of a human? He would tie a woman up underneath a horse or bull, her legs straddling round the animal as it bucked back and forth. The first time the bull crushed her skull against a fence. This made Quintus laugh uproariously. Soon Lucius's perverse curiosity got the better of him, and he began stranger experiments. He tried to mate a woman with a serpent he captured on the farm. Once Quintus stuffed a woman with a male finch and sewed her up to see if she would produce a child with wings. She died of an infection a few days later. The image of her writhing with fever, holding herself between her legs, screaming, still haunts me.

'Lucius would growl guiltily at us when he sensed our disapproval, before he drank too much wine: "Your Zeus always took the form of lusty animals. How do I not know he, or some other god, does not lurk in one of these animals?"

'They spent more and more time at the farm trying their experiments. The Greek pedagogue and I would try to steal away rather than watch the grotesque mating, and most of the time we could because Lucius and Quintus grew more and more creative with their breeding attempts. This is when the Greek taught me about the gods, about Epicureanism, he was like a father. He taught me that the repression of pleasure perverts it, and that if Lucius and Quintus knew peace of mind they would not engage in such sadism.

'One night as Quintus slept, I cut a lock of his hair and took it to one of the slaves. We dipped it in blood and she pretended to give birth to it. Lucius and Quintus stood over her excitedly, as if waiting for the first spoonful from a simmering pot. When they saw it was Quintus's lock of hair, they believed wholeheartedly that they were subjects of divine ire, that this was a punishment for interfering with the gods' authority by mixing mortal and immortal, human and animal. Lucius's wife proved barren, which he took to mean further punishment from the gods. He spent years making offerings, sacrificing anything that moved, but still he had no more children. He donated me to the state soon after the old Greek died. This is how I've come to be here, sitting on the temple steps.'

I reached over and put my hand in his. He sighed, rubbing his face with his other hand.

'The revolt is off. Lentulus and his men have been arrested; all the weapons, spears, armour have been discovered, and an army has been sent to capture Cataline. They're going to be executed without a trial by the end of the week. There is nothing left to do. It's over. And now what will I do?' He pulls his hand away. 'I can't bring my son into this.' He points towards Rome. 'As this.' He points at himself. His head falls into his hands and shakes back and forth.

The revolts are off. I feel as if I am being kicked over and over. It is not as though I can go back. I am irreversibly stained,

383

bloated with consequence. I am dead, my child is dead. I add more kindling, a stream of prayer rolls out of my mouth.

'Stop,' Lysander whispers into the temple.

I fall to my knees, take the purified water and spill it all over Minerva's legs and the floor by her base, where we desecrated her, scrubbing, scrubbing, clawing, my nails snapping. 'I beseech thee to purge me of my impurities ... I beseech thee ... to purge me ...' I think of gods I can blame the child on. Zeus? Who is Zeus? Priapus, Jupiter ... 'I beseech thee to reseal my eye, make me spotless ... Out, forsaken foetus, out.'

'Stop!' He pulls me up. Shakes me back and forth. I begin to cry and would have slumped to the ground if he hadn't held me up by my shoulders. Maybe it is better to die than serve another fifteen years.

'How easily you turn back to your gods!' He says with disgust and waits for me to quieten, to catch my breath. 'We will run away. At least we'll get out. I can sell the knives.'

'To where? How far will we get? Where will we go – a slave and a Virgin?'

'We'll get lost.' He stands up, peers up at the sky. 'I still have some time to get up to Aventine Hill. I'll try to sell them there first.'

'Don't go.' I feel that if he leaves, Vesta and Minerva will over- take me, trample and burn me into nothing, to ashes. I can suddenly smell Sempronia's burning hair again; it fills my mouth.

He presses his lips to my forehead. 'We'll leave as soon as we can, in a day or two.' Then, before slipping again under his cape of shadows, he kisses my stomach.

CHAPTER LXI

For three nights Lysander has tried to sell his sack full of knives, but he has received only a few denarii, much less than they're worth. 'It did not matter when I bought the knives that I was a slave, as long as I had the money, no questions asked. Now, my status is used against me, so I am offered low prices. One man even took a knife right out of my hands and laughed. "What will you do, slave? You shouldn't have knives anyway." Then he rummaged through the sack and took three more. I now have only three more knives to sell.' His whispers are barely audible from where he sits crumpled on the steps. He does not enter the temple. Gone is the boldness of before from both of us. We must tiptoe along the boundaries if we are to get out alive. I make the offerings and he looks away. I tell him about the lyre. Only that I saw it under the willow tree, not that I stole it.

'I'll try that then.' He gets up. 'It costs money to disappear,' he tells me, and I sense a kind of blame and resentment in his voice, and worse, the implication that without money we are doomed.

When I return to the house, I use the chamber room. I bite into myself again, through fresh scabs, swooning with pain. The pain

385

reaches the tips of my fingers, and I can no longer fully bend my arm. The mark is a rippling pool of yellow and purple bruises, the way olive oil looks mixed with a puddle of water under the sun. I streak the blood on a strip of wool; this will be the last. At least the child is hidden inside me like a swallowed heirloom.

Suddenly my stomach begins to churn and empties into one of the chamber pots. I expect there to be bones amid the watery contents, but there is nothing. I tilt the pot back and forth, just in case, to see if I hear any jingling. I've managed to keep the child down.

I tell the slaves to tell the others I am not feeling well and must lie down. I tell them that the temple's vent was blocked again, but praise be to Vesta, it loosened when the sun rose. I need to lie down. I am tired, very tired. Do not bring wine or food, this will need to be starved out.

As the door partially shuts I am for once grateful there isn't any light seeping in from any window. I pull the quilt round me. I feel chilled and scrambled, as if the quilt is also a bag I must slip into, to keep myself together. I want to sleep away the afternoon. Speed up the time between now and seeing Lysander. He will sell the lyre, I tell myself; he will have enough denarii tonight and we will leave. Enjoy the quilt, the quiet, let sleep come. Sleep is something I must convince myself of now.

I hear my door, a light creak. I can hear the most imperceptible sound now that I don't fall asleep completely. I only rest on the feathery pelt around it, unconvinced.

I stay perfectly still, though, pretending to sleep. They are finally coming for me, I think. And then I think, If they were, they'd be louder about it, not this careful shuffle I am hearing now across the floor. Maybe it's an ambush, maybe this is how it happens;

they sneak up on you, toss a net over your head like a wild animal. That is what they would think of me. I've been unchaste, a broken Virgin, and for a moment I think I would deserve it.

My muscles harden, ready to flee or to be hit, or for whatever will be exacted upon my body. No, not ready, one is never ready, not really, my muscles fool me. Or maybe console me.

I will turn to jelly the moment . . .

'What do you do with him?' A high sound floats towards me; I can barely discern it from the whispery steps crossing the room. 'What do you do with him?'

'Who?' I sit up. Priapus is here again. Which means I am dreaming, I must be. All this time I thought I was awake I've been dreaming. Like in the Greek plays, the god has come down to explain it all away. I've been possessed; it's all been a dream. But I don't want Lysander to be a dream. I want this to be the dream I wake up from. I want to wake up in a house next to Tullia, our brood of children playing in the orchards.

'Him. What does he do to you? I will not tell if you show me.' A faint light comes in from the sliver of the door. She's nearly closed it; I can see now it is Julia. She sits on the edge of my bed. Her voice is desperate. I feel her come towards me, the sinking holes in the bed where her hands are, and then her knees. 'Show me, show me,' she is pleading. She tries to lie on top of me, her arms hold me down, pressing on my shoulders, the pain where I bit myself rips down my arm. She is positioning me for something she wants but doesn't understand or know how to get. She knees me in the stomach, as if she is climbing up me, wanting to get into me. She will squash the baby's bones, bend them to clubfoots and snap them to handless arms, its head will be narrow. 'Show me and I will not tell.'

I stay motionless as I feel her hands run up and down my body, searching for something, something to take or maybe give. No, she is here to take. I let her do this at first because I am stunned and don't know what else to do, and then because I don't want her to tell. She is pressing her face against mine and down my neck – not kissing, just pressing – but still I can smell the wine. She must have drunk too much at lunch. She seems to want to grind herself into me, her headdress falling over both our faces, scratching, making rustling sounds like a cricket as her head moves up and down. I suddenly feel I can't breathe, as if her weight is pushing the air from my lungs. 'Stop,' I gasp. I can't hear myself. Stop. I need to think this through.

This is a ruse. It must be. She is here to entrap me, because she could not find out anything definite about Lysander and me. She's been spying and found nothing. So she thinks she can offer up herself as bait. She will tell the others it was me. I manage to get hold of both her hands and stop them. Her. I shake her as hard as I can. 'Why are you tricking me again, Julia? Taking what you want and then blaming me for wanting it? Just as the kiss? Are you trying to put me in the latrine again? You may banish this from your memory as soon as you leave my room, just as before, but I will not. Just as before. I will remember. I should call the others now! Let them see who you really are, under that headdress, under your constant scrutiny of everything I say. You blame me for your wanting and it is not any fault of mine.'

She slumps forward on top of me as if I have stabbed her. I think now of the knife in the potted plant. I could reach over and shove it into her back. But I know I couldn't, and even if I could, it would be the same as if it went into my own back.

Then just as quickly, she leaps from my bed. She steps backward, stumbles, drunk or confused, or trying to appear so. She shakes her head, as if she had been sleepwalking the whole time, then turns and dashes from my room.

I find myself retching up air, emptiness.

CHAPTER LXII

Diminutive chewing mouths and gargled murmurs criss-cross the table as we dine on fattened goose simmered in fish sauce, dried shallots and pickled cranberries. The new Virgin is eating more and much of the conversation is directed towards educating her. The others refrain from fussing over her, from being seen as attempting to mother, but their fussing shows in the occasional way one will interrupt another or add on to their sentences. Not that their fussing is motherly, only their excitement to talk to someone new, with ripe ears, although she is only a child. They chatter at her like squirrels.

I tell her about Sterculinus, the god of manure-spreading.

Julia's face is waxen, as if she is fading away right before my eyes. I notice she takes more wine, cup after cup. She will drink it away. Drink the day upside-down until it breaks apart into fingers of hands that cover the eyes.

'Aemilia, there's a stain on your stola.' Claudia points at my arm. The blood has run through, like a bloody brooch.

'Oh, it's only wine.' My hands shake slightly as I try to dab it off with a cloth. '*The first thing you need to know if you are to take a lover is there can be no sign of it on your body.*'

Fabia watches and I wonder if she sees wine or blood. 'A slave can wash it after dinner, though our stolas should only need monthly washings. You must be more careful.'

I try not to feel any fear; she could sense it. I slowly take a sip of my wine, as if to prove I am heeding her advice, though I am not certain if she was advising or threatening.

Julia looks up and stares blankly at the sore on my arm. I wonder if she thinks she sees an eye, another opening to clamber into? To wound is to be remembered. Maybe this is what she is thinking – that she did this, that she wounded me.

And she has.

After dinner, I go to my room. I put a history book in my lap; the writing blurs and trembles because my legs are drumming up and down. I am finding it hard to stay still. I feel I am waiting for water to boil. What will unfurl in Julia's mind when she goes to sleep? Will she stay silent or will she wake up with another version, one that simmered overnight and will bubble out of her mouth in the morning? Julia knows. This is all that is important; it is only a matter of time before that proves detrimental in some way, even her silence will have a price.

We must go this night.

When I hear someone at the door, I jump. The book falls to the ground, pages curl between its wooden panels like ribbons of dead yellowed skin.

But it is only the blonde slave, who has come to collect my stola. By now her wounds must be healed or at least I hope she is healed. Her wounds are didactic: you will remember not to lose the lyre. But she did not steal, and so she will only remember wounds for the sake of being wounded. 'Please sell the lyre, Lysander.' Let her pain be not in vain, not that this

391

would make her feel better, only me, so her pain is still my vanity.

She seems to move easily as she pulls the stola over my head, though not gently. She scratches, snags my hair in the headdress, pulls it sharply, scratches me again. My under-dress must also be removed; I hope she doesn't notice the stain is thicker there. When she reaches to take it off, I instinctively put my hand over hers, to slow her, to ease her towards the pulsing pain in my shoulder. I am filled with pangs of guilt, that I caused other hands to pain her so, that I should let her pain me back in return. I squeeze her hand. I know your plight, my hand shows, but she snatches it back. She closes her eyes as my under-dress comes off, turns and rolls it up. I wait for her to hand me a clean under-dress, but she just stands there limply, clinging to the ball of my dirty under-dress. My skin prickles. I cross one leg over the other. 'Under-dress?'

She looks back at me. This she should never do – she seems to revel in my nakedness, looking me up and down. 'Turn away!' My voice is pitched high with shock, indignation, as if she is the first person to ever see my naked body.

'Nowhere to hide?'

'I don't understand.'

'Yes, you do. You take and take. Take the lyre . . . and I am whipped because you take.' She notices my arm and gasps. 'You do this for man? You risk all this?' She motions round the room as if it is a palace, and to her it likely is. She shakes her head, laughing. 'But you not know better, no!'

'I don't understand what you are saying. Now turn away!'

'Oh yes, you know. I saw the other one come to your room today; she thinks I did not see. I saw her come in this room, and

I listen, there by the door.' She points to the door as if there were another one to choose from. What I wouldn't do for a back door. 'I hear what she says. I listen. Slaves, we are always listening. That is what you want, no? Us to listen? "Show me what he does, and I won't tell."' She imitates Julia's breathy whisper, adding a churlish giggle. 'Or maybe you do this for woman?' She snorts again at this. 'You are odd women, yes?' I see the clean under-dress folded on the bureau. I try to reach past her, but my arm is too heavy with pain and she snatches it up. 'You give me enough coins to go home, to go north . . . I wait in garden tonight to get it, close to dawn.' Then, as if to explain: 'I watch you, after you take lyre. You watch me be beaten, so I watch you.'

'I have nothing to give you!'

'Coins, to go. Yes?'

She doesn't understand. 'No coins! No.' My palms face up, empty-handed. 'None.' If I had a purse I could turn it upside down.

'I know who *he* is.'

She could be bluffing. She might not, but the *he* – any *he* – is all that matters. My stomach trembles, it must resemble a beating heart or a breathing lung right now. I feel sick, a deep-pitted illness that wants to crawl out. I think it is the child opting out; it's already heard too much.

She laughs again. Her tongue is white, her head nodding. 'Yes, you find way.' She's already made up her mind to triumph, one way or another. She tosses the fresh under-dress at me and leaves. She swings the door wide open as I stand here exposed. I scramble to slip into the under-dress, see a light moving up the hallway. Another slave enters with a tray of fresh candles and blows out the lamps.

I wish I could pace, but there is nothing I can do but turn on my side in my bed.

I push my head against the wall and feel its coolness on my forehead, twist the blanket between my fists. What will we do? What can we do? I feel the taste of goose rise in the back of my throat; my goose is cooked.

It's my fault. He never said he'd die for me.

We must give her the few denarii we have, but it will not be enough to keep her quiet. Then we will have nothing. We will leave empty-handed. Either way, we're both dead. I can smell dirt.

I notice I am tapping my head against the wall. Death's come knocking. I stop.

CHAPTER LXIII

Julia rushes past me in the temple, her face withdrawn and tired. She looks up at me, tilts her head as if she cannot place me; her eyes are still brimming red and bleary from the wine. She will go to sleep now and wake up to her tomorrow, and I will wake up to mine; there will be discrepancies and greater discrepancies thereafter. Also I won't sleep and so I won't wake up.

Peril is coming after me, nipping. How can one sleep under such conditions? But I wish I could sleep through this, come out on the other side. I know there is now only fight or flight, I just don't want to be here for either. I want it to have already happened. I wait for Lysander, trying my best to conjure that moment, after this, when I am fine, sitting in a chair elsewhere, going over our harrowing escape with him, each filling in the other's side with the other side.

Lysander doesn't come, not for a long time. He doesn't know we are on a deadline. From the corners of my sleepless eyes, I keep seeing things move outside the temple entrance – a flash of yellow hair, a shapeless shadow – and I think the blonde slave is here. Startled, I'll drop the sponge or knock over kindling, my legs nearly giving out.

I wish I could pray to Vesta and Minerva to hurry my lover back to me; at least I would feel as if I was doing something. Pray and sacrifice is all I know to do in crises. But even if they do exist, these goddesses are useless in aiding the course of love. I wish I was attending Venus or Flora. I'd have a better chance then.

I look at the sky for the first signs of light and decide to pray to Aurora, goddess of the rosy dawn, to delay her rising. I have to do something. I rip apart a dried brown leaf and toss the pieces through the entrance into the dark night, a meagre offering, but an offering nonetheless. It's all I have.

When he does finally arrive, he flops down on the steps, his beard even longer. He looks haggard. 'I had to go to so many houses. One man set his dog on me.' He lifts his leg to show me two seeping fang marks on his calf. 'I had to break the lyre over its head to get it off me . . .'

'She knows.' My voice is shrill. I stumble down the steps, my arms round his neck. 'She knows. We're caught!' For a moment I don't know if I mean Julia or the blonde slave. I don't want to tell him about Julia. Not now.

'Who? Who knows?' He stiffens, pushes me away and back into the temple.

'A house slave. The blonde one. She said she'll tell if we don't give her enough money to leave Rome. She's waiting in the garden.' I begin to cry. 'It's my fault. I took her lyre . . . I took her lyre.' I am sobbing, dry soundless wheezes. He must find me repulsive, snivelling in this way. But if he thinks this, he says nothing.

'We have only a few denarii; just enough to hire a horse for a day and to eat for two or three days. I still have a knife to sell.'

'We must leave right away! Let's leave now!' I try to run down the steps with his hand in mine, but he pulls me back.

396

'Aemilia, we wouldn't get anywhere fast enough. We must be cunning now.' He leans out of the door, looks up. 'It is near dawn! I still need to find a horse to hire. How do you know she will not tell anyway, before she leaves? If she's found a way to make you suffer, she will make you suffer.'

I never thought of this. I think of her breasts splitting like softened pads of butter cut with a blade.

'I still have a knife,' he says this again, calmly, and I can see something take shape in his face. Another face, a hardened mask, like Sempronia's wax face.

I say nothing. I am wracked with guilt. By saying nothing, by letting him go, I am her killer also. She will suffer again because of me. But I do not wish to end unmourned, unloved, unmoored from the living in death. I want to have an after now, our child. It's us or her. Isn't that how it always is? Us against them.

Lysander presses his cheek against mine, though all I feel is the hard thick brush of his beard. 'I'll come back after and we'll leave. Be ready.'

He moves down the steps stealthily. 'We must do what we must do.' The knife is twisted upward in his hand, parallel to the veins in his wrist. I hear him speak to another slave at the house door, telling him that he will tend the door for a little while. There's some laughter, and the slave brags about winning something in a game of dice. They seem to talk for ever.

I stand by the temple entrance, my heart pounding, pounding. Maybe our hearts do know our lives. I expect to hear a muffled scream. I picture him doing it with his hand over her mouth – at least I hope he puts his hand over her mouth. I hear nothing. It is as silent a night as any. I stay by the door, ready to dash down the steps to him, even when the birds begin to sing and peasants pass by with their squeaking carts and the city begins to wake up, slowly, in fits of shouts and distant hammering, of braying donkeys and bleating sheep.

I wait and wait.

He does not return.

Only Claudia comes. I expect her to tell me something: that the body of the blonde slave has been found in the garden. But she says nothing and I am escorted back to the house. I look back, up at the tall Gaul, but he stares straight ahead, giving nothing away.

CHAPTER LXIV

I eat my lunch, have my bath, deposit a will. I move through the day like a straw doll, an effigy of myself. I feel an ache all through my shoulders, down to the backs of my knees, a slight cramping in my stomach, and again I am worried that it will spill out of me now, that the bathwater will turn red, or that it will drop under the table where I used to fling mushrooms.

I cross my legs to keep it in.

I sit in my room; I don't bother placing a history book in my lap. The bureau is spattered with droplets of oil from the lamps, the tapestry above it hangs flat against the wall. I wish it'd billow and sway, like curtains in the wind. In the corner between the bureau and the wall, there's a small collection of unnoticed dust that I also wish I could see swirling in a gust of air. I crave some kind of movement, even as small as this, anything that shows the passage of time.

I am still waiting.

He must be outside in the garden now, toiling. He had to dispose of the body, after all; the sun must have come up just as he was getting back or maybe he buried her in the garden and had to haul rocks to conceal her grave. We couldn't make a run for it in broad daylight. He would have slipped back into the hut, just in time for their morning repast of water and oats.

Through the chamber-room window I searched for him, but it was raining. It might still be raining now, so maybe he isn't toiling, but is in the hut playing dice, waiting for the rain to pass, for night to thicken.

There's a slave outside my door; she wants me to look up and notice her, to lead me to dinner. She sighs, rustles her tunic, dings her finger against the lamp she is holding as if by accident.

I try to enjoy the last of this: this chair, the warmth of this room, my freshly strigiled skin, the food I am dining on – fish glazed in olive oil with chickpeas and Picene wine. I am eating as much as I can – for two. Who knows when I'll eat again? There will be hardship ahead, of this I am sure, but at least we will endure it together. I look at Minerva, anchored in the mural, stuck for ever in this dining room, never blinking.

'The festival of Janus is again upon us,' Julia affirms. She looks up at me, briefly, but I cannot read whether or not she has tethered what happened yesterday to the truth or a lie, or even if she has let it pass through her completely with the wine.

'May a new year again bring us the gods' good graces,' Fabia recites back.

I take another bread roll, consider shoving it up my sleeve, but cannot risk it slipping out, not now. I picture us eating our meals together, the meandering conversations we might have. We will live in an apartment that has a bed and a crib, a table where he writes. He will make me heat up a flat piece of metal, and I will burn over the branding on the insides of his forearms. A fresh start. Our apartment will be cramped, but there will be a window and we will keep the shutters open so that sunlight streams in all day. Our child, fat and healthy, will sit in the heat of the sun, often giggling. We will be poor and hungry but free, both of us. We will find some land, plant some olive trees. Grow excellent olives. Thick, juicy, salty, but not too salty.

One of the candles has guttered out, wax hardening onto the table.

Fabia motions for one of the slaves to replace it. 'May the new year bring better slaves,' she huffs, taking a sip of wine and dabbing her mouth. 'Two of our slaves have just run away. Caesar has been notified. I am sure they will be caught and thrown into the arena for it.'

'Rightly so,' answers Julia. This time she looks directly at me, a flicker of vicious gloating passes over her face, quickly, so quickly I am not sure I saw it all.

I lean forward. I am jarred as if I had bitten my tongue while eating something sweet and delicious. I feel my hands wrap around the edge of the table. 'Two slaves?' I try to sound astounded, that it is two and not one, that the state has suffered such financial loss.

'Yes, two.' Julia answers, shaking her head with disbelief. 'More wine.' She motions to a slave. 'These chickpeas are quite good. Nice and soft.' Her mundane comments seem to be made on purpose, as if to rub my nose in the endless minutia that I cannot escape.

'Yes, I love chickpeas. We should request them more often.' Claudia nods.

'When did they leave?' I am not sure why I ask this, since I already know. Maybe because I want them to stay on the topic, resist the tide of dullness from sweeping them away, so they can realize they have it wrong, that only one slave is missing.

401

'Some time early this morning, likely just after you finished tending.' Fabia stares at me for a moment. I am showing far too much interest.

He did not come back. He did not come back. A jittery weakness comes over me, as if all my bones have loosened. I try to bring the spoon to my mouth but keep missing, dropping food. My hands are shaking. They are watching me. Sweat beads round my nose, bile rises in my throat, the mural spins. I can feel the bite in my arm ache, open up. I touch it, expecting blood, but there's none. My stomach clenches harder. 'Air . . . Excuse me. Please continue.'

'It is raining out,' I hear Julia call out, her voice pitched with either concern or feigned concern covering for spite, I can no longer tell what is genuine or not. But I am already in the kitchen. The slaves fall silent, their lined faces crouched into their necks, staring at their toes. I push past them and go out into the garden. Round and round the garden I go, looking for Lysander. A heavy rain is falling, and as it pelts down on me, my headdress sticks to my cheeks like wet hair and I can already faintly see the purple dye of my stola running over my hands, onto my white shoes. Good Virgins are dry Virgins. I am dyeing out, I am dying.

I pass the overflowing fountains, glistening sculptures, go off the path, through the leafless hedges towards his hut. I open the door; inside the slaves are huddled together like one fleshy mass, a monster with a multitude of eyes, mouths, noses.

'Lysander, Lysander,' I call out his name, ready to kick at the mass, kick Lysander free of them.

'He is gone,' one of the mouths answers.

He is gone; I will not go on. He knew he would not get far

with a Virgin, so he left me behind, like a sculpture too awkward to carry, too clunky, its colours too obvious to be inconspicuous.

He used me like a drawbridge lowered over a moat; I was his escape, not his accomplice.

I wonder if he is bragging now of duping a Virgin, bragging how he did it. 'All I had to do was look at her, and she fell to her knees. All I had to do was blow on her, and she swooned, returned the next day with six sheets of papyrus. When more was needed – oh, you will not believe this – all I had to do was tell her Rome was nearing a revolt and the Republic would soon inevitably fall. Even the Virgins here are not steadfast.'

He did not bring me because I am misconceived, ill-conceived, have conceived.

He loathes Rome. What did I expect? Maybe I was always part of his revolt, not as an accomplice, but as an act of insurgence. He took me while Vesta looked on so Rome would be vulnerable, even planted his seed to shake Rome's foundation, its infrastructure. He waited for Rome to crumble, and then when it did not, he left.

But then this seems too sinister, too cruel, and I don't want to believe I was duped; it only makes it worse. He killed the blonde and left; he'd had enough of me. He never said he'd kill for me. It was my fault he was forced to turn on his own. I am nothing but trouble now that Rome remains the same. Infallible, un-fallible. He wanted a clear getaway.

We all must do what we must do.

What will I do? I wander back to the house, to the bench under the portico; I seem to tip over onto my side. Rain blows in with the wind like a gentle spray, and I wonder if this is what it must feel like lying on the seashore. I could almost fall asleep here and now, listening to the rain, letting it mix with my tears, drown out my sobs, wash away the wreckage of this trembling body. I could make a run for it on my own, but Virgins can't run. I think of my fleshy legs, soft as veal from disuse; maybe this is why we walk as we do, to keep us tender enough so we can never make a break for it.

Something has snapped off inside me, I can feel it circulating through me, a piece of bone, sharp and unrelenting, until the pain is so great, gash after gash into my sternum.

Tullia said that if a man leaves, make certain it is with consequence. Threaten him with a curse tablet and you'll see how fast he turns back, his tail between his legs, and if he does not return at least he will suffer. They are simple enough. All you need is a lead tablet – the thinner the better, but any will do – to consecrate an enemy to the spirits of the Underworld, to invoke Hecate, the three-faced and three-bodied sister of Latona. She always comes through.

I could sneak down the hall to the classroom. If I am caught, I could claim disorientation. I am ill, after all. I could wander out to the garden again. Of course she is ill, near death, they will say; she is out in the cold garden at night. There will be nails by the fence; I know this because there always are. I will tuck myself back inside my room, hide behind my door, maybe even close it. A closed door. Illness seeks privacy. I could curse his body to a slow illness, his eyes to blindness, his head to baldness, his mouth to muteness, his stomach to emptiness, his legs to limpness, his ears to deafness, his arms to crookedness, his skin to soreness. I could promise my little pup, the one I left behind, though it must be long dead, perhaps Hecate could find it somewhere in the Underworld. But then what good would it

404

do? He'd still be gone and I am so tired, too tired to be vengeful.

I watch the rain for a little while, until I notice a slave standing at the kitchen door. I must go in, up to my room.

Once in my room, I dig up the knife.

I look at my face again, an elongated and bubbling reflection
of a dark-eyed woman with a veil. How different I look now.
Gone is the Virgin on the brink of elsewhere. Gone is the thief,
the secret-keeper.

I tuck the knife in my shoe, as any stray dirt can be expected
there, so I can slip it up my sleeve in the morning. This time I
thoroughly pick my hands clean of soil.

I try to sleep but cannot. When I am about to fall through the
fringes of sleep I suddenly hear his voice, feel his breath, his
hands slipping under my pillow for the papyrus.

CHAPTER LXV

When I arrive in the temple, I add more kindling to Vesta, whisper her praises, bow at Minerva and wipe her down with the purified water. I count the bricks in the hearth, the cracks in the wall and floor, some dried leaves blowing round the box of kindling.

I wish I could say I am reconciled, come full circle. That I am a good Virgin, a Virgin still, that I learnt my lesson, but I am still performing. Always the impersonator, never the original, squeezed between the misalignment of expectations and wants.

There is no other place than here. I should accept this with good Roman stoicism. It is better to think only of what your own hands hold. There is nothing to be pitted against now. I am simply the pit and Vesta is the prune, I am enclosed inside her. A fire pit. The pitfalls of Virginity.

I am held by Vesta, but would rather be held by him. He is gone. All possibility is gone. Anticipation is gone. The after now is now and now and now. Each day after now stretches before me like an infinite line of purple stolas, an unending wall of empty cupboards, a boundless table of cakes. After now is a rotating arrow incessantly circling round, morning, noon and night. Meal after meal. Bath after bath. Eternal fire. Vesta. An after now without him. I slide down close to her circular brick hearth, its heat lapping over my face, burning my forehead and cheeks. I can almost feel the outline of the bricks singeing my skin. Bricks in my head. I am sitting, though it is not permitted, though I should be standing.

Tomorrow will be the first day. Tomorrow I will be a good Virgin.

I build Vesta strong and high. I belong here because I cannot leave. Branded. So here I am, the only way I can be, know how to be. It's been fifteen years, only fifteen more to go. I will wait it out.

I will have the new one, take her under my wing, just as Tullia did with me.

I take the knife from under my sleeve and hold it over Vesta; she will purify it. She will aid me in this murder of my own so she can reclaim my womb. 'I beseech thee, with this knife, bestow upon me a steady hand.'

A heavy sleet begins to fall, beating against the temple as steadily as if it were Vesta's pulse.

I slide down the wall, spread my legs, bend at the knees, my stola a sudden tent. It is better if I can't see. Seeing is believing. I hold the knife against the inside of my thigh. I picture spearing it, like a red grape.

It's not me or you, I tell it, it's me or nothing. It's me, not you.

Just a moment is all I need. My back aches. I will be a better Virgin tomorrow; tomorrow will be the first day. My womb will be picked clean. I feel so heavy. My hands shake – I can't. I put the knife aside. Just for a moment, I'll be there in a moment, I tell it. My legs stretch forward. I slump back. The rain is beating down, filling rivers that lead to other places, upstream. I close my eyes. Let's have these last moments together. I love you already.

I can hear splashing.

A blur, a lifting haze. 'Lysander?'

He is here before me. He's come back. I try to push myself up from the floor, my neck so stiff from sleeping against the wall. 'You're back!' I say. For a moment I realize how absurd this sounds, as though he just forgot something and is quickly popping back in to get it. A few coins, a letter, a book he needs to return to the friend he borrowed it from. I almost laugh with relief, elation. But then I notice he has a bucket in his hands and is holding it over Vesta still dripping. The smell of wet ash fills the temple; it is suddenly dark, so dark.

'It is the only way,' he whispers. One murder has made him crazed, hungry for another. His face seems to be all hair – a savage animal with two black eyes. He is unrecognizable. 'It's better this way.' He drops the bucket, lets it hit the floor with a loud thud.

'I . . . Shhh . . . Lysander,' I say his name again, hoping it will wake him from his violent madness. He looks back at me, his mouth open, as if he is curious to see what will happen now. As if he plans to watch the ensuing chaos from afar, as arsonists are said to do.

He leans out of the door and rings the chimes, then leaps down the steps.

He's killed me.

I stand for a moment in utter disbelief, unable to move.

The male slave is already at the temple door; he does not dare step in, but he peers in and takes in the temple's dimness. I try to move past him, but he blocks the entrance. I pound against his chest, try to scratch his neck, but he pulls my hands away by the wrists and pushes me back in, hard, and I slam against the floor. He can do this now, let loose. He smiles.

I feel like a trapped animal, my legs snared in some trap. The sounds of the bricks, which have been scorching for years, cooling down make an odd croaking song. The others will be a while; they will have to dress first before leaving the house. It would not do, under any circumstance, for the Virgins to be tumbling around in their under-dresses for all Rome to see.

So here I stand, without Vesta. I think of something to say – that a madman entered and just flung water over her. But it would not matter; if I was pure, Vesta would be immune to water. If I was pure, I wouldn't have had a lover who put out the fire. I look for the knife, at least then I can plunge it into my own neck. But Lysander has somehow managed to take that also. He has left me high and dry. Maybe he is snickering in the bushes now. He doesn't want me to kill myself, he wants the whole show.

Fabia and Claudia arrive first. 'What's happened?' Fabia huffs as she charges into the temple. She begins to scream, deep, bloodcurdling screams, as if she's hysterical. A group of people quickly gather outside the temple steps. The sun has risen. The skies have cleared. How long ago did it stop raining?

'*Vesta is out, Vesta is out, Vesta is out . . .*' Fabia begins to chant. The others are all here now, rushing round her, joining in with her wailings. The sound of their shrill howling is too much to bear. I try to go to them, cover their mouths. 'Shhh . . . shhh shhh . . .' But they kick at me, scratch my arms, and now they are all chanting, together as one.

'*Vesta is out, Vesta is out, Vesta is out . . .*'

Julia glances back at me. There are tears on her cheeks, and I know that even if some are tears of sadness, more are tears of relief. I can see a kind of unburdening round her eyes that have now softened, her mouth relaxes.

Caesar enters and already he is yelling, spit sprays against my cheeks and lips.

He knows it is my fault right away because I am standing away from the others. I know he cannot tell us apart otherwise. Veins pop from his forehead and neck, red blotches steam up over his skin. I try to listen, but his words are mangled by his anger, by their throbbing chanting, '*Vesta is out, Vesta is out, Vesta is out, Vesta is out . . .*'.

Caesar pulls me harshly by my arms up to the hearth. 'Rip off a piece of your stola and throw it into the hearth. If you are innocent, Vesta will come alive again. If not, you are guilty and will be punished.' He speaks loudly enough for the growing mass of people at the temple's doorstep to hear, his voice calmer now, his face composed. 'It is unacceptable for Rome to ever be left vulnerable in the dark, without the protective light of Vesta, without the protective fertility of her priestesses. The gods always hold Rome in great esteem because the Roman people are by far the most superior in their care of gods and goddesses. Vesta must be appeased for this Virgin's insolence. She will burn brighter, stronger. Rome will be stronger, greater, even more far-reaching . . .'

He is delivering a speech now, a long-winded, winding speech.

I fall to his feet, begging for mercy, but he barely glances down at me. He expected this, he's used to being begged for mercy.

'Virgins must always remain above suspicion.'

410

I can hear the people outside shuffling up the temple's steps for a better view, waiting. I rip at the cuff of my stola in silence. The hearth is filled with piles of rings, bracelets, pins. Wasted offerings. My hands tremble, but my stola tears. I hold the piece of fabric in my hands, heavy as metal. Vesta will not burn again because it takes flint and stone to make fire, because I am not a Virgin, because I was murdered.

Caesar breathes in, deep, his face contorted, all elbows and knees. 'Now!'

I let go of the fabric and it floats down into the hearth as light and slow as a falling feather.

CHAPTER LXVI

Virgins are disposed of quickly, in innocence and guilt. I am locked in a litter for a short while – not the one we usually travel in but one for prisoners. It is a wooden box with air holes poked into the sides and top, which seems so absurd considering where I am going. Chains and lock slither over it.

I am surrounded by guards, though I suspect it's the same lictors who usually precede our litter, just dressed differently. When I peer through one of the holes, I can see they stand differently too, slouching, spitting into the yellow grass.

I am just outside the temple, in front of the house.

An even bigger crowd has gathered. When the guards notice my peeking eye, they lay a hand flat over the hole. One even threatens me with a stick. 'I'll poke your eye out!' This I cannot help but laugh at. You're too late, I almost jeer back.

I overhear the others as they hurry back and forth between the house and the temple discussing the elaborate ceremony that will be needed to accompany the relighting of Vesta.

This will happen after I am buried.

They've likely had to refer to dusty, nearly decayed scrolls. Caesar is probably consulting the Sibylline books right now to find what it will take to appease Vesta. An augur must be close by, reading the birds flying over the temple. I'll never know what they'll make of me, what will be politically construed. There will be weeks of offerings and prayers, and then things will get back to normal. Bury your shame and it will be forgotten.

The thought of being buried alive brings waves of panic, teeth chattering, the feeling of a stuffed nose and mouth, followed by dreaminess, that this cannot possibly be happening, this body does not belong to me, here, now.

I feel the litter being lifted.

They take me through the Forum, and I can hear the shouts of 'Whore, whore, whore,' matrons crying as if in mourning, though maybe it's because their husbands will take my transgression out on them later. I've shaken their trust in all women; women are sneaks, they'll think, even Virgins. I can hear the constant knocking and thumping of things being thrown at the litter. Rotten apples, I guess. They're long out of season and splatter nicely. Maybe rocks, when the guards aren't looking, though they're wearing helmets. For once people flock towards me. I remember the soft wispy sound of the daisies being tossed in the air, soundlessly landing on the platform, and cannot decide which sounds worse.

I know I should try to kick my way out, or even spew out some curses of doom, if only to spread unease. Stir them up so they can't sleep. I could scream and cry, anguish-filled repentant moans so they'll be filled with trepidation, but I can't seem to muster it. I feel too waterlogged, too cold, and such dramatics seem too pointless. The crowds, in spite of themselves, would enjoy it too much. I am at their level now, soon to be below it.

I'll be put down soon, once and for all. I'll go gently into the ground. There will be no show here.

I rub my arms up and down, slide up my sleeves, feel my skin for particles that will soon break down, disintegrate. There will be nothing left resembling what I once was, and I will recall nothing of here, this place, this life. This is what he meant by it's better this way. He said we reassemble into something else – perhaps a tree. He thought I'd be happier as a tree, so he set me free.

But if I could, I'd prefer to be snow, snow that falls only at night. When I was younger I'd watch the rare snowfalls and think they came from a god's bucket, hidden behind a cloud that would tip over from time to time. I thought snow was really eggs in disguise. Millions of flat, falling eggs. Eggs that would collapse into the ground, disappear and hide until spring, until they grew into trees and shrubs, grasses and flowers, flies and birds. Babies. I would think I was the sole witness to a grand birthing from above: hushing white snow, sowing snow.

I want to be a flake of snow, a seed that will eventually hatch into a bird and fly far away from Rome, high above, until I am only a speck in a blue sky. Mapless. Or maybe a spider building my transparent webs to be suspended between two roses. Or a fish, one that swims only near the bottom of the sea, safe from spears. Perhaps I should like to be a man, a rich Roman citizen, toga flowing, walking about freely in the Forum, speaking leisurely, without any womanly frets. But I don't. I wish to be something much smaller, freed by insignificance.

I lie back on the couch. Dust catches in my throat and eyes. I cough and cough, nearing breathlessness, so thirsty. I pick up the bowl of muddy water – round black insects with orange-spotted shells have drowned in it. I take a sip, thick mud gushes between my teeth. I chew, choke and spit it out. I will die of thirst first. As I put the bowl back, I notice there is something written on the table. Etched in. I pick up the dying lamp from the floor, bring it closer.

I, Tullia, invoke Hecate, the most gracious and clever of all the spirits of the Underworld, to call and empower all barbarians onto Roman soil to bring plague and ruin to the multitudes. Upon Hecate I call, because she is the strongest, to bring inextinguishable fires to the house of Vesta, the Temple of Vesta, to burn all Virgins slowly, when they are awake, to smoulder them slowly until their limbs melt from their bodies, their torsos char and bubble, their hair smokes. With this curse fulfilled, I promise thee, beautiful Hecate, to be your admirer, devout in sacrifice forever.

I stroke the carved letters over and over. Tullia tried her best to have the last word. I can see her, sitting here in this spot, vengeful until the end. My Tullia, once a mother. A slave found her in the cellar at night with her lover and notified the others. Sempronia had her dragged back to the temple. Guilty as sin, she said; found right under our very own noses with a lover.

Or at least they assumed there was a lover, but in fact there was none. Tullia was found in the cellar alone, speaking lovingly to a lover only she could see, kissing a lover only she could feel. Tullia had a lover, that was much true; who it was, only Tullia knew.

I could have pieced it together bit by bit if I had wanted. We all saw the same plays at the theatre, about witches and curses, jokes men made about women. She took what she needed, like germinating seeds, and then hatched her own ideas, making them her own.

415

I believed her because she wanted me to. I believed because I needed to.

They woke me up, sleep still stuck to my eyes, to attend her trial in the temple. The Pontifex Maximus with the mulberry birthmark on his cheek was already there. We gathered near Vesta, still burning; the others refused to acknowledge this contradiction. Tullia was caught in the act, they said; it was only a matter of time before she found a real lover, and in any case her intentions were real – perhaps her lover was an Underworld spirit. It was only a matter of time before something worse would occur. What an embarrassment she is! Regardless of the fact that she had obviously lost her mind. Blemished as a leper.

Blemished as a leper, harmful to Vesta, blemished as a leper, harmful to Vesta, blemished as a leper, harmful to Vesta.

I chanted with them, I had to, though I tried to do so more quietly than the others. I even tried mouthing it at first, but someone pinched my side.

Of course Tullia protested, claimed her innocence. Who wouldn't? For a moment, I could see the fear in her eyes, the same kind of sudden fear seen in a charioteer's eyes as he is about to flip over and be crushed. Then suddenly her fear seemed to dissipate, like smoke in the wind, replaced by a quiet smile, and I knew she could hear her lover again. He was there with her, as she was told that if she was pure, she would be able to carry a sieve filled with the purified water without a drop leaking out. She kept her eyes on him as she held the sieve and the water was poured into it, leaking all down the front of her stola, a puddle round her feet. She kept her eyes on him as she dropped it and turned to run from the temple, calling out his name.

She kept her eyes on him when they grabbed her, carried her out and locked her inside the litter that would bring her to this tomb the

416

following day. That would later bring me here also, to die beside her. I crawl along the tomb's floor and pick up her bones, one by one, from under the couch – no longer a set, a compilation, but Tullia whole – and place her on the couch beside me. Together.

I tell Tullia about Lysander, before he became a murderer. I must leave him as he was on that first day in the garden, the one hunched over, crying, watering radish seeds with his own salty tears, watering his own beard, a hairy vine. Do you understand why it was so easy to love him? I understand, Tullia answers, because she's always understood.

I tell her the middle and the end, because it is necessary for any story, though I change the ending, make Lysander heroic. He tried to save me, the fire was out by the time I woke up, just not enough kindling. He was there with flint in hand, sparking away. It was my fault. I fell asleep.

She coos with admiration, even envy.

Oh, Tullia, remember how you said, 'Not to worry if you cry. Worry only if you stop?' Well, I think we should all be born with a pocket on our hip, a flap of skin, a place we can store all sadness, tucked away. I mean, what good is memory if it is not faulty? What good is memory if it is not malleable, if one cannot select memories? If one's memories cannot be changed, then memory really is no good at all. We are descendants of memory alone. Memories are all I had to choose from.

Tullia, finally you are here. I waited for you. At least you are here now. I place my hand round her dried ribs and curl into her. I tell her I am carrying a child, and she is giddy with excitement. 'Oh, how wonderful,' she tells me.

I am sorry my child will die, but we will die connected. Our particles will always be interwoven, still of the same flesh. If we become a tree, and that is our after-life, at least we are a tree together.

A small mercy, Tullia agrees.

The lamp flame flickers, dims. The tomb hangs, narrows, tilts for a moment then drops off, down. Light bleeds into shadow. Succumbed. Swallowed. The oil is gone. There is nothing I can do but wait. Wait it out. I hold Tullia tighter and can hear her ribs crack one by one in the darkness.

When I wake up I think I am dead and waking up in the Underworld. I don't think I am waking up as a tree, because I still know who I am. I refuse to open my eyes, afraid of what I will see first, afraid that I will wake up in a cave, awake to everlasting pain and suffering. Afraid that my child is no longer with me, afraid that he is – he deserves someplace blissful. I am afraid that my parents will not really recognize me, that I will spend eternity alone. Afraid that I will see Lysander, afraid that I will not. But we all must die sometime, so I will wait for him.

Finally I open one eye, and above, there are stars, beautiful twinkling stars, that seem to explode with starry dust. Oh yes, I've made it to the Elysian Fields. It is Tullia I see first; still in her stola and headdress, she stands before me. She is pointing up. 'Oh yes, such beautiful stars.' Up, up, up. 'Yes, Tullia, I see.' 'Get up, up up.' Her lips do not move and yet she is yelling. 'Up.'

I open my other eye. I am still in the tomb. I am so frustrated I have not died, so disappointed I am not in the Elysian Fields. But still there are stars above me. I look over at Tullia, at the murky outline of her smiling skull. 'Up,' I hear her say. 'Up. Aemilia, come up.'

With the lamp out, I can see light coming into the tomb. I am not down so deep. 'Up,' Tullia calls again. I pull the couch over, tip it onto its side, all her bones falling apart again. I lean it against the wall like a ramp. I stand on the back, my legs caving into cushions, and feel on the tomb's ceiling for the door, grabbing at the top of the tomb, putting down handfuls of dirt and mud, pulling at roots like snakes from trees. I can feel it, some wood, the door. I can barely reach it. I jump up, punch against it, but cannot hit it hard enough. It must be locked. My first locked door. Be careful what you wish for. Was it Tullia who said that, or Fabia? I push up, but lose my footing and slide down the couch. A soft landing. I try again, push, push.

I look at Tullia, still smiling, she has the answer. 'Take me,' she whispers. I pick up her thigh bone, at least that is what I think it is, and climb back up on the couch. I whack it against the wooden door, harder. Whack. I will the door to split in two, rocks to soar up in the air, away. The bone splinters, splits in two. Weak bones, Tullia. I would have done better with a big-boned girl. I go back to her, turn her bones over and over in my hands, feeling their weight as if I am shopping for a good sturdy pitcher. I will try her pelvis this time. I can hold onto it better with two hands. I hit the door again and again, until black dirt begins to stream in. It seems to move, shift a little, the wooden pillars creak and quiver almost as if I've wounded them somehow, plunging a knife into their side. I will dig my way up, out. Again I hit the door, jumping again for more force, my limp legs nearly giving out, my fleshy arms whipping forwards like strings of yarn. Over and over; a good Virgin perseveres.

'Aemilia!' Tullia cheers me on. 'Go up, up.'

Finally, the door splits and dirt rushes in over my face and down my stola, and I am sure my tomb will cave in upon me and I will drown in the earth. I fall back, covered in thick soil, so heavy on my chest I can barely breathe. Up my nose and in my mouth; soil trickles down the back of my throat, in my eyes grittiness blinds. I scoop the soil off the front of me, turn over and wipe it from my face. A powdery light pours in, lighting up the tomb, a dusty corner of the earth.

I feel around for Tullia and kiss her teeth goodbye.

I crawl back up on the couch, reach up and start to pull myself through the small opening, slivers of wood cutting into my hands and arms. I am too weak to pull up my own weight, I kick at the wall, try to run up, pushing and pulling; the slivers now cut into my chest, then stomach. Half in, half out, my legs dangling. Pulling, pulling, slivers cutting into my hips and thighs, into each of my knees. I try to pull myself out from my grave. Then suddenly, I feel hands round my wrists, pulling me up. I begin to kick, no, no. My grave is being robbed. I try to drop back down, twisting my hands.

'Aemilia, come up. I have you. Up. Up.' It's not Tullia's voice but Lysander's.

He pulls me up despite my efforts to break free from his grasp. The sun's white light glares down at me, and I can only see a black outline before me. 'No! Murderer!' I scream. He's come to finish the job. I try to run from him, but he has me tight against his chest.

'I had to do it. Shhh . . . I have you now. It was the only way to get you out of Rome alive. I gave her all the money, the last knife. We'd have never made it any other way. Shhh . . . I have you now . . .' He repeats this over and over, like a lullaby, until I calm, catch my breath and my deep, shuddering cries ebb.

My eyes finally adapt to the light, and I see it is only just dawn. My hands run over his face and chest and ears and nose. He is here, it's really him, the first Lysander.

His hands are covered in dirt up to his elbows. He puts his arm round my waist, his hand over my belly, and I lean into his shoulder. He points and I see it, off in the distance, and we begin to walk to the stony path that leads to elsewhere, to an after now.